Legacy

Michelle Lowe

Michelle E. Lowe

NORDLAND

www.nordlandpublishing.com

Copyright

Published by Nordland Publishing 2016

ISBN Print: 978-82-8331-020-7
ISBN E-book: 978-82-8331-018-4

*To my lovely little daydreamers, Mia and Kirsten,
who, without even trying, inspire me.*

Michelle E. Lowe

CONTENTS

Michelle E. Lowe

ACKNOWLEDGMENTS

I would like to thank those who have helped to make this book possible. First, I'd like to thank my parents, Jim and Janice. To my daughters, Mia and Kirsten, who keep encouraging me to tell stories. And to my aunt JoAnn for always being there.

Special thanks to Jessica Ellis and Kate Hallman for their assistance and advice. Thanks to Amy Coughlin, Elena Lange, Elisa Jiang, Evan Pitman, Heather Pitman, Holly Bagley, Ruth Daly, Glenn Ramos, Kimberley Luce, Landry Prichard, Taunji Hurlbut, Erin Mulligan, Amber Heyman, Russell Hinson, John Cook, Tom and Jennifer Allard for their time and generous support. Although he's no longer here, I'd like to thank Jimmy. Miss you, big brother! A huge thanks and heaps of gratitude to my mentor, Catherine Rudy. And to MJ Kobernus and everyone at Nordland Publishing!

.

Legacy

"The world as we know it is standing on the pivotal edge of change! An evolution is taking shape. This is the climb, my friends! The climb up towards the peak of the Industrial Revolution! I say unto thee, we must contribute to thrive. Contribute to the Age of the Machine!"

—Professor Raphael Brooke

Michelle E. Lowe

The Contract

Thooranu had arrived in the Blue Desert late that evening, but already he'd slain many jackals. After his last kill, he built two fire pits in the sand and gutted the beast. He always ate his final kill, or at least the one that proved hardest to bring down. This particular jackal had been both.

He'd taken the beast bare handed, wrestling the animal until he'd broken its neck. The jackal had gotten in a few good bites, rending deep gashes into his back and crushing sharp teeth through his arm. But the jackal had sensed its attacker was otherworldly and had known it would eventually fail. Nonetheless, that hadn't prevented it from putting up a good fight.

After tossing the lungs, liver, brain, eyes, tongue, balls and heart into a blackened iron cauldron to boil, Thooranu skinned and beheaded the animal, then put the carcass on a skewer to rotate over a second fire.

With most of the work done, he sat and wiped his hands clean. His wounds had already healed. From a rough hessian sack, he brought out a bottle of wine, pulling the cork free with his teeth. He breathed in deeply, the wine's earthy aroma giving clues to its origins. It was old, bottled before his birth. Italian. He poured some into a glass and sipped. It tasted like the beginning of everything.

He leaned back, eying the heavens and the myriad stars, a smile flickering over his lips. Then it vanished. Someone was nearby.

"Mind if I join you?" a male voice asked.

The stranger's abrupt approach startled him, which was difficult to do. It must be the human part of him, he thought. But the stranger could not be human. No mortal could survive this far into the desert without a camel. He wasn't even dressed for the harsh conditions.

The man appeared to be teetering between wealth and poverty. His slashed doublet was a shiny red, embroidered with black skeletons, but his cape was ragged along the hem. The boots were the most sensible thing he was wearing, although they were still too heavy for the day's heat, and a ridiculous hat sat upon his head.

Thooranu breathed deeply, trying to sniff the stranger out. There were many scents. Was he a demon too? A punk? Or perhaps a ghost? Whatever he was, Thooranu sensed no threat.

"Please," he said, gesturing for the stranger to join him.

The flamboyantly dressed man took a seat by one of the fires and poked at it with a shiny black cane. He removed his rabbit fur hat, sporting lively ostrich feathers, and set it down beside him. He was handsome, if a little on the feminine side, with dark hair, a carefully trimmed mustache and beard, along with a charming smile and perfectly shaped eyes that captured the flickering firelight like jewels.

"You've built a couple of nice fires here," the stranger complimented, stroking his beard. He sniffed the cauldron. "Is there a heart in there? I do rather enjoy a good, tasty heart."

"Would you care for some?" Thooranu asked.

"I would, indeed, and perhaps a glass of wine? If you don't mind, that is."

Thooranu did not, for he could obtain wine anywhere with little effort. He poured his guest a glass that he first manifested with a gesture of his hand from the sand and fire.

"Ah," the stranger said, accepting the drink. "Thank you kindly. You are a good host."

The stranger didn't speak with any accent, as though he belonged to no particular region. Then again, neither did Thooranu.

"I'm Jack Pack," the man said, extending his hand.

"Thooranu."

They shook hands then Jack Pack settled back, taking another sip of wine.

"I knew a Thooranu once," Jack Pack admitted. "He was an incubus."

"My father."

"I see." Jack Pack looked him up and down. "It appears that you took after your mother. Human?"

Thooranu smiled. "I suppose I did. And yes."

"That's good for you; for as I said, I've met your father, and I wouldn't curse my worst enemy to inherit his looks."

Thooranu laughed, for he couldn't agree more. "And what of you?"

"Oh, I'm no one special, really. Just a wanderer. A lost soul, if you will. I journey around the universe, seeing what's out there, what trouble I can get myself into, that sort of thing."

"Sounds a bit like me," Thooranu said, looking up again at the star-glittered sky. "Have you ever visited the outer planes?"

The wanderer shrugged. "Sure, a few times. The worlds beyond are interesting enough, but not like this one. Even the best miss the little things that complete this world. I like it here more than most places."

Thooranu nodded. "I concur."

They sat in silence like old friends. Steam curled up from the cauldron. Thooranu glanced at the stranger. Jack Pack had made an impression on him. He hoped the man wouldn't take his leave too soon. It had been a while since he'd had any company.

Thooranu noticed a coil of braided hair pinned by a jeweled brooch onto Jack Pack's doublet. "Whose hair is that?"

Jack Pack raised the braid and looked at it, a smile forming. "It was a gift. It's Guinevere's hair. Fascinating creature."

"Lancelot's Guinevere?"

"The very same. Those two were a good example of how fun mortals are to toy with."

"Oh?"

"Indeed." A shrug. "It passes the time."

"How so?"

"Many years ago, a Trickster, a Dökkálfar and an Adlet beast made a bet on who could find a certain relic that had been hidden; the Holy Grail."

Thooranu's eyes narrowed. "The Grail, huh?"

"Yes, yes, I know; we've all heard stories about the fruitless quests to find it. Not many know how the whole thing got started, though. It's a story wrapped within a story."

"All right."

"Contrary to what many believe, the Grail started out as nothing more than a fallen star. A servant of the Fisher King found it and brought the stone to an artisan, who carved it into a dish. The humble servant then brought the dish to the Fisher King. The king declared the dish to be a grail and kept it for many years until he could no longer carry on with his duties as king. As his kingdom fell into ruin, the Grail passed on to Joseph of Arimathea, who had it made into a cup; and shortly thereafter, it became known as the *Holy Grail* after Christ's crucifixion. Later, the elderly and dying Joseph passed it on to Elaine of Corbenic, and she became the Grail's keeper."

Jack Pack stared into the fire, a wistful look on his face. "Elaine of Corbenic fell in love with poor ole Lancelot. To get him to sleep with her, she twice tricked him into thinking she was Guinevere. She even gave birth to his child, one Galahad by name. When Guinevere discovered this, she cursed Lancelot and he went mad with grief."

"I know the story," Thooranu said. "Later, Elaine finds Lancelot in shambles in her garden. To cure him of his insanity, she lets him drink from the Grail."

"Indeed. Rumors of that spread. In order for Elaine and Lancelot to have a life together without being badgered by those wanting the Grail, Elaine handed it over to a holy court, who hid it away."

"And that's when the Trickster, the elf, and the beast bet on who could find it first?"

"They made the bet long before any of this happened. Each of them was aware of the relic, and when the three attended the funeral of the Fisher King, it became a conversation piece. They knew the Grail would eventually be lost, as most relics are, and decided that when it was, they would race to find. The challenge was, however, that they only use mortals in their search."

"Interesting," Thooranu admitted. "I am intrigued. What happened?"

"When he became a young man, Galahad went to King Arthur, offering to serve him. So, the king put him to the test."

"The old sword in the stone, eh?"

"Indeed, another legend. Now, here is the reason the stories cross paths. A wizard came to Arthur years before and showed him the stone, which was nothing more than a simple boulder by a river. The wizard then presented a sword made from steel that had come from another world. The hilt was wrapped in the hide of a creature that no longer existed, and set inside the pommel was a jewel that once resided far within the earth's heart. The wizard claimed the sword had come from God." Jack Pack took a deep draught of his wine, sighing in appreciation of the vintage.

"The wizard sheathed the sword in the stone and said that only the worthiest knight would be able to pull it free, and that knight would serve Arthur well. Arthur, believing that the sword was indeed a holy relic, held an annual ceremony to find that worthy. Once a year, knights would come to pull the sword free. Legend of the sword spread throughout the lands. No one, however, could get the sword out, and after a while, Arthur stopped holding the ceremony."

"Then one day, Sir Galahad showed up," Thooranu surmised.

"Yes, but he wasn't a knight then, not until he pulled the sword free."

"What made him worthy?"

"Ah-ah, wait," Jack Pack said, wagging his finger. "The king proclaimed that Galahad would become one of the Knights of the Round Table. Shortly afterwards, Arthur had a vision about the Grail and ordered a search for it. The king sent three knights: Galahad of course, Sir Bors, and Sir Perceval. The Trickster, the elf, and the Adlet beast had to choose which of the knights would find the Grail. Whoever's knight found the relic would win the wager. The elf chose Sir Perceval; the Adlet beast chose Sir Bors, and the Trickster chose Galahad."

"How did they determine who got which knight?" Thooranu inquired.

"They went by rank. The Trickster was a god, you see, and being the most powerful, he chose first. The Dökkálfar went next and then the Adlet beast."

Thooranu nodded. It made sense.

Jack Pack continued. "The knights went on with their quest and spent years searching. Then one day, the Trickster became distressed when Sir Bors saved Galahad's life. To show his gratitude, Galahad traded the sword he'd pulled from the stone with Bors."

Thooranu leaned over to pour more wine into his guest's glass. "So what? After the sword had proven Galahad to Arthur, what other purpose did the thing serve?"

"Don't be impatient," Jack Pack said, holding out his glass until it was full. "The Trickster needed the sword returned to Galahad and he found an opportunity for that to happen. After some time apart, the knights reunited when they came across Perceval's sister. She brought them to a ship bound for the Wasteland. When they landed, they continued on their journey together. On the way, the Trickster came to them, masquerading as a holy man and said that in order for them to cross the Wasteland, they first needed the blessing of the sick lady. They went to the sick lady's castle, where the custom was for one of her choosing to drink her blood from a silver dish." Jack Pack paused for a moment, savoring more of the fragrant wine.

"What the knights did not know was that anyone who drank the blood would die. The woman chose Bors. Perceval's sister, who was aware of this custom, offered to drink the blood in his stead. The sick lady allowed it, and when the sister drank, the lady revealed that Perceval's sister would die and that Bors now owed her for her sacrifice. Bors took it upon himself to uphold the dying sister's request to be brought back to the city of Sarras. The sick lady then said that because he had allowed this to happen—even though he'd been unaware of the fatal consequences—he no longer was deemed worthy to hold onto the sword from the stone. Guilt drove him to give the sword back to Galahad."

"You're saying that this Trickster had a hand in her death?" Thooranu asked, amazed. "How could he do that? Did he make a bargain with the Fates?"

"He didn't. Only if the Fates are absent from their realm can the laws of death and life be changed. However, the Trickster was one of the gifted few who had the ability to bend rules."

"I see. If that is so, then why kill Perceval's sister? Why not let Bors drink the blood?"

"It would have suited the Trickster just fine except that Bors might have been buried with the sword that had been given to him. It was customary for knights to be buried with their swords and shields. The Trickster had to make certain Galahad got his sword back."

"What if the sick lady hadn't chosen Bors?"

"She didn't *choose* at all. The Trickster had made a deal with her."

"And the sister couldn't just warn Bors?"

"They had been forbidden to leave until a sacrifice was made—a payment, if you will. Until then, they were bound within the castle walls forever."

Thooranu nodded cautiously and gestured for Jack to continue.

"The sword was returned to its rightful owner and Bors left to take Perceval's sister's body back to her homeland," Jack Pack went on, "leaving only Galahad and Perceval to continue the search for the Grail. After years of adventures, the pair finally came to the court of King Pelles and his son, Eliazar. These two holy men were the Grail's keepers. They told the knights that only a blessed man, a man of pure heart, could see the Holy Grail. Galahad then presented the sword he had pulled from the stone."

"Wait, I thought it was the Sword of David, the one given to him on the ship of faith."

"That's one version of the story, but it's not true. It was really the sword that proved his salt to King Arthur. The Trickster then won the contest the moment Galahad showed the king and his son the sword."

"What?" Thooranu said. "How is that?"

"It was rather simple, actually," Jack Pack said with a mischievous smirk. "It was the Trickster who had come to King Arthur with the sword. The wizard presented the sword that he, himself, had forged. In telling the lie that it had come from God, it helped to get the tale out into the world, where it was eventually brought to the attention of the holy court."

"Why go through the trouble with the sword?"

"Well, because of the love affair between Lancelot and Guinevere, Arthur was reluctant to allow the son of the man who stole his woman's heart to join his circle of knights. The sword convinced the King that Galahad was the knight he needed."

"Why did the Trickster want Galahad to be chosen to look for the Grail? Wouldn't any knight do?"

"No. Even with the sword, no mere human could be allowed to see the Grail, which had become much more than a fallen star. The sword was designed to release itself from the stone only by someone with a special bloodline, which Galahad had."

"Did this Trickster have a hand in Galahad's birth?" Thooranu asked, sensing a deeper history to this god's involvement.

"Very good guess, young man," the wanderer praised. "He most certainly did. To win the bet, the Trickster needed a mortal with an edge over the other two knights. He decided to use the love that Elaine had for Lancelot as a means to bring forth said mortal. He'd portrayed himself as a servant girl and told Elaine that if she wanted Lancelot to lay with her, she needed to give him wine and to wear a certain ring. The wine and ring were utterly useless, merely a ruse that gave her the confidence to go forth with the plan. It was the Trickster who'd led Lancelot to believe that it was Guinevere he was laying with. When their son was born, the Trickster made the sword and presented it to King Arthur."

"Then the Trickster was pulling the strings the entire time? Why?"

"To win the bet, my boy."

Thooranu snorted. "Not much of a challenge if he was going to cheat."

"Oh, but it was. The bet wasn't just about winning; it was a way for the Trickster to test his scheming skills, and what better way to do that than with a fixed wager?"

"Huh. So Galahad saw the Grail for himself. What happened then?"

"Not much; he died."

"And who gave Arthur the vision?"

Jack Pack smiled. "The Trickster, of course."

"And the Dökkálfar and the Adlet beast never suspected?"

"*That* was the real challenge, being able to do all of that trickery without getting caught."

"You mean all that backstabbing, it seems."

The wanderer shrugged. "No one said the Trickster was honest."

Thooranu raised his glass, and gave a wry smile. "Well played."

They both drank.

"Who gave you Guinevere's hair?" Thooranu asked.

"The Trickster. It was the only thing he requested of her when she asked him to convince Elaine to kill herself, which wasn't hard seeing how she was utterly heartbroken. Lancelot never stopped loving Guinevere, you know."

"So you met the Trickster?"

"I did, indeed." Jack Pack took a long drink of wine and turned to Thooranu. "Now, let's have some of that heart."

They spoke for hours on many topics: the places they'd seen, women they'd seduced, and mischievous deeds committed. Several bottles of wine and one jackal later, they were conversing on matters that Thooranu had never discussed with anyone. As the sun began to rise over the sandy hills, Jack Pack told him that he was going to explore the moons of Jupiter and invited him along.

For the next few years, the two were inseparable. They traveled together, sharing adventures that Thooranu hoped would never end. He felt he'd found a true friend in Jack Pack.

One hot summer's day in Greece, they were enjoying coffee at a café when Jack Pack offered a proposal. "Have you ever thought about running a business?"

"Pardon?" Thooranu said, setting his cup on its saucer. "A business?"

"I've been flirting with the idea for quite some time now. I was once an architect, you know."

"An architect?" he chuckled. "Why?"

"Sometimes I like to grow roots. It's a change of pace. I like to keep myself busy, and what better way than running a business, eh?"

Thooranu's curiosity was piqued. He had never tried such an endeavor. "What sort of business?"

"I was thinking of a tavern and brothel."

"Where?"

"Here, in Athens. I've already picked out a place."

Thooranu leaned back in his chair. "A brothel, eh?" he said, rubbing his chin.

"We'll only employ the finest women," Jack Pack added slyly.

Both the human and incubus side of Thooranu liked that idea and he grinned. "Where is it?"

Jack Pack took him to an abandoned brick building in Piraeus. Fragments of pottery lay everywhere, and a couple of amphora stood against one wall.

"It used to be a warehouse," Jack Pack explained, walking farther inside. "Until last year, when the owner committed suicide after he lost two of his ships."

Thooranu imagined how it might be, not as the hollow forgotten place it now was, but as a fully stocked tavern, filled with people drinking and singing. He smelled cigar smoke and heard music. There would be blood on his face from a fight. Once in a while, he'd sneak off with one of the whores for a good fucking. Seeing everything so clearly got him excited. What did he have to lose?

"What say you?" Jack Pack asked. "Are you game?"

"Sure. Why the hell not. We can just walk away from it when we're bored."

"Ah," Jack Pack said, coming back. "That is so, but we need a signed contract for the building."

Thooranu's eyebrows knitted together. "Why?"

"To make it legal, of course." He reached into his inside coat pocket.

"I don't understand. It isn't as if it matters if we lose money. I sure as hell don't care. Why sign a contract?"

"As you pointed out, we can leave the business anytime we wish. The contract is simply a formality to the owner of the property. It's meaningless to us, but the mortal I leased the building from needs it." Jack Pack brought out a rolled up piece of paper. "Have a look and see."

Thooranu took the paper and unrolled it. He had never read a legal document before. The single sheet was indeed a lease for the building, the price paid for it each month, and other legal jargon that bored him. Jack's name was already scrawled in black.

"How come you've already signed it?"

"I want it," Jack Pack said. "Do you?"

Thooranu thought on that for a moment, then turned his eyes back to the contract and to the blank line next to Jack's signature.

"You can sign it later, if you want," Jack said. "I don't want us to be late for the matinee."

Seven against Thebes. Thooranu had nearly forgotten about the play. He checked his pocket watch. It was already one-twenty-three.

"Got a pen?" he asked.

Jack Pack smirked and handed over a quill. Thooranu took it and carefully signed his name. Instantly he felt woozy, suddenly weak.

"What is it?" Jack asked.

"I'm not sure," he muttered, almost falling, catching

himself against a support beam at the last second. "I feel off somehow."

"Oh?" Jack crossed his arms. "Do you feel a bit hollow, as if you've just lost something?"

Thooranu did not like the tone in his friend's voice. Nevertheless, what Jack Pack had said captured his attention. Something was terribly wrong. He felt a sense of loss.

"What have you done?" he asked fretfully.

"It's not what *I've* done, per se; it's what you just did."

"What?"

"Look at the contract."

Thooranu did so—immediately—as if obeying Jack Pack's command. He read the contract again, only it wasn't a deed to the ownership of the building they stood in, but a deed to ownership of *him*! Thooranu's name was printed before a statement that he had surrendered his freedom to whoever's name was on the deed. The other name was none other than Jack Pack.

"I . . . I don't understand," Thooranu stammered. "This isn't what I just read."

Jack began jumping up and down, clapping his hands while laughing. "I got you! I did it! I caught a demon!"

Reeling from what was happening, Thooranu shifted his wide eyes up to him. "Why have you done this?"

"Why?" Jack said, stopping his excited jumping. "Because I wanted to. Because I've never done it before. You're my property now, for an entire year. Until the contract expires."

Thooranu's face was stone. He looked at Jack Pack through slitted eyes. When the deed finally expired, he would tear his betrayer to bits.

"Oh, but you won't," Jack Pack said, catching his thoughts. "All I need to do is sign my name again."

Thooranu was still holding the contact. He tried to rip it to shreds, but his arms locked up. No matter how hard he struggled, he couldn't tear up the piece of paper.

"You're not allowed to do that," Jack Pack said with a wagging finger. "If you read on, you'll see why. Also, if the deed is destroyed, you will be forced to destroy yourself in the most painful way that a demon can die."

Thooranu lowered the paper. His whole body was numb with shock. "How did you do this?"

"Well, first I had to gain your trust," Jack Pack said, taking the paper from Thooranu's hand. "Then, when the time came, I drew this deed up and put an illusion over it that kept you from seeing the real meaning."

"An illusion?"

Jack Pack winked. "Yes, just like Elaine and Lancelot."

"Fiend! *You're* the Trickster!"

"Indeed. And I have succeeded in my scheme."

Being a demon, emotions usually didn't penetrate Thooranu's cerebral cortex. Yet the human side of him felt the sting of betrayal that this *thing*, this petty god, had inflicted upon him.

The Trickster lost his smile. He leaned in closer, his face now only inches from the demon's.

"I have you, Thooranu, you're mine. Until I sell you to the highest bidder."

Chapter One
Mother of Craft

Spring, 1843

Mother of Craft's garden smelled like new life in the fresh afternoon air, growing everything from local to exotic plants; from peas to poppies, orchids to onions, daisies to dwarf apples. The plot was vibrant with a variety of colors, an Eden overlooking the sea. Her garden was a place where life began. And sometimes where it ended.

Tarquin Norwich rode up the lane toward the modest cottage. For years, he had come to Mother of Craft, seeking guidance. Today, he'd come with a special request.

He dismounted. The roan was shiny with sweat. He started for the front door when he spied Mother of Craft on her knees, at work amongst the flowers. She didn't greet him, continuing to weed. Norwich was allergic to pollen, a fact she knew, and no doubt was why she was waiting for him in the garden. She smirked as he approached, as if she sensed his discomfort.

"Mother of Craft," he said, clearing his throat loudly.

"I'm not deaf, Tarquin Norwich," she retorted, pulling weeds from amongst the chamomile.

Norwich sighed, then sneezed. "Mother of Craft, *please.*" His tone hardened.

She rose and examined him. Norwich's eyes were red and glossy, like freshly spilled blood. But despite his sniffing and heavy breathing, he stood arrow straight, head high like a proud, albeit sick, lion.

"Let's go inside," she said, heading for the back door, a bouquet of white chamomile in her hand. "The water will be boiling by now."

As she knew he would, he hurried to follow.

Her home felt like an ancient memory, an echo of a past life. A few glass plated daguerreotypes of her and her daughter hung on the dark blue wall, along with oil paintings of forested landscapes and abstracts of cities. Twisted vines cradled glass lamps in their green fingers. Inside, living plants thrived, yet the lamps still gave off a low glow.

Norwich hung his coat and hat on a rack, then went to the kitchen and sat at his usual chair. It was the most inviting room in the small cottage. Freshly baked biscuits sat within a small wicker basket, giving it a homey aroma. Through a wide window above the counter was a view of an endless ocean.

While she removed her sun hat and loosened the ribbon around her long red hair, Norwich took out a handkerchief and blew his nose.

"Tell me, Tarquin," Mother of Craft said, tearing flower pedals from their stems, dropping them into a small bowl, "what is it you seek?"

"The Toymaker," he said, his voice clear now. "Can you help me find him?"

"Indigo Peachtree, eh? Has he gone missing?"

"Yes," Norwich admitted. "In truth, he escaped from me last night."

The iron kettle hanging over the range began to whistle sharply. It was sculpted like a short twisted tree with roots snaking its body, with a branch for a handle. It was half covered by small tesserae with tea-leaves painted on. She dumped the bowl of petals into a matching teapot, then grabbed the kettle with a cloth and poured in the steaming water. She smiled wistfully, breathing the heady aroma as she stirred the brew.

"No," she said, pouring the tea into a cup.

"No?" he exclaimed, his face reddening. He slapped his hand down on the table.

"Don't you be hitting anything that belongs to me, Tarquin Norwich!" she admonished fiercely. Although her anger was feigned, it was enough to put him in his place.

Norwich was deemed an important man. He was also power hungry, ambitious, cruel, and deadly. Mother of Craft helped him because he played a vital role in her plans.

Norwich's face softened and he looked away, not meeting her gaze. He cleared his throat as if to say something, but no words were forthcoming.

"I don't know where to find Indigo Peachtree," Mother of Craft said. It was a lie, but he could not know that. She placed the teacup down before him. "But"— she hesitated, relishing the little torment it gave him— "there are those who do."

Norwich leaned over his cup, wafting the steam up with his hands, breathing deeply. He spoke in a casual tone that barely masked his profound interest. "And who might they be?"

"The Landcross brothers."

Norwich sat bolt upright. "Landcross," he gasped. "How can that be?"

"The two have crossed paths with Indigo."

"I see," Norwich said, nodding solemnly. He took a sip of tea. "Do you know how to find them? Either, I don't care which."

The sun vanished behind a mass of grey clouds, a warning of oncoming rain. Mother of Craft lit candles inside several yellowing glass lanterns that she placed upon the table. "Not just one, but *both* of them."

"I only need one," he replied, taking a biscuit from the basket. "The one who will best cooperate, that is."

"You'll find that both will cooperate in their own way," she said.

"Why do I need both?" He chewed the soft biscuit, letting its sweet taste lighten his mood.

"The oldest knows where to find the Toymaker. However, the younger knows where to find an important item you seek."

She looked him in the eye, but he turned away. Her unusual violet eyes unnerved him.

"The journal?" Norwich asked in a whisper. "He knows where it is?"

"Indeed. As well as the masks. You'll need those, too, Tarquin. Do not misjudge their importance."

Norwich could not hide his excitement. "And you can locate them?"

"Yes, I believe I can."

She left the kitchen with the teacup in hand, walking over to a bookshelf in the other room. "They're many miles distant, but not for long." She stopped in front of a map of England painted on a burlap canvas that hung on the wall like a ragged curtain.

"Are they together?" Norwich asked.

"No," she said, planting her finger on the map. "One is here."

He stood up and came over to her. "Bristol? It'll take me a week to get there and back. "

"That's why you'll wait a week until he arrives here," Mother of Craft said, sliding her finger down to the forest area of Ampfield. "On this road, at Pagan Tree Dressing Church, you'll be able to capture him when he and his gang of highwaymen try to rob you."

"Which brother is it?"

"The oldest."

"Right," he huffed. "Where's the other one?"

She sipped her tea, then turned to face him. Just mentioning the younger brother boiled her blood. The years she'd invested in that boy! It kept her awake at nights.

"He's in France, on his way to Le Havre. You'll find him in an inn by the sea."

"How is it that you can tell me exactly where those two are, but not Peachtree?" His tone conveyed more than simply suspicion; there was a threat there too.

"The brothers were touched by the supernatural many years ago, and that allows me—and any good witch or warlock—to sense them. I have an insight into their futures."

What she told him was only half of the truth. Indeed, the Landcross brothers had the cloak of craft over them. Like most enchanters, she was able to look into the kaleidoscope of someone's future and see the many different outcomes in their life. Contrary to what many believed, there was no such thing as destiny, only random acts that kept the future constantly shifting. Consequently, one's future could not be told in a single path. The only certainty was death, the time of which was determined before birth.

Mother of Craft was a talented witch. Like most with magical blessings, she did not need a lot of paraphernalia to use her power. It simply resided within her like a vital organ.

And she didn't mind the term witch. She was who she was, and she had no quarrel with that. After all, she had let herself die in order to become an enchantress.

"How will I know him?" Norwich asked. "The one in France."

"He has a scar across his throat. This is common knowledge so he will try to hide it, concealed under an old scarf. He also wears a Greek coin on a chain around his neck; a stater. When you find him, he'll be eating soup."

"Eating soup?"

She nodded.

"Is he not in Le Havre now?" Norwich asked with a dash of impatience in his tone.

"No, Calais. He arrived after a narrow escape from the royal guards. He will be heading south to Le Havre." She went back to the kitchen and poured herself more tea. He followed slowly, with a last lingering look at the map.

"These are the closest locations that the brothers will be to you. Try not to be so impatient. Let them draw themselves in on their own." She turned her eyes up to him. "Besides, do you not have business at your summer estate?"

His look betrayed his thoughts as he frowned. "Ah, yes. I do, indeed."

Norwich drained his last drops of tea, and Mother of Craft poured more for him. "Another shipment coming in, yes?"

He snorted. "I confide too much in you."

He was obviously feeling better now.

"And for good reason," she replied. "If you had not confided in me about what Indigo told you, I could not have explained what I knew—and the power that could be gained from what he has. You're crossing dangerous ground, dove, and you need all the help you can get."

"I'll be fine."

She raised her chin. "Just in case, I will give you something."

She headed to the spice rack, with him following closely. She could feel his strength whenever he was near, and not just his physical might. His willpower was an unbreakable force. His stony grey eyes matched his salt and pepper hair, set within a majestic warrior's face. Physically, he was a handsome man, yet he was a hardened soul who had not even mourned the death of his lovely wife when she'd taken her own life.

But, however strong, Tarquin Norwich was an automaton, a mindless machine for her to use.

She took a small, pink vial from the rack. She popped the tiny cork and poured out the fine anise seeds. She moved over to the counter near the window and lifted the lid of the largest of the matryoshka nesting dolls lining the wall. From it, she brought out a round, midnight blue jar. After twisting the cap off, she poured what looked to be black oil into the vial. She pressed the cork back and placed the pink container in front of Norwich. "Use it well."

Norwich picked it up, studying it, his face scrunching in distaste. "What is it?"

"Demon's blood."

He laughed, thinking it a joke. But when she didn't join him, he fell silent.

"Mix this into something when you use it. It'll be easier for the individual to drink it if they don't know what it is. Afterwards you'll have complete control."

He nodded. "The color of the bottle makes me half believe it's a love potion."

She snorted. "*That* doesn't exist. Otherwise, I would have sold you some to use on your wife."

He grimaced and placed his cup on the counter. "I must go. It's a long ride to Southampton." He set a coin purse down next to his teacup and headed for the coat rack.

"One more thing," Mother of Craft said, paying no mind to the purse. "It would be best to send all three of your children out to find the brothers."

Norwich turned to her as he donned his coat. "Archie? He's a weak imbecile. Useless on all fronts. And Clover? She's a ten-year-old girl. Just as useless."

"Trust me," she said earnestly. "You'll need them. And if you think so poorly of them, send them after the easiest one to catch."

He didn't seem convinced, yet she knew that his trust in her would outweigh his doubt.

She saw him out and watched him ride down the lane through the sprinkling rain. As she did every time he'd come to seek guidance, she thought it was funny that he never asked if he would succeed in his plan. It wasn't fear that kept him from inquiring. Tarquin Norwich simply had too much damn self-confidence. A flaw, for that blinding buoyancy would be his undoing.

Vela, Mother of Craft's daughter, emerged from the woods in time to see him leave. She carried two limp, dangling hares. The mirror image of Mother of Craft, but at only eleven, she still had a lot of growing to do. She also shared some of her father's features, like his wild heart and slender build. Mother of Craft had to admit she missed him sometimes.

"Was that Norwich again?" Vela asked.

"Aye."

"What did he want this time?"

"He wants many things, as most men do. None of which concern you."

"Yes, Mother."

"I will say this, child," she added. "This may well be the last you'll ever see of him."

Chapter Two
Let it Begin

Seven days later

Archie Norwich lay in bed, his chest heaving from the love making with the beautiful woman beside him. He adored moments like these. Being with Eilidh took his mind off the bruised eye and equally bruised ego.

"Archie?" Eilidh whispered from beside him, "have you made plans for us to leave, yet?"

It was a question that jabbed a thorn into his side and he frowned. "I have to map it out, but I thought we would start in Paris."

"Paris?"

"We'll go to Rome from there, then to Venice."

"Then where?" she asked, sitting up.

He turned to look at her naked body glowing in the afternoon light, examining her greedily, feasting on her perfection. A smile flit across his lips. She had a face like a pixie, with large royal blue eyes and a small but vibrant mouth that offered the most charming smiles. He pulled her to him, the fingers of his right hand interlacing with hers.

"Umm, the Netherlands. Then to Prague."

"Prague? That dreadful city?"

"It's interesting."

"Have you ever been to Prague?" she challenged.

"No, never."

"Then how do you know it's interesting?"

"You haven't been there, either. How do you know it's dreadful?"

She chuckled, low in her throat. "Fair enough. After we've traveled to Paris, Rome, Venice, the Netherlands, and . . . Prague, what's next?"

He knew where this was going and dreaded it. "Where else would you like to go?" he asked to prolong the conversation.

"Someplace where you and I can have a life together." She pulled away, then rolled onto him, propping herself up with arms on either side of him, her long hair brushing his face. "You know, start a family." She leaned in and kissed his chest. "Like we discussed, remember?"

He had no plan and she saw it in his hesitation.

"You promised!" she accused, slapping him hard on the chest. "You said that after we got married, you'd find a way to get us away from here so we could start a life together!" She flung herself out of bed and began dressing. "We should have left while your father and brother were gone."

"There were two reasons why we couldn't," he said, sitting up. "One, I'm not going anywhere without Clover; and she's just gotten over an illness."

Eilidh's expression softened. "I know you'd never leave your sister behind, Archie. I adore her as much as you do, and I would never ask you to abandon her."

"Thank you." He sighed. "Also, my father told me that he has an important mission for me when he returns. If we were gone when he needed me, he would undoubtedly send a hunting party after us." And he knew exactly what he was talking about. "I need time to get enough money so we can get as far away as possible. I must have the means to provide for us."

"We don't need a lot of money," she said, putting on her black long-sleeve blouse. "We only need each other. Even if we end up living in a quaint little farm cottage, it doesn't matter as long as we're together."

That was one reason he loved her. Despite seeing the luxurious life and all the benefits of being a Norwich, Eilidh had never wanted any of it. All she wanted was love, family, and honesty.

She had been a maid in his father's household for five years, since she was sixteen. When she'd arrived, it had been love at first sight and they had become lovers, marrying each other in secret. Even now, she wasn't fully aware of what his father was capable of. Just learning about their secret marriage would spark a merciless reaction in Tarquin Norwich.

Archie had been frightened of his father his entire life. If he and Eilidh ran away together and his father caught up to them, he'd kill Eilidh, perhaps them both, and bury them in shallow graves. He knew his father could do such things; he'd done it before.

"It won't be long before he finds out about us, Archie," Eilidh said, slipping her wedding ring off its proper place and setting it on her index finger. She glanced out the window as she tied her white apron around her waist. "Your father and brother are back."

Struck with panic, Archie jumped from the bed and ran to the window. His father and older brother, Ivor, were riding up the gravel lane toward the house. The sound of a servant announcing their return made his stomach twist.

"Goodbye, my lord," Eilidh said in her servant tone.

"Eilidh, wait."

But she had already left the room. Being naked, he couldn't very well go after her. Yet even if he did, what could he say?

He cleaned up, dressed then hurried downstairs with his shotgun. He went out back, to the shooting range. He needed to appear as if he was doing something, anything, other than making love with his secret bride, as well as make it easy for his father to find him.

He stood near a hand-crank machine with eight brass cylinders that could send clay disks sailing into the air. A servant was at the crank, waiting for his command.

Archie raised his shotgun. "Loose!"

The servant turned the metal crank several times until a disk was hurled into the sky. Archie fired and the disk shattered. The servant turned a wheel attached to the side of the machine and rotated the brass cylinders as Archie reloaded.

Archie hoped the gun smoke would mask his fear.

He fired another shot before he heard his father calling. Tarquin Norwich was standing on the stone steps leading up to the back entrance of the house. When his father beckoned him forward, Archie raced up the steps with the shotgun in hand and stood before him, almost at attention.

He hated being face-to-face with the man but he plastered on a smile. "Welcome home, Father. I hope your time at the castle was restful."

Tarquin had been going to Castle Norwich on the Isle of Wight more often these days. Archie didn't know why, and he'd been forbidden to go himself, which suited him just fine.

"I want you to go to Le Havre and apprehend Pierce Landcross," his father ordered. "Tell the Harbormaster to have one of his captains take you across on my personal ferry."

Archie thought he must have heard him wrong. "Pierce Landcross? The thief who—"

"Yes, the one and the same," his father said. "He's going to help find the Toymaker's journal. Once you have him in custody, bring him here, where he can be interrogated. Understood?"

"Father, what if I can get him to talk?"

"Absolutely not! He may try fooling you, boy; and knowing how gullible you are, you'll fall head first for his lies. Besides, you don't have the stomach for what I have in mind if he refuses to cooperate."

His father's words washed over him as they normally did. Tarquin Norwich had said far worse things to him in the past. Yet he was curious about this journal that Pierce Landcross was supposed to find, although he knew better than to ask. Why had Indigo Peachtree, the Toymaker, been invited to the mansion to begin with?

Peachtree had seemed nervous when he'd been at the estate, especially around Archie's father. Something Archie could well understand. His father had had a special feast prepared for Peachtree, which the Toymaker had attended dressed in an old, cheap tweed suit, his hair wildly disheveled. Clover thought he was amusing and wanted to stay, but when their father wanted to speak business with Peachtree, Archie had been told to put his sister to bed. Archie hadn't minded much. He never wanted to be involved in any of his father's affairs. That was a task best suited for Ivor. Archie much preferred spending his time listening to Clover's stories than listening to his father.

Peachtree had left the mansion sometime during the night. The next day, Tarquin had sent a search party out. Archie had asked what had happened and it had earned him a black eye. It wasn't the first time his father had struck him and it most likely wouldn't be the last. Therefore, he kept his inquiries about his father's mission to himself and simply said, "Yes, sir. How shall I find him?"

"Late afternoon tomorrow, Landcross will be in a tavern near the sea. He has a scar across his throat, hidden under a scarf. And he will be wearing a silver coin, a stater, on a chain."

Archie furrowed his brow. His father saw his confusion. "It's an ancient coin from Greece," he explained.

Archie knew what a stater was and that Landcross was scarred. What puzzled him was how his father knew the man's location.

"Oh, and apparently he will be eating soup," his father added, deepening Archie's curiosity.

"Yes, sir. I will bring him here to you."

"Good. Take some of my soldiers with you, as well as your sister."

"Clover?" he asked before he could stop himself. "Why?"

"Don't question me!" his father bellowed. "Just do as I say."

Archie looked down at the ground. "Yes, sir."

"Your brother and I will be traveling north. We will most likely not be back by the time you arrive with Landcross, so make sure he's well secured until our return."

"Yes, sir."

"Leave before nightfall," his father ordered. "And don't fail me or I shall have you severely punished. Understood?"

Archie understood all too well.

As his father left the yard, Archie headed for his sister's room. He found her at her desk, scribbling in her journal.

Clover loved writing, especially fantasy stories about dragons and lost worlds, where she cast herself as the protagonist, traveling from one adventure to another. He envied her imagination. The stories set her free to live in other places and took her away from the harsh world she actually inhabited. Although their father had never laid a hand on her, he ignored her. Clover's only parental affection had come from their mother, but Archie doubted if his sister even remembered her.

When their mother died, Archie tried to fill the void the best he could by buying her books, getting her journals and listening to her stories. It had kept them both sane. He only hoped that he could soon work up enough courage to take her and Eilidh away from all this.

"Writing your adventures again?" he asked, standing within the doorway.

Clover raised her head and twisted around to look at him.

She was beautiful, just like their late mother, with large dark eyes and hair like red wine, tied back in a striped ribbon that matched her dress.

With a smile, she said, "I just started a new story. This time, I'm a mermaid and will explore the depths of the ocean."

"Is that so?" he said with unfeigned interest, stepping into the room. He wanted to hear more, as he always did. She would get animated and act out her ideas as they came to her. But there was no time, not if they were to be off before sundown.

"How would you like to go on a real adventure?" he asked.

"What do you mean?"

Archie took a seat by the window. "Father wants us to go to Le Havre."

"Why?"

He'd rehearsed his answer before coming to the

room. If only he didn't have to bring her with him. Aside from fearing the worst to happen to her during the mission, she had just gotten over a bad cold. Even the color of her face had yet to return in full. Crossing the Channel could bring back her illness.

He cleared his throat and said, "Um, to catch a man who Father wishes to question."

"What sort of questions?"

"He wants to ask him about Indigo Peachtree."

She giggled. "Mr. Peachtree? He was so funny. Remember when he gave me this?"

Archie looked at the mechanical rabbit on her desk. When wound, it would bounce straight up in the air and flip backwards. The amazing automaton was an example of the Toymaker's talent.

"Too bad Father scared him away," she said. "Why does he want to find him?"

"You know he doesn't confide in me."

"What else does Father want with him?"

"He wants to know about Peachtree's journal."

"A journal? What's in it?"

Archie shrugged.

"Right." She sighed. "And this man knows where Mr. Peachtree and his journal are?"

"I'm not sure if he knows the whereabouts of Peachtree, but Father believes that he knows where to find the book."

"And I'm sure that Father told you where to find this man. Have you ever wondered how he acquires such information?"

"I do. If I were to ask him, though . . ." He trailed off, looking away. The bruise around his eye began to throb.

"Why does he hate us so much?" Clover asked.

It was a simple question but Archie found it difficult to answer. He shrugged. "I think it's because we remind him too much of her."

"Mother?"

"Aye. We are a reminder of the one person in his miserable life that he could never fully control." He stood and headed for the door. "Take only what you need. We leave within the hour."

Back in his own room, he began packing his things into a small rucksack when a movement from the corner caught his eye.

"Eilidh," he said, "you shouldn't be in here."

"I'll only be a moment," she whispered, rushing up to him. She hugged him tightly, and although it was dangerous, he embraced her in return.

"I'm sorry about earlier," she said, pulling him tighter.

"For what?"

She pulled away and looked him in the eye.

"I saw you and your father speaking in the yard. I heard him yelling. It reminded me who he really is. We shouldn't take the chance of him finding us when we leave."

Her understanding thrilled him, yet the pressure to come up with a plan still weighed heavily. Then he recalled what his father had said.

"Eilidh," — he spoke urgently — "pack your things and be ready to leave when I come back."

"What?"

"My father told me that he and Ivor won't return until after I bring back a prisoner."

"A prisoner?"

"Yes, I am to travel to Le Havre and capture Pierce Landcross, and bring him here."

"Landcross? Is your father planning to take him to the Queen? I'm sure she'd love to get her hands on him after what he pulled."

"No, he wants to question him about Indigo Peachtree. Listen, after I return with Landcross and he's securely under lock and key, you, Clover, and I will leave."

"To where?"

"Dublin. From there, we'll board an Atlantic steamer."

"America?"

"Yes. And if we hurry, we can be in Ireland by the time Father and Ivor get here. Who knows; perhaps he'll be so preoccupied with Landcross and what he wants with Peachtree that he won't bother with us."

He felt an electric charge surge through him. It was a good plan. As long as he could deliver what his father desired, there stood a chance they could make it.

"Do you really think so?" Eilidh asked, eyes wide.

"You were right before, my love. It won't be long before my father finds out about us." His mouth went dry and the words rasped. "I don't want to imagine what he'd do if that happened."

She placed a hand on his shoulder. "I'm not afraid of your father."

He took her hand and held it over his heart. *If you knew what he has done, you would be,* he thought gravely. He kissed her hand.

"You should go. I'll see you in a few days."

She took the bedpan and as she left, Ivor entered the room after her. For a moment, Archie feared that his brother had heard their conversation.

"Ah, little brother wants his room nice and tidy when he returns?" Ivor finally said.

"Shut it," Archie seethed, shoving a folded shirt into his bag, relieved that his and Eilidh's conversation hadn't been overheard.

"Father told me that you are going after Pierce Landcross," Ivor said. "Think you can handle it?"

Archie glared at him through narrowed eyes. He never wanted to, but he'd grown to loathe his older brother. Ever since Ivor had become their father's lapdog.

"Don't look at me like that," Ivor said, approaching him. "I only ask."

His brother smelled of brandy. It only took a couple of drinks to prompt Ivor to badger him.

"The maid who just left," Ivor said. "Are you fucking her?"

Archie continued packing, trying desperately not to betray any emotion, when all he wanted was to slam his fist into his brother's face and break his skull wide open. Instead, he replied with a smirk, "What if I am?"

Ivor chuckled. "Bedding the help, eh? Maybe you're more like Father than you think." He leaned against the bedpost. "If she's that willing, perhaps I'll have a go at her."

Archie's fists clenched involuntarily. *One more word . . . just one.* He swallowed thickly and said, "When do you and Father depart?"

"This evening, same as you. He's in quite a hurry."

"I see."

Ivor's lips tended to loosen with drink. Archie wondered if he could get anything out of him that his father had refused to share. "He ordered that I bring Clover."

Ivor snorted. "I know. What good she'll do is beyond me."

"Then why do I have to take her?"

"That isn't the question you ought to be asking."

"Really?" Archie said, tying off his rucksack. "What should I be asking? What is Father's business with the Toymaker, anyway? What's in this journal that Landcross is supposed to help Father find?"

Ivor smirked. "It just kills you that Father entrusts me with his plans and not you, doesn't it?"

Damn it, Ivor hadn't drunk enough to spill secrets, just enough to be obnoxious. It was no secret that their father favored Ivor more than his other children, but Archie could not care less.

"I need to get going," Archie said, slinging the pack over his shoulder.

He started for the door when Ivor stepped in his way.

"What Father has built, I will inherit after his death. What will you receive, little brother?"

"If I'm a thousand miles away from you, then I'll have just about everything I could ever ask for."

Archie pushed past him and didn't look back.

Having found Clover, he and his sister went outside to be met by four house guards. Everyone saddled up. Clover rode beside him with two guards in front and two behind. Archie twisted in the saddle, looking back towards the house. Was that his father? He turned back to the road, falling quickly into the familiar rhythm of his horse's gait as they began their journey south, towards the coast.

Tarquin Norwich watched from his bedroom balcony as the group made their way along the gravel lane.

"You think he'll succeed?" Ivor asked, stepping up next to him with a glass of brandy in his hand.

Norwich had never approved of his son's excessive drinking, but he also didn't condemn it. Whenever he looked at his eldest child, he saw his own father; a strong, chiseled featured man with eyes like black glass. He'd admired his father and had adored his mother, whom Ivor had inherited his wheat-colored hair from. Both had been strong and intelligent people who'd taught their only son to take whatever he wanted.

Regardless of his love for his own son, he dared not to fill him in on the most vital part of his plan, mostly because of Ivor's talkative nature when drunk.

"He better. Too much is at stake," he replied, taking Ivor's brandy glass. "Do not allow drink to compromise our goal."

"I won't, Father," Ivor promised.

"Go downstairs. Be ready to leave when I come down. We'll rest at the inn at North Baddesley."

"Yes, Father."

As Ivor left, Norwich turned back to watch the group now on the thoroughfare.

If everything goes as planned, I'll become much more than any mortal monarch. Norwich's lips twitched into a leering smile as he knocked back Ivor's brandy in one swallow.

Chapter Three
To Catch a Thief

Archie had devised a plan to catch Landcross before they'd crossed the Channel. They stayed the night in Southampton, where Archie had explained his idea. He'd brought common clothing for himself and Clover, for she too was a necessary part of the plan. The soldiers had been instructed to leave behind their grey leather uniforms and wear their own clothing instead. The following morning, the group left for the harbor and boarded a steam-powered ferryboat.

The day was fine, the ferry gliding across the flat of the English Channel with ease. Still, Archie was nervous for Clover. She hadn't been out at sea in years, and he feared that the brisk, wet air would cause her to fall ill again.

But Clover was unaffected by the climate and her excitement appeared to grow as they drew closer to Le Havre. The port was full of ships, a forest of tall masts rising like pikes. Sailors bustled about, loading and unloading cargo. Black smokestacks jutted up from both buildings and steamships. The air smelled of the sea and its myriad creatures.

The ferryboat reached the dock and a crewman threw a line to a dockhand to tie off.

"Where do you think Landcross is?" Clover asked Archie.

"This is one of the largest commercial harbors in France," he said, scanning the marina while taking her hand as they crossed the gangplank. "There are a lot of inns, but most likely he'll be here, by the docks. I'm thinking that he's going to try boarding a ship, so he will want to be close."

His soldiers joined them on the dock, and Sergeant Arran Derby nodded. "Right," he said. "Let's scout the dockside inns."

Sergeant Derby was a tall burly man with stark black hair and thick muttonchops.

"Good," Archie said. "Remember, we're looking for a man in his mid-twenties with a scarf hiding a scar across his throat. He'll also have a coin on a chain around his neck."

"And he'll be eating soup," Clover threw in.

Archie smiled down at her. "Aye, that he will. Don't get anxious if you spot him," he said to his men. "Let's keep this capture discreet to prevent any unwanted attention."

"Aye, sir," the sergeant replied.

"Right then, let's get on with it."

Clover tugged his arm and pointed. "Archie, look."

He followed her finger to a ship docked a little ways down from them. Black-skinned people—men, women, and children—trailed down a ramp to the pier. Awaiting them were several groups of people; French humanitarians, unless he missed his mark.

Archie studied the ship. It was a late 1700s Spanish galleon with many feathers and animal bones tied everywhere along the gunwales. Large brass piping ran down the ship's sides, and the engine from a steam locomotive was mounted on deck. But what caught Archie's attention was the ship's flag; three wavy lines, the ancient symbol for water, with two arrows crossing each other.

Some Indian tribes had been drafted into the colonial defense, and they had fought the British Royal Navy at sea. After the Seven Years War ended, some of them kept their ships, dubbing themselves the Sea

Warriors, attacking European settlers sailing to the New World. Yet on their own, they were no match for the strongest naval fleet in the world, and the number of Sea Warriors had dwindled over the course of the last hundred years. Now only a handful remained, with a new battle to fight—attacking slave ships and freeing people who'd been kidnapped from their homeland. Instead of fighting against the English, they helped uphold the loosely followed Slave Trade Act that had been put into law in 1788.

Sometimes the Sea Warriors brought people back to their homeland, risking being taken themselves; but most often they were taken to a country where they would remain free.

"Were those people going to be slaves?" Clover asked.

"Yes," Archie said with heaviness in his throat.

"Bloody hell," one of the men said. "I wonder if that's ole Captain Sea Wind, himself."

The soldier indicated a man sporting long black hair, wearing a large brimmed hat adorned with feathers. His clothing was an outdated French great coat and buckskin breeches. He stood by the railing, observing his crew helping the Africans to the pier.

Captain Sea Wind, an Apache, was the most infamous of the Sea Warriors. Tales of him and his wife were printed in novelty pamphlets almost every year. Their ship, the *Ekta*, which meant Unity, was known to have successfully attacked over forty slave ships throughout the course of her thirty-five years under Captain Sea Wind's control.

Archie and the others headed into the city on foot. He was prepared to search every tavern along the coast until he found his quarry. Landcross was his ticket to freedom. Once he had the outlaw safely in his father's mansion, he, Eilidh, and Clover would leave and make a new life together.

Pierce Landcross had dreamt again of strange flying machines. He tried to hold onto the images, yet they slipped away. As his eyes reluctantly opened, he remembered nothing.

He'd awakened in his chambers after a full day's sleep. With a groan and a deep yawn, he got out of bed, stretched, and went over to the washbasin. After scrubbing his face and the rest of the sleep away, he looked at himself in the mirror. The room glowed with the afternoon light, and his scar stood out, livid white, a brutal reminder of betrayal and heartbreak. Every detail of that night played out in significant fragments; the punch that had brought him down, the knife, the look on his assailant's face, and then the abandonment when it was all over. Every time he touched the scar, he could almost feel the jagged blade tearing across his skin.

He shook off the memory and splashed more water on his face. A pang in his stomach reminded him that he needed food. He also needed to find a ship willing to let him board before the royal guards caught up with him. He was willing to take passage anywhere so long as it was hundreds, or even thousands of miles away.

A week and a half ago, he'd crossed a line, earning him a hunting party on his tail, aiming to bring him back to London. He'd managed a razor-thin escape in Aylesham, before crossing the Channel, where he'd traveled down the coast, only stopping to steal a horse to keep up a steady getaway.

The only issue looming over him was money. Without money for passage, he would have to offer to work his way. He hadn't even paid for his chambers.

He'd simply entered the hotel, gone up to the rooms and picked a lock. After establishing that the room wasn't occupied, he'd spent nearly the rest of his cash on a meal and gone back up to sleep.

He went downstairs and found a small table in the back room. On the way there, he picked the pocket of a guest. After he'd taken a seat at the table, he ordered a cup of clam soup and a pint of ale.

He'd always been a good thief. He'd been stealing since childhood after he and his brother had been separated from their parents and the gypsy family they'd been traveling with. Such nimble fingered skill had served him well over the years, but he'd taken it too far.

He kept his old Quaker hat low over his face while he was sitting at the table, his scarf wrapped snugly around his throat. Another problem with the scar was that it had become a permanent tag, like a tattoo or a brand, one that Queen Victoria had noticed when he'd stood face-to-face with her.

His popularity had become widespread in England and other parts of Europe throughout the years, especially after his unexpected return from having been sent to a notorious penal colony. But after what he'd just done, that popularity would undoubtedly increase ten-fold.

Clover's eyes watered as she crossed the smoky room. No one paid her any mind as she weaved between tables. She could no longer stand the cigars and loud, drunken laughter, so she headed for an archway leading into a back room. The moment she crossed the threshold, she stopped dead in her tracks.

Sitting at a small table in the corner was a man eating soup and reading a book. He wore a linen shirt with copper buttons and a grey paisley vest. He also wore a dapper black coat with slender sleeves and wide cuffs, dark pinstriped breeches with the suspenders hanging down on either side, and scuffed boots with spats. The brim of his well-worn Quaker hat hovered low over bright-green eyes, yet she saw his face clearly when he took a drink from his ale. He had a smooth, youthful face, sculpted in all the right places. His hair had many shades, from golden brown to auburn, with some locks as dark as coal.

And just below his ratty scarf hung a silver coin on a chain.

With every sip of his drink, Pierce scanned the room. He wasn't too worried because he'd put a great distance between himself and his pursuers. By the time his trackers reached Le Havre, he'd be out at sea. So while there should not be any danger, he caught sight of a young girl staring at him. He lowered his pint and stared back from beneath the brim of his hat.

She was a tall and skinny thing, with deep red hair pulled back in a ponytail. She wore a drab dress, black stockings and well-worn shoes.

Does she recognize me?

Then he realized that her eyes weren't on him, but on the stater hanging from his neck, visible just below his scarf. The girl appeared to be an orphan and sickly. Her skin was pale and there were dark circles under her hungry eyes, which were riveted on the coin. Even though it had no value here, he'd never part with it willingly.

She must have wandered in looking for scraps or to beg, so he reached into his pocket for a shilling before she came over to bother him. He flicked the coin into the air toward her. It spun and then descended. She didn't even try to catch it as it fell. Instead, it hit the floor and stayed there. As for her, she turned, vanishing into the crowd and tobacco smoke.

"Unbelievable," he muttered, standing up. He retrieved the shilling and returned to the table to finish his meal. A few minutes later, a young man dropped into the seat in front of him.

"Bloody hell!" Pierce said with a start. He reached for his flintlock pistol when the young girl appeared beside the table.

"*Guten Abend,*" she said to him.

Germans, he reckoned.

"Sir," the young man said in a thick accent, "forgive our intrusion. My name is Hansel and this is . . ."

"Hansel?" he snorted. "Is this your sister, Gretel?"

The youth appeared confused but the girl giggled.

Hansel shook his head. "No, she's my sister, Magdalena. We need help."

The boy's claim that the girl was his sister seemed true enough. They both shared the same eyes and hair color. The lad seemed no more than twenty, a handsome boy whose clean face and healthy glow didn't match his own drab wardrobe. He had a bruise around one eye, faded enough to indicate that he had gotten it a little while back.

His gut warned him to be wary.

"Pardon?" Pierce said. "You need help? How does that concern me, eh?"

"You are British, *ja?*"

"*Ja,*" he answered, "*Ich bin.*"

Hansel seemed surprised by his use of their language. In German, Pierce added, "And I am also French on my mother's side."

Hansel and Magdalena looked at one another.

"*Welche art von hilfe suchen?*" Pierce continued, leaning back in his seat.

The young man replied; "We need a guide to help us escape to England."

"Escape?"

"*Ja*. We are homeless. Last night, we stole from a dangerous man who is now searching for us. If we can get across the Channel, perhaps he will not find us."

"Board a ferry," Pierce said bluntly. "You don't need help for that."

"We need someone who speaks fluent English," Hansel went on with urgency. "We cannot speak it as well as French and our accents will identify us as Germans. This man is very dangerous, you see. If he finds us, we are dead."

Pierce glanced at the little girl. Her sickly eyes were wide with fear. "Look, chum," he said, reverting back to English. "You got the wrong Brit. I ain't going anywhere near that country ever again."

He began to stand when the lad blurted out in German, "We can pay you!" He threw down a coin purse on the table. "And there is more for you if you can safely get us across the Channel."

Pierce couldn't resist a peek inside the bag, where there were thirty or more francs. If he did cross the Channel to Southampton, he could simply exchange the money for British pounds and buy himself a ticket, securing his own escape. Traveling back to England may not be a bad idea, as the guards who were after him weren't likely to suspect such a move. Regardless, he hadn't survived this long by taking chances while under so much pressure.

He opened his mouth to decline the offer when Hansel said in English, "I will get you a drink. Think it over, yes?" The boy shot up from his seat and hurried toward the bar.

Pierce sighed and snatched the coin purse from the table to look inside it again. He took out a gold coin and bit into it.

Magdalena narrowed her eyes at him with a grin. Pierce scowled back at her.

"I picked you out," she said in German. "When I saw you, I told my brother that you'd be perfect."

He almost felt sorry for her. Clearly, she had no one else but her halfwit brother who'd gotten her involved in a dangerous situation. The pair reminded him of himself and his brother when they'd been children. In any case, he had no intention of getting mixed up in their problems, no matter how much money they offered him.

He lowered the coin from his mouth and said, "Is that so? Then you are a poor judge of character, darling."

He shoved the coin purse into his pocket and reached for his bag, ready to leave the tavern when he heard someone say in French, "There you are, you little shit!"

A tall man with thick black muttonchops grabbed the girl by the arm. "Where is the money you stole from me? Tell me, or so help me . . ."

"Stop it! You're hurting me!" she cried.

"I want my money back," the man bellowed, raising a hand to strike her.

The man froze the moment Pierce shot up from his seat, a flintlock pistol pointed unerringly at his face.

"Get your hands off her, *monsieur*."

"This isn't your concern," the man hissed.

Realizing he was drawing attention to himself, he jabbed the muzzle under the man's chin and pushed him back. He slammed him against the nearby wall and struck him on the head with the gun. Then he hit him again and the man fell. To make certain he stayed down, Pierce whacked him a third time.

He grabbed his bag, ready to dart out of the building, when the girl called out to him, "Don't leave me, please!"

He stopped and looked at her. He just needed to get out the door, yet her large eyes held him in place.

"C'mon," he said.

She followed him out, passing her brother on the way.

"What happened?" the lad asked, holding a pint of ale in each hand.

"Let's go," Pierce grumbled.

Without argument, Hansel handed the drinks to the man closest to him and followed them out the door.

"All right," Pierce said, hurrying away from the building, "I'll help get you across the Channel and into a carriage headed for London. In the city, you'll be able to blend in."

"Thank you, sir!" Hansel said. "Thank you!"

Hansel gave Pierce money for tickets to board a ferry bound for England. They then separated while Pierce went to purchase their way across the Channel. After that, he met up with Hansel inside a small alehouse by the docks. Hansel bought a pint and came over to the table where Pierce sat, reading a book.

"The boat will depart in a half hour," Pierce said without looking up.

"Thank you again for your help," the young man said, placing the mug in front of him before taking a seat across the table.

"*Bitteschön*," Pierce said petulantly.

"You speak German very well. Where did you learn it?"

"I spent some time in Germany." Pierce flipped a page. "I picked up some phrases here and there. Enough to get by. But it was a woman who taught me how to speak it."

"Was she your paramour?"

"In a way she was, I reckon. But that was years ago."

Frederica Katz passed through his thoughts. Never could he forget the sanctuary she'd offered him when he'd been a young outlaw and she an aspiring actress. He missed her and hoped she was doing well.

"Really?" Hansel said, shifting his eyes around.

"Aye," he said before taking notice of the missing girl. "Where's the other one? We ought to stay together."

Hansel folded his hands on the table and grinned widely. When Pierce saw the foreboding look on his face, the bad feeling returned.

"You know where I learned German?" the youth asked in an English accent as he stood up. "My mother was German."

Pierce realized the danger instantly. He shot up from his chair the moment footsteps surrounded him. He grabbed for his pistol, but the gun never left its holster before it was seized from his hand and he was shoved face down on the table, a hand gripping the nape of his neck. Another person took his arms and pulled them behind his back, where cold iron clamped around his wrists. Fingers went through his pockets, finding weapons and whatever else he had. Someone ordered him to stop fidgeting.

Christ, who are these people?

They weren't royal guards, that was certain. They wouldn't have set a trap to catch him; they would have simply ambushed him back at the inn. Bounty-hunters, perhaps?

Once he was secured in manacles, he was hoisted up from the table and turned to the tall man with muttonchops who'd attacked the girl. His face was battered from where Pierce had struck him. Pierce really didn't like that he was the one holding the gun on him.

"Let's see if you're really him, eh?" the man said, unwinding the scarf from around Pierce's neck and tossing it to the floor. "Aye, it's Landcross for sure."

"Pierce Landcross," the young man known as Hansel said. "My name is Archie Norwich and you're coming with us."

Chapter Four
A Misstep on the Highway

By the time Joaquin Landcross and his gang arrived at the old church, the cloudy afternoon was threatening rain. They settled in to wait by the gravestones.

There were hunting parties searching for Pierce everywhere, as well as a price on Joaquin's own head. Things had gotten perilous for them, more than he was comfortable with.

"You think anyone worth robbing will come this way?" Luca Smith asked.

Luca and his cousin, Giles Summerfield, had been at his side since the days when he and Pierce had been together. With them were three others they'd picked up in various parts of England.

"The wealthy from Ampfield travel through here," Joaquin said. "We just need to be patient."

He hadn't been on this road since it had been just him and Pierce. The two of them had had modest luck on this stretch of highway in the past. Thinking about it, though, the road leading into Crampmoor would most likely be more profitable, yet something had drawn him to this spot.

Soon, two carriages approached, heading toward town just as Joaquin had said. They looked ripe for the picking.

"You three," he ordered the others, "dismount and take the rear carriage. Luca, Giles, we'll handle the leader."

Everyone dismounted, tying up the horses at a hitching post in by the lichgate. They covered their faces with scarves or sacks with eyeholes.

When the coaches came close, the gang sprang into action. Joaquin, Luca, and Giles surrounded the first coach, with Luca grabbing the lead horse, while the rest went for the other. Giles ran in front with his loaded flintlock and ordered the driver to stop. Joaquin opened the carriage door and aimed his gun at the passengers.

"Give us your loot!" he commanded.

When he saw the guards' grey uniforms with the crossed double-headed axes emblazoned on them, he lowered his gun.

"Good morrow," one guard said sardonically. "We're looking for Joaquin Landcross. Are you he, by any chance?"

The guards all aimed their guns at both him and Luca, who now stood on the other side of the carriage.

Thinking fast, Joaquin slammed the door and fired through the window.

"Trap!" he shouted.

There was no time to react as the guards burst out of the second stagecoach. Alan was immediately tackled, Augustine surrendered at gunpoint, and the third, Evert, darted off into the forest with the guards at his heels. Luca took off into the thicket. Giles fired upon the driver but missed. The older man flinched, then drew a pair of pistols. Seeing that, Giles turned and ran, following Joaquin to the cemetery.

They made it to the horses, and mounted quickly. Giles rode toward the woods beyond the boneyard, while Joaquin headed for the road. The coachman opened fire, hitting Joaquin's horse in the neck. The animal went down, sending Joaquin tumbling to the ground.

Before he had a chance to recover, the guards were

on him. They disarmed him, ripped the mask off his head, and shackled him in irons before dragging him back to the carriage. There, they forced him to sit beside his other men. Once they were all lined up, the driver of the first carriage stood before them. He had a Colt revolver in his hand. Joaquin had never seen the new revolving cylinder pistols before, which far outmatched the simple one-shot flintlocks he and his men carried.

"Gentlemen, I am Tarquin Norwich, cousin to her Majesty, Queen Victoria."

"Shit," Joaquin muttered under his breath.

He should have known that a trap like this would have been set to nab the brother of the most-wanted man in the country. But why had the Queen commissioned her cousin to come after him?

"I am looking for the Toymaker, Indigo Peachtree," Norwich said.

That was a name Joaquin hadn't heard in ages. Despite himself, he said, "Indigo?"

Norwich's eyebrows hiked. "Know him, do you?"

Realizing his error, Joaquin cleared his throat. "No, the name is odd, is all."

The three gang members smirked and snickered.

"Oh," Norwich said, "I see. So, you're *not* Joaquin Landcross?"

Joaquin gave no answer.

Norwich turned to the man next to Joaquin on his right and aimed his revolver at his face. "Are you Joaquin Landcross?"

Evert pulled his head back from the barrel and looked away without an answer.

Norwich turned the gun on Alan next. "How about you then, eh?"

"No!" Alan declared.

"No," Norwich said. "I didn't think so. You're too scrawny." He lowered his gun. "Joaquin Landcross is wanted dead. If you tell me which one he is, I won't have to kill *all* of you."

"It's him!" all three exclaimed, pointing at Joaquin despite their manacles.

Their betrayal came as no surprise to Joaquin. They were, after all, cutthroats who would murder their own family if it benefited them.

Norwich knelt in front of Joaquin. He stared him straight in the eye. "Is this so?"

The game was up. "Aye," he grunted.

Norwich stared at him for a moment longer before he rose. "I thought as much." He aimed his pistol at Joaquin again.

The second before Norwich pulled the trigger, Joaquin's life didn't flash before his eyes, just a single nagging question: *Why is he looking for Indigo?*

A blast rang out and Augustine fell dead to his left. In a blink, two more shots split the air, sending Evert and Alan twitching to the ground.

"Fuckin' hell!" Joaquin exclaimed.

Grey smoke rose from the end of the barrel like the spirits of the newly dead. The smell of gunpowder dominated. A light rain began to fall, like a punctual maid cleaning away the stained air.

"As I said, Mr. Landcross," Norwich continued, holstering his pistol, "I am in search of Indigo Peachtree. I understand that you've crossed paths with him before?"

Joaquin took a deep breath to collect himself. "Aye," he answered calmly.

"Good. Then you must know that Peachtree has

more than one home. I only know of his apartment in London. I need you to lead me to his other domicile. Help me find him and you might live. There are uses for a man like you."

Was Norwich suggesting he work for him? Fat chance! But he had little choice at the present. At least helping Norwich would give him time to think of a way to escape.

"All right," he agreed.

Norwich nodded to his men, who hoisted Joaquin to his feet.

"Get him into the carriage," Norwich ordered.

Joaquin was shoved into the first stagecoach and seated between armed guards. Instantly the carriage lurched into motion. Joaquin stared out the window, catching a glimpse of Giles hiding in the forest, watching. Luca had also escaped, yet neither man would do him any good now. The drizzle turned to rain and Joaquin sat back, getting as comfortable as possible on the hard bench, ignoring the leers of his captors.

Chapter Five
The Agreement

First mate, Wind in the Sails, strode along the dock on his way to the tobacconist. Many stared as he passed; an Indian dressed in a British great coat with Apache symbols daubed on the sleeves, a warrior's bone breastplate across his chest.

Wind in the Sails, once named Bipin, had been sailing since he was fifteen. He'd fought alongside Chief Sea Wind for the past decade. He hated what the Europeans had done to so many people throughout the years since their crossing the Atlantic: the stolen land, the true people slaughtered, the promises broken. The years he'd spent taking slavers had given him great satisfaction, yet nothing would give him more pleasure than sending every last one of the so-called New Americans back to their own homelands.

Through it all, though, he'd learned to forgive, thanks to Sea Wind's teachings. Wind in the Sails had come to understand that not everyone followed the same cruel mindset as others, and after meeting and getting to know those who he'd once considered his enemy, he truly realized the power of compassion.

His musings were cut short as he saw something odd. Four guards were escorting a shackled man onto a ferry, with a young girl following them. A prisoner transfer did not pluck any particular strings in him; it was *who* the guards had that made him turn the other way and dart back to the *Ekta*.

Pierce knew that if he struggled, it would only earn him a beating. Clearly, they wanted him alive, yet he doubted they needed to deliver him in tip-top shape. He could do without any broken bones. So he allowed himself to be taken aboard without incident, saying and doing nothing as he was unshackled and re-shackled to the ship's only mast.

As Pierce was forced to sit on the main deck, hands cuffed behind him, the captain approached Archie Norwich. The young man had changed into something more befitting his station, and looked the part of a gentleman now, with a blue frock coat and stylish vest.

"Are you certain you wish to sail at this hour, sir?" the captain asked Archie. "I feel a storm brewing and it'll be dark by the time we reach shore."

"I need to get this man to Southampton as soon as possible. On my father's orders."

"Aye, sir," the captain said, then left for the pilothouse.

"Who's your father?" Pierce asked.

The young man turned as if he was going to answer him. Instead, he shifted his eyes to the tall man with muttonchops. "Keep an eye on him at all times, Sergeant Derby. Make sure he doesn't try anything."

"Yes, sir."

Pierce drew the sea air into his lungs, held it for a moment, then released it slowly. The gig was up. Soon he'd be back in London, facing trial. The Queen herself might just bless him with her presence at his hanging. But something that son of a German bitch had said to the captain prompted him to reconsider. *Why is he taking me to his father in Southampton instead of sailing straight to the Port of London?*

The steamboat was large enough to hold fifty passengers, yet no one other than the few crewmen,

Archie, his sister, and the guards with him were
aboard. Black smoke plumed out of the single stack and
the stern wheel began turning. The ferryboat made way
from the dock, heading for the Channel. The first touch
of sea spray reminded Pierce that death waited for him
in Southampton. He would wallow deeper in despair if
not for the girl.

"Hello, Mr. Landcross," she said sweetly, as if they
were on good terms.

With a frustrating sigh that described his mood, he
hissed, "Hello, miss?"

She grinned. "Clover," she said. "My name is Clover
Alice Norwich and I'm ten years old."

"Hello, Miss Clover Alice Norwich and I'm ten years
old."

She approached and sat cross-legged next to him,
resting her chin on her palm, shook her head. "It is
rather a shame that we have to take you to our father.
You're awfully cute to meet the likes of him."

"Cheers, I reckon. Who is this father of yours?"

A certain tragedy flashed within her dark eyes. He
saw it despite her grin. He felt the same heartbreak in
himself from the night when he'd received his scar.

"He's a lord," she said at length. "And a distant
cousin to Queen Victoria."

Pierce remembered now where he'd heard the name.
Clover's father was none other than Tarquin Norwich,
founder of the British Guardians. They were nothing
more than a band of thieves and murderers, turned
thief-takers. Norwich had cherry-picked them from
prisons in order to hunt fugitives down and dispose of
them. They were easily identified by the pins they wore
on their vests and coats: a double headed axe.

Any crime received the same ruthless punishment.
Without the luxury of a trial, prisoners were usually

tortured before death, or sometimes *to* death, their bodies displayed as ornaments, hanging by the neck from trees on the sides of highly trafficked thoroughfares. There were cases of charred corpses, some still smoking from the fire they'd died in, hanging at intersections. When King William received complaints about the bodies from family members protesting the unjust way their loved ones had died, Norwich had reluctantly disbanded the British Guardians. He'd even had some of them hanged as a show of solidarity, and threw in a promise to end their cruelty.

"He's a nasty man," Clover said. "He doesn't really care for Archie and me much. He never even cried when my mother died."

"I see. Is your father the one taking me to London?"

"You're not going to London. My father wants you to tell him where a book is."

"A book?"

"Yes. It's a journal that Mr. Peachtree has."

"Peachtree?" he repeated in disbelief. "Indigo Peachtree?"

Clover giggled. "Funny name, isn't it?"

Pierce quickly put the pieces together. He understood why Norwich would want it. Yet he wondered how in the world he had even found out about the journal, much less that Pierce knew where it was. Had Indigo told him that he'd taken it? Did Norwich have Indigo?

"I knew it was you the moment I saw you in the tavern," Clover said.

"Why? Because of my likeness in the newspapers?"

"No, because you were eating soup."

"Soup? I beg your Pardon?"

"Yep. My father said to look for a man eating soup and wearing a coin as a necklace."

Pierce looked down at the silver stater lying against his chest. Never had it been mentioned in any of his descriptions before. In fact, he'd only had the damn thing in his possession for a couple of years, and he hadn't been arrested during that time. Aside from the coin being a protective talisman against someone he'd crossed in the past, he'd started to consider it his little good luck charm. That apparently had changed. How the hell had Tarquin Norwich known such a detail?

He opened his mouth to ask that when Archie returned. "Clover, don't sit so close to the prisoner. He's a dangerous fugitive."

"He's not dangerous," she protested. "He's merely a thief."

"Yeah, *Arch*, I'm just a thief," Pierce said with a dash of resentment. "We were just havin' a little chat about a certain book."

Archie crouched down next to him. "Is that so? What's in the journal?"

Pierce tilted his head and arched an eyebrow at the lad. "You have no idea what's in the bloody book, yet your father sent you off to catch me for him to . . . I can only assume, torture me until I tell him where it is?" He did know where the book was and he feared for the person who now had possession of it.

"I couldn't care less," Archie said with a dismissive wave of his hand.

"Then why did you ask, you whore pipe?" he asked tersely.

Archie shrugged. He really didn't seem to care. It appeared that he had other things on his mind aside from his father's interests.

"What about Indigo?" Pierce asked. "Does your

father have him?"

Archie seemed to notice the concern in his tone, making Pierce cringe. As a fugitive, it was best not to show vulnerability of any sort, for it could very well come back to haunt him later.

"No," Clover chimed in. "Mr. Peachtree was at our house a while ago, but he absconded during the night. Father is searching for him right now."

Shite!

If it hadn't been for Indigo, Pierce and his brother might not have survived the winter of 1826; a harsh, bitter bastard of a winter that had proven too much for a pair of orphaned kids. Indigo had not only taken them into his home, but he'd cared for them.

The Toymaker was a peace-loving man who wanted to spend his life making remarkable toys for all children, no matter their background. If he'd run away from Tarquin Norwich, it was because Norwich must have wanted him to do something Indigo didn't want to do. And since Norwich was searching for the journal as well, Pierce could only imagine what he needed from the kindly old man.

"Sorry, chum, but I don't recall where the journal went."

"I don't care," Archie said, rising to his full height. "Tell it to my father when you meet him." He held out his hand to his sister. "Come, Clover, you need to get inside."

"Aw," she whined. "I want to stay here."

"We need to get you out of this cold," he said almost pleadingly. "Please, Clover."

The girl huffed petulantly. "Oh, all right," she said, slipping her hand into his and allowing him to pull her to her feet.

Archie led her to the passenger lodge and she went

inside. When she was gone, he turned back to Pierce as if he had something else to say, but then went to the railing instead. Sergeant Derby suddenly loomed over Pierce, his arms crossed over his chest.

"How's the face?" Pierce asked with a grin.

"I'm going to request of Lord Norwich that I be the one to hurt you if you fail to cooperate," the man said, his voice as deep as the English Channel. He seemed rather excited at the thought.

Pierce looked away. So, this was it. The end. For the sake of the journal's keeper, he hoped that whoever tortured him would botch it, killing him before he cracked.

Half hour into the voyage, and everything was quiet, except for the rhythmic thump of the steam engine. The sun slid slowly across the sky towards the horizon. Rain clouds from England casually rolled their way. A chilly breeze caressed Pierce's neck. He shuddered, staring forlornly down at the deck.

The breeze grew stronger, stirring up the waves, causing the steamboat to buck. Pierce looked to the stern. Were those sails? He had good eyesight, one of his blessings. Seeing another ship on the Channel did nothing to raise any eyebrows, yet this particular one appeared to be chasing after them. Soon he heard the deep rumble of blades chopping air.

It can't be, he thought.

Sergeant Derby heard the noise too. "Looks like they're in more of a hurry then we are," he remarked. "What the devil is that sound though?"

The ship was catching up at a rate that belied the advantage its extra masts gave it. White smoke billowed from the smokestacks.

"Lord Norwich," Sergeant Derby hollered from the

stern.

Archie craned his neck around. "What is that ship doing?"

A wicked grin stretched clear across Pierce's face. Perhaps his coin was lucky after all.

The rumbling sound, which had become nearly deafening at this point, slowed until it finally ceased completely when the ship came close enough that the Apache symbol on the sails could be seen.

A battle cry screeched out, letting everyone on the ferry know that Death had come for them.

The other three guards rushed over to the stern.

"Best get ready, lad," Pierce warned Archie.

Archie tore his gaze away from the ship and saw the grin on his face. All the color drained from his own.

Archie shouted to the guards, "Get away from the railing!"

They stood gawking. The guards were military trained but they weren't true soldiers. They served only as escorts and protectors to a home that even Pierce dared not intercept. None of them had ever been in a life-or-death situation before—until now.

A group of Sea Warriors rose from behind the *Ekta*'s railing with rifles and opened fire on the men. Two went down; another wounded in the arm. Sergeant Derby grabbed the wounded man and pulled him away as the Sea Warriors reloaded.

"Take cover!" Archie ordered, pulling his pistol from its holster and running across the bow.

Pierce tripped him as he passed. Archie hit the deck, firing a shot into the air.

"Let me go, boy," Pierce demanded hotly. "They're here for me."

Archie aimed his gun on him. It shook in his face.

"No! I must take you to my father!"

A handful of Sea Warriors aimed large, bulky rifles at the sky and opened fire. Iron grappling hooks launched into the air, their ropes falling in a spiraling arch towards the deck. The men on the other ship hauled the lines back, scraping the jagged flukes of the grapplers across the deck until they caught the railing in their hooked teeth.

The ferry was dwarfed by the great galleon, and the Sea Warriors slid down the lines, landing lightly on deck.

Archie had no time to take a precise aim before the tribe scattered over the deck. Everything happened so fast. Clover came outside and Archie rushed to her. The two Norwich siblings vanished into the passenger lodge. Behind the pilothouse there were shouts, then gunfire, and then quiet.

The storm clouds steadily rolled over them and dark spots dotted the deck as rain began to fall.

"If it was my decision," a woman said in French as she rounded the corner of the passenger lodge, "I'd let them take you away."

Pierce grimaced. "Waves of Strength," he said with contempt. She was the last person he wanted to see while he was in this position. She approached with a smug look on her face, relishing the moment.

She knelt beside him, holding the keys that Sergeant Derby had carried, as well as a blood-soaked knife in her other hand. For a moment, Pierce wondered if Waves of Strength was considering which to use.

"Mind unlocking me?" he said.

She narrowed her eyes. "If I did not love my husband as much as I do, I'd jab this knife into your chest and claim you were a casualty."

The key finally slid into the lock and Pierce was

freed. He stood up, rubbing his sore wrists. "Cheers," he said icily. He spoke to her in English; a language that both she and her husband, Chief Sea Wind, understood but rarely spoke.

With a snarl, she walked away. He could practically feel her hate like a physical presence.

"Landcross," came a strong voice.

Pierce turned. "Chief!" he exclaimed.

Sea Wind approached him with arms wide open. They embraced, patting each other's backs. Chief Sea Wind had ten years on him, yet his brawny embrace reminded Pierce of the man's strength.

In French, Chief Sea Wind said, "I see that you've gotten yourself into trouble again."

"Just the usual," he replied in kind. "How did you find me?"

"I saw you being led away," came another familiar voice.

Pierce caught sight of the *Ekta's* first mate, Wind in the Sails.

"Fuckin' hell," he exclaimed, hugging the first mate as well. "*Merci, mon ami. Merci!*"

Relief overwhelmed him. By sheer luck, Wind in the Sails had spotted him being shipped off to face a horrible and painful end. He turned back to the chief and said gleefully, "*Merci, Chef.*"

"You saved our lives. We owe you much," Chief Sea Wind said.

Pierce didn't wallow in the reunion for too long. There was something he needed to discuss with Archie Norwich. "Can I borrow your rifle, Chief?"

Chief Sea Wind handed him his weapon and Pierce went inside the passenger lodge. The chief, Wind in the Sails, and two other Sea Warriors followed him. By then, the rain was pounding over the ocean and the skies had darkened almost to night.

"Archie! Oh, Arch," Pierce called with the rifle's barrel resting on his shoulder. He grinned, enjoying this turn of events. The lodge was just a small room with a wraparound bench and windows lining the walls. Archie and Clover were sitting in the corner. The lad still held his pistol and it was aimed at him.

Archie had no clue just how fortunate he was. If Clover hadn't come out, Archie would most likely have done something stupid, like fight back, getting himself killed in the process. But in that moment, Archie's only objective was to keep his sister safe.

"Stay right there," Archie commanded. "I *will* shoot you."

Pierce stopped and shook his head. "No, you won't, lad. You kill me and you kill yourself. Do you want your sister to see her brother get cut down?"

Archie remained still, eyes locked on the muzzle of his gun. Clover was sitting right behind him, pressed into the seat corner. She peered over her brother's shoulder at Pierce but she didn't appear frightened. Pierce gave her a wink.

"It'll be all right, love," he said soothingly to her.

"What do you want, Landcross?" Archie demanded.

Pierce returned his attention to him. He took a chance and stepped forward. "We need to have ourselves a little chat, boyo. A kind of *tête-à-tête*, per se." He propped his foot on the bench with the rifle resting across his leg. Hawk and crow feathers hung from the long barrel.

"About what?" Archie asked.

"Indigo Peachtree and his journal."

"I'm listening."

Pierce did his best to ignore the gun aimed at his face. "I think your father is being a tad greedy."

"What do you mean?"

"He wants the book and Indigo, eh?"

"What are you suggesting?"

Pierce straightened up. "I'll help you get the book, but you have to help me get Indigo if your father already has him."

Archie's frown deepened. His eyes studied him in wonderment. "You would go after Peachtree rather than escaping?"

Pierce didn't give him an answer. He understood the risk he was about to take. He had a chance to leave with the Sea Warriors to wherever they were bound.

"Peachtree is a friend of yours, isn't he?" Archie guessed with some confidence.

"Don't get any ideas, chum," Pierce said darkly. "My freedom is also part of this agreement. Once we find Indigo, he and I are leaving without you on our tails, got it?"

Archie finally lowered the revolver and stood up. "I don't care what happens to you, Landcross. If you can get me the book, I'll help you save Peachtree."

"Marvelous!" Pierce held out his hand. "Then we have an agreement?"

Archie studied Pierce's extended hand for a moment before he took it and shook.

"Well then," Pierce said. "Let's get to it, eh?"

Chapter Six
Oak Leaf

The inn at Romsey was small, but they had a room suitable for the occasion. Joaquin was shackled to a chair. He looked about with contempt wishing for free hands and a pair of pistols. Tarquin Norwich was speaking with his son. The guards stood about, not hiding in the least their pleasure at his discomfort.

The room became darker as dusk drew near. A guard lit the lanterns until the soft light swallowed up the shadows. Another guard checked Joaquin's bindings, while a third entered with a heavy trunk and set it near the bed.

"I want you men to take shifts on guard duty tonight," Norwich ordered. He held his hand out to the one who'd bound Joaquin to the chair.

"Yes, my lord," the guard responded, handing him a set of keys.

"I'm going to my room to clean up," Norwich said to his son. He shifted his attention to Joaquin. "When I return, I advise that you start talking." With that, he and the guards left the room.

Since his capture, Joaquin had said very little. Ivor had asked him questions about Indigo. Not many, but he hadn't answered any of them. In truth, it wasn't that he wouldn't talk; he just needed guarantees first.

Ivor fell back into a plushly upholstered chair, easing a leather bound copper flask out of his coat pocket. Embedded in the leather were a couple of jewels and a cameo of a woman in the center. Joaquin had seen the like before. Most likely custom-made.

"Best do what he says," Ivor said. From another

pocket, he brought out a bottle of Scottish whisky and poured it into the flask. He'd been doing this throughout the entire trip and he'd been drunk for at least an hour.

"What will he do to me?" Joaquin asked, unafraid. "Hurt me?"

Ivor dripped the last drop of whisky into the flask then tossed the bottle to the floor. He shrugged. "Likely, yeah, and worse." He slid his black glassy eyes to Joaquin and said with a sadistic smirk, "Ever met anyone without a lower jawbone?"

Joaquin stared at him, his eyes widening.

"I'm serious," Ivor said. "I've seen my father dissect a man. Well, not exactly dissect in terms of study, but he's cut a few blokes' jawbones right out of their faces for holding in their tongues. It takes skill, mind you. Granted, most died from the pain alone, but the ones who survived have to shove food down into their own throats just to get it into their stomachs. Very nasty sight."

Although Joaquin didn't want to give it any credence, he didn't put it past someone with Norwich's reputation. He shifted uneasily in his chair, sorely wishing that the beast had come out at Pagan Tree before he'd been grabbed.

The beast always began as a sickening flutter in his gut that would grow until it took him over. Once the beast was free, he lost all self-control and acted without fear or remorse until he became himself again.

He hadn't always been cursed with the beast. It had only been in the past decade that it had taken up residence. It had once caused him to do something that he could never fix nor ever forgive himself for. Controlling it proved difficult at times, but it had failed him now. In his hour of need, the beast had lain docile, refusing to unleash itself on Norwich and his men.

"I'm dead as soon as I tell you what you want," he said.

"Not necessarily," Ivor said and took a drink. "We're in need of more strong backs like yours in the workshop."

Joaquin snorted. "Work for you? What makes you think I'd ever work for the likes of you?"

"Oh, it wouldn't be by choice. More like forced labor at my father's summer home."

"Where's that?"

If the dolt hadn't been drinking, he'd most likely say very little. But the whisky's seductive touch had loosened Ivor's lips like the threads on a sack of grain.

"Norwich Castle," Ivor replied. "It's on the Isle of Wight. It's been in our family for five hundred years."

"What would I do there?"

Ivor blinked slowly, as if he was dozing off. With a smack of his lips, he opened his mouth to say something, but the door opened and he remained silent. Norwich entered and shook his head at his son's inebriated state.

"Has he said anything?" Norwich inquired.

Ivor slouched comfortably in his drunken stupor, flask held lovingly in his grasp. "Hasn't said much, Father."

Norwich shut the door behind him. "I see."

"Exactly what is it that you want to know?" Joaquin asked brusquely.

"As I mentioned before, Indigo Peachtree has an apartment in London. I received a telegraph from my men there, informing that he hasn't returned, which tells me that he's hiding at his country home."

"And you need to know where that is, eh?"

"Indeed," Norwich said. He smiled thinly, but there was no mirth in his voice. "And I need to know right now, before he vanishes."

"How'd you come to find out that I knew him in the first place?"

Norwich swung hard, hitting Joaquin square in the face, rocking his head back. It was a hard punch, but Joaquin had taken worse.

"Ouch." Ivor snickered and leered up at Norwich.

"Where is the house?" Norwich asked, his voice frighteningly calm. He leaned over, almost whispering in Joaquin's ear. "Tell me if you don't want to spend the last hour of your life in the most exquisite pain."

Joaquin had no doubt that Norwich would mutilate him if he didn't give him something. "It's south from here, towards the coast." He lifted his head and stared Norwich in the eye. "I won't tell you where, but I'll show you."

Norwich rose to his full height, his tight expression loosening a bit. "You know exactly where it is?"

"Aye, and I'll take you there, provided that you cut me loose when we arrive."

"No," Norwich said, placing his hands on the arms of the chair and leaning forward. "You'll earn your freedom when we find Peachtree, understood?"

Joaquin pulled back. He didn't doubt that once Norwich got his hands on the Toymaker, he'd either butcher him or send him off to the Norwich Castle, just as Ivor had said.

"Understood," he said.

Norwich pushed off the chair and took a step back. "Good. We set off in the morning."

Ivor had already passed out in the chair when Norwich left. A guard entered after him and stood watch, his eyes never leaving Joaquin's face. His jaw hurt from where he'd been struck, but at least he still had one.

Lieutenant Darius Javan and his men finished searching another street in Berck. They had spent two hours in town with no luck in finding Pierce Landcross.

Javan and the other royal guards with him had been assigned to hunt down the thief who'd broken into Buckingham Palace and had attempted to steal the Queen's jewelry. They'd nearly had him in Aylesham, but Landcross had managed to vanish before they'd caught up with him. They'd then tracked him to Dover and along the French coastline. Javan had come to learn that Landcross was known to visit Berck occasionally. He was known there as the thief who had once stolen a carriage with a baby inside. He'd been arrested when he'd returned the infant to its parents— but he escaped a short time later.

Javan had hoped that there'd been recent sightings of the fugitive in Berck, but no one had admitted to seeing him.

Realizing that he was wasting time, he pulled his men together and headed back to the coast, stopping at every house along the way.

The Sea Warriors disabled the ferry's steam engine and cut the sails from the mast. The ship was dead in the water now. The four crewmen, including the ferryboat's captain, were tied up inside the passenger lodge, left to be discovered by whoever came across the ferry.

Everyone else boarded the *Ekta* , which made steam, turning for France.

The *Ekta* creaked and groaned with every wave. Chief Sea Wind had gained possession of the galleon over thirty years ago. Despite being built in the previous century, the *Ekta* was a sturdy old girl. A Spanish jewel in craftsmanship, she had been beaten down by storms and clashes with other ships, and patched up many times over. But Chief Sea Wind wouldn't trade the Spanish galleon for a newer steam-powered vessel. The chief disliked the idea of billowing coal-burning smoke into the sky. Although many sailors found steam power technology useful and, more importantly, profitable, Chief Sea Wind saw it as the beginning of a destructive path. However, that didn't mean he hadn't found other ways to modify the old vessel.

On deck, Pierce went over to the steam engine that had come from an old steam locomotive. It had now been converted into a fully functioning power source for the *Ekta*. Pierce rested his hand on it. The engine was still warm.

Whenever the crew needed that extra lift of speed— as in the case of when they had been sailing against the storm's winds—they simply fired up the huge fans. Pierce took a moment to examine them. The brass guards that encased the steel blades were securely strapped and bolted to the main and mizzenmast. To power them, the chief's engineer had found a solution other than burning coal. The answer was all around them. Water.

When he'd sailed with the Sea Warriors for a time, he'd inquired of the engineer how it worked.

"The secret is in the centrifugal pumps," the engineer had explained to him while they had stood on the upper deck. He stomped his foot. "The water pipes are hidden just below the decking."

He showed Pierce where one of the pipes came out through a hole located above the portholes.

Wide, solid brass pipes ran down both the port and starboard side of the vessel, vanishing into the water below.

"The pipes end near the keel and bend bowwards, where water is sucked in through iron impellers," the engineer went on. "The water travels up to the steam engine, where it boils as wood burns inside the firebox. The heated water inside the boiler turns into steam and is sent through the pipes up the masts to each fan."

He pointed up to thinner piping that fastened to the main mast by rivets nailed into the wraparound strips of metal that kept the pipes in place.

There had been more to it than that; the engineer had tried explaining to him, such as pistons, valves, the way the boiler tubes were arranged. By then, Pierce had stopped listening, wishing he hadn't inquired.

All-in-all it was a nifty device and in spite of himself he was impressed.

Pierce crossed to the helm where Wind in the Sails stood at the wheel. Since the rain had passed, Archie and his sister were now on deck. Clover was listening to a crewmate playing a flute. She seemed mesmerized by the music, like a cobra to a snake charmer.

Chief Sea Wind climbed the stairs and came up next to Pierce. He was a powerful looking man with much wisdom stored in a soul that was kinder than the world around him. He'd been born on his father's ship, the *Sonsee-array*, which meant Morning Star. He had come into the world during a rough storm that had nearly taken the vessel. His parents had then named him Sea Wind. He always smelled of the ocean he called home.

"You should come with us," Chief Sea Wind said to Pierce. "We can take you to the islands in the Pacific."

The chief stood a good four inches taller than Pierce,

forcing the thief to tilt his chin a tad to meet his gaze. "Oi, to those Hawaiian Islands?"

The chief nodded. "They are surrounded by sand the color of fresh fallen snow and the ocean is like clear glass. There are mountains and plenty of space to roam. I can introduce you to an old friend of mine, Chief Ailani."

Pierce was intrigued. To be far away and living on a tropical island would be a dream come true. Not to mention that sailing with Chief Sea Wind and his crew was the safest bet he could hope for.

The *Ekta*, despite her age, was fitted with the best and most up-to-date firepower. Behind him were a pair of three-barrelled cannons. Each cannon could shoot multiple cannonballs into any pursuing ship before having to reload. The same went for the other rotary cannons at the bow.

"We could even bring you to our home in Sonora and teach you how to live off the land," the chief offered. "What you are doing right now isn't wise."

"Aye, true enough," Pierce agreed wholeheartedly. "But the book they're looking for is held by my friend; and if they've managed to find me, they'll very well find him."

"How *did* they find you?"

"It's strange. The girl told me that her father knew exactly where I'd be and when. Even knew what I'd be doing."

"Mmm," the chief mused. "It seems like this man has a connection with the spirits."

Pierce thought on that. Growing up in the type of family he had, it made sense. "Maybe. I need to get that book away from my mate and go after Indigo." He studied Archie. "The lad is hiding something."

"What do you mean?"

"His father hasn't told him anything about the journal's contents, and yet he doesn't seem to give a toss about it as long as he completes his mission." He slid his eyes over to the chief. "I reckon that I'm trying to figure him out, 'tis all."

"Everyone has secrets, Landcross. Perhaps for your sake, you should learn his."

"*Oui*," Wind in the Sails spoke up. "You might be able to use it to your advantage when he tries to betray you."

"And he will," the chief warned.

If anyone could sniff out a traitor, it was the Apache.

Pierce headed down to the hold to search for a gun. While he rummaged through one of the crates, the deck creaked behind him.

"Why is it that idiots like you live so long?" Waves of Strength asked, standing in the doorway.

"Dunno," he said, his back still facing her. "Is that a question you ask yourself every morning?"

He lifted another crate lid, only to find spare engine parts inside. "Bugger," he said, closing it.

He caught the sound of her approaching footsteps and turned, expecting a knife in her hand. If she wanted to kill him she could do so easily enough, especially since he was unarmed. To his relief, her blade was tucked into her turquoise belt.

She stepped halfway into the cramped hold, placing her hands on her tiny waist. "One day, someone will cut out that sarcastic tongue of yours, Landcross," she said in the angriest French he'd ever heard.

Her resentment radiated off her like a furnace. He wanted to throw something back at her in return. Instead, he tried another approach. He casually leaned against the crate with his hands on the lid.

"Listen, love, I know you're sore at me, but you know as well as I do that it was an accident."

"What if I had done it to you?" she retorted. "Would you be so forgiving?"

"I reckon I would be," he said as she turned and stormed out. "We were under attack," he called out after her. "Things got bloody chaotic. You just got in the way, 'tis all."

Waves of Strength returned, holding a branding iron that glowed brighter than the lantern overhead. In her other hand, a bucket of water.

"Whoa! Whoa!" Pierce said, holding out his hands.

She stopped, placed the bucket down, and held the red, smoldering brand like a sword. "I've had this burning since I learned that we were coming to save you."

"What the bloody hell are you doing with that?" he asked, swallowing nervously.

"You shot me in the ass, Landcross! I couldn't sit properly for months."

Despite himself, he snickered.

She took a step forward, her eyes narrowed. Pierce's lower back slammed into the crate when he jumped back.

"And I've apologized for that more times than I can count. Not to mention that I did save the entire crew, including you and your husband, remember?"

The heat of the glowing brand warmed his extended palms.

"When you shot me, it felt like *fire*!" she exclaimed. "You burned and scarred me!"

He lowered his hands and set his eyes on her instead of the brand.

Waves of Strength was in her mid-thirties. Her skin

was hard and dark like wood. Her straight black hair reached the middle of her back with many blue, yellow, and green threads woven into several braids. The buckskin dress she wore hugged her slender frame, as did the black leather knee-high Italian boots clinging to her calves. Her high cheekbones met up with her light brown eyes. The years at sea had turned her into a true warrior without stripping away the years from her face.

There was only way to make peace. Whether he liked it or not, he needed her blessing to keep her from interfering with Chief Sea Wind's decision to wait for his return to the shores of Berck.

The burn would hurt like hell, but he'd dealt with pain before. At least he would see this one coming.

"Where? My arse?" he asked.

"Your chest. So I can *see* it."

He nodded submissively and unbuttoned his shirt. Spreading the edges apart, he exposed his chest to the brand.

"Mind the chain, eh?"

Searing heat roasted his flesh and sizzled the skin over his heart. He screamed while she howled with satisfaction. Smoke rose from both the iron and him as he slid down the crate, hollering. The heat hit every nerve in his body and traveled like burning coals throughout. He swore that she held it against him longer then she needed to.

When the terrible brand finally lifted, he collapsed to his knees, sweat drenching him. His first instinct was to put his hand over the wound, but the raw, burning flesh wouldn't allow any contact. There was now a five-inch figure-eight on his chest.

Between heavy painful breaths, he asked, "What . . . what does this mean?"

Waves of Strength shrugged and said, "It's the

symbol of the Apache. We paint our horses with it. I suppose it means that you're our property now." She looked a little closer at the brand she'd created. "Strange, but the brand didn't form like it should."

He studied it himself. She must have pressed it against him wrong. He raised his chin to her, tears and sweat rolling down his face.

"Are we even?" he hissed through clenched teeth.

She plunged the brand into the bucket of water, which hissed and steamed.

"*Oui*, we are even. Go to our physician, Heals with Nature. She will soothe the pain and bandage the wound." Waves of Strength turned to leave when she nodded to a crate in the corner. "The weapons are in there."

When she left, he slowly got to his feet and staggered to the crate. Every nerve in his left side felt like it was fried, preventing him from lifting his arms.

He pushed the lid off the crate and found it full of guns and ammo, which had been looted throughout the years from slave ships. There were even pistols and rifles dating back to the last century.

Among the cluster of firearms, he found a copper-plated six-cylinder revolver. Carved into the copper were tree branches that wrapped around the muzzle. Embedded into the stained black cherry handle was an oak leaf within a small plaque bolted on with miniature rivets. The words Oak Leaf were engraved into the frame.

He reckoned that the Oak Leaf was the name of the manufacturing company, perhaps a new competition for ole Samuel Colt himself. In any case, the gun was a fine discovery.

As he rolled the cylinder to test its rotation, he suddenly discovered that he was holding another gun;

a shiny black metal handgun. On the barrel, the name Smith & Wesson was engraved, along with MADE IN USA carved into the frame.

Then the gun was gone and he again held the Oak Leaf pistol.

He blinked and tried to make sense of it. In the past four years, he'd been experiencing strange dreams and flashes of images. He tried figuring it out, especially the dreams that escaped him upon waking, leaving the residue of their presence inside his head. He had a superb memory and usually recalled most of his dreams, as well as nightmares, but these strange images and brief flashes were like shredded memories that made no sense unless he could piece them together. If only he could remember most of them.

Recovering from the strange occurrence, he searched the crate and found an old black leather gun belt, as well as a box of ammo, which he placed in his coat pocket. He slipped the gun into the waistband of his britches and went to find Heals with Nature.

By the time the *Ekta* dropped anchor, night had pulled its star-sprinkled sheet over the dimming sky. Pierce waited irritably as a few crewmembers prepared the dinghy. The ointment that Heals with Nature had given him helped, yet the wound still stung, thumping and pulsating with pain under the bandage.

"I'm sorry, Landcross," Chief Sea Wind said, coming up alongside him. "She felt it was her right to punish you."

"You knew she would do this, eh?"

"She has been traveling with that brand ever since we last went home, in case the two of you ever crossed paths again. It was the only way to make peace between you both."

A snap of hot pain struck the wound, causing Pierce to suck in an anguished breath.

"At least it wasn't your ass," the chief added facetiously.

"Aye," Pierce said with a chuckle.

"The boat is ready, Chief," one of the crewmen said.

"In consideration for your condition, Wind in the Sails will help you row to shore," the chief said.

"No need," Archie said, approaching from behind with Clover. "We're coming along."

Pierce's face grew hot. He didn't like the idea of having the lad come to the home of the very person he was trying to protect. Besides, after everything that Archie had put him through, he preferred the company of a venomous snake to young Norwich.

The chief whispered in his ear, "Learn his secrets."

Pierce's tight expression relaxed. If he was truly going after Indigo, he'd need leverage.

"All right," he said to Archie. "C'mon, then."

The two siblings got into the dinghy, while Pierce shook Chief Sea Wind's hand.

"We shall be here when you return," Chief Sea Wind promised.

"*Merci.*"

Pierce stepped into the boat, while Archie sat at the bow.

"Get up from there, you wanker, you're bloody well rowing," Pierce commanded.

Once the three were in the boat, the crew lowered the dinghy into the water. The trip to shore didn't take long, although to Pierce, it felt like an eternity. He rubbed just above the edge of the bandage covering his burn.

"What happened to you?" Clover asked, pointing to

the bandage, which was barely visible through the scant light cast by the single lantern on the prow.

"Nothing, lass," he said. "Just an old debt that needed to be paid, 'tis all."

When they reached shore, he grinned in anticipation. He and Archie pulled the boat onto the beach.

"Where are we?" Archie asked.

"France," he answered simply, grabbing the lantern out of the boat.

"I mean *where* in France," Archie specified, helping Clover out.

"On the shore," he replied, striding away with the light.

Chapter Seven
Clover's Plan

Archie's feet hurt. They had been walking for an hour on a dark country road that Landcross had led them to after cutting through a wheat field. The only light was the lantern that Landcross was carrying.

"Where are we going exactly?" he finally asked. "Is this a trick?"

"Yes," Landcross said sarcastically, walking ahead of everyone. "I bloody well brought you way out here, away from the safety of my mates, in order to make my daring escape."

Archie tripped over a large rock. "Watch your step," he said to Clover. Then he addressed Landcross. "Mind slowing down a bit?"

"You're in a hurry to get the book and take it to your father, aye?"

"Yes, but—"

"Then step lively, man," Landcross said. "Why are you taking the book to your father?"

"He ordered me to."

"Why send you?" Landcross prodded. "He obviously doesn't trust you enough to tell what it contains, and yet you're scurrying off to obey. Are you trying to get into his good graces?"

"That is neither here nor there," Archie said hotly. "I just need to—" He stopped himself. The plan to leave his father's estate with his sister and new bride was a secret that could blow up in his face if he didn't keep it to himself.

"Have to what?" Landcross asked over his shoulder.

"Nothing," he said, tripping over another rock. "Slow down, we can't see."

"Walk faster."

"My sister can't keep up."

"I can try," Clover whispered.

"You wanted to bring her along," Landcross pointed out.

"I couldn't leave her on that ship with people I don't know. What if they changed their minds and sailed off without us?"

Landcross stopped short and turned on him. "You risked her safety back at the inn."

Archie and Clover came into the lantern light. The welcoming warm glow attracted many flying insects that circled them. "How's that?" Archie inquired.

"I could have walked away when that giant attacked her."

"He was *acting*. She wasn't in any real danger. Plus, I knew you wouldn't just leave."

"Oh? Do tell."

"The baby."

Landcross seemed confused.

"The one you accidentally stole," Archie clarified.

"Oh, bloody hell." Landcross turned to press on.

Archie and Clover followed.

"You *stole* a baby?" Clover asked.

"I didn't . . ." Landcross started to say and then continued, "I didn't realize that she was in the carriage, all right?"

"The child was missing for nearly a week before you returned her," Archie went on. "You could've abandoned her anywhere, but, instead, you cared for her. And then you risked yourself by bringing her home."

"What happened, Mr. Landcross?" Clover asked.

"I got arrested. Apparently, sticking my neck out for others is a weakness that I need to eradicate."

"You escaped," Archie threw in. "Which got your name in the papers for the first time."

"Wasn't the first," he muttered.

"You should have books written about you, Mr. Landcross," Clover said excitably. "You must have led an awfully adventurous life."

Archie agreed about the adventurous part. However, he didn't want to become too engrossed in Landcross' reputation any more then he already was. Landcross was a legend in his own right, which had come from a decade of thefts, arrests, escapes, and tall tales that no one knew for sure were true or not. Archie had been keen on actually meeting him, especially after the incident between Landcross and the Queen. Even so, no legend would prevent him from completing his mission and starting a new life with his wife and sister.

"Well, my life has been anything but boring, love," Landcross stated.

"Going back to the question at hand," Archie said. "Do you even know where we're going?"

"Aye," Landcross replied. "Over there."

Up ahead, tall torches burned off to the left side of the road. A high hedge appeared in the yellow glow of the lantern. Lights shined through many windows coming from a house beyond that. The house itself was surrounded by a tall brick wall covered with vines.

"Is the journal in there?" Archie asked.

"If he still has it."

"If who still has it?"

"Mind your business, boy," Landcross growled over his shoulder.

It was apparent that Landcross was protecting someone, so Archie didn't press him. Whoever this person was, it didn't concern Archie in the least. He only needed the book and return with it to England before dawn. Once he accomplished that, he needed a way to shake off Landcross, because he had no intention of helping him find or save Peachtree as they'd agreed.

A carriage came towards them. Landcross halted, reaching for a gun. The stagecoach turned for the gate of the house and came to a stop in front of the torches. Archie's small group stood in the shadows and watched as the driver spoke to a pair of footmen. One accepted an envelope from the driver.

"It must be a party," Clover surmised.

"Aye," Landcross said, handing Archie the lantern. "Wait here."

Landcross headed for the gate.

"What's he doing?" Clover asked.

Archie stared after Landcross' back as it disappeared into the darkness.

"I wish I knew."

Pierce waved at the footmen when they spotted him. Since putting down roots in France, Robert Blackbird had accumulated a lot of security—and for good reason.

"*Bonsoir*," Pierce greeted. "Er, Fable and Eric, is it?"

"*Bonsoir*, Landcross," Fable greeted mildly. "Back so soon?"

"It's been a year. I need to speak to your master."

The pair turned their rifles on him the moment he tried to go through the gate. "Our master is holding a social gathering this evening," Fable said. "Outlaws are *not* invited."

"Ah, *oui*," Pierce said, raising his hands. "I only need to pop in, get something of mine, and leave."

"He doesn't want you around anymore," Eric said. "He's even given us permission to shoot you in the leg if you return and refuse to leave."

Pierce dropped his hands, his mouth hanging open. After a moment he gathered his wits. "He actually said that?"

"Go away, Landcross," Eric ordered. "Your presence here endangers our master, and he's a man we'd give our lives for, if need be. Go, or we'll be forced to shoot you." The guard aimed his rifle down at Pierce's crotch. "And in such low lighting as this, we might miss your leg, *non*?"

"All right!" Pierce spat. "No need for threats. I'll crack on."

Fearing the loss of his manhood, he practically sprinted into the darkness. When he reached the corner of the wall, he spied the lantern.

"We need a plan to get inside," he said to Archie.

"I thought he was a friend of yours."

"Y'know nothing about this person, understand?" Pierce seethed.

Archie sighed with contempt. "In any case, you're a thief. Can't you scale the wall and break in?"

"First off, that's a twenty-foot high wall. Second, even if I did get over the blasted wall and dropped down without breaking a leg, there are guards on the other side who will put a bullet in my . . ." He trailed off when he remembered that he was in the presence of a young girl. "Er . . . put a bullet in me. And third, I'm not entirely sure *where* the book is in that house. So, if you have any ideas, I'm bloody well listening."

"I have an idea," Clover spoke up. She pushed her way between him and Archie.

Intrigued, Pierce gave her his full attention. "What's on your mind, love?"

She smiled broadly in response. They listened in rapt attention as she outlined her plan.

They ran through the field across from the château and up the road, away from the place. Pierce and Archie waited at the side of the road, hidden in a ditch. Though the plan wasn't bad, Pierce was skeptical that the girl could pull it off. After some time passed, the rattle of a stagecoach caught their attention.

"Are you sure they're going to the house?" Archie asked.

"There's nothing else here but a few farmhouses," Pierce whispered. "Stagecoaches like that come from other mansions, or the town."

"You seem to know this area fairly well," Archie remarked.

"Shut it," he said. "Your sister can speak French, right?"

"Yes, we both can."

"Bien."

As the coach began to pass, Clover moved. She scampered down the road, waving her hands. "*Stop! S'il vous plaît, arrêtez!*"

The coachman pulled on the reins and the slow-moving carriage eased to a halt. The moment it did, Pierce sprang out from his hiding place and hurried up behind the carriage.

"What is it, girl?" the French coachman asked.

"*Monsieur*, my father is mad at me and has thrown me out of the house. Could I ask for a ride into town and perhaps some money for food?"

As she spoke, Pierce silently climbed up the rear

boot of the carriage. He slid down on his belly atop of the roof and stayed as flat as humanly possible. From where he lay, the back of the coachman's head was just in sight. As long as Clover kept the driver's attention on her, he might not notice the extra traveler behind him.

"What goes on here?" a woman demanded from inside the carriage. "Driver, let me out."

The coachman leapt down and opened the door to help the woman out of the coach. She was dressed in what appeared to be a costume. Even in the muted light, he could see it was too ornate for a simple dress.

"*Mes excuses, mademoiselle,*" the coachman said. "This child suddenly came into my path."

The beautifully dressed woman approached Clover. "What is the matter, child?" she asked, her voice softer.

"My father threw me out, *Mademoiselle*. I am cold, hungry, and in need of a ride into town."

"Oh, you poor dear. What a cruel father you have to cast out such a lovely child as yourself. I am attending a party at Anatolie Hagi's estate. Would you care to join me? You can get some food there."

"Say no," Pierce muttered to himself.

"*Oui,*" Clover said. "I would love to. *Merci!*"

Damn and blast! This wasn't part of the plan. He only needed Clover to stop the carriage long enough for him to climb onto it. The coachman was supposed to yell at her to piss off and she'd run away.

Something caught the corner of his eye. To his dismay, Archie slid on his belly next to him. "What are you doing?" he whispered angrily.

"If Clover goes, I go," Archie whispered back.

Unable to argue without running the risk of being overheard, Pierce kept his tongue.

The elegant woman led Clover to the carriage, and

once they were inside, the coach went on. Pierce and Archie hugged the roof as the coach stopped at the gate. The roof was high enough where the firelight couldn't reach, keeping them hidden in the shadows. The coachman handed Fable an envelope.

"Good evening, *Mademoiselle* Penelope Reine," the footman said, "the master will be most thrilled that you have decided to attend."

"I wouldn't have missed it for the world," the woman said from inside the carriage. "I have brought a little friend with me, though."

"Very good, *Mademoiselle*, anything is permitted."

The carriage passed through the gate and drove up the lane toward the house, where a servant opened the door for the woman and Clover and helped them down from the coach. Even though no one ever thought to look up, nor was anyone standing on the balcony to see them from above, the lights from the house made Pierce nervous.

The coachman drove the carriage towards the stables where other liveries were lined up outside. The moment the coachman stopped the carriage and climbed down, Pierce rolled off the roof, landing silently on the other side. Archie followed suit as Pierce peered around the back of the carriage to scout out the yard. The coast appeared to be clear enough.

He looked over his shoulder and whispered to Archie, "Follow me and stay low."

The coachman joined a group of other servants smoking pipes and drinking from hip flasks. None of them noticed Pierce or Archie crossing the yard to the side of the house. There, Pierce found an open window, and slowly lifted it all the way up. He slipped inside the dark room.

"C'mon," he ordered.

Archie quickly followed suit, keeping as quiet as possible. In spite of himself, Pierce was impressed with the lad. He seemed to be able to hold his own under pressure and take orders without argument.

After Archie clambered inside, they crept toward the other side of the room, feeling around for any obstructions in their way. Pierce touched a wall and slid his hand over it until his fingertips touched a doorframe. His hand searched a moment longer and found the latch. Low light melted into the darkness as the door slowly opened. He peered out into the hallway.

"Let's go," he whispered, stepping out.

Down the short corridor was the busy kitchen, and at the other end, the entrance hall, where laughter and conversation drifted out like ghosts. The ballroom would be the next room over, where the gathering was being held. Keeping his back pressed against the wall, Pierce crouched down and peered around the corner.

The entrance hall had been decorated with several naked mannequins wearing masks. Clearly it was a masquerade. A servant stood next to the front door, while a couple of footmen stood at attention by the open ballroom entrance.

Pierce had a sudden inspiration. He turned to Archie. "What's the caliber of your thespian skills?"

Archie looked at him, clearly befuddled. "Pardon?"

"Wait here."

He darted down the hall towards the kitchen. The staff were bustling, barely taking notice of anything or anyone unless it had to do with their duties. It was all too easy.

He returned to Archie with a bottle of wine, digging a corkscrew into it. By the time he reached the lad, he'd pulled the cork out.

"I need you to go out there and pretend that you're

drunk to draw the attention of the footmen. Get them away from the door, eh?"

"Why me?" Archie argued.

"'Cause look how you're dressed."

In his royal blue frock coat, ornate vest, black trousers, and new leather shoes, Archie looked the part of a young aristocrat. And although he smelled of sea and sweat, he had more respectable attire then Pierce.

"Not to mention the servants know me," Pierce went on.

Archie seemed less then convinced. "The bottle is full. They'll never believe that I'm a blundering drunk with an untouched bottle."

"Fine, drink," Pierce said, handing the bottle over.

Archie raised an eyebrow.

Pierce sighed deeply and said, "We'll drink together, eh?"

He tipped the bottle up and took in several large healthy gulps. After letting out a burp, he handed the bottle over to the lad. "Go on, drink," he ordered with another burp.

"I don't care much for wine."

"You want the journal?" he pressed. "Take it."

Someone knocked on the front door and a servant opened it. More costumed guests entered.

"C'mon, drink," Pierce urged as the servant took the guests' coats.

Archie took the bottle and drank quickly. Pierce nodded approvingly. The lad needed some liquid courage.

"Keep drinking," he whispered. "Good, now get out there." And he shoved him out.

Exposed, Archie had little choice but to go along with the plan. He slackened his straight posture and stumbled across the room. "Hope yu donna mind, my good fellows," he said to the footmen. "I helped myself to da wine in da kitchen."

His performance caught not only the attention of the servants, but of the guests as well. Pierce was impressed as well as amused.

"I seemed to have lost my mask," Archie said, heading up the stairs. "I wonder if it's up here."

"No, *monsieur*, you're not allowed up there," a footman said, moving from his post.

"It's quite all right, my good man," Archie said, continuing his ascent.

That prompted both footmen to go after him. Archie had already made it well up the stairs when they took up the chase.

Pierce quickly left the hall, hurrying over to one of the mannequins. He snatched off a silver long horned mask and slipped it over his face. Then he causally strolled over to the now unattended ballroom door. The guests were amused by the drunken young man arguing with the footmen at the top of the stairs.

"I lost my mask!" Archie shouted. "Has anyone seen it?"

"Some buffoons can't handle their drink, *non*?" Pierce remarked as he passed by.

"*Oui, monsieur*," the door servant agreed, unable to pull his eyes away from the spectacle.

Pierce went into the ballroom, the mask over his face.

The hall was the largest in the château and had been renovated since Pierce had last seen it. The old wooden floors were now marble. The staircase railing had been replaced by a pair of sinuous steel dragons. The dragons' heads served as the downstairs stair posts with front legs reaching to the floor.

A bar was set up under the upstairs balcony, decorated with helium balloon lamps that hung on wires from the ceiling. A uniformed bartender wearing a plain red mask, mixed drinks and served champagne. On the other side of the hall, a long table with a lavish spread of food and drink attracted many guests. Overhead an ornate crystal chandelier drifted slowly through the great hall, suspended from a hot air balloon.

More mannequins, much like the ones in the entrance hall, lined the walls, naked but for masks. A quartet of musicians, also in costume, played at the far end of the ballroom.

In the years since inheriting the mansion, Robert Blackbird had filled it with color and life.

Clover sat comfortably in a chair in a corner, eating cake. Leaving her to her bliss, Pierce went in search of Robert. He moved casually through the crowd. With all the decorations, dancers, tables, and guests just standing about, space was a luxury.

As he glided through the ballroom, he wondered how he would find Robert amongst all the guests. He eventually made his way to the base of a staircase that led to the wraparound balcony. There, beside the dragons, he found the kindly Mademoiselle Penelope Reine.

She was as beautiful as her temperament was delightful. She wore a low-cut silver dress with gleaming dragonflies starting at her shoulders and running down to the hem of the dress, where the silver darkened to black. About her wrists were diamond bracelets that stood out in dazzling contrast to her black lace gloves. Her mask was hardly a mask at all, but a well-crafted accessory made of slivers of black wire webbed over half of her charming face. He couldn't help but to steal a glance at the dragonfly charm resting between her perfect breasts.

She was speaking to a man in a dark blue coat embroidered with gold thread and a pocket watch hanging from a vest pocket. His mask was a bird's face, complete with a long beak. The mask prevented Pierce from identifying him, and yet his voice was familiar.

"I must say, Anatolie," Mademoiselle Reine cooed, "you have certainly outdone yourself. I cannot wait for your annual All Hallows Eve party."

Anatolie laughed in obvious relief. "I am thrilled that you like it. I know how much you enjoy costumed festivities."

Pierce had to admit it; his mate could pull off a Romanian accent while speaking French very well.

"Are you saying that you did this for me?" Mademoiselle Reine exclaimed, one hand going to her mouth.

Anatolie fidgeted with his rings, apparently nervous that he had said too much. "Well, I . . . uh," he began as Pierce approached.

"Monsieur Anatolie Hagi, how wonderful it is to see you again," Pierce said in French, bowing deeply.

Robert turned to him and Pierce raised his chin, showing the scar across his neck. Robert's jaw went slack.

"It was so kind of you to invite me to your beautiful home," Pierce said.

Robert's mouth remained hanging open.

Pierce cleared his throat and took Penelope by the hand. "And who is this fairytale vision?"

"Reine," she answered. "Mademoiselle Penelope Reine."

"Charmed, Mademoiselle Penelope Reine," he said

before placing a kiss on her hand.

In the course of his lifetime, he'd learned how to play many roles, from a commoner to a proper gentleman. His true personality was somewhere in between.

He rose to his full height. "I must say, you have the most fascinating costume."

Mademoiselle Reine's eyes crinkled as she smiled. "*Merci, Monsieur*, I designed it myself."

Pierce stole a glance at Robert. His shock was subsiding. "I stand amazed, my lady. You should go into business making costumes, if you haven't already."

"That is not such a bad idea," she said with exuberance. "And what of your, er . . . costume?"

"Oh," Pierce said, looking down at his disheveled clothing. "I decided to attend the festivities as a commoner masquerading amongst the wealthy."

"How original," she complimented. "Don't you agree, Anatolie?"

Robert shook his head slightly. "Ah, yes," he said after finding his voice. "Darling, would you excuse us for a moment?"

Robert's feet moved before she answered. He grabbed Pierce by the arm and led him toward the exit.

"Of course, darling," Mademoiselle Reine said as they left.

"She's really quite lovely, Robert," Pierce whispered as they made their way past the guests. "You ought to hold on to her."

Robert Blackbird retained his calm demeanor, even waving at a guest who called out to him. "Wonderful party, Monsieur Hagi."

"*Merci*." To Pierce, Robert whispered, "Don't call me Robert here. Just keep moving."

Robert escorted him out of the ballroom, passing

Archie along the way. After his stunt, it surprised Pierce that the lad had been allowed to stay. Yet there he was, standing by his sister in the corner, a smug smile on his young face.

Chapter Eight
The Late Edgardo José

Pierce and Robert exited the ballroom, where Robert ordered a servant to follow them, and the three went upstairs to a small library.

"Allow no one to enter," Robert ordered the guard.

"*Oui, mon seigneur.*"

Robert slid the double doors shut, which rendered the room pitch-black; at least until he struck a match, lighting another hot air balloon lantern.

Pierce slipped off his mask. "You've certainly fixed up the place since I last saw it."

"Aye," Robert said in his native British. He walked over to the next lantern, protecting the tiny flame at the end of the match with his hand. "The late Edgardo José left this place in a wretched state."

"I remember. It was a good plan to befriend the old cocker."

"It wasn't difficult," Robert said. "The man was sick and lonely, and with no family. All he wanted was for an ear to listen to his stories. In truth, I'm grateful to have been here during his final few years."

"You bloody liar. You drafted a new will and then forged his name on it."

Robert lit another lantern and threw the fire-eaten match into the fireplace. He lit another match and continued going about the room, making it brighter.

"Of course I did, after what I allowed that sodomite to do to me. I had to make certain I got everything. Besides, he'd completely lost the plot. He planned to leave his entire fortune to his bloody terriers, which I am now caring for."

Like Pierce, Robert Blackbird had been a thief since childhood. If his folks had been able to send him to school, undoubtedly, he would have had a comfortable life. Instead, he'd spent years scraping by, trying to attain the money for the lifestyle he desired. In the end, it only took a little whoring to get his piece of heaven.

Pierce walked over to a small table sitting between two cushioned armchairs and picked up a golden Egyptian bust.

"Why did you decide to portray yourself as a Romanian, anyway?"

Robert reached the last lantern and placed the match to the wick. "Anatolie is my grandfather's name on my mother's side. Her parents didn't care to be poor in Romania, so they decided to migrate to England and be poor there instead." He shook the match until the flame went out, then slipped off his mask. "I told you not to come here anymore. I thought we had an understanding."

"Aye, that we did, I only came for—"

"Came for what?" Robert demanded tersely. He held a small loaded crossbow that he'd taken down from a bookshelf. He could fire it and no one would ever hear the shot.

"Whoa, mate," Pierce said, raising his hands. "I'm not here to stir up shite, eh? I just—"

"Dropped in to blackmail me?" Robert cut in vehemently. "Is that it? You want *money*?"

Pierce lowered his hands with a quizzical expression. "You've become paranoid over the years, Rob."

"And for good reason," Robert said, advancing. "I've worked hard to get my fortune. I'll not have it threatened!"

Pierce backed up to the bookshelves. "Look, I haven't come seeking money. All I want is the book."

"The book?"

"Aye, the journal you won from me, remember?"

Keeping the bolt aimed at Pierce's chest, Robert slowly approached. "Explain."

Pierce's back hit the bookshelf and he began sidestepping along it. "I've been found by a nasty man named Tarquin Norwich. Know him?"

Robert stopped and lowered the crossbow. His disquieted expression answered the question.

Pierce stopped as well. "He sent his boy to nab me and drag me back to England to have a not-so-friendly chat with Norwich about the whereabouts of the book. The book *you* have."

Robert chewed his bottom lip.

"Norwich's kid brought up the whole baby-stealing bit, which I still get blamed for, by the way," Pierce threw in. "But it was *you* who stole that bleedin' carriage with the child inside."

Robert raised his weapon once more. Pierce grabbed a book and held it against his chest as a shield. "Er . . . to make a long story short, it's best if I get that bloody thing far away from you."

Robert didn't seem convinced.

"You saw the book's contents, Rob," Pierce said in earnest. "And if someone like Tarquin Norwich is interested in it, chances are, he'll stop at nothing to get it."

A brief silence fell like an autumn leaf. Pierce thought that he'd finally gotten through to him—until Robert raised his weapon again. This time, he took aim and fired.

Pierce turned away with his book covering his face.

The passing bolt splitting the air sounded close. He opened his eyes, expecting stabbing pain somewhere in his body. Instead, the bolt had become lodged in the spine of a book near his head. He needed only to reach over his head to touch its feathers.

"Take it," Robert said, lowering the crossbow to his hip.

Pierce looked at his old friend and then back at the bolt, which was protruding from the journal itself. He slipped the book off the shelf. It was black leather, with polished steel corners. He opened the journal to where the tip had struck.

"Nice shot," he grumbled, taking hold of the bolt to remove it.

"So you haven't come for money?" Robert said, taking a seat on one of the cushioned armchairs. He appeared to be a mythological monarch in his costume.

Robert was a handsome gent, with bright clear eyes and flawless skin. Even when he ran with Pierce, dressed in rags, Robert's good looks were never in dispute. Sometimes, he made Pierce envious.

"Never have I asked you for any of the loot you swindled from that old goat. Why would I do so now?"

"The Queen. Remember that?" Robert said, running his hands through his perfectly coiffed hair.

Pierce gritted his teeth as he struggled to pull the bolt out of the leather spine. "Heard about that, did you? You make one mistake and no one lets up about it."

"Pierce, you tried stealing Queen Victoria's necklace, which Albert gave to her as an anniversary present. And out of her own bedchamber, no doubt!"

The bolt grudgingly came out of the spine. Frustrated from both the struggle and the topic, Pierce tossed it away. "It wasn't an anniversary gift; it was a birthday gift." He took a seat on the other armchair with a contemptuous sigh. "The rest of it is true enough."

"Why did you do it?" Robert asked.

"I wanted to see if I could."

"You do realize the trouble you're in, right? Christ, you've become a retirement ticket for anyone who brings you back to London—dead or alive."

"I would've pulled it off if her Highness hadn't walked in on me," he explained. "Besides, that fuckin' necklace was made from forty aquamarines. *Forty*! That there would've been *my* retirement ticket."

Robert waved his hand dismissively at him. "You've never stolen just for the money. You enjoy it. Always have."

Robert had something there. Never in his life had Pierce searched for the kind of wealth that Robert had made. Mainly, he'd stolen to put food in his mouth and to get a room for the night. He got by just like his gypsy parents had. As a younger man, being an outlaw thief had thrilled him. It was a high, living so close to death. Foolish now when he looked back on it, for he could have died many times over. Perhaps that was the real reason why he'd gone after the necklace, one last rush before retiring and finding a spot somewhere in the world to call his own.

A smirk touched a corner of Robert's lips. "I apologize for doubting you. What are you going to do, now that you have the book?"

"I'm going back to England," he said, flipping through the pages. He was in awe of the genius behind each description and every sketch, as much now as he had been when he'd first looked through it.

"England?" Robert blurted out. "Are you mad?"

"Norwich is after someone I know." He closed the

book and raised it slightly in one hand. "The author of this very journal."

Robert's eyebrows hiked up. "Peachtree? But he's the gent you stole the book from."

"I didn't steal it," he said. "I *mistakenly* loaded it into my bag while packing my gear when Joaquin and I were leaving. It was in the middle of the night and I thought it was one of my own books."

"You ought to destroy it," Robert recommended.

"Not yet. I may need it to bargain with." As he said it, a thought occurred. "Do you have a journal somewhat similar to this cover, one with empty pages?"

Robert cocked an eyebrow. "Ah, I see." He stood up and walked over to the bookshelf. "I may have something."

"It's not another crossbow, eh?" Pierce said, twisting around.

Robert slipped a book off a shelf. "Now who's paranoid?"

Pierce took the book. It was a little larger then Indigo's journal, and it had no steel corners, yet the cover was similar enough. He flipped through the pages. The journal held nothing but blank sheets.

"It'll do just fine. Cheers."

"Pierce," Robert said with sincerity. When Pierce tilted his chin up, he saw Robert looking at him with concern. "You're playing a dangerous game. My heart would bleed if something terrible befell you. Do be careful."

Robert had long ago become one of the few friends that Pierce could trust with his life. He was like a brother, and when someone of such rarity drifted into his life, Pierce valued them more than any gold coin in his possession.

"I'll do my best."

Robert embraced him tightly and Pierce returned the favor, slapping his back. A knock came at the door.

"What is it?" Robert demanded.

"*Mon seigneur*," the servant outside said. "There are British soldiers here. They are looking for Pierce Landcross."

Chapter Nine

The Story of the Priest

Summer, 1639

When it was made known that the Teller of Forgotten Tales was returning, Temenitis' soul filled with excitement beyond measure. She had waited a long time for this. It had been twenty years since the Teller of Forgotten Tales had wandered through this realm. For one night, he would tell the most amazing sagas under his oilskin tarpaulin. But once the stories ended and the audience stepped out from under the tent, the stories would be forgotten by all who'd heard them.

On the night of his coming, Temenitis asked her sisters, the Pegaeae nymphs, if they wanted to join her.

"What is the point, little sister?" Euneica, the eldest asked, while standing in the spring with the others. "No one remembers what that old storyteller says."

"Exactly," Nycheia concurred as she lovingly combed her wet hair. Temenitis was a hundred years younger than her sisters, yet she felt like she was the wisest amongst them.

"It is a waste of time," another sister said, stretching her body out over the sun-warmed rocks.

Her sisters were pure perfection of the female form. On the surface, they had no flaws. It was no different for Temenitis. She had the smoothest skin, warm colored hair and eyes like lilac flowers.

"It is not a waste of time," Temenitis argued. "And it isn't about remembering the stories. It's about living in the moment. To be taken in by the seconds as they pass you by."

"Go if you wish, little sister," Euneica said, turning her back on Temenitis with a flick of her wrist. "Go waste your time."

Temenitis snarled and retorted, "Time better spent then here with you!"

She darted into the forest, tears of anger stinging her eyes. She hated the narrow-minded nymphs who never wanted anything more for themselves then to look pretty. And she hated that she was one of them.

For some time, she'd been desiring something else for herself, to become more then a nymph with little thought or power to do anything. Even for deities, they were weak. With everything out there in the world, why did she have to have been born a nymph?

When she finished crying, the moon was already up. It lit her way through the thick Forest of Forgiveness, until it opened up into the Field of Uncertainty, where anything was possible as well as impossible. It was there that the oilskin tarpaulin came into view. Her mood lifted at the sight of it.

Many had already gathered there, faeries, trolls, other nymphs, goblins, spirits, and elves, even animals of the forest, a human woodsman, a woman, and a couple of imps. They sat, or flew, or stood around while chattering amongst themselves. Everyone was packed in tight, for if anyone stood outside the tarpaulin, they wouldn't be able to hear a single word.

She made her way as far into the crowd as she could, toward a small clearing directly under the center of the tent. When the throng got too thick, she settled down on the grass and waited.

Soon afterward, fires burst to life in mid-air around the small clearing. With the fire came the moths.

There were hundreds, swarming in and gathering within the circle of flames. A twisted walking stick rose from the ground. Tied to the stick were countless quills and ink jars. The nib of each quill was black with ink, droplets still dripping.

The moths coalesced into the shape of a man, their little wings fluttering as it took form. A hand clutched the walking stick. When it did, the moths' wings closed and each insect faded from view, leaving the Storyteller in their wake.

He wore a waist-length coat with over-sized sleeves, stripped breeches, and buckled shoes, and his felt cape came down to the back of his knees. His hair was black and shoulder length. He had no hat, but he did wear a mask of glossy black metal that covered his entire face: Temenitis could just make out the words from different languages carved into nearly every inch of it. The mask's eyes were closed but the mouth was open. The opening was too dark to see anything, as though no face existed behind it.

"He does like to make an entrance, doesn't he?" the spirit next to Temenitis said.

"Welcome, story lovers," the Teller of Forgotten Tales said in a voice deep yet gentle. "I am humbled to have you here."

Temenitis sat with her knees clutched to her chest and stared up in rapt attention.

The Teller of Forgotten Tales raised his hand theatrically toward the ceiling.

"Tonight, I have a special tale for you. A tale that is as entertaining to tell as it is dangerous."

The fires around him dimmed to glowing beads of light, giving way to images manifesting overhead.

"This tale is titled, *The Story of the Priest.*"

Temenitis listened to every word, letting herself be taken away by the animated show playing out above her and in her mind.

It began with the galaxy. "No one knows how they obtained their powers," the Teller of Forgotten Tales began. "Some speculated that they came from another plane of existence, perhaps one that no longer exists. One in which they may have destroyed themselves. They were destructive creatures and were in need of a new home. They found it here where they declared themselves gods . . ."

The images continued to change. There were dark figures fighting with a jackal headed man, a god. Other deities sought help from a man in a grey robe, who lived in a temple on top of Mount Dai. There was trickery and more deaths.

His words created moving images as he spoke each sentence. What he told them that night gave reason for why his stories were meant to be forgotten. And yet the story also needed to be told. Yarns lived through ink and through words spoken by storytellers who cared enough to spin them. Even if it was forgotten, as long as it passed between someone's lips, the story survived.

The images burst and vanished when the story came to an end. The fires brightened once again. The Teller of Forgotten Tales thanked everyone for coming. As his audience cleared out from under the tent, Temenitis approached him. He stood unmoving, leaning against his tall, twisted walking stick as if he needed it for support. His metal mask glimmered in the firelight and she wondered why he wore it.

"Is it true? Is *The Story of the Priest* true?"

The Teller of Forgotten Tales raised his head as if waking from a slumber. "Never speak of the stories I tell, child. Even the title."

She didn't understand, yet she did not ask him to explain what he meant.

"Yes," he answered at length. "It is a true tale. If the

story was not true, there would be no need for it to be forgotten. It is a story that happened a very long time ago, so long that only a few even remember the truth of it."

"It seems impossible, though."

"Many impossible things have happened."

She left the tent, and in the moment she did, the tale faded from her memory.

The Story of the Priest.

Perhaps she remembered the title because she had spoken it out loud, keeping it alive in her head. Along with the title, she carried the imprint of the tale and how it had made her feel when she'd heard it.

She felt liberated.

Chapter Ten

Run

Ramirez Tajo's lungs burned as he hurried through the dark countryside of Cowes. His spirit remained young but his body was growing old and weary. Unlike his master's. The high wet grass dampened his trousers, the fabric sticking to his legs. Still, he ran through the field until he came to the road where his horse was tied to a tree. He mounted the mare and rode a few miles until he spied emerald light coming from an ornate wagon. Sitting atop of the wagon was his master, smoking a pipe.

"I made it to the castle, master," Ramirez announced, halting the horse near the wagon.

"What did you find, my friend?" the man asked, exhaling smoke.

"It's as you suspected. He's holding prisoners there. I saw someone being brought in."

The master bowed his head and rubbed his temple. "Norwich has gone too far this time."

"What are we to do?"

The master lifted his face to him, his pale complexion now green in the glow of the lanterns mounted on either side of the wagon.

"I cannot shake the feeling that there's more. We shall wait until Norwich returns. I want to find out everything he's planning."

Ramirez Tajo's chest swelled with prideful air. Since his youth, he'd served this man, this legend.

Many years ago, as a drunk angry young man, Ramirez headed toward his own doom, until one night, when a performing wagon had come into his small village. A magician and his elderly assistant, whose stage name was the Fire King, performed magic that intrigued him. Curiosity and drunkenness prompted him to sneak into the magician's wagon to uncover clues of how he'd done his tricks. Being a clumsy and intoxicated boy, he'd been discovered by both the magician and his assistant.

Instead of killing him, the magician had seen something in him. Understanding Ramirez's true character, the magician had taken him in, sobered him up, and the three had traveled together to lands that Ramirez had never believed were real. When the Fire King died and Ramirez had taken his place, he'd learned the most vital secret about the magician—and it was no trick.

"I've learned that he was here recently, *señor*. When do you think he will return?"

"Soon, I hope." The magician leapt off the wagon, almost floating to the ground. "We'll stay close until then."

Archie stayed by his sister while Landcross was gone. In the meantime, he helped himself to some food to fill his stomach and to clear his head from the wine. He felt foolish for letting a few drinks consume his senses so. He didn't touch alcohol often, save for a glass on special occasions. Though the wine in his head now made him feel somewhat jovial, he kept his mind on the mission.

"Stay here," he said.

Clover nodded as she continued to stuff her face with mini cakes and fruit.

Archie went to the open doorway, ready to search for Landcross, when the sight of British soldiers held him at the threshold. The leader of the group, a dark-skinned man, spoke to the servant at the front door. If it wasn't for the band playing and people chattering around him, he could have heard what they were saying. He could only assume that the soldiers were the same group that had been chasing Landcross as far back as London.

Archie had no intention of going against the Crown, especially since he was related to the Queen; but if they found Landcross before he could get the book, then he risked returning to his father empty-handed. Even if he managed to get home first and take Eilidh and Clover away, chances were that his father would find them; and like his mother, his father would make him suffer a fate worse than death. He needed either the book or Landcross to distract his father; and at that moment, he didn't care which.

A footman standing in front of the double doors stepped forward to listen in on the conversation between the servant and the soldiers. He seemed to be able to hear them and then knocked on the door behind him. The dark-skinned soldier, a Persian, Archie surmised, showed the servant at the front door a wanted poster with a likeness of Landcross. The servant shook his head. Yet the Persian was persistent and marched himself and his men into the entrance hall.

It dawned on Archie that this must be one of Landcross' frequent haunts. That was the reason why he knew so much about the area, even in the dark. Berck was a place reputed for misdeeds committed by Landcross, as were other parts of France. The Persian obviously had his suspicions to warrant such an intrusion.

Before they reached the ballroom, Archie grabbed a mask from one of the mannequins and put it on. It was a long shot that the soldiers would recognize him, yet he'd been to the Queen's palace enough times to know it wasn't impossible.

"There are soldiers here searching for Landcross," he whispered to Clover, handing her a mask.

Her eyes grew large. "What are we to do?"

"Put the mask on and come with me."

The soldiers entered the ballroom and stopped several feet inside, where they attracted everyone's attention. Archie and Clover slipped out while the soldiers' backs were turned. The footmen at the ballroom doorway were now watching the English soldiers in return. The footman at the top of the stairs came down to join them, giving Archie and Clover clear passage up the staircase. They ascended, then slipped through the door, entering what appeared to be a library. Clover bumped into Archie's back as he stopped dead in his tracks. She peered around him, straight into the muzzle of a large pistol.

"Easy, Landcross," Archie said, holding up his hand. "It's only me."

Landcross didn't look happy that Archie had caught him with the person he wanted to protect. That man rushed over to the doors and slid them shut.

"What the bloody hell are you doing in here?" Landcross seethed.

Cradled in Landcross' hands were two books. One had to be the journal he needed for his father.

Before Landcross could see that he had noticed, Archie lifted his eyes up to him. "There are at least twenty or so soldiers down there looking for you."

"Aye, I know," he grumbled, holstering his gun. To his companion, he said, "Is there a balcony I can scale down?"

"Only in the bedrooms," the man said, grabbing a satchel hanging from a wall and tossing it to him. "But you won't make it without being spotted. My men out in the yard may draw attention to your presence."

"Wonderful," Landcross said, shoving the books into the bag.

"Is that the journal?" Archie inquired.

Landcross glared at him. "Maybe."

"It's too risky to have it on you," Archie said. "Give it to me and I'll get it to the ship."

"Like bloody hell you will," Landcross said, shouldering the satchel. "The minute you get your hands on this, who's to say you won't turn me over to that royal throng down there, eh?"

"Is this the lad you told me about?" the man in costume asked.

"Aye," Landcross answered irritably. "He's become my bloody shadow."

"Be that as it may, we need to think of a way to get you out of here without detection," Archie said. "As of now, they're questioning the guests; and I'm sure that even with the mask, someone might have seen that scar on your throat."

That sparked fear in Landcross' eyes. "S'pose you were right about my being here endangering you, eh?" he said to the man in costume.

"Mr. Landcross?" Clover spoke up.

All eyes turned to her as she stepped closer to Landcross.

"Maybe we can get you out as well as protect your friend."

Landcross folded his arms and said, "Got something in mind, love?"

She nodded. "I do. But it's a tad risky on your end."

He smiled. "Risky I don't mind. It's suicide where I draw the line."

Robert Blackbird composed himself the best he could as he made his way downstairs to confront the soldiers in his home. Behind him were the young man and the girl he'd just met, who separated from him at the bottom of the steps in order to make their escape through the kitchen. Before he entered the ballroom, Robert slipped on his mask. He could hear a soldier speaking to his guests and he whispered instructions to one of his servants. The servant nodded and signaled the others to follow him out of the house.

Robert took a deep breath just before he fixed a grin on his face and stepped inside. "I was not aware that I would be entertaining members of the British soldiery tonight," he said in his Romanian accent. "What an honor."

When the troop of red uniforms turned his way, Robert thought his heart would explode. One soldier turned away from the couple he was questioning and spoke to him with a distinctly foreign accent. "Are you the master of the house?"

"I am," Robert answered. "I am Anatolie Hagi. And you are?"

"Lieutenant Darius Javan."

"Ah. Well now, Lieutenant Darius Javan, to what do I owe the pleasure of this invasive visit?"

"We are in search of Pierce Landcross. We have reason to believe that he may be passing through this area on his way to the coast, perhaps to acquire revenue to go underground. This party drew our attention to your home." The soldier lifted a wanted poster with a drawing of Pierce on it. "Have you seen this man around recently? A few of your guests stated that they saw a man here in worn clothing, with a scar across his neck."

Robert glanced over to Penelope, who must have mentioned it to the lieutenant. He held his composure when he answered, "Yes, that man is here. He said he was a guest of a guest and claimed to be an art collector. I took him up to my library to see some of my own collection."

The lieutenant's dark face hardened. "Where is he now, sir?"

"He's still upstairs."

The soldiers hurried past him. Robert followed them out of the room, and as they prepared to climb the stairs, Pierce came out of the library. He was holding the gold Egyptian bust, which he was putting into his satchel. He stopped dead in his tracks and stared at the soldiers, who also halted at the base of the stairs.

"Oh, bugger," Pierce said with his eyes widening.

"You blasted thief!" Robert shouted, pointing at him. "You lied to me!"

The soldiers drew their guns. When they did, Pierce threw the statue at them and took off running.

"Halt in the name of the Queen!" Lieutenant Javan demanded.

Pierce vanished into a bedroom, slamming the door. When the soldiers reached it, they discovered it was locked.

"Open this door!" the lieutenant demanded before he crashed his own shoulder against it.

As Robert watched nervously, Penelope wrapped her arm around his. "Forgive me, darling," she whispered, "I did not know he was a friend you wanted to protect."

Robert whipped his head around to her. "How did you . . ?

She tilted her head sideways and smiled coyly.

"Sweetheart, he said nothing about being an art collector."

His jaw dropped and fear flashed in his eyes.

Penelope slid a comforting hand along his chin. He shuddered at her warm touch. "You have nothing to worry about from me, darling. Whatever skeletons are in your closet, rest assured that you can trust me with them."

And right then, Robert knew that he wanted to spend the rest of his life with her.

Seconds after Pierce locked the door, the soldiers reached it, ordering him to open it. He crossed the room to the bay windows leading to the outside balcony. There was two dogs inside wicker cages. They barked enthusiastically at his presence, making him jump. Robert's inherited terriers. He clambered over the stone railing and lowered himself down as far as he could, dangling from the ledge. Pushing the fall from his mind, he let go, dropping into the bushes below.

The shrubs broke his fall but not without a price. Every little branch scratched him. Groaning, he rolled onto the lawn, then staggered to his feet and stumbled a ways, until he ran into a group of Robert's footmen.

"Bugger," he said with hands raised, thinking that he was dead, or worse.

"Come with us," one of the footmen said. "Hurry!"

A gunshot came from inside the house. It jolted him to move and he followed the footmen to the wall. Only a single lantern lit their way.

Under a thick barrier of ivy was a small wooden door. An escape route? He wondered if the door had always been there or if Robert had had it installed when he'd taken over the château. That was a possibility, considering Robert's past.

"Go," a footman ordered. "Run to the road. Keep going until you see a carriage."

"What?" he said.

"He's not in the room!" a soldier yelled from the balcony. "Search the yard!"

"Go!" the footman urged.

Pierce wasted no more time as he opened the door and ducked to get through it, then ran as fast as he could through the field beyond. The door slammed shut behind him. Voices were soon yelling in French, shouting that someone had stolen a horse and was now heading for the road.

By the time Pierce reached the road, his heart was bursting. He continued running along the path, ready to fall on his belly and hide in the tall grass if he heard the sound of hooves. Instead, he came upon a carriage traveling towards the coast.

"Hurry up," Archie ordered from his seat beside the driver. "Get in."

The moonless night made it difficult to identify Archie, but the light offered by the carriage lanterns helped. Pierce ran up to the door while the coach was still in motion and swung it open.

"Hello, Mr. Landcross," Clover said, sitting next to a whale-oil lantern.

He grinned before jumping in. "'Ello, love."

The stagecoach continued toward the coast. No horsemen came their way, which meant that the soldiers must have ridden towards town instead.

Before long, they reached the shoreline, where Pierce bid farewell to the driver. The servant quickly left to return the carriage before its owner noticed it was missing. Pierce, Archie, and Clover jumped into the dinghy they'd left on the beach and rowed back to the waiting ship.

The constant rumbling coming from that daft drunk, Ivor, kept Joaquin from sleeping. It also made his blood boil. After Tarquin Norwich had left the room, Ivor had awakened briefly to finish explaining why they needed forced labor at the Norwich estate. Joaquin had never been one to be easily shocked, but the scale of their plan would have floored him if he wasn't tied to a chair. If only his hands were tied with rope instead of bound by iron, he could slip them out, kill the exhausted guard at the door, then slit Ivor's throat with the bugger's own knife. But his bonds tied him securely. He had no chance of escaping. He wondered if this was karma for his wicked deeds.

He had long since developed a hardened soul, especially after he'd committed the unforgivable sin on the first night that the beast had surfaced. For the first time, he tried summoning it. He would gladly let it take him over if it would help get him out of this mess, but there was nothing, not even the sickening flutter.

He'd been suffering from stomach cramps for a long time even before the beast had taken up residence inside him. Sometimes the pain was enough to drop him to his knees. He actually considered seeing a physician about it.

Now the pains served as a warning whenever the beast was going to come out. A hell of a time for this curse to be lifted, he thought grimly. Or perhaps the beast needed more incentive to come forth. When it took him over, he felt nothing but rage. Fear and second-guessing would be an afterthought.

He leaned his head back and closed his eyes, trying to ignore the earthquake snores coming from Ivor.

Never in all his years had Lieutenant Darius Javan been so infuriated. Twice, Pierce Landcross had escaped him. What made this time worse was that he'd been much closer to catching the thief. Darius could kick himself for not splitting up the troops when they'd been in pursuit, which he had done all too late, it seemed.

When he was just seventeen years old, five years after coming to Great Britain, Darius had fought in the Third Anglo-Maratha War, and then had gone to fight in the hellish conditions of the Gold Coast jungle during the First Ashanti War. Yet capturing this thief had proven more trying then both!

He'd set many goals in his life for himself, some he'd already achieved, but now his newest goal was at the top of the list. Bring Pierce Landcross back to London. He was fully prepared to scour the world over to find him.

Landcross must be heading south, he surmised. They had encountered a coachman on the road who'd admitted to seeing a horseman riding swiftly towards the coast. Javan figured the outlaw was now heading for a port. If Pierce Landcross truly wanted to disappear for good, Le Havre was where he'd be heading.

Chapter Eleven

Finding the Secret

Pierce's heart was still pounding well after the *Ekta* made way. After boarding the ship, he collapsed on the deck and lay on his back, recuperating. He ignored all offers of drink or food, simply relishing in the fact that he had escaped.

"You're a ruin," Waves of Strength said.

He slowly opened his eyes to see her standing over him with hands on hips. Suddenly the burn began to ache.

"Flattery will only get me to fall in love with you, y'know?" He rolled over and climbed to his feet, placing a hand over the bandage on his chest. "Maybe that's what you wanted all along, *non*?" He walked away.

She said something to him in her native language. Although he didn't understand, he was sure that it wasn't anything good. He doubted that true peace would ever exist between them. At least he didn't have to worry about her killing him anymore.

At least, he hoped.

He spotted Clover sitting on the steps next to a lantern, writing in a book. He had to admit that the child possessed a brilliant mind. In one night, she had not only helped him retrieve the journal, but she'd saved his life as well. He didn't come across intelligent people every day, but it was a treat when he did, especially when they were on his side.

"What are you writing, love?" he asked.

Clover seemed so engrossed in her writing that she hadn't noticed him. He cleared his throat to catch her attention.

She snapped her head up and said with a start, "Oh, hi, Mr. Landcross."

"Just call me Pierce."

She smiled shyly. "All right, Mr. Pierce."

"Are you writing your autobiography or something?"

"Oh, um, kind of," she said, hugging the book against her chest as if she wanted to hide it. "I'm crafting an adventure story."

"Ah, writing a manuscript, eh? Using our little escapades as inspiration, no doubt?"

She giggled. "You can say that."

He rarely expressed his gratitude, mostly because when he did, people shrugged it off. "You saved my life tonight, little lassie. Cheers."

Even through the low amber light from the lamp, her cheeks burned brightly. "You are most welcome," she said softly.

Seeing her fountain pen, he remembered the idea he'd gotten at Robert's place. "Do you have a spare pen by any chance, love?"

"I most certainly do," she said, reaching into a bag next to her. "A good writer always travels prepared." She found one and handed it to him.

"Cheers. I'll give this back once I'm done with it."

He walked up the stairs, patting her on the head as he went. Now he needed to have a chat with her big brother. Archie stood at the helm, looking out into the blackness. The ship's second mate, Waban, was steering the *Ekta* with one eye focused on the stars. Pierce couldn't imagine sailing a ship in complete darkness.

"Landcross," Archie said as Pierce climbed his way toward him. "Landcross, what sort of name is that, anyway?"

"It's a gypsy name. It means crossing lands."

"Your family were gypsies?"

"Aye," he said, folding his arms over the railing. "My mother, father, grandparents, and my brother, we all traveled with a large troupe comprised of several families. The tribe had been together for so long that my folks had grown up knowing each other."

Growing up, it had been an adventurous childhood, indeed. Not a day went by that he didn't think of the family. They had lived off the land, educated their own children, and loved and cared for one another, with the exception of his uncle, who left the group years ago.

"Huh," Archie said with a shrug. "Explains a lot, I suppose. Where is this ship going exactly? The steersman doesn't seem to speak English or French."

"To England," Pierce answered.

"Not this again," Archie grumbled. "*Where* in England? Southampton?"

"No, Lepe."

"Lepe? I thought we agreed to go back to my father's home to save your friend?"

"Aye, *if* Indigo isn't at his country house, that is."

"Country house?"

"That's where we found him," Pierce explained. "My brother and I, that is. We were hungry and freezing, so we broke into an old man's house. We were discovered, but instead of giving us the boot, he fed us and allowed us to stay with him. Indigo saved our lives."

Archie stared at him, but in the shallow lamplight, it was difficult to read his expression.

Pierce decided that this might be a good time to try and pry out that one vital secret—if it even existed.

"Is there something you need to get in Southampton?" he asked.

"No," Archie answered a little too quickly. He turned back to the dark sea. "I only want to get this entire mess over with."

Pierce nodded, but he was convinced that Archie was hiding something. "Aw, come off it. I told you bits about myself. Tell me, what's the real reason you need to get back, eh?"

"I just told you," Archie said distinctly.

"Fair enough," Pierce said, turning to leave. "Just making conversation. Best get some rest, eh? We have a long day ahead of us tomorrow."

He went into the chief's quarters, lit a couple of candles and lanterns, and sat at a table. There, he brought out Indigo's book and looked through it.

"All right," he said, studying the first page before he set the book down. He brought out the other journal and opened it to its first blank page. Taking the pen in hand, he began copying Indigo's book.

He was no artist, but he managed to roughly duplicate the sketches. Since Tarquin Norwich most likely had never seen the book, he probably couldn't tell the difference.

Inside the journal were dozens of weapons that Indigo had designed. Some were improvements to old weapons, such as a repeating crossbow that was designed to fire off arrows as well as bullets; and rifles with scopes for shooting far distances. Grappling hook guns, armored locomotives, tanks, and submersibles made of metal.

Indigo had even drawn a cyclic multi-barrel gun controlled by a wired remote, powered by a source called a voltaic pile. The shooter could hide in a ditch on the battlefield a hundred feet away and simply press a button on the remote to fire the weapon. Even the voltaic pile that charged the entire thing had extended wires on it, and could be kept away from the enemy's gunfire.

He could only imagine what that bastard, Norwich, wanted to do with such things.

Pierce copied the pictures and jotted down the plans on how to make these machines of mass destruction. When he flipped the page over from the last weapon, he saw something he hadn't seen in years. He picked up the book in disbelief and gaped at the image.

"*Qu'est-ce que c'est?*" Chief Sea Wind asked as he entered the room.

"I forgot about these," Pierce said, showing him the page.

The chief reached the table and took the book to study the images more closely. "What are they?"

"Masks," Pierce said. "Indigo had 'em years ago."

Chief Sea Wind shifted his eyes to the next page where some kind of foreign language was written. "Do you know anything about this writing?"

"*Un peu,*" Pierce admitted, taking the book back. "Indigo told me something about it. Now that I remember, he was trying to translate it."

"Let me fetch Sees Beyond," the chief said.

Pierce grinned widely. "Aye, do, *s'il vous plait.*"

Moments later, the chief returned with a young woman no older then Pierce. It had been four years since he'd last seen her.

Sees Beyond was a psychic of sorts. She helped the crew of the *Ekta* avoid storms and to steer them to the next slave ship and away from any enemy vessels, using the help of spirits. Sees Beyond had received her gift at birth. A gift that only grew stronger with each year of her life. She was also very lovely.

Pierce straightened his coat collar a tad and tried

smoothing out his hair. "'Ello, Sees," he said, grinning.

She looked at him with those brown eyes of hers, making him feel lightheaded. "Hello, Pierce. It's good to see you again."

Sees Beyond was one of the few of the crew who spoke English. She was wise beyond her years and Pierce had enjoyed their insightful conversations during his short travel onboard the *Ekta*.

"What can you tell us about this writing?" the chief asked, breaking their locked gaze.

Sees Beyond studied the page after taking the book from Pierce. Her initial reaction was confusion. She placed her hand over the writing and closed her eyes. "It's written in an old language," she explained, saying nothing that Pierce didn't already know. "It's a language that has not been spoken out loud in thousands of years. The writers—" She paused, her expression tight as if she was in pain. "The writers of this weren't simply mortal men or women. They were powerful beings. Something created, in a way."

"Something created?" Pierce asked. "What does that mean?"

Chief Sea Wind said something in Apache to Sees Beyond. She opened her eyes to him and replied in the same language. Pierce wished he spoke Apache, or at least understood it.

"What?" he demanded. "What are you saying?"

Sees Beyond shifted her eyes to him, and said, "This is a spell."

"A spell?" he said, utterly gobsmacked by that. "What sort of spell?"

"I cannot read what this says, but I can tell you that this spell is made to do something dangerous, and not for anyone to possess, even by those who wrote it."

"How do you know that?"

"My messengers tell me."

People like her seemed to have a connection to spirits or other entities from different worlds who told them things. Pierce's own grandmother had been like that, although he barely remembered her, for she had fallen seriously ill and had gone to live with her son in the Netherlands when Pierce had only been four years old.

"You should destroy the book," Chief Sea Wind suggested.

Pierce took the book from Sees Beyond and studied the illustrations of the masks and the spell on the next page. "I can't. Not now, anyway."

"Just be careful, Pierce," she advised.

She began to leave and Pierce rushed over to stop her. "Hey, you want to sit with me for a while? Catch up? It's been ages, eh?"

A beautiful smile touched the corners of her lips and she placed a hand on the side of his face. A passionate heat ignited within him, so much, in fact, that he wouldn't be surprised if his skin burned her hand. They'd had a brief history that had left a lasting impression on him, and their deep conversations weren't the only delights they'd shared.

"I would love to, Pierce, but I am wedded now."

His passion immediately cooled. "Wedded? To whom?"

"To my soul mate, Mohin."

"Mohin?" he said with a snarl. "Isn't he the one with the lazy eye?"

She laughed and shook her head. "No, you never met him. He lives in our village in Sonora, taking care of my son, Tarak."

Pierce remembered her speaking about the boy. He was her son from her first marriage when she'd only been seventeen. Her first husband, Cochise, was also a Sea Warrior onboard the *Ekta,* who had died along with many of Chief Sea Wind's crew during a hurricane in the Atlantic. After his death, Sees Beyond had joined Chief Sea Wind, using her gift to protect others from sharing the same fate.

He turned sulky. "So, you found your soul mate, eh?"

"Worry not," she said, "I have seen it in one of your paths that you will soon meet yours." With that, she walked away, leaving him bewildered.

He headed back to the table, setting Indigo's journal down beside the other book.

"Did you find out anything about the young man?" Chief Sea Wind asked.

"No. Whatever he's hiding, he won't tell me. I don't think he would even if I tortured him." He took a seat. "Which I'd bloody well do at this point, just out of spite." He snatched up the fountain pen and began sketching the masks.

"Maybe his secrets will come to you without his words."

Pierce snorted. He then thought back on the short discussion he'd had with Clover about her story.

"Hmm," he said, rubbing his chin.

The *Ekta* continued making its way across the Channel. The blindness of the night and the soft winds made for a slow but steady passage. Archie had fallen asleep against a mast near the steam engine, with Clover sound asleep against him, wrapped snugly in a thick quilt. Pierce crept up on them from behind. Sitting on the railing nearby was the engineer, smoking a pipe. The feathers tied on the brim of his hat fluttered in the breeze, as if to follow the smoke he exhaled. Pierce put a finger to his nose in a shushing gesture and crouched next to Clover's bag. He reached inside for her journal. Without disturbing either of them, he slipped the book out and went over to a nearby lamp next to the crewman. There, he opened the book and searched for where the girl's new story began.

"The child has good handwriting," the engineer commented in French.

"*Oui*, that she does," he agreed.

He turned the pages, hoping to find something useful. Then he came across a title that read: *The Adventurous Pierce Landcross,* and there, on the first bloody page, titled Chapter One, The Secret Wedding, he found what he was searching for.

He had to admit, the child had skill with a pen. He found himself reading the story to the point where she'd left off earlier that night. When he was done, he returned both the journal and the pen he had borrowed, and went below deck to find a vacant hammock for a few hours of sleep.

"Landcross," came a voice in the randomness of his mind.

"Lucy?" he said, seeing a woman's face.

"Lucy?" the voice said in a masculine tone. "Who's Lucy? Come on, man, wake up!"

He suddenly snapped awake and sat up. "I had nothing to do with that!" he yelled.

"What?" Archie said.

"What?" Pierce said back.

Archie shook his head and said, "We dropped anchor hours ago."

Pierce recovered from his rude awakening and yawned while stretching his arms overhead.

"All right," he said in mid-yawn.

"Who's Lucy?" Archie asked again.

"Eh?" he said groggily. "Dunno. Why do you ask?" He got out of the hammock and put on his dapper coat, which he'd used as a blanket. He went over to an empty barrel, lifted the lid, and reached inside.

Archie huffed when he brought out the satchel, holding the journal.

"You think I'd keep it on me while I was asleep?" Pierce asked. When he turned to see the youth's annoyed expression, he snorted. "Aye, you hoped as much, eh?"

"We have to go," Archie said peevishly.

Pierce grinned and followed him up to the deck.

The sky was iron grey. The crisp air told Pierce that daybreak couldn't be more than an hour old. The shore had patches of greenery showing through a curtain of thick fog. A finger of light from the lighthouse on shore penetrated the moist haze. Pierce wished that he could be thousands of miles away, on an island of blue sky and white sand.

Chief Sea Wind and Waves of Strength stood near a longboat.

"Chief," Pierce said as he approached them.

While Archie helped his sister into the longboat, Chief Sea Wind whispered, "Did you find something?"

Pierce smirked deviously. "*Oui*. And it's enough to keep him in line if he tries anything."

"Good. I wish you a safe journey, my friend."

They shook hands. "*Merci, capitaine*."

"We are heading back to Le Havre for supplies," Waves of Strength informed. "We'll be there until tomorrow afternoon. If you make it, you can come with us."

Did he hear her correctly? Had she *actually* invited him to sail with them?

"Peace is between us now, Landcross," she said, holding out a tiny bottle to him. "Take this ointment for your wound."

"Uh, *merci*," he said, accepting the vial.

"Good luck, my friend," the chief said. "May we see each other soon."

The crew lowered the longboat into the smoky water. First mate, Wind in the Sails, along with the second mate, Waban, rowed the boat to the sandy shore.

"How did you meet these people?" Archie asked Pierce.

"Pardon?" Pierce said, sitting with his chin resting on his palm, wondering what the hell he was doing.

"The Sea Warriors. When did you meet them?"

"Oh, some time ago, I got arrested for thievery and sentenced to a penal colony. On our way to Norfolk Island, the Sea Warriors attacked the ship, thinking that it was a slave ship. I managed to get free and made my way up to the helm. The crew was about to fire cannons at the Sea Warriors' ship, so I killed the captain and took the wheel, turning the vessel the other way before they had the chance to do too much damage. The chief spotted me doing so. He, in turn, offered for me to take up arms and fight alongside his crew. We managed to take the convict ship and ole Sea Wind allowed me aboard the *Ekta*. They eventually let me off in France when we brought the poor sods we saved from an actual slave ship there."

"What happened to the crew on the ship you were held on?" Archie asked.

Pierce shuddered. The events that had led him to being transported in the first place had been a long line of unfortunate occurrences that had included kidnapping, psychological torture, and dismemberment.

Those were the darkest parts of his past that he'd never disclosed to another living soul. And he had one albino bastard to thank for it.

"We left them to fend for themselves on the ship," he said simply.

"What is the story between you and the chief's wife?" Archie demanded.

"Oh, that? During the skirmish, I accidentally shot her in the arse."

"You shot the captain's wife in the rear?" Clover exclaimed, one hand going to her mouth.

"Aye, but as you can see," he said, pointing to his bandaged wound, "she got her revenge, well and truly."

"At least she didn't take your scalp," Wind in the Sails offered unhelpfully, a sly smile on her face.

"Unbelievable," Archie said. "You have led quite the life. Is there anyone you haven't pissed off?"

"Sure, but it ain't over yet," Pierce said, with a smile. "Knock on wood!"

The boat reached the shore and Pierce bid the Sea Warriors goodbye as they jumped down onto the stony beach.

"Where to now?" Archie asked.

"First to Exbury for food. And we're in need of horses. Perhaps we'll pass some in a field on the way into town. If not, I'll pluck a couple from a stable."

"Pluck? You mean *steal* them?" Archie demanded appalled.

"Aye, what did you think I meant?" he said defensively. "Pick them off a tree?"

"We're not stealing horses. I have money. We'll buy them, understand?"

Pierce placed his hand on his chest, the other behind his back, and bowed deeply to him. "Yes, my liege."

"You're a fool," the lad said, walking to the road.

"Only for you, boyo." Pierce said playfully.

Clover snickered and followed her brother and the thief.

"Wake up, Landcross."

With a snort, Joaquin raised his head. His sleepy eyes needed a few minutes to adjust to the waking world. When they did, they didn't like the face staring back at him.

"Time to go," Tarquin Norwich declared severely, as if announcing that it was time for Joaquin to go to his execution. He placed his hands on the arms of the chair and leaned toward his face. "I warn you, Landcross; you best know *exactly* where Peachtree's home is or the consequences will be dire."

Joaquin's jaw ached just thinking about those consequences. *Where are you, beast?*

The soldiers re-shackled his hands in front of him so he could ride. He was allowed a short time to take a piss beside the stables, and without a scrap of breakfast, he was forced to travel south.

Chapter Twelve
Masks

By mid-morning, Pierce and the Norwich siblings had reached the town of Exbury, where Archie bought everyone food at a tavern. The professional thief in Pierce noted which pocket Archie kept his coin purse in. Afterwards, they were directed by the barkeep to a stable on the outskirts of town. Archie again warned Pierce not to steal anything. Instead, the lad negotiated with the rancher and bought two mounts. The three headed north into a forested area, running alongside the river to Beaulieu.

"Where is this house you're looking for?" Archie asked.

"Not far, on the other side of the river. First we need to make a detour."

"To where?"

"The museum. More specifically, the Beaulieu Art Museum." He reached into his satchel to answer the question he knew was coming.

"For what?" Archie asked.

"To get these."

He brought out the forged book and showed Archie the picture of the masks that he'd drawn himself. Archie reached for the book but Pierce quickly pulled it away. "No touching."

"Why do we need those masks?" Archie asked.

"I believe your father wants them."

"What are you talking about? Does the book tell you where the masks are?"

"No," Pierce said, showing him another page. "But

your father wants weapons as well. Weapons that Indigo designed."

"Mr. Peachtree designed weapons?" Clover asked from her seat in the saddle in front of Archie.

"Aye. Indigo isn't just a maker of toys. He wears many hats. He's a bloody genius, I daresay."

"Like Da Vinci," she said.

"Exactly."

"And what are you proposing that my father is planning to do with the weapons?" Archie asked.

Pierce gave him a sidelong glance. "I see that you lack both imagination and common sense."

Archie looked at him crossly. "You think he plans to start a war?"

"There you have it," Pierce praised sarcastically.

The lad was quiet for a while. "My father isn't after masks, Landcross," Archie finally said irritably.

"Maybe not, but think about it. Why go after Indigo? If all Tarquin needed was for me to tell him where the journal was, why does he need the Toymaker at all, eh?"

Archie shrugged. "He needs someone to build those weapons."

Pierce snorted. "Any bloody engineer can do that."

"Then what?"

Pierce flipped back to the page with the masks. "I think it has something to do with this strange writing," he said, showing Archie the script on the page.

"And the masks are linked?" Clover asked.

Pierce smiled at her. If he was ever to have a daughter, he hoped she'd be just as inquisitive as her.

"Aye, I believe so."

"How do you know?" Archie asked.

Pierce sighed, readying himself for the brief journey

into his past. "When my brother and I stayed with Indigo, I'd seen him from time to time trying to translate these words. When I asked him about it, he told me that it was an ancient language, a dead language. Something he'd found years ago in Egypt. The same antiquities dealer, who convinced him to buy it, also sold him the masks."

"What are they?" Clover asked, completely fascinated by the tale.

"Dunno. But one day, Indigo came to me in a panic and gave me the masks. He told me to get rid of them and not to say what happened to the bloody things. When I asked, he only said that they were dangerous. I reckon he'd translated the language and had found out something about them."

"So you took the masks to the town's museum?" Archie guessed.

"I didn't know what else to do. I sold the entire lot to the museum's curator for a shilling."

"What did you tell Mr. Peachtree?" Clover asked.

"I told him that I'd gotten rid of them and that was the end of it. It wasn't long afterward that Joaquin and I left."

"Why retrieve the masks now?" Archie challenged. "Why not just leave them in the museum?"

"I'm sure your dad will eventually find them there. Indigo was frightened enough to hand 'em off to me. I can only image what they could be used for." Pierce paused a moment, remembering what Sees Beyond had said. "I reckon that they aren't meant for anyone in this world to possess."

They entered the quaint town of Beaulieu and followed a road that led to a stone house with a sign at the front: *The Beaulieu Art Museum*. The house itself had been converted into a museum some time back, after the owner had gone insane with mad hatter disease.

"How do you propose we get the masks?" Archie asked as they hitched the horses to a post. "That is *if* they're on display."

"I have my ways," he said, securing his mount to the post.

"What way is that?"

Pierce stepped around his horse and headed for the museum's entrance. "You are aware of my reputation, eh?"

Archie slapped his hand against Pierce's chest, right against the still painful brand.

"Ow!" Pierce shouted, shoving Archie back. "Keep your bloody hands off me!"

"You're not going to steal anything."

"Don't be telling me what to do, boyo." Pierce seethed, angered by the hot pain in his breast. "You need to take that self-righteous stick outta your arse and learn a thing or two about the real world and the people in it. We weren't all born to wealthy families. Some of us have to do unscrupulous things to survive."

"I know plenty about the real world and I'm quite aware of what people are capable of doing. Don't mistake me as ignorant, Landcross. You choose to steal instead of working for a living. No one put a gun to your head to thieve."

"Well, there was this one time—" Pierce began.

"Go back to your wicked life once we're through with you. Thieve your way into a noose, for all I care; but while you're with us, you're going to keep your sticky fingers inside your pockets, understand?"

The cocker was adamant, Pierce had to give him that. He thought about arguing with the lad, but refrained. It'd be a waste of time. If he was to dispute

Archie any further, he'd point out that this was an art museum, not an art gallery, and therefore would not sell the masks. Besides, after purchasing the horses, he doubted that Archie carried enough money to buy them, even if the curator was willing to risk his job by selling them.

"Fine," Pierce said. "You speak to the curator, then."

They went to the ticket booth where the seller told them the price for admission.

"Well," Pierce said, folding his arms, "pay the man."

Archie rolled his eyes and reached for his purse. The lad had far more loot left then he'd thought.

They entered the art museum. In the first room, they were greeted by a large sculpture of a half-naked woman with the body of a snail shell. Her arm was stretched towards the inside of the building, as if showing visitors where to go. Clover gasped with excitement.

The museum had a variety of artwork: sculptures, glass art, even oddities of stuffed animals dressed in clothing. There were paintings from all over the world mounted on the walls; and hanging from the ceiling were four giant horses made from pieces of cut mirrors.

"It's incredible," Clover exclaimed.

The girl's eyes were so wide that Pierce half expected them to pop out. Clover Norwich was filled with talents that demanded a wide range of exposure. Sadly, judging by her reaction, he imagined that she wasn't ordinarily exposed to much creativity. Her excitement was genuine and refreshing to see, much different from the jaded lot Pierce was used to running with. Her love for every exhibit was instant and he was charmed.

As they ventured farther into the place, Pierce took time to absorb the artwork as well. Inside a conjoined room was a special exhibit. The banner read: *Industrial*

Art. Since the birth of the Industrial Revolution, Europe had entered a new-age of machines like never before.

He peeked in and saw strange paintings depicting hybrids of half-animal and half-mechanical creatures. Many sculptures were put together out of machine parts to represent insects, jewelry, even people wearing the latest fashion in clothing. As he was admiring a couple of human-like sculptures made of scrap locomotive parts with brass plated chests and gears for eyes, Archie urged him on.

They continued their search for the masks. After looking through a room of marine art, Pierce began to doubt that the masks were even on display. That gave him some relief, thinking they were locked in a vault. Perhaps the curator that he'd sold the bloody things to had tossed them out?

Then he stepped into a small room filled with an array of masks, and there at the very back hung the three from the notebook.

"There you are," Pierce announced.

Hanging within a silver frame against a black background were the three masks that Pierce hadn't seen in eighteen years. Two of them were fashioned to look like men's faces, and the third a woman. The masks were pearl white with shiny blue grains interspersed throughout. The mask that hung in the center above the others depicted a strong featured man with a beard. The other male mask had a youthful face, as did the woman. Pierce remembered the way the masks had felt when Indigo had tasked him the mission to stash them away. They had vibrated against his hands as if they'd been humming, almost like a live wire surging with electricity.

"Are those the masks?" Archie asked, coming up and

peering over his shoulder.

"Aye, that's them."

"They look like death masks," Clover put in.

Pierce studied them a tad harder. She was right. He'd never noticed it before, mainly because he'd only been a child who didn't know what death masks were at the time. Now that Clover mentioned it, though, they did look that way. If they were masks from the faces of some departed society, who on earth had they been?

"Right," Archie said. "I'll go find the curator."

"You do that," Pierce said as he walked away. He had other plans, though.

While searching the museum, he'd observed more than just the artwork. Guards stood in each room, watching over everything. One even stood in the corner of this room. To snatch the masks, a simple distraction was in order.

He walked over to a large display of African tribal masks suspended by wires in the center of the room and stood where the guard couldn't see him.

"Clover," he whispered.

She turned from studying an exhibition of Mexican Mayo tribal masks and came over to him.

"Listen. We need to get those masks and we're not going to get 'em with money or kind words," he said.

"We can't steal them," she whispered back.

"No, *we* can't, but I can. I need your help, if you're willing."

It was obvious by her expression that she was apprehensive. "What would I have to do?"

After his instructions, they left the room. Pierce stepped over to a Chinese oil painting of a dragon near the mask room's entrance, seemingly to admire it, while Clover left for the room of human anatomy.

He waited. Then an ear-piercing scream echoed throughout the entire museum. The guard in the mask room hurried off. He clearly understood that it was coming from the human anatomy room and raced that way.

Pierce slipped back into the mask room and quickly took the ones he wanted off the wall, replacing them with other masks. The replacements didn't even come close to resembling the ones he took. He only needed something to fill the empty space to prolong detection of the missing trio.

He shoved the real masks inside his satchel and hurried out of the room. From there, he darted over to the human anatomy exhibit, where Clover was putting on her show.

"They're so horrifying," she hollered, pointing at the skeletons in display cases, the graphic paintings of autopsies, and the sculptures of human organs. "So horrifying!"

The guards, who had no idea what to do, tried consoling her.

"Child," one said, "let's get you out of here. Come along now."

Clover stayed in place, crying until she spotted Pierce. He nodded. She ran to him and cried, "Father!"

Pierce picked her up and held her. For a ten-year-old, she was quite tall, so holding her proved a tad challenging, especially with his freshly branded chest.

"There you are," he said. "I told you not to wander off." He put her down and took her by the hand. "I think you've seen enough for one day."

He quickly led her out of the room and headed for the exit. On the way, they ran into Archie, who was running toward them. "What was that? It sounded like you, Clover."

"She just got a little scared," Pierce said, keeping his steady pace up as he hurried for the exit. "Time to go."

"But what about the—"

"No worries," Pierce said, cutting him off. "Come along."

Outside, they hurried to their horses.

"Pierce Landcross, you thieving cur, I demand that you return those masks at once."

"Nope," Pierce said, letting go of Clover's hand.

Archie jumped in front of him, stopping him short. "I told you that I was going to speak to the curator."

"No, *I* told you to speak to the curator. I needed to get you off my back." Archie opened his mouth to speak but Pierce raised a finger at him. "*And* even if I was inclined to give them back, I'd be arrested on the spot, which is not what I had planned for today. Not to mention her plans, either."

Archie's eyes went to his sister and his face blazed red with rage. "You bastard!" he swung at Pierce, who jumped away. "What the hell is wrong with you?"

"Stop it!" Clover demanded angrily. "What's done is done."

Archie faced her. His fists were clenched but Pierce doubted he'd attack again.

"We need to go," Clover said.

Archie sighed and stepped forward. "I'm *very* disappointed in you."

"Archie?" she said dolefully.

He didn't respond, only went over to the horses.

Clover sniffed and Pierce patted her on the head. "You did good, lass. C'mon, you can ride with me."

Chapter Thirteen
What Needed to be Done

Summer, 1815

The summer heat forced the gypsies to seek cover within the forest. They found a lovely spot where the trees stood far enough apart to offer plenty of space for their wagons, while providing much needed shade from the sun.

Once the travelers settled themselves, Joaquin left to explore the surrounding area. He ran past wide trees with patches of green moss on them, and frightened a few elk grazing in a small meadow of grass and bright chive flowers. The air smelled of sap, rain, and foliage. Rays of sunshine cut through spaces in the thick leaves, dappling the earth with soft light.

In a forest like this, he hoped to see a fairy or an elf, like his grandmother had told him about. Maybe he'd meet an imp. But he didn't find anything so exciting. Instead, he came upon a stream flowing between two short embankments where he unearthed loads of worms. He put them in a jar that he'd brought with him. He did his best to accommodate the worms by including some dirt. When the jar was full, he sat on a moss-covered rock by the water and observed some of his worms through the glass as they burrowed tunnels in the black dirt. Those little squirmy things fascinated him to no end.

"Hello," a girl with hair the color of poppies said. She stood on the far embankment, dressed in a long black tailcoat with the tattered train stretching over the ground as long as a wedding dress. She wore a deep red gown beneath that and torn striped stockings. She was holding a basket in her lace gloved hands.

"Hi," he said curiously. "Are you a fairy?"

She laughed. "No, silly boy, I'm just a girl."

He frowned slightly, scrunching his face in disappointment.

"How old are you?" she asked.

"Five. How old are you?"

"Thirteen. What's your name, little boy?"

"Joaquin, Joaquin Landcross."

She smiled. "Pleased to meet you, Joaquin Landcross. I'm Freya Bates." She spied his jar. "What do you have there?"

"Worms. I collect them."

"Can I see?"

She climbed down the grassy embankment and stepped through the small stream. It was narrow enough that she could have leapt over it, but she didn't seem to mind getting her feet or the incredibly long tail of her coat wet as it dragged through the water. She smelled of chamomile. He soon realized that the scent was coming from the white flowers in her basket. She set that down on the mossy stone and reached for the jar. "May I?"

He usually didn't like anyone messing with his worms. The other children, and even some of the adults, mocked his hobby, calling him names, like Wormy, but Freya seemed genuinely interested. He handed the jar over. As she looked, he noticed that her fingernails were as dirty as his, as though she'd also been doing some digging.

"These are good worms," she praised. "Fat and healthy. You ought to take good care of them."

"Thanks," he said.

As she handed the jar back, he looked in her eyes. "You have purple eyes?"

"Oh," she said, touching her face right below one eye. "Yes. It's rare to be born with eyes of violet, but it does happen."

"I should say it's rare. I've never seen anyone with purple eyes before."

"My mother used to call them my twilight eyes."

"I like that. Where is your mother? Do you live close by?"

"Yes, in a cottage in the forest. But my mother died last winter."

"What about your father?"

"I never knew him."

"Oh," he said mournfully. He couldn't imagine being without his own parents.

"You should come visit me," she said.

"I'm not supposed to go too far from the familia."

"Your family?"

"Yes. We made camp at the edge of the forest."

"Bring your family then," she offered, picking up her basket. "I would love to meet them. My cottage isn't far, just head east from this stream and you'll come across it."

"Which way is east?"

"Here, take this," she said, reaching into her pocket. She produced a compass and set it in his hand. "It was my father's. I carry it with me to keep from getting lost in the forest when I go out walking. Use it to guide you and your family to me."

Joaquin was intrigued. Holding the compass made him more adult, more important. Like he was an explorer.

When she was gone, he ran back to camp and told

his parents about the girl and her invitation.

"You shouldn't talk to people you don't know," his mother chided.

"She's just a child, like me," he explained. "She lives in a cottage in the woods. Her name is Freya and she wants you to meet her."

"Son," his father said, "I'm not sure that her folks would be all right with us just showing up at their doorstep, all unannounced."

"No, it's okay. Freya doesn't have any parents. She told me her mother died last winter and that she never knew her father."

His mother looked over at her husband with concern. "Perhaps we should go, Jasper. I mean, if she's all alone?"

"Aye," Jasper agreed. "You show us where she lives then boy."

Joaquin led them to the stream where he'd met Freya, and from there, he followed the compass east. They traveled no more than half a mile before they came upon a grave marker.

"Oh, my," his mother said, staring down at the stone with the name Rosie Bates engraved on it. The ground where the body lay beneath was clear of leaves and outlined by smaller stones.

"That must be Freya's mum," Joaquin said. He looked up at his own mother with great affection.

They pressed on, and not much farther, a cottage appeared. It looked like it was part of the forest itself. The wood from the outer walls had moss growing on it all the way up to the roof. Fungi sprouted from the cracks between the boards and vines twisted their way up and over the roof.

"Are you certain that someone lives here?" Nona asked her son.

Even Joaquin seemed unsure.

Freya appeared around the corner of the house. She no longer wore her incredibly long tailcoat.

"Freya!" Joaquin called out.

She spotted them and waved them to come over.

"C'mon," Joaquin said, darting off in Freya's direction. He met her near the corner of the house.

"Hello, again, Joaquin," Freya said. "I'd hug you but my hands are absolutely filthy." She showed him her dirty hands. "I've been tending to my garden."

He peeked around the house. A small garden grew within the limited space where sunlight shone through the trees. However, she had managed to grow a lot in the small spot. She had tomato plants, green beans, cucumbers, some heads of cabbage, and potatoes.

"You must be Freya," Joaquin's mum said when she and Jasper reached them. "Joaquin told us about you. I'm his mother, Nona Landcross."

"And I'm Jasper, Joaquin's father."

"Hello, and welcome to my home," Freya said. "Would you like to come inside?"

They followed her to the front porch where part of the rotten wood gave way and Jasper's foot shot through the boards.

"Are you all right?" his wife asked, holding his arm as he pulled his leg free.

Jasper set his foot slowly back on the floor. "Aye, fine. Don't think I even got a scratch." He sounded greatly relieved for that. A cut had the potential to cause a nasty infection.

"Oh, Mr. Landcross," Freya said from the front door, "I'm so sorry. This cottage has fallen under the strain of neglect for quite some time now."

"Aye, I can see that."

Nona slapped him on the arm. "Jasper," she snapped in a whisper.

As Freya went inside, he said softly, "What? My bloody foot went right through the rotten mess."

"Don't be rude."

They entered the house, where bowls of chamomile flowers perfumed the air, masking the moldy, musty smell. Dead flowers were everywhere. It appeared they had been collected for many years. The place was neat enough, simply because there weren't many items in the house. An old rug lay in the center of the room, with broken twigs from the broom scattered about. The mangy old broom was propped up in the corner. There were melted candles and a pair of broken china cups on the fireplace mantel. The furniture appeared makeshift, just branches tied or nailed together. A grandfather clock without a pendulum stood against the wall next to a solid black chest. Mounted on the wall were the stuffed heads of a red deer and a grey fox. The flooring inside seemed sound enough, although Jasper stepped lightly anyway.

"I'm so glad you came by," Freya said, entering the kitchen, which was nothing more than a little iron stove in the corner, near a small round table. "I never receive visitors."

A chipped basin sat on a rickety old cutting table, where Freya washed her hands. "It gets awfully lonely sometimes," she added softly.

"Joaquin tells us that you live here alone," Nona said, approaching the table.

Freya bowed her head. "It's true, Mrs. Landcross. Ever since February, when Mother was mauled to death by a pack of wild dogs that roam these woods. There wasn't much of her left, but I wasn't able to carry her back, so I buried her in the spot where she was attacked."

"Bloody hell," Jasper gasped.

"Oh, darling," Nona said woefully. "Dear, I'm so sorry."

Freya dried her hands on an old rag as she turned around. "Your son was the first person I've spoken to since her death."

Joaquin smiled at her.

"Don't you have any other family?" Jasper asked. "Someone you can stay with?"

She shook her head. "If I do, I don't know who they are or where they could be. Mother never spoke about any family. I suspect that she and Father weren't married, or even in any kind of relationship, I daresay."

"I see," Nona said, going back to her husband. Again, she whispered in his ear, "We need to talk."

As his parents chatted among themselves in the Romani tongue, Joaquin went over to Freya. "Have you lived here your whole life?"

She hung the rag back on the rusted oven handle. "Mother was a hermit until I came along. She lived here since she discovered the cottage abandoned years ago. She never did fancy being with other people."

"Oh. What about you?"

She gently gripped his chin. Her touch was cool from the water she'd washed her hands in. "I think I would like to be around other people. It would be rather nice to see what else is out there in the world."

"Freya," his mum said.

"Yes, Mrs. Landcross?" she said, letting Joaquin go.

His parents approached and stopped at the table. "Jasper and I discussed it, and we want to ask you to live with us."

Freya looked stunned. "Really? You would take *me*

in?"

"And accept you as one of our own," his dad said. "I noticed your garden out there. We could use a competent gardener."

"That's a great idea," Joaquin said with exuberance. "Freya, you ought to come live with us."

"Now, son," his dad said, "it's up to the young lady to decide."

Joaquin turned to her with pleading eyes. In Freya, he'd found a friend, someone he could connect to, and possibly to hunt worms with. He also found her interesting and wanted to learn more about her.

"I . . ." she began to say, "I would love to live with you. All of you."

Freya packed what little she owned, mainly plant pots and gardening tools. Everyone helped to harvest the edible plants from the garden and carried them back to the gypsy camp, where Freya met Grandmother Fey.

"Welcome, child," Grandmother Fey said, seeming to understand everything at once.

That night, they made rabbit stew, using potatoes and cabbage from Freya's garden. It was enough to feed the entire troupe. Joaquin was thrilled to have found a genuine friend.

The next two years flew by. Joaquin and Freya were practically inseparable. They played together, studied reading and writing, and tended to the garden in the bed of an old horse cart, which they were able to haul around with them.

When the gypsies went into towns and villages, Joaquin and Freya sold trinkets to the locals. Sometimes, Freya would tell fortunes like Grandmother Fey had in her youth. She really seemed to have a knack for it.

At this time, Joaquin's mother was with child. Grandmother Fey estimated she would give birth in June.

The gypsies left Blandford, and made their way to Andover. Days before reaching Salisbury, they made camp in a wide open field. During the night, Joaquin was awakened from his slumber near the burnt remains of a fire. Only a few glowing embers remained.

"Joaquin," someone said, "wake up."

Startled, he quickly sat up.

"Shush," Freya said. "Come quickly. Hurry, before they vanish."

"Before *who* vanishes?" he asked, rubbing his eyes.

"Come with me and find out."

Curious, he followed the firelight dancing on the head of a candle in her hand. They went out of camp and into a dark field.

"Where are we going?" he asked.

"Quiet, you'll scare them away."

He held his questions until he saw whatever she wanted to surprise him with. At least until they came to a dry stone wall, where Freya crouched.

"Get down," she whispered urgently.

He did and she blew out the candle. The smell of burning wax filled his nostrils.

"Look over the wall," she commanded.

He peered over but saw nothing but darkness. "What am I looking for?"

"Just wait."

Several minutes ticked by before she said, "There. Look! See it?"

At first, he didn't see anything until a light flickered. It flashed again, then appeared and stayed.

What is that? Joaquin wondered.

More little dots of light flickered, the color of limes and the size of apples. They zipped through the night and twirled around. Joaquin could have sworn he heard signing.

"They're fairies," Freya explained.

His mouth dropped. For years, he'd wanted to see such creatures and now here they were, spinning and dancing with each other. Many more appeared, setting the wide field aglow as far as his eye could see.

"They're beautiful," he said in awe.

"Oh, look," Freya said, "this one is pretty close." To the fairy, she said, "Come here. Come, come, my sweet."

A glow jumped around in midair before it gradually drew close.

"That's it. Come to me."

The glow got a little closer, then suddenly leapt back.

"Ah, ah," she demanded softy. "Come here."

The glow continued its approach.

"Unbelievable," Joaquin whispered. "It's as if you're controlling it."

She said nothing, only kept coaxing it along. As the glow got closer, a little figure began to emerge. It was a male fairy. He had a thin body with hair that floated around him as if he was underwater. He also looked petrified.

"Is he all right?" Joaquin asked just before Freya snatched the little creature out of the air.

"Got you!"

Her loud voice caused the other dots of light to flutter back. Hundreds moved like an ocean wave. They backed off and twinkled brightly.

"Freya, what are you doing?" Joaquin asked in

alarm.

Her fist closed around the fairy, his light shining between her fingers. "I wanted you to see one up close," she explained, its green light glimmering in her eyes. "You always wanted to see one, yes?"

"Not like this. Let him go."

She scrunched up her face at him. "Fine."

She opened her hand, and he expected the fairy to zip right out and rejoin the others. Instead, the little creature stayed in her palm, barely moving.

Joaquin leaned in to examine it closer and he discovered that the fairy's wings were bent like crumpled paper. "He's hurt," he said in dismay. "You broke his wings."

"I did?" she said, looking down for herself.

He sighed and shook his head. "S'pose we can put him into one of my jars and wait for him to heal. Then we can set him free."

"A fairy isn't like one of your worms, Joaquin," she said bitterly. "They're more like butterflies or moths. Once their wings are damaged, they'll never be able to fly again."

"What do you suggest we do then?"

Freya smashed her fist down on the fairy, grounding it around in her hand. Most of the squished creature had splattered on it. Some had hit Joaquin too, covering his chest with glowing ichor. Green slime dripped from Freya's chin.

"What have you done?" he shouted in horror.

"What needed to be done. It could no longer fly. To a fairy, it's the same as if we had lost the use of our arms or legs. Trust me, it was for the best."

He looked toward the field. He no longer heard singing—only crying. Their sobs rang in his ears all the way back to camp.

"Goodnight, Joaquin," Freya said, leaving for her tent.

He was stunned by her abrupt departure. When the glow of the dead fairy vanished, he returned to the blanket on the ground where he slept. He wiped cold moisture off his cheek and stared at the fading glow on his hand. He wrapped himself up and cried himself to sleep.

On the road, Joaquin could hardly look at Freya. He told no one about what had happened. In fact, he spoke little to anyone. A day before reaching Salisbury, he found a place under a tree to sit alone and stare at nothing.

A hand full of dirty, squirmy worms suddenly appeared in front of his face.

"Look at what I have," Freya said, holding the worms in her gloved hand.

"Go away," he ordered.

"What's wrong?" she asked, sitting down next to him. "You haven't spoken to me in days."

"You know why. Don't play daft."

"And I told you why I had to kill it. I did it a favor."

"He was a boy," he snapped. "And you didn't even give him a chance."

"You're right," she agreed unexpectedly. "I didn't. But he wouldn't have lived much longer. Sometimes we have to kill to show mercy."

"He didn't have to die."

"I know. I shouldn't have snatched him like that. I just wanted you to see him. I'm sorry."

Her apology surprised him. He craned his neck around and actually looked at her for the first time in a long while. Her lovely face that he'd adored since the moment he'd seen her was very somber and remorseful.

"I don't want to lose your friendship," she admitted.

She made it hard for him to stay mad at her. "Just promise me that you won't do anything like that again."

Her lively lips curled at the corners. "I promise."

They went back to camp as if nothing had happened. As the day ended, Joaquin and Freya sat on a short hill that overlooked the camp.

"Are you excited about becoming a big brother?" she asked him.

He shrugged. "I s'pose."

"Well, I'm absolutely thrilled. I bet he'll be the best little brother ever."

"How do you know it's a boy?"

"It's the way your mother carries the baby. Her belly is quite low. Haven't you noticed?"

"Em, no," he laughed. "So, if her belly was high up, it'd be a girl?"

"Indeed it would. Your mother should be going into labor soon. I can't wait to meet him."

"You *are* excited about it, eh?" Joaquin noted. It was as though she had been waiting for the baby for many years.

She gave him a sidelong glance. "Maybe I am. Joaquin, do you trust me?"

"Trust you?" he asked quizzically. "What do you mean?"

She brought out a knife she had inside her pocketbook. "Can I have some of your blood?"

"My blood? Why?"

"I want to make sure that no matter where I am, I will always have part of you with me."

"No matter where you are?" he said worryingly. "What are you talking about? Are you leaving?"

"Of course not. The future, however, is a mystery. In time, who knows what will happen?"

"I thought you told fortunes."

"I tell people what *could* happen in their lives," she explained. "A person's life can take many routes. There is no certain destiny save for the time of their death."

"You mean it doesn't matter what course you take in life, you will die at a certain time?"

"Yes. There are many different ways that a person can die, but never on a different day or time, since our deaths are predetermined." she stated matter-of-factly.

He didn't quite believe that. "And you don't tell real fortunes?"

"I do, they're just events that might happen, as I said. When I tell fortunes, I only tell what I see from one possible path in someone's life."

"Tell my fortune," he said. "Tell me the paths you see."

"I can't tell you all of them."

"You want my blood?" he said, holding out his hands, palms up. "Then tell me."

Seeing that there was no changing his mind, she sighed. "Fine, I'll tell you a couple." She enfolded one of his hands in both of hers. "I really don't need to look at your palm. We only do that for show."

"Oh."

She held his hand anyway and looked him straight in his bright green eyes. "I see exploits in your life. Both for you and your brother, Pierce. You will have many adventures together."

"With Pierce?"

She nodded, still keeping eye contact.

"Are we with the family?"

She slowly shook her head. "You get separated from them."

He looked at her with dread. "What about other paths? What do you see?"

Freya leaned forward, searching deeper into his eyes. "You stay with the familia, living the Romani life."

"I like that one much better."

With a pat on his hand, she said, "Then I hope it comes true. Now," She picked the knife up, "may I?"

He looked down at his palm, where his hand still rested in hers.

"Go ahead," he said warily.

The cut across his palm was swift and it stung. When blood seeped, she brought out a vial and collected some inside it. "Thank you. Now I shall always have you with me."

She brought out some of her healing herbs, as well as cloths to clean the wound, binding it expertly.

The Romani troupe reached Salisbury by mid-afternoon and arrived at Stonehenge. Nona went for a short walk when she suddenly went into labor.

Joaquin, who wasn't too far away, was the first one at her side. Her labor came on so fast that she couldn't be moved. Grandmother Fey had barely enough time to gather everything needed for the birth before Nona was ready to push. With Joaquin and Jasper by her side, and Grandmother Fey ready for the delivery, Nona pushed her new child out into the world.

"It's a boy!" Grandmother Fey said excitedly, holding the babe up to show everyone.

Freya had been right!

When the newborn was cleaned up and wrapped in

a blanket, he was handed over to his mother. Jasper was seated behind Nona with his legs spread out on either side of her, offering himself as a backrest. He looked at his new son from over his wife's shoulder.

"He's perfect," his mum said joyfully.

"What should we name him?" his father asked.

"How about Pierce?" Joaquin suggested.

They looked at him with approval on their faces.

"Pierce," his mum said. "That's a wonderful name. *Merci*, Joaquin."

That night, the familia built a bonfire and held a celebration for the new child, Pierce Landcross. Joaquin was standing by the fire, listening to his father play his violin, when he spotted Freya walking with her bag. He hurried after her as she headed for the road.

"Where are you going?" he asked.

"Your grandmother told me to leave."

"Leave? Why?"

"I was only holding your brother," she said heatedly. "That's all."

He didn't understand, but before he could ask, she said, "I have to go. You and I shall meet again someday. Farewell, Joaquin."

He stood and watched as she vanished into the darkness.

"Don't go," he said somberly, but she did not turn back.

He went to the tent where Grandmother Fey stood over his baby brother, who was resting peacefully inside a bassinette. She was holding her hands over him, whispering something with her eyes closed.

"You told Freya to leave?" Joaquin said hotly. "Why did you do that?"

She turned to him, her face grave with concern.

"Freya is a clever one. I never even suspected."

"What do you mean?" he demanded, his eyes full of tears. "Suspected what?"

"You're too young to understand, Joaquin. The best way to explain it is that some people are not what they appear."

"I . . . I don't follow."

"You will someday," she said calmly. "Please, leave me now. I must finish placing protections over your brother, for his life is in danger."

Chapter Fourteen
The Bomb

Pierce, Archie, and Clover rode out of Beaulieu, and from there crossed a bridge traveling down to New Forest. The fog had long since dissipated and the sun had risen to the center of the sky by the time they reached a cottage tucked away under many tall trees. Some were in bloom, displaying pink and white blossoms. The secluded cottage seemed to sit a world away. A stream that broke away from the Beaulieu River drifted gently in the backyard.

The house had Celtic symbols carved into every board. Stones plucked from the riverbed had been used to build the chimney. The entire house had been built by Indigo Peachtree, who'd used materials from the surrounding land.

"It's so charming," Clover cooed.

"Aye," Pierce agreed.

"You lived here?" Archie asked. "Why didn't you stay?"

Pierce's blissful expression stiffened to anger. "My brother wanted us to leave. Said we needed to keep looking for our family. All we achieved was to become common criminals."

How things could have been different. He often wondered what his life would have been like if he hadn't allowed the influence of his older brother to take him away from Indigo. He never doubted that the Toymaker would have adopted him as his own son, for he'd stated as much when he'd asked the boys to stay. Pierce could have learned the art of toy-making, perhaps even gone to school and opened his world up to other possibilities then stealing. Instead, he and Joaquin had slunk out of the house during the night and vanished.

"If Peachtree is here, will you give me the book?" Archie asked hopefully.

Pierce nodded.

When they dismounted, he and Archie led the horses to the stream to drink. Clover stayed behind with the animals while they went to the back door. Pierce knocked, but no one answered. He tried looking through the small window set in the kitchen door, but the outside light shining through the house revealed little.

"See anything?" Archie asked.

"No," he said, trying the door latch. To his surprise, it opened. "Well, look at that, eh?"

Archie seemed apprehensive.

"We're not robbin' the man," Pierce told him.

Archie said nothing, only followed him in.

"Indigo!" Pierce called. "Oi, Indigo, are you home, boyo? It's me, Pierce."

They passed through the kitchen into a short hall leading to the front door. Pierce stopped. "Indigo!"

No answer.

"You think he stepped out for a moment?" Archie asked.

"Dunno."

They went upstairs to the master bedroom. Shelves from the dresser gaped wide, and clothing and other items were strewn all over the place.

"Left in a hurry," Pierce remarked, turning to Archie. "Your father must have scared the bloody hell out of him."

Archie sighed petulantly. "Do you have any idea

where he went?"

Pierce scanned the room. "Not off the top of my head, lad."

When they exited the room, Archie spotted a ladder. "What's up there?"

"The attic. Indigo keeps most of his faulty creations up there."

Archie expressed interest and went upstairs alone. Pierce left the house through the back and followed a narrow trail, barely visible between the trees and thick foliage. The path was traced out by stones, some sinking into the soft earth. A modestly sized shed lay about twenty paces into the forest and the unlocked door opened with a loud creak. A strong earthy smell wafted out. The dust in the air made his eyes twitch and tickled his nose. He suppressed the urge to sneeze.

He stepped further into the workshop, where Indigo created his wonderful mechanical toys. As a lost boy of nine, Pierce had been utterly fascinated by how the man was able to construct elegant playthings with moveable parts.

The light was minimal but he saw everything: the work desk covered with mechanical parts, gears, paints, and tools; toy designs tacked on a wall; cottage-shaped lanterns hanging overhead, and pools of dried melted wax with the nub of a candle sticking out on the desk. Indigo would work into the late hours most nights.

Memories of watching the Toymaker came back to him. Pierce had even assisted him at times and had cooked him meals when the man had simply forgotten to eat. This little shed was Indigo's favorite place in the entire world. His flat in London was merely where he stayed when he'd reveal a new toy to companies in the city. Not many people other than Pierce and Joaquin knew where he really lived, and that was how Indigo liked it.

The one-room shed had a bookshelf, housing many things that Indigo had made. Pierce made his way around barrels and crates to get to it. He picked a round object up from a shelf and examined it. It was the size of a turnip with a metal safety pin in it. He knew what it was and chuckled.

Indigo indeed possessed many talents. Engineering and improving the performance of weaponry was one of them. He was a modern day Da Vinci, just like Clover had said. Although he was a peaceful man who enjoyed making children happy—rich or poor—with his high-tech toys, the urge to build modern weapons had tugged at him.

He set the object down beside another invention. It was slightly smaller than a typewriter, with a copper cone resting on black iron legs, set on top of a wooden platform. Behind it was a cylinder, also set on short iron stilts, with a single turning crank on its end. Over the cylinder was a shiny black tube. It was what Indigo had called a *phonautograph*.

A couple of years before Pierce and Joaquin had arrived at his cottage, Indigo had spent time in France. There, he'd met a young inventor, Édouard-Léon Scott de Martinville, who had an idea to record sounds. Together, they'd built prototypes until Indigo decided to go back to England, leaving Édouard-Léon to continue working alone. The Toymaker had brought one of the prototypes to tinker with on his own. Later, when the boys turned up, he showed them how it worked.

Pierce put his ear to the larger end of the cone and slowly turned the crank. This was what was done to listen to the phonautograph. To record something, one only needed to speak into the cone and the vocal vibrations caused a stylus, which was connected to the small end of the cone, to etch wavy lines into the lampblack paper wrapped around the black tube.

When Pierce turned the crank, the sound that met his ear was low and scratchy. He remembered that he needed to turn the crank at a certain velocity to hear the recording clearly.

It took a little time, but he eventually got the hang of it. What he heard was the voice of the Toymaker; a voice he hadn't heard in many years.

The recording was brief, just notes on things that had happened throughout the day, a few reminders of what needed to be done. The voice sounded far off, crackly, and hollow, as if Pierce was listening to Indigo inside a tomb.

On the same shelf was an old box with a dozen or so black tubes, each labeled with a date. One caught his eye. *March 8, 1826.*

That was the spring when he and Joaquin had lived with Indigo.

Pierce brought it out and carefully replaced the delicate cylinder. Once he set it in place, he put his ear to the cone and turned the crank.

"Joaquin has been doing repairs on the house and even on my workshop," Indigo's voice said from within the cone. *"The boy has a stone exterior but a heart of gold. He is a good lad, yet has trust issues, so he has kept a certain distance. He watches over his younger brother. He cares for the boy and loves him. I daresay, the lad would kill to keep him safe."*

Pierce snorted at that.

"Young Pierce, however, is not only good-natured and appreciative, but a smart and inquisitive lad. He's truly the son I always dreamt of having.'

A string in Pierce's heart tugged at him.

"The boys and I are going on a little trip. Throughout the winter, they have been very helpful around this old place. They deserve some adventure. It will be a real treat for them to explore the cave."

The cave!

It dawned on him right then. Indigo lived a secluded life. His friends were the creations manifested inside his own head. He had no family that Pierce knew about. What other sanctuary would Indigo go to for safety?

Clover stood beside the small stream out back, throwing stones into it. She breathed in deeply, taking in the scents of trees and grass. If only this were her home. This quiet, tucked-away place was ideal for a creative mind such as hers. Here, she could sink happily into her own imagination and lose herself for hours. And at the end of the day, she could write down her stories. It was far better than where she lived at the present. Although her father's house was large, with acres of property, she had only a few minutes in the day where she could escape the pressures of being the daughter of a noble lord. She was no more than a speck of floating dust to her father. He barely gave her the time of day, yet because of his status, she was constantly required to act accordingly, especially during her father's boring gatherings.

She wished her mother were still alive. Clover was so thankful for Archie. He was her rock—her only true connection to any idea of what it was like to be part of a happy family. He protected her from everything he could, even knowing about what had happened between their parents that had caused her mother to take her own life.

With so many raw emotions sweeping over her, as well as being in this quintessential landscape, the urge to write suddenly came over her. She went to Archie's grazing horse to retrieve her journal from the saddlebag but stopped when she saw horsemen riding up the lane. She squinted a bit to sharpen her sight and didn't like the faces that came into view.

Before anyone spotted her, she dashed over to the hidden path where Mr. Pierce had gone and followed it to a shed. She burst through the door, only to meet the barrel of a gun head on. Her already pounding heart jumped into her throat.

Mr. Pierce quickly redirected his gun away from her with an annoyed sigh. "Bloody hell, child," he scorned, "don't do that!"

Clover gulped hard and said between hasty breaths, "My father and brother are here."

Never had she witnessed the color drain from someone's face so fast. Mr. Pierce peered through the window beside him, which overlooked the main house. She looked out the window on the other side of the door. Through the rich spring foliage, she saw soldiers heading for the house. The rest ran toward the backyard. Mr. Pierce needed only to get a glimpse of them before he began searching for a place to hide.

"Quick," he whispered to her, "over here."

She hurried over to him and went behind a series of barrels and crates. Mr. Pierce pulled one of the barrels in front of them, enclosing their hiding spot. He grabbed a round device from a bookshelf and handed it to her.

"If things go to pot, pull this pin here and throw it to the floor as hard as you can."

Before she could ask him what it was, he said, "Can I trust you?"

Her heart melted as she looked into his green eyes. Damn, if only she was a young woman!

"Yes," she said softly.

His smile nearly made her knees buckle.

"Good, lass," he said, just before footsteps sounded nearby.

Mr. Pierce crouched down, and she did the same. As the door creaked open, Mr. Pierce raised his pistol to face level. Through a slender space between the crates, she saw her father and brother entering the shed. Two soldiers followed, pushing a man she had never seen before.

The stranger was tall and handsome, wearing an old brown coat. His hands were shackled before him. His long dark hair reached well past his shoulders. When he stepped, his heavy black boots shook the ground. He had a long nose, high cheekbones, and eyes as green as Mr. Pierce's.

Clover caught sight of Mr. Pierce's gun shaking. His face was a mixture of bewilderment, rage, and fear. At first, she thought that it must be because of her father, yet Mr. Pierce's eyes weren't on him, but rather on the stranger in shackles. If they weren't so close to her father's men, she would ask him who the stranger was. She held her tongue, crouching lower when her father spoke.

"It doesn't seem that Peachtree is here, Landcross," her father said, looking around the one-room workshop.

Landcross? Clover wondered. Is he a relation to Mr. Pierce?

"Maybe he's in the house," the stranger said. "Or he isn't home at all. I never said he'd be here."

Her father stood by a work desk with his back to everyone, seemingly admiring the unfinished toys. He picked up a wooden mallet. "If he isn't here, where else could he be?"

Mr. Pierce shook his head. Did he know where the Toymaker had gone?

"I dunno," the shackled man said. "I only stayed with him for a handful of months. I know very little about him, all right?"

Clover's stomach twisted at the brusque tone the man used. Judging by the shackles, she surmised that he wasn't there willingly, which meant he was in no position to be cheeky.

Her father swung around with the mallet raised and brought it down on the prisoner's head. The stranger acted quickly, guarding his head with his arms, but the mallet hit his elbow and he cried out. He doubled over, cradling his wounded arm. The mallet then crashed down on his back, sending the poor man to the floor. Ivor laughed maliciously and even kicked the wretch in the stomach. The soldiers with them stood like statues, unwilling to do anything while her father loomed over the stranger, holding the mallet high, ready to strike again.

"If you cannot tell me anything, then I have no further use for you!"

Mr. Pierce took a deep breath and rose. "Drop the hammer, chum," he shouted, pointing the gun at her father.

Everyone froze, surprised by the order. Mr. Pierce turned the gun on the soldiers and Ivor. "Go for your guns, you bloody bastards, and I'll put bullets in ya."

The shackled man on the floor looked up. He appeared more surprised than anyone else in the room.

"Pierce?" he said weakly.

Tarquin Norwich lowered the mallet and said, "Ah, Pierce Landcross, is it? I expected you to be in Southampton under lock and key."

"Change of plans," Mr. Pierce said through his teeth.

"Now, cut my brother loose, eh?"

The prisoner began to get up, but her father held him down with his boot.

"I think not. He's disappointed me and will therefore die. You, however, know where a certain book is. Once I get my hands on you, I will introduce you to pain that you never knew existed, unless you tell me where it is."

Clover knew that Mr. Pierce was in way over his head. Even with a revolver, he couldn't shoot all four men before someone shot him. She already envisioned Ivor using the soldier next to him as a shield to hide behind in order to shoot at Mr. Pierce. Her brother was a drunk, but he was a precise marksman. Even if her father was shot dead, Mr. Pierce would most certainly follow suit.

She pulled the pin on the small device.

"I don't think so," Mr. Pierce said. "Get your bloody boot off my . . ."

Clover sprang up, throwing the device at Ivor's feet. She caught a glimpse of her father staring wide eyed, before a heavy, noxious smoke suddenly filled the room.

It was the worst thing she had ever smelled! An overpowering rotten egg stench that made her gag and her eyes water. Hot stinging tears even tasted like the smell. Yellow smoke engulfed the entire room, blinding everyone. She groped around, trying to find her way out when someone grabbed her arm. Men shouted, coughed, and shouted some more. Sparks from gunfire lit up the room like fireworks in the thick, sickening fog. A cry of agony howled out. Clover's heart pounded. Both tears of irritation and fear streamed from stinging eyes. She didn't even know who had her by the arm.

The front door swung open and she was pushed out. The fresh air helped soothe the rawness in her throat and burning in her lungs. She wiped the tears from her eyes in time to see blurry shapes slamming the door closed.

"Have you gone round the bend, girl?" Mr. Pierce shouted, then coughed.

"You said to do it!" she argued, stumbling around a bit. "My father would have killed you if I hadn't."

"Father?" Mr. Pierce's brother said softly.

Mr. Pierce grabbed a shovel that was propped up against the wall of the shed and wedged it under the doorknob, planting the end of it deep into the earth.

"Go! Go!" he ordered, taking her by the hand and dashing off into the forest.

"Always an adventure with you ain't it, little brother?"

"Shut it, Joaquin," Mr. Pierce snapped with indignation.

They reached the stream and splashed water on their faces. Joaquin had keys in his hand and he chuckled in spite of the tears in his puffy red eyes.

"Fuckin' hell, I think I'm gonna be *sick*," Mr. Pierce moaned, spitting water out of his mouth. He turned to Clover. "Go to your brother."

"What about you?"

Joaquin Landcross unshackled himself, then tossed the manacles away. He got up and ran back in the direction of the house.

"I have to go, lass," Mr. Pierce said, ignoring his departing brother.

A twinge of pain struck her in the chest. He was telling her goodbye. Before her emotions got the better of her, she shrugged them off, bringing herself back to reality.

"Good luck, Mr. Pierce."

Mr. Pierce's eyes were bloodshot, yet the green still glowed through. He gave her his signature smile.

"You, too, love."

She darted off toward the house. On the way, she spotted the other soldiers who'd been inside the house were now heading toward the path. Passing by the shed, she could see Ivor through the trees and brush, clambering out of a small window. Yellow smoke poured from the opening. Apparently, Mr. Pierce's shovel trick had worked well.

Archie rushed out of the back of the house and spotted her. "Clover! Thank God you're all right."

He took her by the shoulders and examined her critically. He must have thought the worst when he'd heard the gunshots. His concern, however, soon turned to confusion and disgust. "Why in God's name do you smell so bad?"

"Father is here!" she exclaimed. "Mr. Pierce and I were in the shed when Father and Ivor came in. Mr. Pierce was in trouble, so I threw a stink bomb."

As she explained, her brother's focus shifted to something behind her. She twisted around to see Mr. Pierce heading for his horse.

"Go to the house," Archie ordered.

He didn't wait for a response, striding off towards the horses. Clover thought about staying put to see what would happen, but she wanted to find something to wash off the stink. Perhaps if she was lucky, she could find some clean clothes to change into.

She entered the house, searching for a washroom, when someone grabbed her and lifted her off the ground.

"You're coming with me," Joaquin Landcross said, carrying her to the front door.

She began struggling, kicking and jabbing her

elbows back. At ten years old, she was tall for her age, so her feet nearly touched the ground. But Landcross was even taller than Mr. Pierce, and strong to boot. Carrying her didn't seem to be much of a task for him.

"Stop your struggling or I'll shoot you dead," he said grimly.

He had a gun?

It was very possible that he did. After all, he'd managed to get keys to free himself during the struggle in the shed, so perhaps he'd taken a gun, too.

She offered no more resistance as he carried her outside to the horses. Clover wondered if she would survive the day.

Chapter Fifteen
To the Isle of Wight

After Archie instructed Clover to go into the house, he intercepted Pierce Landcross just as the man was just about to mount on his horse.

"Where do you think you're going?" he demanded.

Landcross turned sharply around to him. His eyes were red and he had the same rancid smell about him as Clover. Landcross stomped over to Archie.

By the time Archie noticed his dark expression, it was too late. Landcross swung a fist and struck him in the face, the impact rattling Archie's brain. He stumbled back, but kept on his feet.

"You never fuckin' told me that my brother was involved in this!" Landcross bellowed.

Archie charged, tackling the man. They fell to the ground, where rounds of punches were thrown. One landed on Landcross' bandaged chest, causing him to cry out. They rolled around, each trying to get the upper hand, until eventually they tumbled into the stream. Archie hoisted Landcross to his feet and punched him hard in the gut. Landcross doubled over, yet he had one last punch left in him. He brought up a closed fist and slammed it into Archie's chin, sending him flying back into the water. Archie shook off the dizziness and grabbed a stone, ready to bash Landcross' head when he saw the gun.

"This is where we part ways, mate," Landcross said, stepping out of the stream. He clutched his stomach with one hand, the other aimed the pistol unerringly at Archie. He spoke between heavy breaths, but it didn't slow him down.

Archie slowly stood up and took a step forward. "I can't let you leave."

"I think you will, not unless you want your father to learn about your secret marriage, eh?"

Archie dropped the rock, stunned. "How do you know about that?"

"Never mind how. You just bloody well stay there," Landcross ordered.

Archie didn't worry so much about being shot, for Landcross could end him right now if he wanted. Even so, Archie knew better then to test him.

As he stepped out of the water, Landcross unfastened his satchel's strap with his free hand and reached in. He brought out the book and held it up. "You want the bloody thing?" He tossed it into the thick brush. "Take it."

Landcross mounted his horse and rode through the stream. Archie thought about going for his pistol, but there was no point now that Landcross had given up the book.

He stepped out of the shallow water and retrieved the book from the bushes. "Finally."

"Find that bastard!" Tarquin Norwich shouted to his men.

Soldiers raced out from a wooded area and headed for their horses. Moments later, his father, brother, and a soldier supporting another wounded man emerged from the woods, coughing and spitting.

If Clover wasn't in the house, Archie would ride away before they noticed him. But he headed up the short hill to his father instead. The decaying smell of sulfur arrived long before he reached them.

"Archie," Ivor said, "where the hell have you been while we were being ambushed by that little bastard?"

Archie had hoped that the marks on his face and his drenched clothing would give evidence that he'd been doing something, but apparently not.

"What happened?" he asked to distract his brother from the question.

His inquiry seemed to make his father more livid.

"What happened is that we lost *everything*," his father shouted, coming face to face with him. "Where's your sister?"

"Clover?" he said, trying not to show his disgust at the smell emendating from his father. "Why?"

Norwich grabbed him by the lapels, pulling him closer, a fist looming over his head. "Where is she?"

His father wasn't asking out of concern for Clover; he was enraged about what she'd done. Archie could only imagine what he would do if he got his hands on her.

When Archie didn't answer, he was met with a hard blow that came crashing down on his head, dropping him to his knees as waves of pain washed over him.

"Are you and your sister against me?" his father screamed in venomous rage.

"Maybe she went into the house," Ivor suggested casually.

Their father immediately headed for the back door.

"No, Father!" Archie cried, staggering to his feet.

"You're a traitorous little scum," his father said over his shoulder.

Ivor laughed loudly.

Archie followed, feeling the ground shift beneath him. He needed to do something, anything before it was too late. "I have the book!"

His father stopped and turned around. His expression didn't alter, but his eyes shifted to the book that Archie held up.

"Give me that," his father demanded, snatching it from him. He flipped through the pages, and for a moment, it seemed as if everything would be all right.

"I can't believe you got it." He smiled thinly, then spun around. "Clover!"

Archie knew he was the only one who would protect her. He reached for his pistol.

"Sir!" a soldier yelled out as he rounded the corner of the house on horseback.

"What is it?" Norwich snapped, stopping before he reached the back door.

Archie also stopped, dropping his hand from the butt of his gun. He pushed the thought of what he was about to do out of mind in order to have the strength he would need if he was forced to use the gun. If he put too much thought into it, he might lose his nerve.

"Did you find Peachtree?" his father demanded of the soldier.

"Nay, sir," the man replied. "When we searched the house, we found no trace of him. Judging from the state of his chamber, it appears as if he's fled."

Norwich's face flamed hotter.

"Also, one of our horses is missing, sir," the man reported.

"Pierce's brother must have taken it," Archie said, trying to redirect his father's anger toward someone other than his sister.

Norwich turned, studied Archie and said brusquely, "From the looks of you, I sense that the other brother got away as well?"

"Aye, sir," Archie said. "Most likely, he's heading back to France."

Archie needed his father to forget about Clover and

refocus on his mission. "He has the masks, sir."

Landcross was right about his father wanting the masks after all, and Archie saw it in the flashes of his father's stony eyes.

"Let's go," Norwich ordered the soldier holding the wounded man up. He had a bad wound, but one he would survive if he received the proper medical care.

"Sir, what about Trotter?" the soldier asked, gesturing to his comrade.

Norwich marched over to the hurt man. He pulled his gun and shot the injured man in the head. A cloud of red dispersed from the back of his skull.

"Fetch the shovel and bury him," Norwich snarled at the soldier, who now had blood flecking his shocked face. "Then you can *walk* back to Southampton."

"Y-y-yes, sir," the man stammered before rushing away.

Archie stood his ground as his father marched back toward him, while Ivor went over to the body lying on its back. Ivor took his flask out of his pocket and drank as he stared at the corpse.

"Get your sister and return home immediately," Norwich commanded Archie. "I'll deal with you both when I arrive."

"Yes, sir," Archie said.

The soldier returned with the horses, and both his father and Ivor mounted.

"Perhaps we can catch both brothers," Ivor said.

"I only need one now," his father stated. To Archie, he asked, "Which way did he go?"

Archie pointed toward the field. "He went that way, heading for the coast."

Without another word, his father kicked his horse into a gallop and rode toward the small meadow. The rest of his men followed.

Once they were out of sight, Archie realized that he'd come very close to killing his father. He wanted to gag at the thought. Never had he been so close to killing anyone before, yet if his father had gone into that house, he would have put a bullet through the back of the man's skull.

Clover's life was his to protect. It was his duty. His promise to his mother on the night she'd taken her own life. If Clover died, not only would he lose one of the two people in the world he cared the most about, but he would have failed to keep his promise.

He doubled over and dry-heaved, which left him shaking. He entered the house on wobbly legs, breathing heavily.

"Clover!" he called. "Come out. We must go."

He had to act fast. He and Clover needed to return to Southampton, collect Eilidh, and leave for Ireland to catch a ship in Dublin. There was now a small window of time to do so. If his father captured Landcross, he would without a doubt acquire the masks and head for home—unless he took time to torture the blasted thief to get Landcross to tell him where he could find Indigo first. Even if that did happen, it would only gain Archie an extra sliver of time.

"Clover!"

He searched the house, calling for her to let her know that their father had left in case she was hiding from him. He went out into the front yard and called for her there.

Imprinted in the dirt were many horse tracks. A horse had gone missing. He hadn't given it much thought other then that the other Landcross had stolen it, but had the man taken Clover as well?

"But why?" he whispered to himself, feeling the

tremors of panic return.

Had Joaquin Landcross taken her to use as leverage in case his father came after him? That didn't make sense. How would Landcross even know that she was Tarquin Norwich's daughter? What would he do to her?

The fear of that last question prompted him to follow the only horse tracks heading away from the house. On the main road, the tracks continued north.

"Where are they going?" he asked himself.

He raced to his horse in the backyard and rode up to the main road. There were other horse-and-wagon-wheel tracks in the dirt. He kicked his horse's flanks and followed the tracks back to the bridge leading over the Beaulieu River.

The sun was setting by the time Clover and Joaquin reached Lepe. The exhausted horse had run for miles and was panting harshly.

"We should walk for a little while," she said as they rode slowly over the quiet seaside road.

"I don't think so," Joaquin replied.

"Your horse will collapse and die before long."

"It can rest once we're on the ferry. Besides, I want to get out of Lepe."

"Why?"

He looked around as if he was searching for something. "Dunno actually. It's as though I've been here before."

"Did something happen to you here?" she asked, noting the strange tone in his voice.

He looked at the palm of his hand and a scar that stretched across it.

"I . . ." he began, as if straining to remember what

had happened. "Nothing." He lowered his hand. "Forget I said anything."

"Where are we going exactly?"

"To the Isle of Wight."

Her eyebrows came together. "Why there?"

She no longer feared him as she had when he'd threatened to shoot her. She still didn't know whether or not he had a gun, yet she sensed he wouldn't murder a child.

"I want you to show me where your father's summer home is."

She snorted. "I could try. I haven't been there in ages, though. Why on earth would you want to go there?"

"I reckon your father never told you his plans, did he?" When she gave no answer, he chuckled. "No, I thought not. Your dear old dad wishes to build specialized weapons."

"And?" Clover said, waiting to hear something she didn't already know.

"And apparently he's holding prisoners there to start building them once he has Indigo."

"You're lying. My father is a dangerous man but he's not stupid enough to kidnap people."

"Oh?" Joaquin challenged. "Is that so?"

"Yes," she answered flatly. "Besides, why does he need Indigo to help build the weapons when all he needs is a good engineer?"

Joaquin seemed stumped. "I don't know," he replied petulantly. "Maybe he wants to make certain they're assembled correctly. That bomb of holy hell you threw at us back in the shed was just an example of what the man can do."

"How do you know all this?"

"Your belligerent brother talks a lot when he has a head full of whisky."

Clover considered that for a moment.

"I don't believe you," she squeaked out. "About the prisoners, that is."

"Really now? Show me to your father's summer home and I'll prove it."

Any thought about escaping left her then. Regardless of what she believed, or wanted to believe, she had to see what was behind the walls at Norwich Castle.

"Fine. I'll take you there," she said with forced strength.

On the outskirts of Holbury, Norwich shot his horse in the head after the animal broke its leg in a rabbit hole.

His rage from the events back in the New Forest pumped his blood hot like molten steel throughout his body. When anger like this came over him, it took a lot to calm him.

"Sir, the horses are too tired to ride at this pace anymore," one soldier stated. "At this rate, they'll be dead before we reach shore."

"He's right, Father," Ivor slurred. "We should trade them off in Holbury."

If his son hadn't spoken, Norwich would have pulled the soldier off his mount and pistol-whipped him. With his teeth gritted tightly, he stared at Ivor sitting on his own sweaty steed. The animal breathed deeply, with foam dripping from its mouth.

Ivor's black glassy eyes flashed, almost as if Norwich's own father was the one trying to talk reason to him. Was he going mad? Sometimes, he questioned just how sane he really was. But he always reminded himself that it was the world that was crazy and he merely acted as the world around him allowed.

He viewed the situation with the horses from a different perspective. The stupid beasts would indeed drop dead before long, leaving them without transportation to get them to port in order to catch a passage to France. Landcross would most likely have already switched horses by now and would be nearing the shore, while he was standing here thinking about it. They wouldn't be able to catch him on English soil, but if they hurried, they'd be able to get Landcross on the other side of the Channel.

"Right," Norwich said at length, pointing to the soldier who'd spoken earlier. "You, dismount."

The man obeyed.

Norwich mounted his horse and said, "Move out."

The horsemen walked their horses at a relaxed pace, with the soldier trailing on foot behind.

Pierce traveled down the river past Eling. He stopped at Applemore to switch horses, leaving his exhausted animal to rest and graze in the same field from which he took his next horse. It was a tad time-consuming, putting the saddle and bridle on the new mount without being seen, but it was necessary. He knew Norwich and his lot would most likely be tailing him, but after hours of steady riding, Norwich's horses wouldn't be able to keep up.

In Black Water, he caught the last ferryboat out of port. Black smoke poured from the stack as it sailed over the steel grey waters of the Solent.

He stood at the bow, keeping clear from everyone either inside the passenger cabin or at the stern so they wouldn't smell him. Although he wasn't anywhere near used to the stench himself, which had become worse since his dip in the stream with that twit Archie, he did find some amusement in it.

As the boat cut through the cold water, he took out Indigo's book and opened it. The Toymaker's genius was represented on every page. The fact that Indigo had kept it hidden must have been because the Toymaker didn't want to let people know how smart he was. It was no wonder that Indigo kept his weapon designs a secret with a madman like Tarquin Norwich after him. A wiser choice would have been to never put any of this down on paper in the first place. But looking at it from an artist's perspective, he could understand Indigo's urge to get all his designs out of his mind by way of print. Pierce wasn't an artist; he couldn't draw unless he copied an image, or paint, or write poetry, or anything of that nature, but he'd been around enough artists to know how they thought—to a degree—and how their art could physically and mentally hurt them if they ignored it.

The smart thing for Pierce to do at the moment was to throw the damn journal into the Channel and let the ocean devour it before it could be used to create havoc. The world simply didn't need any more bloody weapons.

He held it out over the railing, the freezing saltwater spraying his hand. All he needed to do was to let it go.

But he couldn't. He pulled his arm in and flipped to the pages where the masks and writing were. What were they and what did the spell do? Was this the reason why Tarquin Norwich wanted the book? If he could find Indigo, he could find out once and for all.

He placed the journal back into his satchel and continued watching the Isle of Wight grow larger.

Chapter Sixteen
The Workshop

"Lord Norwich," the harbormaster said, "how are you, sir?"

As Tarquin Norwich approached the man at his desk, Ivor waited by the door, watching. He cracked a smile when the harbormaster scrunched up his face at the rotten egg smell that radiated from them.

"Sir?" the harbormaster said, holding a handkerchief to his face, "what in God's name happened?"

"It is of no concern of yours," Norwich snapped. "I need a ferry to take us to France immediately."

The man leapt up from his chair, abandoning his work to open the windows behind him, allowing the ocean air to enter. The scent of the sea breeze was not strong enough to mask the gut-twisting stench. A man in a captain's uniform entered the room.

"Bloody hell, chaps, what beast died in here?"

"Behave, Jeffery," the harbormaster warned. "This here is Lord Norwich, the Queen's . . ."

"I know who he is," the gruff old captain interrupted. To Norwich, he said, "Pleasure meeting you, milord."

Norwich ignored the uncouth sea captain and said to the harbormaster, "Why are you standing there, Jackson? Go arrange for my transportation to France. We are after a dangerous man who has quite a head start on us."

"Does he smell as bad as you lot?" the captain asked.

Ivor could sense his father's patience running out.

For some reason or another, his father loved him above all his other children. No matter how drunk or useless he got, his father treasured him and kept him around. Ivor simply played the role of the obedient son, but deep down, his resentment toward his father was great.

"Do you wish to spend the remainder of your wretched life in prison?" Norwich seethed to the sea captain. If the harbormaster wasn't in the room, Ivor knew that his father would murder the man.

The harbormaster seemed to understand the thin line that Jeffery was walking. "Jeffery! Belt up!"

"No offense, milord," the cocky captain said, setting down a log of daily reports on the desk. "I only ask because there was a gent who boarded a ferry two hours ago who reeked like one of Satan's farts! That ferry wasn't headin' for France, though."

"How do you know that?" Norwich demanded.

"'Cause I saw 'im going up the ramp to the boat, I did. To my ill-fortune, I'd been standing downwind of the bastard."

Norwich crossed his arms and asked with skepticism, "What did he look like?"

The old bugger shrugged. "Medium height, brown hair, wearing a black coat and pinstriped trousers. He carried nothing more than a satchel, he did."

Norwich seemed more inclined to listen to the man. "A satchel, you say? Where was he heading?"

"For the Isle of Wight."

Norwich turned to Ivor. "Why on earth would he go there?"

"Maybe he went looking for someone," Ivor said cryptically.

"Yes," his father said almost pleasantly. To the harbormaster, he said, "What time is the next ferry to the island?"

"I'm afraid the man you're speaking about left on the last one, Lord Norwich," the harbormaster said. "That ferry won't return until morning."

"I'll take 'em," the sea captain offered. "Won't take me long to get me boat ready."

"How much?" Norwich demanded.

The nervous harbormaster looked uncomfortable with this discussion, as if he couldn't believe the gall of his captain to negotiate with someone like Tarquin Norwich. Ivor, however, liked the ballsy man.

The shabby captain casually shrugged and said, "Not much. Fifty pounds."

"Bloody hell, Jeffery," the harbormaster gasped. "That's far more then what you make in a year."

"Aye," the sea captain said. "What's your point?"

"Done," Norwich said, clearly ready to be underway. "Have your boat ready to depart for Cowes in no less than twenty minutes."

"Aye, milord," the sea captain said with a crooked grin. As he headed out the door, he stopped at the threshold and said, "I'll, um, find you both some clean duds as well, eh?"

The afternoon had turned into evening by the time Indigo Peachtree reached the shore where the cave was located. In his hand, he held a burlap sack containing food and a newspaper. It had been a long walk to the nearest store and carrying the heavy sack had made the walk back feel even longer. His body had gained too many years.

Before entering the cave, he went to a circle of stones that surrounded a grill nestled within the larger rocks near a woodpile. Indigo placed three logs under the grill and lifted his cast iron cook pot onto the grill. The old thing had worked well over the years, now he looked at it with remorse. With a huff, he brought out his newspaper. On the front page, there was an illustration of a man he didn't recognize except for the name. He read the story about how this man, once a boy he'd known, had broken into the royal palace and attempted to steal Queen Victoria's jewelry. He'd been caught by the Queen herself but managed to get away.

Shaking his head, Indigo slipped out a section of paper and struck a match to it. He lit the paper on fire, tucked it under the logs, and blew on it until the flame grew over the wood. Lifting his creaky body, he rose with joints popping and made his way to the cave. This night would mark the eighth since he'd fled his home.

He should have known better then to have gone to the lair of a man like Tarquin Norwich. Norwich would never want toys for the poor children of Southampton, as he'd claimed when he'd summoned him from London. Norwich wanted his journal, but thankfully, it had been taken from him years ago. He only hoped the damn thing had been destroyed.

He regretted how he allowed himself to be convinced in buying those blasted things.

The day was hot. Midday had settled, turning the marketplace into an oven. Even the shade and closed in spaces offered little relief. But Indigo was content. He sat alone at El Fishawi's coffeehouse, drinking lethally strong coffee, reading a book, and enjoying a toke from the house hookah.

He had been busy. Awaking at dawn, he had gone about Cairo, visiting various sections of the city before coming to the suq, the famous Khan el-Khalili. Indigo had enjoyed his time in Egypt. He'd taken a camel into the desert to see Giza and the Great Sphinx for himself. He even helped dig out the sand that had covered nearly the whole statue. The work was tough and after so many years, the workers had only unearthed the Sphinx down to its chest. After a week, Indigo left them to it and returned to Cairo.

At the suq, he bought many wonderful little trinkets, including a nice cook pot. The well made cast iron item would be worth hauling back to Britain.

He left the coffeehouse and joined the bustling throngs, passing shops selling exotic lamps and colorful spices. The smell of cloves and cinnamon filled his senses. People smiled at him, the phrase *as-salaam 'alaykum* on many lips. Children stared at him curiously. Although his skin had darkened, thanks to his time in the desert, he was still the palest amongst the locals and he was sure his pith helmet with goggles resting on the bill, tan slacks and Safari vest seemed peculiar. He gave anyone who waved to him a friendly wave back and responded to the greetings with the traditional response, *wa 'alaykum salaam*, before continuing on his way.

He mentally prepared himself for the ferocity of the heat that waited for him just past the archway. He passed glittering trinkets, sparkling in the sun just before the light and brutal heat washed over him as he stepped outside suq's limits and into direct sunlight. He pulled the goggles over his spectacles. The tinted lenses shielded his eyes from the intense brightness. He heard his name uttered.

"Indigo Peachtree."

He stopped short and scanned around.

"Peachtree," the voice said again, this time coming from a man sitting cross-legged on the ground under a parasol. Beside him was a glass hookah. The man wore a white Jellabiya with embroidered cuffs. Although his garb fit in with the other vendors' modest clothing, it was the fur hat with feathers that struck Indigo as most odd. His complexion was dark with a neatly trimmed mustache on a face that still managed to look girlish.

"Do I know you?" Indigo said in Arabic.

The man removed the hookah pipe from his lips.

"Know me, sir?" he said with smoke breezing from his mouth and nostrils. "Why should I know *you*?"

Bloody hell, Indigo. The heat has made you delusional.

"Ah, well then, pardon me, my good man," Indigo said as he turned to leave.

"Must you go before seeing what I have to offer?"

"Thank you kindly, sir, but I have quite enough keepsakes."

"Not like these, you don't."

If he had been a wiser man, he would have pushed on. Instead, his curious nature urged him to have a look.

"All right, what do you have?" He went over and peered at the seller's wares.

"These," the man said, gliding his hand gracefully over four items that lay on a small rug.

Three white masks and a rolled up scroll. He had them displayed out in front of him. They appeared to be the only items he was selling. Indigo had to admit that the trinkets were interesting.

"What are they?" he asked, strictly out of curiosity.

"These are masks. They have a legend dating back thousands of years."

Indigo listened intently as the man spoke about the legend. It intrigued him so much, that he nearly forgot about the heat. He did, however, remove his heavy pack and sat with the man under the shade of the parasol. He even partook of the hookah.

"That is a fascinating fable, young man," Indigo said when the seller finished.

"Oh, it's no fable, sir," he proclaimed. "It's all quite true."

Indigo arched a suspicious eyebrow at him. "Is it? And the writing is linked to the masks, you say?"

Indigo glanced down at the parchment now unrolled and laid out over the masks. A strange script, written in black ink, like nothing he had ever seen. Could it be some kind of ancient Greek?

"Indeed," said the seller with a sincere nod.

"But you don't know what the writing says or what it does?"

The vendor said nothing, only took a long toke from the hookah. The smoke inside swirled like a desert djinn.

The fact that the writing was a mystery piqued Indigo's interests. He loved puzzles. Even so, he wasn't some wide eye, wet behind the ear lad. He thought the whole story was a crock and the scroll was something the seller may have created himself.

"In any case. I thank you for the story."

He reached for his bag but suddenly the vendor was handing him a pair of twenty-sided dice made of green serpentine with what looked like Demotic carved on each face.

"These items are special. They belong with someone worthy."

Now Indigo knew the man was a con merchant. "I see."

"Roll the letters of your choosing and you can have the masks and scroll for nothing."

Indigo lowered his goggles. "Is that so? And if I lose?"

"Then choose whether or not you're willing to buy them."

Indigo didn't fully believe that, but decided to play along. "All right. It's a deal."

He took the dice and shook them in his enclosed hand.

"X and H," he said, tossing them down.

They tumbled a bit and then landed on the symbols that represented those sounds. He couldn't believe it.

"That was lucky," said the seller nonchalantly.

"Impossible."

"Is it?" the vendor challenged. "Try again with different letters."

Indigo shook the dice. "B and Q."

He rolled, and sure enough, they landed on those very letters.

"It appears that you have won," said the seller. "Take care of them."

"Wait. This isn't fair to you," Indigo said, his honest, good-natured self coming out. "I can't just take them."

"We had an agreement. They are yours."

Although it appeared that he had won the trinkets fair and square, he still felt he should give the man something.

"Here," he said, reaching into the pocket of his vest. "Take this."

He put some silver coins into the man's hand. He accepted them with a slight nod of his head.

Indigo loaded the masks inside his rucksack. They felt strange to the touch. He carried everything back to his hotel room, and there he studied the writing on the ancient scroll.

Old fool, Indigo thought to himself. He was only

thankful for the dream that had warned him of Norwich's true intention. A redheaded woman came to him in a blur and informed him that Norwich wanted him for something dangerous.

During his visit at Norwich's estate, he'd realized that the dream had indeed been a warning, which had prompted him to flee during the night. What angered him more was how Tarquin Norwich had found out about the book in the first place.

He'd put the entire world in jeopardy, and worse yet, he didn't know how to fix it.

After a choppy and cold journey across the Channel, Joaquin and the little brat arrived at Cowes harbor. She'd wanted to go inside the passenger cabin, but he'd denied her request in fear that she would try communicating to someone that she was a hostage. He'd shown her that he indeed had a gun, one that he'd stolen from a soldier during his escape. Even so, he wouldn't put it past her to try something.

By the time they'd made their way through town, she was coughing and had a fever. He couldn't wait to be rid of her. When they finally left town, they headed into the outskirts, where the countryside opened up.

"There," the brat said, pointing to a gate ahead of them.

Two guards were at a black iron gate set amidst of a vine covered stone wall. When the guards spotted them coming, one of them stepped forward.

"Halt," the guard ordered. "What's your business here?"

"Lord Norwich has instructed me to deliver this girl to work at the castle," Joaquin said with authority. "She's to help in building weapons."

The guards laughed.

"Help build weapons?" one guard mocked. "*Her*? What good would she be, eh? Lugging heavy stuff around?"

It's true! Joaquin thought excitedly.

"She can fetch things and squeeze into nooks and crannies to fix stuck gears," he explained. "I don't know. I just do what I'm told."

"Be quiet, Euan," the other guard snapped. To Joaquin, he asked, "Sir, where is your uniform?"

"I needed to change on the way here," Joaquin said. He turned his horse so the men could see Norwich's insignia embroidered on the side of the saddle. He hoped it would be enough to fool them.

"What are you talking about?" the brat asked.

"Silence, slave," Joaquin ordered. To the guards, he said, "She's a bit mad. She thinks she's Lord Norwich's daughter. Don't believe her."

"I am his daughter. I brought *you* here."

"I said to be quiet," he yelled, shaking her some. "I'll not tolerate this nonsense any further."

She tried prying herself away from him. "Let go of me! Let go, I say!"

"Are you going to open the gate or not?" he bellowed angrily. "I've put up with this shit since Southampton." Before she could scratch him or get away, he pressed the barrel of the gun under her chin. She stilled instantly.

The guard seemed unconvinced and craned his neck over to the other guard behind him, who only shrugged. Receiving no opinion from his comrade, the guard sighed. "All right, push on."

The guards opened the gate and Joaquin rode forward, keeping the gun wedged under the brat's small chin. She began crying, then coughing.

"Stop that," he demanded as they neared the Gothic-style building up ahead. "The world is a cruel and hard place, where you must adapt or die, understand? Quit your blubbering and be strong. You wanted proof; I'm simply giving it to you."

The brat took some deep breaths and said in a quivering tone, "I hope you're shot dead for this, and I'm there to see it."

"There you go!" he praised. "That's the attitude you need. Now play along. I'll get you out as soon as I have enough evidence to take down your father."

"Is that why you're doing this?"

"Aye. And once you see that, you'll believe everything I've told you. Do you want a man like your father to succeed?"

The brat was quiet for a moment.

"No," she said at length.

"Good, then behave."

They said nothing else as they reached the front entrance to the estate. The building looked as though it had been carved by demons. The medieval walls were dark grey, almost black. Patches of vines clung to the dark walls. It wasn't a terribly large castle, but it had a domineering personality that dared anyone to enter.

"How long has it been since you were here?" he whispered to the brat as a stable boy approached to collect the horse.

"Five years, I believe."

He was relieved to hear that. He feared that someone in the castle, a servant perhaps, might recognize her on sight. All he needed was a little time inside to learn details of what was happening so he could give a clear description to the authorities. If someone knew her and identified her as truly being Norwich's daughter, he'd no doubt end up imprisoned

The Legacy

and building weapons after all. That, or be killed on the spot.

Inside, they were met by a hard faced woman dressed in a similar uniform as the men. Evidently it had been tailored, as her outfit hugged her body perfectly. When she walked, the leather creaked. Her bright blonde hair was pulled tightly back.

"What is this?" she asked in a thick Dutch accent. "Who are you and why is this child here?"

"This girl was caught stealing from Lord Norwich's home," Joaquin said. "I was instructed to bring her here to work."

When the woman came a little closer, she threw a hand over her nose and mouth. "Why on earth do you both smell so bad?"

"We, uh, ran into some complications on the way here, milady. In Southampton, she got away from me for a time and ran onto the beach, where I caught up to her. We struggled, and both of us fell onto the rotting corpse of a sea lion."

"Just one?" the woman quipped through her hand.

"Please," he said, "it's has been a very long day. Could we possibly move this along?"

"You're not dressed like a servant of Lord Norwich," she continued to challenge.

"My clothes were covered in dead flesh, milady. I paid a drifter for his." He stepped forward with his arm out. "These clothes smell a little cleaner. Would you like a whiff?"

She instantly backed away, waving her hands at him. "No need!" When he stopped, so did she. "How will this child serve us?"

He looked the woman over in appreciation. The figure hugging the leather looked good on her. He gave her a leer. "As I pointed out to your guards at the gate, she is small and able to reach into certain places where a grown person cannot and . . . Look, Lord Norwich believes she is valuable enough for me to bring her here. If you have objections, I suggest that you take them up with him, eh? Either way, the girl stays."

He waited for her response. There appeared to be very little resentment in her plain pale eyes, although that didn't mean she trusted him entirely.

"The girl may remain," she said, "and I shall send a telegraph to Lord Norwich about this. Guard," she called to someone else in the room with them, "take this child upstairs and have a maid bathe her."

The servant bowed. "Yes, milady." He snatched the brat by the arm. "Come along, girl. This way."

"Get your hands off me!" she shouted. "I can very well walk on my own."

She shook off his grasp and walked out of the room with her head held high. Joaquin couldn't help but to be impressed by her gall.

"She has spirit," the woman said, turning to leave the room. "Now then, if there isn't anything else . . ."

"Actually," he said before she could walk away, "Lord Norwich has also instructed me to take a look around at the prisoners and the workshop to make sure that everything is in tip-top shape."

"Lord Norwich was here not even a fortnight ago. He saw nothing wrong."

"He complained about sanitation. Did he not explain that to you when he was here?"

"Sanitation?"

"Yes, the stench of the laborers. Lord Norwich said it was unbearable. He doesn't want any of his workers getting ill."

The woman narrowed her eyes at him. "The

prisoners' conditions aren't *that* bad."

"Just a quick look to see."

She sighed vexingly. "If Lord Norwich wishes to have an up-to-date report, then, by all means, come this way."

When she turned her back to him, he let out a relieved sigh.

He followed her through the castle, towards the back and down a flight of spiral stairs to a short corridor, where a guard stood in front of a doorway. Joaquin followed her through the doorway and down another flight of narrow steps leading deep under-ground. The dank staircase was ancient, yet the lanterns set in alcoves carved into the walls were modern. They lit the way with an eerily pale red glow. Finally, Joaquin and the woman reached an old wooden door. She pulled down the latch and opened it, passing one guard on the way. After taking a few steps inside, she stopped and said, "Go on, take a look."

Joaquin sucked in an anxious breath and proceeded into the medieval dungeon. He feared that the woman suspected that he might be lying and had only brought him down here to corner him before she summoned the guards. He pressed on, looking from side-to-side at each cell. Eight cells stocked full of dirty men and women, each of who peered back at him through the old bars.

"There are so many," he observed.

"They are gifted with many different skills," she said. "They range anywhere from chemists to welders, engineers, and blacksmiths."

He fixed his sight on every cell; four on either side. Each cell held between seven to a dozen gloomy and angry faces. Women and men were kept separately. Despite their predicament, they appeared well-fed, which wasn't surprising, considering they were here to serve as a labor force. The reek of human waste was surprisingly low for so many prisoners, though. He himself smelled worse, which wasn't lost on the woman.

"If your nose can reach past your own stench," she said petulantly, "then you'll notice that there are no neglect violations here."

"Are they up for the task at hand?" he asked over his shoulder.

"Why is Lord Norwich suddenly distressed? He seemed perfectly confident that everything was in order when he was here."

"Because, milady," he said in a testy tone that wasn't entirely forced, "he *has* the Toymaker and he wants a full report before his arrival. Understood?"

His tactic seemed to work. "Lord Norwich has Peachtree?" she said in a small voice. She cleared her throat as if she had a stone stuck in her windpipe. "Um, everything is ready, I assure you. Come. I'll show you to the workshop."

He followed her back upstairs and down the hallway, through the entrance hall and into another corridor. Another ancient door waited at the end of the hall, guarded by two men. When the guards saw them, they opened the double doors for the woman.

Beyond the door was a banquet hall. Portraits that Joaquin surmised were Norwich's relatives hung on the cold dark walls. There was even one of Tarquin Norwich over the mantel of the grand fireplace, no doubt put there by the ole bastard, himself.

On a long table sat sheets of metal: copper, silver, and bronze, engine parts and two hollow shells of tank bodies. There were jars filled with bolts and nails, as well as measuring sticks and tools lined up nearby.

Large wooden and steel wheels where stacked in at least a dozen piles on the floor. Nearby were blacksmith and alchemical workstations. On the wall hung many rifles and crossbows, as well as pistols resting on another table under them. In one corner, farthest from the hearth, were barrels of gunpowder. Joaquin was impressed.

"As you can see," the Dutch woman said, twirling around to him as smoothly as if she was standing on ice, "when Lord Norwich arrives with Peachtree, we'll be ready. And if any other materials are needed, we shall get them."

Joaquin checked his excitement. Inside he was bursting with glee at the tangible evidence he would need to earn him a pardon from the Queen herself. "Very well. Now, could I trouble you for a bath and some clean clothes?"

She crossed her arms and said, "I suppose. Shall I fetch a maid to scrub your back?"

"Actually, I think you'd be much more thorough," he said playfully.

Her thin lips rose slightly in a lopsided smile, and she looked him up and down. "I think not," she said, turning away. "I'll arrange for your bath."

Chapter Seventeen
Robin the Magnificent

The sun had set completely by the time Pierce's ferryboat had reached port. His stolen steed was famished, so he paid for oats and water at the first stable he came across. After the animal had had its fill, Pierce walked the mount through the streets of Cowes. The town was already aglow with street lamps and fire-lit windows. Carriages, horsemen, and pedestrians were out in numbers on the thorough-fares. Loud chatter and booming laughter came from inside taverns.

Pierce rounded a corner and spied a group of people gathered in front of what appeared to be a circus wagon. A man dressed in a pinstripe suit stood on a small stage high enough to be seen by his audience. He was telling a story while juggling three glass balls with glowing white liquid sloshing around inside them. By his accent, Pierce judged the man to be Spanish.

"Many years ago, a young man went out alone to hunt. In the forest where he knew every tree and rock, he became hopelessly lost. It wasn't until the sun came to meet the eastern horizon that he returned home, where an elderly man, his lifelong friend, waited. Drenched and utterly spent, the youth refused to explain his lateness until after he was dry and fed. After dinner, he and the old man sat by the fire smoking pipes, with a dog at their feet and an old cat sleeping blissfully near the flames.

'Stupid old cat, the old man grumbled. Worthless beasts, the lot of them.'

'I beg to differ,' the youth spoke up.

'Oh? the old man said. You, sir, have never favored these creatures in all your years of life. Why the change of heart now?'

Pierce couldn't decide whether it was the tale that captivated him or the hypnotic movement of the glowing orbs that danced in the air.

"To this, the youth said, 'I had quite a curious day today. I hardly know what to say about it. I went and wandered, not knowing where I was, 'til at last I saw a light and made for it, hoping to get help. As I came near it, the light disappeared and I found myself close to a large oak tree. I climbed into the branches, the better to look for the light, and, behold, it was beneath me, inside the hollow trunk of the tree. I seemed to be looking down into a church, where a funeral was taking place. I heard singing and saw a coffin surrounded by torches, all carried by . . .'" He shifted stance, becoming crooked with age, '*Out with it!*' the elderly man demanded. '*Dammit, man, what did you see?*'"

The crowd laughed at the Spaniard's changing voices.

"'Oh, but you will think me mad if I tell you!'

'By this time, the cat had awakened and sat up, seeming to be listening to their conversation, while the youth continued. 'The coffin and the torches were both borne by cats, and on the coffin was the mark of a crown and a scepter!'

'He got no further in the story before the cat started shrieking, 'By Jove! Old Peter's dead!,' the cat declared. 'And I'm the King o' the Cats!'

'With that, the old cat rushed up the chimney and was seen no more.'"

The crowd laughed and applauded. Pierce stood behind the crowd, anxiously waiting for the Spaniard to go on.

"Now that I have your full attention," the Spaniard said, "it is my pleasure to introduce to you the great and powerful, the *mysterious*, Robin the Magnificent!"

Pierce mouthed *Robin the Magnificent,* sensing some familiarity with the name.

The Spaniard juggled once more, then let each ball fall to the stage floor. When they landed, the balls burst into thick smoke that completely engulfed the man.

The audience gasped. It took only seconds for the smoke to clear, but as it dispersed, another man stood in the Spaniard's place. He was dressed in typical magician attire: a black suit with a blood red tie, black top-hat, and a cape. His face was ash white, and his eyes were lined in black kohl, enhancing the blue in them. His goatee and mustache were well-trimmed.

When Pierce saw him, his grin vanished. Fear exploded in his heart, causing his chest to ache.

"Ladies and gentlemen," Robin the Magnificent said loudly, spreading his arms wide. "Welcome to the show."

Pierce turned and slunk away, returning to where he'd come from. Icy shudders danced up his spine as he hurried toward the intersection. Any second, he expected the sound of rushing footsteps to come up behind him. Yet if that man—if Pierce could call him that—*was* coming after him, though, he wouldn't hear a thing.

Fortunately, no one followed and he made his way safely down another road.

"Spare change, sir?" a homeless man begged after Pierce rounded a corner. "Any change, please, sir."

As Pierce got closer, the beggar covered his mouth. "What the devil? Did you climb your way out of the sewer, young man?"

Pierce grimaced. That blasted stink bomb may have

saved his life, but he was paying for it everywhere he went! Having a homeless beggar take offense only added insult to injury.

Regardless, he reached into his pocket and brought out a few pennies. "Here, ol' boy. Could you tell me where a good hotel is around here?"

"One with a bath?" the beggar added.

Pierce sucked in a deep breath and said with barely controlled irritation, "Preferably."

"Stay on York Street and bank right on Bridge Road. There, you'll find Hotel Joubert. It is the only hotel company in town with indoor plumbing. Very fancy, indeed."

Joubert? Pierce thought. That name sounds familiar.

He was too tired to think on it so, instead, he grumbled, "Cheers," and continued down the road.

At last, Archie reached the shoreline. He'd asked the ticket seller in Lepe if a man and a child who smelled like rotten eggs had bought tickets, and, if so, to where. The ticket seller acknowledged that she'd sold them boarding passes to the Isle of Wight. Archie asked her to describe the man. She told him he was tall, with slightly wavy hair, a dark brown beard and mustache, green eyes, and wearing a brown coat.

Archie absorbed that while remembering the illustrations on Joaquin Landcross' broadsheets that he'd seen long ago. The ticket seller also informed him that the steamboat ferry that had left for the island was the last one of the day, and if he wanted to cross the Channel that evening, he needed to speak to the captain when he arrived. An hour later, Archie did just that, and he paid the sea captain every penny he had left.

He could have sworn that he had more money, but it seemed that much of it had gone missing. Pierce Landcross, up to his old tricks, no doubt.

Nevertheless, what was left was enough to convince the captain to make one last voyage to the island.

When he finally reached land, he went in search of the older Landcross brother and Clover. In order to find the rogue, he needed to deduce why the man would come to the island in the first place.

There was only one possible explanation. He was heading for the castle.

Although Archie didn't understand why Landcross wanted to go there, or how he even knew about it unless Clover had said something, it was at least a logical place to start looking.

As he rode through Cowes towards the castle, he spotted a man matching the description the ticket seller had given. He was dressed in the grey leather that his father's men wore, yet Archie felt sure it must be Landcross. He needed to question the man, yet his instincts warned against approaching him out in the open.

Landcross dismounted in front of a hotel, tying his horse to the hitching post, then went inside. Archie led his horse over and tied the animal to the same post. The urge to charge after the man tugged painfully at him, but he listened to his gut and stepped over to the window to peer through it.

Whoever he was, the man was signing the hotel's log. When the clerk gave him a key, Archie slipped in and followed, striding confidently as if he was a guest himself. They went up to the second floor. When Landcross reached the door to his room, Archie slowed his approach. The moment he had the door unlocked, Archie pulled his gun and jabbed it in the man's back.

"Get in," he commanded, shoving Landcross into the dark room.

Through the dim light of the hallway, he spotted a lantern on the small table. He grabbed Landcross' gun from its holster as he pushed him away. He ordered him to light the lantern. With two guns on him, Landcross sighed and complied.

Archie closed the door and demanded, "Where is my sister?"

"Who?" Landcross asked, blowing out the match.

"The girl you kidnapped. Don't play me for a fool. I know you're Joaquin Landcross."

"That I am," he said almost proudly. "And I did take your brat sister. She's now a slave in your father's castle."

"What are you talking about?"

"Your dear ole dad is building weapons and is using his summer home as a factory. He has workers locked away in there, your sister being the newest member."

Archie did his best to stomach the news. At first, he didn't believe that Landcross had taken Clover there, but where else would he have gotten the uniform?

"Why did you go to the castle? Why not run when you escaped my father?"

"I wanted to see it for myself, and I needed your sister to get me in."

Archie sensed that Landcross' purpose for going to the castle ran deeper than mere curiosity. "For what reason?" he pressed.

"If you must know, I'm going to take my findings to the Queen in exchange for a royal pardon."

The answer surprised Archie. Thinking on it for a moment, he didn't see that Landcross' plan was impossible, but it was most certainly risky.

"And good luck trying to get her out," Landcross added. "No one there recognized your sister. I doubt they'll believe that you're Norwich's son. Most likely, they'll lock you up as well."

Archie thought on that. If what Landcross had said about Clover was true, then everything else he said was a possibility. And the last thing he needed was for his father to find him locked inside the castle when he was supposed to be in Southampton.

"You ought to find my brother," Landcross suggested. "He'll be more inclined to assist you then I will if you plan to break her out."

"Your brother is on his way to France."

Landcross cracked a smile.

"What?" Archie demanded. His arms were growing tired of holding the guns.

"Not without Indigo, he's not." Landcross said.

"Are you saying that your brother is *here*?"

"Most likely. He and Indigo were very close. I know my brother, and he ain't the type to abandon his mates when they're in trouble."

"Indigo is on the island as well?"

"He brought us here once. I won't say where. You can speak to Pierce about that."

Could Pierce Landcross truly be on the island? It seemed like both brothers loved tempting fate.

"How will I find him?" he asked.

Joaquin Landcross chuckled. "He'll most likely try to find a place to bathe. Why did you drag him into this in the first place? Your father already had me."

"He wanted a book."

Landcross narrowed his eyes and rubbed his chin. "Ah, Pierce has the journal, eh?"

Archie found his reaction strange and asked, "Are

you sure he's here?"

"I wouldn't doubt it. My brother is very loyal to his mates." Landcross' tone held a hint of sadness to it and his eyes flickered with regret.

"What happened between you two?" Archie asked.

"I tried to kill him," Landcross answered tersely. "I put a knife to his neck and cut 'im."

"The scar across his throat? *You* did that to him?"

"Aye, when we were highwaymen together. He and I, along with a few others, we were a gang, and one night during a botched heist in some rich bloke's mansion, we were being chased by the owner and his sons. They managed to catch one of us, but the rest of us got away. Pierce wanted to go back to the mansion and rescue him. The rest of the gang disagreed but Pierce tried to get me to come with him. You see, the others got scared that he'd tell where our hideout was if he got caught. They looked to me as their leader to stop him, so I did."

Archie nearly fell over in disbelief. "You tried killing your own brother just to keep him from going back to rescue someone?"

Landcross blinked slowly. "I . . . I wasn't myself that night. To his good fortune, my blade was too dull to cut his windpipe. I left him there in the forest, bleeding. I hadn't seen him since, not until this afternoon when he saved my life."

Archie could only imagine the betrayal that Pierce Landcross must have felt when his own brother had turned against him.

Their falling-out struck close to home. He and Ivor had never gotten along, especially after what he'd done to their good-hearted uncle, who had only wanted to help them.

"You see," Landcross went on, "my brother is a

swindler, a smuggler, even a cocky thief, but he's honorable."

"That's a bold claim coming from someone who tried opening his throat," Archie said with malice.

Landcross slumped. He suddenly seemed old and frail. "I've done many ungodly things in my lifetime. The only thing I truly regret was what I did that night."

As far as Archie could see, he had two choices. He could take Landcross hostage and risk going to the castle and get himself locked up, or he could search for the brother. Each path seemed bleak. However, he favored one over the other. Pierce Landcross had expressed in minor ways that he cared for Clover. Either that, or he'd simply needed to stay in her good graces to use her as he had at the museum. Remembering that, he figured that Landcross owed her for saving him the night before, and for having her assist him in stealing the masks. If what Joaquin Landcross said was true, then his brother would feel obligated to help.

"Trust me," Landcross said, "he's here." Then to Archie's amazement, he added, "Come along then; we'll find him together, eh?"

Landcross marched toward the door, despite the guns on him. He flung the door open and headed down the hall.

Archie holstered the pistols and followed.

"You'll need more then soap and water to wash that smell away, sir," the lofty clerk at the front desk of Hotel Joubert said. She was short in stature, wearing a deep green uniform that resembled a military jacket, with a chain clasped to her shoulder and a pocket watch hanging by her breast. Her dark hair was done up as high as she could get it, with thick curls draping on either side of her face. She also wore too much powder and rouge. She was pinching her nose, which made her tone sound nasal and annoying to Pierce.

"It's mostly the clothes," he justified.

"Then may I suggest a *very* deep steam cleaning for them?" she said. "That is, if you can afford it."

Hotel Joubert was not without its swank. The lobby walls were adorned with paintings of different sections of the city, the sea, and the countryside. Red leather chairs clustered by large ottomans, where guests sat drinking brandy and blowing smoke to the ceiling from their cigars. Above the guests was a chandelier in the form of an octopus made from blue crystals, holding gas lit torches coiled around its arms. The furniture appeared to be good and sturdy, and clean rugs covered the entire floor without a speck of dirt visible. The ceiling above Pierce had a large stained glass skylight with elaborate flowers within a colorful Celtic pattern. Across from the front desk was an archway leading into the hotel tavern, which was lit by bright blue glass lamps.

The fact that Pierce had paraded into such a high-class establishment dressed as he was and smelling like a rotting corpse surprised him. He would have thought that he would have been tossed out already. In a world where money spoke louder than any clerk's complaining, he pulled out a fat coin purse, compliments of Archie Norwich. He dropped the coin purse on the counter. "Aye, I have enough."

With her nose still pinched between her long fingers, she said, "Very good, sir. Just sign in and I shall have someone show you to your room."

He forced a smile. "Much obliged."

He only had his satchel since losing his belongings back in France, leaving nothing for the bellboy to carry as he led the way down the first floor corridor.

"You will like this room, indeed, sir," the bellboy said, pulling a key out of his red coat pocket. "It's not only spacious, but it has its own Water Closet, equipped with indoor plumbing. You can actually turn on the faucet and water comes out! It's quite modern."

"Actually, the Romans had indoor plumbing centuries ago, lad," Pierce said as the youth unlocked a door near the end of the hall.

"Pardon?" the bellhop said, opening the door.

In no mood to give a history lesson, Pierce shook his head and started in. "Nothing."

When he entered the room, the bellboy quickly fluttered about, lighting gas lanterns mounted on the wall. "And here is your Water Closet, sir," the lad said, vanishing into a dark adjoining room.

As he lit lamps inside, Pierce threw his satchel on a small table and began shucking off his clothes.

"The tub is made of copper," the bellboy explained. "The wall tiles come from the island of Rhodos. You can adjust the temperature of the water using these glass knobs. The boilers in the hotel basement heat the water rather quickly."

The bellhop turned the knobs, running the water. Pierce entered the washroom, naked except for the silver stater around his neck.

"Aye, and I'm sure the soap is made from the finest fat in all of France," he said, ignoring the shocked expression on the boy's face. "Now be a good lad and take these to be washed, eh?"

He handed his clothes to the boy, amused that the youth strained to keep his composure after smelling their stench. He dropped a few pound notes onto the pile of stinking clothes. "And throw in a pair of new undergarments, too. You can keep the change."

The money prompted the boy into action. "Yes, sir! Right away, sir!"

The bellhop sprang out of the room and Pierce stepped into the tub. The warm water embraced him, unknotting his tense muscles. He couldn't remember the last time he'd felt so good.

Chapter Eighteen
Obligation

Clover's skin and scalp were tender to the touch after her bath. The maid who'd been appointed to wash her had scrubbed her from top to bottom as if she were a stained rug. When Clover had protested that she could very well bathe herself, it had only earned her a slap. After the bath, another maid had arrived with her clothes, which were damp and still smelled bad.

"We have no children's clothes here," the maid snapped when Clover asked. "Put these on or walk around naked."

Now Clover's chest was burning with the sickness. When she coughed, her throat seemed to tear and the cool air felt like burning gas when she breathed in. It would have helped if the bath water had at least been warm, but instead of taking the time to heat it, the hasty maid had brought the water straight from the well outside. The chattering of her teeth echoed in her head the entire time. Dressing in damp clothes and being brought down to the dank dungeon had done nothing to help, either.

When she was pushed into a cell containing women, they flocked to her and wrapped her in a blanket. One heavyset woman held her against her bosom for comfort and warmth. As the woman gently rocked her back and forth, Clover doubted that Joaquin Landcross would ever come back for her. She closed her eyes and allowed the rocking motion to take her away.

Ivor, Tarquin Norwich, and the remaining soldiers

rode through Cowes, heading for the Norwich summer estate. Ivor couldn't wait to reach it. The journey across the Channel had been dicey, causing him to vomit over the side of the ship many times. Like most days, he'd filled his stomach with more liquids then food, so the rough sea had wreaked havoc on him. When they'd finally reached port, his father had bought them both a hot meal at a seaside restaurant. His father didn't mind the lost time. He had a deep suspicion that Pierce Landcross was somewhere in town. And with no more ferries leaving until morning, they had the entire night to search. Once they arrived at the family estate, his father would order a massive manhunt for Landcross. While that went on, Ivor would be soaking in a hot bath, drinking away his memories.

After their meal, they resumed their journey to the castle. When they came to York Street, a beggar appeared between his and his father's horse with a filthy hand outstretched. "Spare a copper, sirs?" the beggar asked, walking alongside the horse.

Before his father had the chance to tell the man to piss off, the beggar said, "Ooh. Blimey! You almost smell as bad as that young feller who just came through here."

Norwich snatched the beggar by the lapel and yanked him forward. "What young fellow?" he demanded. "What did he look like? Come on, man, speak up!"

The beggar, not expecting this manhandling, quivered and stuttered when he spoke. "He . . . he was around my height, smelled like rotting death."

"Did he have a scar across his throat?" Norwich asked, shaking him a tad.

"I . . . I dunno, sir. It was dark, you see."

Norwich looked to Ivor for help. The man had the

mind of an evil genius who understood how to use fear as a weapon. At times, however, his brilliance refused to see the most obvious solution. That was where his drunken "loyal" son came in.

Ivor rolled his eyes and asked with a sigh, "Do you know *where* he went?"

"Yes, sir, he . . . he went to the Hotel Joubert, down on Bridge Road."

Norwich threw the beggar away and he fell against Ivor's leg.

"Get off," Ivor said, kicking viciously.

"Let's go," Norwich ordered.

Exhausted, Ivor followed.

"Yes, sir," the desk clerk at Hotel Joubert said when Joaquin described Pierce to her. "That man checked in about an hour ago."

"What room is he in?" Archie asked.

"I'm sorry but I cannot give out guests' room numbers."

Archie was going to say something to her when Joaquin stepped in. "You're lucky to be alive, you know."

The clerk turned her big eyes on him. "Come again?"

"The man you gave a room to. You're lucky he didn't hurt you. He must be calm now."

"What are you talking about, sir?"

Archie seemed to understand his strategy and said, "Yes, you are fortunate, indeed. I'm his doctor. Doctor Laird Harris. You see, he's escaped from Beldam. He's mentally disturbed and requires medical attention."

The clerk blinked and looked between the two men. She took a step back as if they were dangerous. Her stiff pose began to waver. "What was he in for?"

"Evaluation of the psyche," Joaquin said. "He needs to be contained immediately, before the killer in him resurfaces again."

The clerk placed a hand on her chest, trying her damnedest to stay calm. "Before the *killer* in him does *what*? Are you saying that he's possessed?"

Joaquin found her distress amusing. "Indeed. We've been tracking him since he brutally murdered several people in Newport."

She seemed reluctant to believe them. But as her gaze flicked over Archie's expensive attire and Joaquin's uniform, her eyes opened wide.

To press a little more fear into her, Joaquin added, "He's a dangerous man, ma'am. No telling what unspeakable acts he'll commit against your guests or staff if they cross him during one of his dark moods."

"Ah," she began when her eyes shifted to someone behind them, "Willard."

"Yes, Mrs. Brome," a bellboy said. He carried a set of folded clothes in one hand and a dapper black coat and vest on a hanger in the other.

"Those belong to our guest in Room 119, yes?"

"Yes, ma'am," the young man said. "Just retrieved them from the cleaners, I did."

"Would you show these gentlemen to that room, please?"

"Certainly, ma'am," the chipper lad said. "This way, gentlemen."

Archie and Joaquin followed the bellboy down the first floor hallway, listening to him ramble on and on about the clothes he carried. "The cleaner said it was a bit of a challenge to get the smell out. Said it'd cost less to toss 'em out and get new clothes rather than to clean them." He stopped at the door to room number 119. "Guess the gent is fond of them, I suppose." He folded the coat and vest over his arm that held the other clothing and knocked hard. "Sir, I have your clothes ready."

"Aye, c'mon in, lad," Pierce said from the other side.

Hearing his brother's voice caused sweat to form on Joaquin's skin. Ever since that night when he'd left Pierce dying on the forest floor, he'd wanted nothing more than to take it back. As children, he'd been willing to die to protect his little brother, so his actions that night had surprised him. He blamed it on his accursed beast. It had been the first time the beast had come out, committing an act that he'd otherwise would never have done. Deep down, he wanted Pierce's forgiveness more than anything in the world, even more than a pardon from the Queen, but how could he explain to anyone what dwelled inside him?

The bellboy unlocked the door and was about to enter the room when Joaquin and Archie grabbed the clothes from him. "We'll take it from here," Archie said.

The bellboy started to protest when Joaquin tapped his finger to his nose. "Official business," he said, slipping inside the room and closing the door in the lad's face.

He reached under his coat for his spare pistol that Archie had failed to find on him, just in case Pierce went mental when he saw him. The room, however, was vacant.

"Just leave the clothes on the bed, mate," came Pierce's voice from another room.

Archie threw the clothing onto the bed and headed for the adjoining room. Joaquin briefly scanned the place until he spied a satchel on a small table. He looked inside it to find the book. He also found some masks, but saw no value in them. He slipped the journal out of the bag and left the room.

The bath water had cooled, which made the bellboy's return most welcome. Pierce had scrubbed himself clean, shaved, and applied fresh ointment to his burned flesh. He'd been soaking for nearly an hour, and had even caught a few minutes of sleep. It made getting blasted by that stink bomb *almost* worthwhile.

But his time of rest wasn't completely tranquil. Seeing Joaquin today had only reminded him of that bloody dreadful day in London when they were kids.

The gypsies had arrived in the city for the music, and crafts festival, where people from all around gathered to sell jewelry, play music, display their artwork, and perform small shows.

Festival season was always the best time of year for the gypsies when it came to making money. During spring and summer, they worked tirelessly to have enough to survive the upcoming winter.

This was the first time they'd come to London without Grandmother Fey. She had become gravely ill years back and had later succumbed to her illness.

In Abney Park, Pierce's family had set up on the edge of the cemetery on Stroke Newington Church Street. Pierce, only eight at the time, and Joaquin had gone to the candy store and afterwards went to explore the cemetery. After spending some time playing games around the tombstones, they headed back to their encampment. When they arrived they were horrified at what they saw. The area was littered with broken wood from the stage and torn props and clothing. Even their organ was toppled over and smashed to bits. There was no sign of the gypsies, only a pack of constables and a woman holding a black lace parasol.

"There!" the woman shouted, pointing at the boys. "Officers, there! That's them!"

They had no chance to run before they were apprehended. Their bags of candy fell to the ground.

"Get your hands off me," Joaquin demanded.

"Search them," a heavyset constable ordered as he approached with the woman. He had a thick mustache and a shiny tin badge pinned on his chest.

The officers' hands rifled through Pierce's clothes.

"Stop it!" he hollered when a hand searched too close to his crotch.

"Found it," an officer said.

"Give that back," Joaquin cried, trying to snatch back his compass from the officer.

It was the little brass compass that he always carried around with him. He had it for as long as Pierce could remember.

The fat constable looked at it, and then at the woman. She was a tall lady, wearing a sleeveless taffeta dress, black lace gloves, a hat, and purple-tinted spectacles.

"Is this it, ma'am?" the constable asked.

She looked at it and then at the boys. Pierce and his brother's reflection showed in her large round violet glasses.

"It is," she claimed. She pointed at Pierce. "This one here distracted me by asking if he could dance for a penny. I didn't have the heart to turn him away, so I took a penny from my pocketbook and allowed him to dance for me. After he was gone, I discovered that my compass and all my money was missing."

As she spoke, Joaquin examined her intently, as if trying to place her face, while the mustached officer eyed the scattered candy on the ground. "Aye," he said, "and I can only imagine where they spent it."

"It seems as though this one," the woman continued,

referring to Joaquin, "was the one who actually stole from me."

"Working as a team, eh?" the officer said. "That's what these gypsies do."

"We didn't steal anything," Pierce declared. "Where are our parents?"

"Those nasty gypsies that were here?" the fat officer said. "Run out of the city, by now. We received complaints of thievery and hustling."

"That's a lie." Pierce seethed.

"What was that you said, you little bastard?" the officer growled, leaning in nose to nose with him.

Pierce saw the man's eyes turn red, like ink spilling from the pupils and spreading over the entire eyeballs. Only the pupils and veins, which were now black, remained untainted. Pierce looked at his brother, who was gawking at the other constables. They all had the same eerily changing eyes.

"Officer," the young woman said.

The constable rose to his full height, blinking until his eyes returned to normal. "Yes, ma'am?" he said, like an obedient servant.

"Since they're just children, I do not wish to press charges."

"Are you sure, ma'am? Some time locked away in Newgate might do these guttersnipes some good."

Pierce had heard enough stories about Newgate Prison to know that he never wanted to go there.

"I am, Constable," she said. "However, I don't believe they ought to be allowed to return to that family of thieves and beggars they were spawned from. Isn't there a place they can be taken?"

The husky officer with the shiny badge rubbed his chin in thought. "I believe there is. The Foundling

Hospital Orphanage. They'll take these troublemaking brats in. Put them to work, they will."

"You can't," Joaquin shouted, desperately trying to break free from the man holding him. "We haven't done anything."

"That will do just fine, Officer," the woman said. "A little discipline will serve them well, I think. Good day." With that, she turned and walked away.

Pierce sighed. But those days were over. Now he had other problems to worry about.

Under the washcloth that rested over his face, he sensed a presence in the room.

"Is this where my money went?" Archie asked.

"Fuckin' hell!" Pierce exclaimed, snatching away the washcloth. He nearly went for his gun belt hanging on the doorknob, but Archie had him dead to rights with his own pistol.

"I thought you were going back to France," Archie said.

Pierce narrowed his eyes at him. "Once I get what I came for, I will."

"Meaning the Toymaker?" the lad inquired.

Pierce tossed the washcloth into the water. "What are you doing here? Came for the masks, I reckon?"

"Clover is in danger."

Pierce wrapped his arms around his knees. "What happened?"

"Your damn brother, that's what happened. He kidnapped her and brought her to Norwich Castle."

"Wait a tick," Pierce replied, holding up a hand. "Did you say Norwich *Castle*?"

"Yes, it's here on the island. It has been in our family for centuries."

"Right," Pierce grumbled. "A castle. Bloody perfect. In any case, she's safe there, yeah?"

"Pierce, your brother turned her in to be used as slave labor," Archie said with malice.

It was the first time Archie had called him by his first name.

"Well, go get her out then," Pierce retorted. "Surely, the guards there will recognize you."

"I haven't been there in many years. Before my mother kill—" Archie stopped, shying away from the memory. His pained expression betrayed him. "I can't risk them thinking I'm an impostor. I might be killed or imprisoned. My father is very upset with Clover at the moment, and when he's upset, people get hurt. *Badly.*"

"What makes you think I can help?" Pierce asked, not liking this conversation one bit.

"I don't know," the lad said in a testy tone. "We can think of a plan together." He then threw in. "You owe her, Pierce Landcross. She saved your life more than once, remember?"

Pierce gritted his teeth and huffed vexingly. "Bastard. Are my clothes out there?"

"Yes."

He stood up and grabbed a towel. "This better not be a trap."

"If I wanted you prisoner, I'd put this gun to your head and put you in shackles." Archie holstered his weapon and stepped out of the room to let Pierce dry himself.

"What do you propose we—" Archie started to say from the other room, but then stopped, leaving the sentence in limbo.

"What?" Pierce demanded, stepping out of the WC, carrying his gun belt while rubbing the towel over his wet hair. The lad was scanning the room as if searching for something. "What are you looking for?" he asked, reaching for his clothes on the bed.

"Sorry?" Archie asked, turning back to him. "Oh, um, nothing. I'm not looking for anything."

Pierce sniffed the clothes and relished the fresh scent of his newly washed duds. "Don't think I've ever had clothes so clean before."

"Congratulations," Archie said. "What do you propose we do?"

Pierce mulled it over while he put on new undergarments. "That arsehole brother of mine turned the little lass over as slave labor, you say?"

"Yes. Apparently, my father has converted the castle into a weapons factory, which remains at a standstill until Peachtree and the book arrive."

Pierce fastened his gun belt around his pinstripe breeches, leaving the suspenders hanging over his sides as he normally did. "Sounds like the whole place will be heavily guarded then, eh?"

"Most likely, yeah."

Pierce returned to his thoughts. Even if they managed to enter the castle through deception, he didn't see how they could rescue Clover from wherever she was being held, nor get out without drawing attention to themselves. Also, there was a chance that Tarquin Norwich was either there or on his way. He envisioned Archie turning against him if they encountered his father, especially if it meant saving his sister. In order to push toward a successful rescue, they would need help.

As he pulled his shirt on, he knew of only one person who was equipped for what they needed. The price, however, for this kind of help from this particular individual would be the ultimate one for him.

Damn that girl for saving my life! He buttoned his vest savagely, nearly tearing one button free.

He slid the drawer of the bedside table open, where he'd stashed the coin purse he'd stolen from Archie and took out a silver shilling. On the bright side, Pierce knew what he'd have to give in order to obtain help from this person and therefore had already thought of how to get around it. He didn't fancy the idea of putting himself in such a risky situation, yet to stick it to that bastard, Norwich, he'd pay just about any price.

"Let's go visit a magician, eh?" he said, taking his coat off the hanger.

"A magician?" Archie said, brows hiked up to his hairline.

Pierce headed for the door as he slipped his arms through the coat's sleeves. "Just follow. Don't ask too many questions."

He put the coin in his pocket and opened the door, then suddenly stopped. The feeling that someone else had been in the room rushed through him. His eyes went immediately to the satchel on the table.

"What?" Archie asked.

Pierce studied the satchel. It sat in the exact same spot as he'd left it, the flap still buckled.

"We have to go," Archie nagged.

He shook off the urge to check inside the bag, dismissing it as paranoia, and left the room. He locked the door and started down the hall when Archie said, "Maybe we ought to go out the back way."

"Why?"

"Uh, I might have led the desk clerk to believe that you're a madman."

"*What*? Why the bloody hell did you tell her that?" Archie was about to answer when he waved him off. "Never mind. Let's just crack on, eh?"

They left through the back and headed toward Medina Road. The wagon no longer sat in the middle of the street, but had been moved and parked off to the side; the horses had been unhitched and most likely taken to a stable for the night. The crowd, of course, had vacated.

Pierce reached up to the wagon's door with a shaking fist, ready to knock, when Archie said, "Do you know this man? And how will he help us?"

Archie's sudden inquiry made him jump. The danger he was about to place himself in had frayed his nerves.

"Fuckin' hell," he said through gritted teeth. "Yes, I know 'im. And once you meet 'im, you'll understand, all right?"

"Who's out there?" someone asked before opening the door.

Pierce again jumped and felt his insides dry up. He began to tremble. His voice was dry when he spoke. "I wish to see Robin the Magnificent?"

"The master is not receiving guests at the moment, señor," the Spaniard said. "If you want an autograph, then return for tomorrow night's show."

The short man was about to close the door when a voice from inside the wagon said, "Wait, Ramirez. Allow the gentleman in, please."

Ramirez turned back to Pierce and moved aside. "Come in, señor."

Pierce gulped hard as he climbed up the short steps leading into the large wagon. To his relief, when he entered, Archie was right there beside him.

Despite his terror, he was impressed with the size of the wagon. The inside was large, crammed with all sorts of things. Clothes and costumes hung on a long iron rod, stretching from the front of the wagon to the back. There were long shelves attached to the wall, housing many knickknacks. The floor was old dark wood, and gold decorative trim traced out the ceiling, with the air smelling of incense. He spotted an ancient longbow resting on hooks on the wall and couldn't help but reach over and touch it.

Sitting in front of a mirror, with a pair of green glass lanterns mounted above, was the magician. He was dressed in a dark red robe; shoulder length hair tied back, pulling every strand away from his pale face. He was wiping the blush from one cheek when he spied Pierce's reflection. His grin split his face.

"Pierce Landcross," the magician said in his magnificent voice. After all these years, the authority in his tone hadn't withered.

Pierce fixed a smile to his own face and said, "'Ello, Robin. It's been a long time, eh?"

The man turned in his chair, his smile widening, showing his teeth. "Has it?"

"Well, perhaps not for you," Pierce replied.

"No," Robin said.

Robin the Magnificent was not a tall man. In fact, he stood a little shorter then Pierce. That didn't stop Pierce from holding his breath when he rose, however.

"Em, nice wagon," he muttered.

"Ah, thank you. I had it commissioned in Romania. It's a Burton Vardo."

"We could've used these in the family," Pierce remarked.

"If the Romanians continue to manufacture them, I'm sure their uses will legion." Finally, he shifted his bright blues over to the Spaniard. "Ramirez, would you be so kind as to go to the restaurant across the way and fetch some hot water for tea?"

"Sí, mi señor," Ramirez said with a slight bow. He

plucked a kettle from one of the shelves and headed for the door.

As his servant left, the Magician gestured to a small red table. "He'll not be long. The restaurant always has boiling water ready. Sit, please. We have much to discuss."

Pierce looked at Archie, who kept his silence. His expression, though, told of his confusion.

"Aye," Pierce said, "s'pose we do."

He moved over to the table and sat on a wooden stool. Archie sat beside him, and Robin took a seat directly in front of them. Robin folded his hands on the table and said, "I see that you still have it."

Pierce looked down at the coin hanging on the chain around his neck. He folded it tightly in his trembling hand and turned his chin up, meeting the magician's gaze. "Of course," he said with a forced grin, trying to keep things light.

"How do you two know each other?" Archie finally chimed in.

"You should tell him," Robin said.

Pierce sighed. "Everything?"

The magician nodded slowly. "Why not? I sense he is the trusting sort."

Although he disagreed, Pierce had to admit that when it came to reading a person's true nature, Robin was always spot on.

"All right," he said, steering his attention to Archie. "A couple of years back, when I was twenty-five, I broke into his house in Nottingham."

"Don't be shy; tell him what you were after," Robin said.

Pierce cleared his throat. He could really use that tea right about now, with some brandy in it as well. "It was rumored that the master of the estate," he gestured toward the magician, "owned the thirty pieces of silver. I thought I could get a pretty penny for it."

"Wait," Archie said. "Thirty pieces of silver? *The* thirty pieces of silver? From Judas?"

"The very same," Robin said. "I acquired the coins many years ago when I was in the Holy Land."

"The Holy Land? When were you there?" Archie asked.

"When I fought in the Crusades, my boy."

Archie's face went slack, his mouth hanging open. Pierce couldn't blame the boy. He decided to stop beating around the bloody bush and just tell him.

"Archie Norwich," he said, "meet Robin of Locksley, vampire."

Chapter Nineteen
The Deadly Debt

"Yes, Lord Norwich," Mrs. Brome said at the front desk, "that man checked into Room 119 a little over an hour ago. But you see, he—"

"Where is the room?" Norwich demanded sharply.

Mrs. Brome quivered. The night was shaping into one of the most unusual and frightening events of her life. "It . . . it's down the hall, on the left." She pointed to the corridor on the other side of the lobby.

"Give me the key," he demanded.

She handed the room's spare key over to him without protest and kept her mouth shut as Lord Norwich stormed away. When he and his guards disappeared down the hall, she released the breath she had been holding. After tonight, she wanted to find a new job.

Norwich marched down the hall, scanning each room number as he passed. He arrived at number 119 and jabbed the key into the lock.

"I want him alive," he ordered.

The instant the lock clicked, he swung the door open and hurried inside. Everyone poured in and began searching the spacious suite.

"No one here, sir," a guard informed as he came out of another room.

Norwich spied a satchel on a table and his heart knocked hard against his ribcage. He stepped toward it and unbuckled the flap.

The masks!

Slowly he reached in, biting his lip as he brought two out. They vibrated against his fingertips.

"The water in the tub is a bit warm, Father," Ivor reported. "He must have just left."

Norwich had just about everything he needed: the book and the masks, even prisoners waiting to build his weapons. Yet he still needed the Toymaker and there was only one person who could help find him.

"He'll return," he said. "And when he does, we'll be waiting."

"Norwich?" Robin said to Archie. "Are you any relation to Tarquin Norwich?"

Throwing the question at the lad, who was still reeling from Pierce's introduction, was like asking a fingerless person to play piano. The lad just couldn't get the words out to answer.

"I-I-I . . . Why do you ask?" Archie stammered.

Pierce watched Robin study the lad. As the vampire's ancient eyes dug into the youth's soul, Pierce slipped his hand to the butt of his Oak Leaf pistol.

"Take your hand off your gun, Landcross," Robin said. "This young man possesses a good heart."

The vampire shifted his eyes back to Pierce, who slowly removed his shaky hand from the gun.

"I'm sorry," Archie said, regaining the ability to speak. "You're Robin of Locksley? Robin *Hood*?"

"Also a vampire," Pierce reminded.

"I was, yes. Now I am Robin the Magnificent," Robin said in a theatrical tone.

"And Landcross tried to steal from you." A statement, not a question.

"Indeed. I caught him at it. He had my coins and was about to make a hasty exit, but I grabbed him."

"He lifted me right off the ground, he did," Pierce said, looking at his hands now folded on the table, trying to keep them steady. "I shattered the coin box over his head and that's when I realized."

"What happened?" Archie asked, shifting on his stool.

"The coins burned me," Robin explained, showing a few scars on his face. "You see, before Judas killed himself, he cursed the thirty pieces. When he died, he came back as an immortal—a vampire."

"Was he the first?"

"No, silly boy, vampires had been around forever. It was the chief priests who turned Judas, wanting him in their fold. But Judas' guilt over his betrayal of Jesus ran deep, and in the light of his first sunrise, he allowed himself to be engulfed in flames."

Archie gawked at Robin.

"So the legend goes," Robin added. "I do not know if it's true. I wasn't there."

"Then the coins are harmful to your kind?" Archie asked.

"Even more so then any other silver. They can even scar us." He again pointed to the marks on his face. "Just having one of the coins in your possession will keep you safe from ever being touched by a vampire."

Archie turned to Pierce, looking at the necklace he wore. "I see. So you got away with them?"

"No," Pierce said, "just the one. Robin was crippled long enough for me to grab a single coin and flee."

"Who was it that turned you?" Archie asked Robin.

"A monk who'd been searching for the coins for centuries. His search led him to me. I tried fighting but he easily subdued me. At the time, I had my lands back, and Marian and I were married. We even had a child," he said soberly, with a hint of longing. "Being the legend I was, the demon monk couldn't resist forcing me to drink from his veins under the threat that he would kill my family if I refused."

"Why did he want the coins?" Archie asked.

"To destroy them," Robin said. "In doing so, it would lift Judas' curse."

"What would happen then?"

"Silver would once again become just another metal to vampires," Pierce answered.

"Yes," Robin said. "Shortly after turning me, the monk demanded that the coins be brought to him. I did so, fearing for my wife and babe. I sensed a danger in the coins that I had never noticed before. When I came close enough to him, I grabbed one, burning myself, and crammed it down his throat. I watched him run out of the house and into the forest, bursting into flames as he went."

He smiled grimly at the memory. "I knew the racket had awakened Marian, but before she came down to investigate, I fled after the vampire who'd made me. I found his charred corpse miles from the house. I ripped open his throat and snatched the coin out of it." He raised his hand to show the burn marks on his palm. "I returned home only to retrieve the rest of the coins. I could no longer stay with my love, nor leave the thirty pieces to be discovered by another immortal. On that night, I left Nottingham."

"You never went back?" Archie asked. "Not even to see how your own child was doing?"

"I saw him once when he was a young man living in Paris," Robin said fondly. "However, I wanted Marian to remember the man I was and not the demon I had become."

"Why did you not destroy the coins? Free vampires

from the curse of silver?"

"Vampires need a weakness. More than they already have, in my opinion. It helps even out the order of things."

"Really?" Archie said, unconvinced. He stood up. "Well, Mr. Locksley, lovely meeting you, but we must be go . . ."

Before he could finish speaking, Robin snatched him by the wrist with a preternatural quickness and thrust him back down into his seat. Alarmed, Archie grabbed Pierce by the arm with his other hand.

"No need to rush off," Robin said as the door opened and Ramirez entered the room. "Ah, tea time."

Robin rose and took the rest of the tea set off a shelf. He placed it on the table and lifted the lid off the teapot to pour the hot water into it from the kettle.

"Tell me, Pierce, why did you come?"

Ramirez set the kettle back on the shelf and went over to a cot across from a coffin at the back of the wagon. He plucked a guitar off the wall and lay down on the bed, strumming.

"We need your help," Pierce said.

"*We*? Since when is it 'we'?"

Pierce turned to Archie and nudged him with his elbow. "Tell 'im."

Archie looked him dead in the eyes. "Right," he said weakly. He cleared his throat and said to Robin with renewed focus in his tone, "My sister, Clover, is in danger. She's being held in my father's castle."

"You know a thing or two about bustin' into castles, don't you, Rob?" Pierce said jocularly.

Robin gave him a level look before licking one of his long fangs. Pierce gulped audibly.

With a loud click of his tongue, Robin said, "I

suppose I do. What sort of danger is she in?"

"She was taken by Pierce's brother and turned over to use as slave labor to build weapons for my father."

"Yes," Robin said, stirring the tea leaves. "Tarquin Norwich. I have been suspicious of that man for many years. I'm very aware of what he's capable of doing, as I'm sure you are, young man. I came here to the Isle of Wight to investigate what he was up to. It was not until last night that we discovered part of his plan."

"What will you do, then?" Archie asked. "Kill him yourself? Drink his blood?"

"I have thought about it on numerous occasions. He most certainly deserves it. Not to mention that I have been dining on the blood of animals for weeks now," He glanced at Pierce with hunger in his eyes, "which isn't at all fulfilling. However, I cannot, for he has protection."

"Protection?" Pierce muttered.

"If he returns and finds my sister at the castle, he'll murder her," Archie said in earnest. "She apparently helped this idiot—"

"Hey!" Pierce said defensively.

"—to escape him, and I have no doubt that she'll die by his hand if they encounter each other."

"Is that so?" Robin said, taking the spoon out and pouring tea into cups. "And what of you, Landcross?"

"What of me?"

"You brought him to me asking for help when you didn't have to. You must care for this girl, as well?"

"I owe her, all right? Just repaying my debt, is all."

"Ah. I see. Well, Mr. Norwich, will you kindly excuse us for a moment?"

Archie had just lifted his cup to his lips. "Pardon?"

"You may take the tea with you, of course," Robin

said. "No sense in wasting good tea, eh?" To Ramirez, he said, "You too, my old friend. I must speak to Landcross alone."

"Sí, mi señor," the Spaniard said, getting up with his guitar in hand. He walked over to the door and said to Archie, "Come, I will play for you."

Archie looked at Pierce as if asking for permission to leave. Pierce nodded, and without protest, Archie left with the Spaniard, carrying the teacup as he went. Pierce took a drink from his own, trying to hold himself together. The effort didn't prevent him from jumping at the sound of the door closing.

"You were going to shoot me if I attacked that boy, weren't you?" Robin said.

"Come again?" Pierce said, lowering his teacup.

"When I peered into his soul, you were ready to defend him if I felt like he took too much after his father."

"It's not him I aim to protect."

"The girl, then? She needs her brother, yes?"

Pierce had walked into that one.

Robin stood, causing Pierce to jump to his feet. As the vampire walked around the table, Pierce struggled to maintain control of his bladder.

"Do you remember what I told you in York?" Robin asked.

"Aye," Pierce said softly, backing away. "Like it was yesterday. You said that the moment the coin was out of my possession that you'd have me. That's why I nailed a hole in it and have worn it around my neck ever since."

"Yes. Then you know what I want in exchange for my assistance." Robin gestured to the coin with his pale hand. "That . . . off."

Pierce's back hit the wall. Even with the protection of the coin, the fear made him lightheaded, to the brink of fainting. "Aw, come off it, Rob, you're not still sore about that night, eh?

"That," the vampire repeated, "off."

Chapter Twenty
Getting Out

Clover opened her eyes. It proved a bit of a challenge for they were crusted shut. Thanks to the kind woman who'd held her snug in the blanket, she had gotten warm and her clothing was dry. Regardless, her body felt wrecked. The burn in her chest set her lungs aflame whenever she inhaled. The pounding in her head clubbed her brain every time she moved. A tickle in her throat caused her to cough, which sparked harsher ones to follow.

"There, there, child," the woman said, cradling her in her thick arms. The woman had nothing at her disposal to soothe her illness other then kind words. Clover welcomed them and allowed herself to be rocked a little while longer.

"What a cruel, cruel thing to do, locking a child up in such a place," another woman remarked. "May Tarquin Norwich burn in hell for this."

"Aye, Ruth," the busty woman said, rocking Clover. "He has most certainly gone mad."

While they spoke ill about her warmongering father, an idea came to mind. "This castle has secret passageways," she said in a scratchy voice.

"What did you say, child?" the woman holding her asked.

Clover pulled herself away from the woman, already missing the comfort of her loving embrace. She cleared her sore throat and said, "If we can get to the hallway above us, there is a hidden door that will take us into a secret passageway. We might be able to get out that way."

"How do you know that?" the other woman asked.

"My mother was a servant here when I was younger," she lied. "I used to play inside the tunnels."

In truth, the passageways had been known to the Norwich family for generations. One of her vague memories as a child was of her and Archie playing hide-and-seek in a maze of passageways that webbed throughout the entire building. The closest entrance from the dungeon was located in the upstairs corridor, next to a stuffed wolf.

"Are you sure, lass?" the matronly woman asked with a hint of fear and excitement in her voice.

"Yes, and I have a plan. Just follow my lead."

Minutes later, a guard came running to the cell in response to frantic screams.

"Good God, woman," he said to the busty lady. "What is it?"

"She's not breathing," the woman shouted with tears streaming down her face. "I think she's dead!"

"What?" the young guard said, peering into the cell where Clover's lifeless body lay on the floor. "Bloody hell," he said, taking out his keys.

He unlocked the door and entered the cell, apparently unconcerned about the women. He approached Clover and stopped a few feet away from her. "What happened?"

Ruth, who stood near the door, moved silently toward him from behind and pulled his flintlock pistol from its holster. His reaction wasn't quick, and he froze when she pressed the muzzle against his head.

"Move and I'll put a lead ball in your brain," she said.

"Take it easy," he said, raising his hands.

Clover coughed and got to her feet. The expression

of disbelief on the guard's face caused her to smile. She snatched the keys from his hand and said, "Let's go."

After locking the guard in the cell and releasing the other prisoners, they all headed upstairs. To her relief, no other guards were in the corridor, which gave them clear passage to the stuffed wolf. She always hated that dead thing. Archie had told her that it had been hunted down and killed by their great, great grandfather. Age had caught up to the old hide and the fur was now straggly. Dry dead skin around its glass eyes was peeling upward.

When she reached it now, she ignored the hideous thing and pushed in a large stone on the wall beside it. The stone, wide but only an inch deep, slid in and over. She pushed it into a carved out slot in a thicker stone next to it. A cool musty breeze blew over her as the entrance to the tunnel opened up.

"Come on," she whispered as she ducked inside and led the way into the darkness.

Pierce stepped out of the Burton wagon. He could hear the Spaniard playing his guitar and singing a song in Spanish. He looked around and found both Ramirez and Archie sitting on the wagon's roof.

"Arch," Pierce called, trying to contain his anger, "let's go get your sister, eh?"

"He's going to do it?" Archie asked, setting his cup of tea aside and climbing down the ladder running alongside of the wagon. "He's going to help?"

"Aye," he grumbled, keeping his back to the lad.

"Incredible," Archie said, coming up behind him on the sidewalk. "What did you say to convince him?"

He wanted to throw a punch at Archie so hard that he'd break the lad's teeth. If it wasn't for him, he'd be on a ship sailing to some place far and safe away from anyone who knew his name. Instead, he'd been dragged back into a country with people who either wanted to hang him or force him to make deals with legendary demons.

Then he thought about that even more. It wasn't the lad's fault, really. It was Tarquin Norwich who'd set this entire nightmare into motion. Archie, and even Clover, were simply puppets dancing at his command. That thought kept him from striking the lad. Barely.

"I told him he could turn you into a vampire in exchange for his help."

"You did *what*?" Archie yelled so loud that Ramirez stopped in mid verse.

Pierce secretly grinned. It wasn't broken teeth, but the lad's reaction was a good second best. "You want to save your sister, yeah?"

"Yes, but . . . but . . ." Archie sputtered.

"You want her safe and sound, eh?"

"I do . . . but . . ." Archie faltered in what he was about to say when he realized there were other people within earshot. He took a step up to Pierce and whispered to him, "I don't want to be a vampire."

"It's done," Pierce said with fake sincerity from over his shoulder.

Before Archie mouthed another word, the door to the wagon opened and Robin emerged, dressed in a long black coat and gloves, a green velvet vest, a linen shirt and dark brown breeches.

"No hat with that outfit?" Pierce asked as Robin stepped onto the sidewalk.

"It will only get lost during the rescue," Robin explained.

"Are you going out, *mi señor*?" Ramirez inquired.

"*Sí, mi amigo*," Robin said, looking up at his

servant. "I shall not be long."

"Shall I come with you?"

"No, stay with the wagon and have everything ready for our departure when I return." He turned to Pierce. "*We* will be leaving tonight."

"Umm, Mr. Locksley," Archie began.

"I will meet you both at the castle," Robin said as he marched off, disappearing into a nearby alleyway.

"Wait," Archie said, running after him.

Pierce stayed in place and watched the lad follow the vampire. A moment later, Archie reappeared, shaking his head. "He's gone."

"Let's go," Pierce said, walking away. He took out the silver shilling from his pocket and looked at it. He hoped to find a hammer and nail in the stable when they retrieved their mounts.

The lit torches at the gate announced the border of the castle's grounds.

"What do we do?" Archie asked, staring at the guards.

"Wait," Pierce said.

He and Archie stayed saddled on their horses far enough away so not to be detected by the night guards. Yet, considering what was about to happen to them, it mattered little if they were spotted.

"Wait for what?" Archie asked.

"That," Pierce said, pointing ahead.

A shadow emerged next to one of the guards, and in a blink, that shadow had him down. The second guard leapt into action and aimed his musket at the assailant when the shadow jumped, taking him down as well.

"Well, that was easy enough," Pierce said, riding on.

They completed the distance to the gate where

Robin stood, wiping blood from his mouth with a handkerchief. Pierce had no idea if the renewed color in him was due to the feeding he'd just accomplished or the firelight from the torches. He tried to ignore the bodies lying on the ground, not because they were dead, but because it served as a reminder of what Robin wanted to do to *him*.

"The gate is open," Robin announced, tucking the bloodstained handkerchief into his breast pocket in a poised manner.

Pierce and Archie dismounted and the three entered the inner courtyard of the castle.

"You there," another guard at the front door leading into the castle called, "state your business!"

The poor sod didn't have the foggiest notion about the murders just beyond the front gate. Pierce almost felt sorry for the wanker.

The man let out a small cry as Robin latched his teeth into the guard's neck. It happened so quickly that only one second earlier, the vampire had been standing between Pierce and Archie. The guard struggled before he fell to his knees. Only when he ceased to move did Robin release him. The vampire rose and turned to face the stunned men.

"Christ almighty," Archie whispered.

"That's the sort of thing you'll be doing soon enough," Pierce quipped.

Archie looked at him with wide eyes, his face pale.

"Keep your head in the game, gentlemen," Robin said, pushing the double doors open, breaking the thick bar that locked them on the other side. "We have only just begun."

"Halt!" someone on the inner curtain wall shouted from above, aiming a musket at them.

Pierce pulled his gun and took a potshot at him. He

missed, naturally, but it was enough to scare the guard and ruin his own shot.

"Get inside," Robin ordered, breaking the bar completely in half with a deafening crack.

"Sound the alarm!" the guard above yelled while reloading his musket.

Robin snatched the last man he'd killed and swung the body, throwing it toward the screaming man. The guard was struck by the corpse and fell back.

"Incredible," Archie said. "Can you also fly?"

"No, but very close to it," Robin said before he rushed off for the wall. When he neared the barrier, he leapt high and caught the stones near the top. He then scaled the wall and attacked the dazed guard standing atop it. Screams followed Pierce and Archie as they raced inside.

"Where would the prisoners be?" Pierce asked.

"The dungeon," Archie answered, hurrying down a corridor.

"Dungeon? Really?" Pierce huffed.

They scurried through the old hallways. Stomping footsteps coming their way got Archie to shove Pierce into a room.

"Hands off," Pierce ordered.

"Shush," Archie hissed, moving away from the opening and into the shadows.

A handful of guards ran by the door, never even looking into the room.

"This place is gonna be on lockdown soon enough," Pierce whispered. "We'll never get to the other side of the castle with these blokes buzzing about."

"Follow me," Archie said, leaving the room and going back into the hallway.

Pierce sighed irritably and followed him. After

turning the corner where the guards had come from, the lad went to a stone in the wall and pushed it in.

"A secret passageway?" Pierce said as the stone moved to the side and vanished within a slit carved into the stone block beside it.

"This will take us there," Archie said, crawling in.

Pierce shrugged and went in after him. The narrow and low ceiling of the tunnel forced him to hunch over and walk slightly sideways as they made their way between the walls.

"The entire castle has tunnels," Archie explained as if Pierce had asked the question about them. "There's at least forty ways in and out of here."

"Grand," he said apathetically.

They snaked their way through the castle and finally came out beside a stuffed wolf. Pierce snarled at the dead thing, then followed Archie down the hall to a spiral staircase. When they arrived in the dungeon, they discovered that all the cells were empty.

"This is just bloody perfect!" Pierce complained. "There ain't no one even here."

"No, they have to be," Archie said in disbelief. "There isn't any other place for prisoners to be."

"Oi, who's out there?" someone called from the cell near the back wall. A hand appeared through the bars. "Come get me out, eh?"

Archie rushed over to the cell. "Where are the prisoners?"

"They have escaped! Overpowered me, they did."

Archie looked over to Pierce, then rushed at him and said as he passed, "They must've taken the tunnels out."

"Then why didn't we run into them on the way here?" Pierce asked.

"I told you, the entire place is riddled with tunnels. They most likely took another route. Let's head back in to see where they might have gone."

Clover pushed another stone in and slid it sideways. She stepped out and found she was in the kitchen.

"Hurry," she said, waving everyone out. "Go out through the door over there. It leads to the garden."

Everyone clambered out of the tunnel and headed for the door at the back of the kitchen. The hefty woman was the last one in line and was crawling out when her wide hips caught in the opening.

"I'm stuck," she whispered, trying to force her way through.

Everyone else had already left the kitchen and vanished into the darkness of the night outside. Clover took the woman by the wrists and pulled, but the woman seemed completely locked in. Clover gritted her teeth and pulled harder when she was yanked up by someone.

"You there!" growled the cruel maid who had nearly scrubbed her skin off during her bath. "What are you doing out of your cage, you stupid girl? You're coming with me."

She wasn't going to let this woman take her anywhere, so she sank her teeth into the maid's arm as hard as she could. The woman let out a howl but didn't let her go. Instead, she raised her hand, ready to strike Clover, when someone beside her exclaimed, "Don't you *dare!*"

The maid craned her head around, only to be punched in the face by the busty woman, who had finally gotten herself out of the tunnel. The crack made from the impact made Clover cringe. The maid went down, blood gushing from her nose.

"You all right?" the matronly prisoner asked Clover, shaking her hurt hand.

Clover nodded. "Yes. Come on; we need to catch up with the others."

They went outside to where everyone was standing around a man holding a gas powered lantern.

"Ah," the man said when he saw Clover. "You must be the young lady we've come to save."

"Who are you?" she asked, stepping forward.

"I am a friend. Come, let me lead you all out of here."

"What about the guards?" someone asked.

The man chuckled. "You need not worry about them anymore. Let us be away."

No one argued or asked any more questions as they followed the mysterious stranger to the front gate.

Poppy Gillis didn't know what hurt more, her nose where she'd been hit by that brick of a woman or the bite mark where that little brat had chomped down on her arm. If she ever got her hands on that girl again, she'd break *her* nose.

With wet eyes stinging with tears, she stumbled out of the kitchen and began making her way toward her own room. On the way, she caught the sound of moaning coming from the dining hall. Curious, she went in and found three guards sitting on top of the table, gagged and tied together by rope. One was Gerdi Citroen, the captain of the guards.

"Oh, my," she said, approaching them. She lowered the gag from the Dutch woman first.

"Who on earth did this, now?"

"Where is it?" the captain demanded.

"Where's what, my lady?"

"The vampire, you fool! The one who killed nearly

every guard in the place."

Poppy thought her mad. "I'll go fetch a knife and cut you loose," she said, walking away. "By the by, all the prisoners have left through the kitchen door."

Archie crawled out of the passageway first. He recognized the kitchen immediately.

"They must have come through this way," he said as Landcross crawled out of the hole next.

"How do you figure?"

"The tunnel door was already open."

Landcross rose to his full height. He placed his hands behind the small of his back and cracked it.

Archie glared at him and thought about shooting him in the head for the arrangement he'd made with the vampire. He should have known that a man like Pierce Landcross would make such a deal. For all Archie knew, it could have been Landcross' plan all along when he'd gone to Locksley in the first place.

"Ah, food," Landcross said, stepping over to a basket of apples. "I'm bloody starving."

The moment he took an apple, guards came down the hall toward them.

"You there," a yellow haired woman yelled with a Dutch accent. "Stop!"

"Shite!" Pierce exclaimed, dropping the apple.

Both Archie and Landcross pointed their guns at the guards and fired, slowing the guards down for the moment.

"Quick," Archie said, running to the door. "This way!"

They went out into the night and ran as fast as they could toward the main gate. The guards took chase. Landcross turned as he ran and fired at them. It was dark and Archie doubted that he'd hit anyone. The darkness also didn't help him find his way, and his foot landed in a hole, pitching him forward. Landcross tumbled right over him.

The advancing guards closed the gap between them, and Archie thought he was dead—until a shadow came out of the darkness and lifted one of the guards up and threw him straight through a second floor window. The remaining guards stopped and aimed their pistols at the first floor window when it shattered, and the Dutch woman was taken away somewhere in the dark. The last man standing opened fire, lighting up the yard with the muzzle flash from his flintlock. The guard then ran back toward the kitchen.

Archie was shaking, his knees weak and standing was not as easy as it should have been. He staggered as he found his feet. Landcross jumped like a startled cat when Robin of Locksley appeared.

"I heard shots," Locksley said. "We must go before those guards return."

"They're not dead?" Archie said.

"Of course not. Their hearts were not filled with evil. Well, the woman sort of. In any case, I never take the life of the good-hearted."

"Aren't you a saint," Landcross grumbled.

"A saint with devil's blood," the vampire remarked icily. He set his reflecting eyes on Archie. "Someone is waiting for you just beyond the gate."

Archie headed that way and found Clover mounted on his horse outside the castle walls. The other prisoners were standing around nearby. The bodies of the guards were no longer in view. Archie briefly wondered if the vampire had hidden them.

"Archie," Clover said as she jumped down from the horse and ran up to him with her arms wide open.

His whole body sagged with relief. He almost thought it was a trick until her arms were around his neck.

"You feel awfully warm," he noted, removing her hands from him. Her forehead felt damp and hot.

"I'm afraid she has a bad fever," a heavyset woman said.

The vampire suddenly appeared out of nowhere and placed his hand on Clover's forehead. A look of urgency on the demon's face frosted Archie's heart with dread.

"You need to get her to my wagon," Locksley said. "I have medicine there."

"Where are you going?" Landcross asked Locksley.

"I'm staying with these people," he said. "I'll make sure they reach the town safely. On foot, we can cut through the fields and get there faster. I'll meet you back at the wagon." As Archie mounted his horse, Locksley stepped in close to Landcross and said softly, "Do not forget our bargain."

Landcross said nothing, only watched Locksley move toward the group of prisoners.

"Come, people. Follow me," the vampire said.

Without protest, the group began following him into the dark open field. As they did, the heavyset woman approached Clover and took her by the hand. "Be well, little one."

"Thank you," Clover rasped.

When the group had vanished with the vampire, Archie and Landcross rode over the dirt lane, heading for the main road. On their way, a rider rode by them in a hurry. Archie only caught a flash of him in the light of the lantern he held.

"That was one of my father's soldiers," he said. "That means he's here."

Chapter Twenty-One
I'll Tell You a Secret

Pierce didn't know which was worse: having a vampire wanting his life or facing Tarquin Norwich. He thought about finding Indigo, but if he crossed Robin, the vampire would hunt him down. But he had one last trick up his sleeve, a trick that might work so long as Robin's honor existed after seven centuries.

When he and the Norwich siblings arrived at the wagon, Robin was waiting for them.

"Bring the child to the table," the vampire said to Archie as they stepped inside. "I have broth ready for her."

Clover didn't need an escort. When she spied the bowl on the table, she went to it and sat down. Archie shook his head as Pierce closed the door. "She was sick before we went on this blasted mission."

Ramirez reclined on the bed, playing his guitar. The gentle notes soothed Pierce—until he noticed Robin staring at him.

"While I was leading the hostages to safety," Robin began, "some stated that they were going to the authorities to speak of the atrocities they experienced. However, in light of what Tarquin Norwich is doing, I feel it is best to keep it secret, so I promised those he held that I would take care of Norwich personally if they kept their silence."

"You said he was protected," Pierce reminded.

"He is. Yet I have confidence that what he is planning will backfire on him. Perhaps even fatally."

"How's that?" Pierce inquired. "What do you think he's planning?"

"Never mind that now," Robin said. "It's time to pay up."

Archie looked up sharply. He turned his attention to Robin, a look of horror on his face. It wasn't as amusing as it once was. "I don't agree with the bargain you and Landcross made without my say so, but I shall honor it."

Robin gave him a perplexed look. "What are you talking about, boy? This has nothing to do with you."

"What?" Archie said, looking over at Pierce, "I . . . I thought . . ."

Robin ignored him and stepped over to Pierce. The Spaniard stood up and joined them, closing in on the thief. The wagon suddenly became very small.

"Hand it over," Robin ordered.

Pierce took the coin in his hand and looked at it for a moment. He raised his chin to Robin and said, "No, I think I'll hold on to it a tad longer."

Robin—no doubt expecting this—smiled slyly. He could have ordered Ramirez to take it from Pierce, but instead, he sighed deeply and said to Archie, "Your sister has pneumonia. Without proper treatment, her illness will get quickly worse."

"You said you had medicine," the lad said hopefully.

Robin didn't reply. Instead, he kept his bright blue eyes on Pierce. Pierce knew that for Clover to live, he would have to surrender the coin.

Ramirez held out his hand. Pierce glanced at him, and then back at Robin, who held his stare.

Grudgingly, he unclasped the necklace and dropped it into the Spaniard's extended palm. Ramirez took it away to the other side of the wagon, leaving Pierce to stand defenseless against a vampire who wanted his blood. A rhythmic pounding began knocking hard from behind his ribcage.

Robin's handsome grin stretched a little wider. He moved toward a set of shelves on the wall. "I lied," he said, plucking a vial from a shelf. "She merely has a cold. Give her a teaspoon of this, and after some rest, she will be right as rain."

"You bastard," Pierce said through gritted teeth.

Robin craned his neck around to face him with that grin of his, while handing the vial over to Archie. "You're not the only experienced liar in the room. As an ex-thief, I had to do quite a lot of it myself."

Either it was a natural instinct or something that was granted to him when he'd become a vampire, or perhaps a little of both, but Robin had the gift to peer into a person's true self. He saw Pierce's weakness.

"You mean the agreement was for the coin?" Archie said. "Why?"

"You should take your sister and find a place for her to rest for the night," Robin suggested.

Archie looked at Pierce, who merely nodded in agreement. "Go on, lad."

"No," Archie said abruptly. He looked at Robin. "You cannot."

"Can't what?" Clover said, standing up from her seat.

"It's all right," Pierce said, pulling out his room key from his coat pocket. "I'll catch up with you, eh?" He put the key in Archie's hand.

Archie stared with his mouth hanging agape. At the same time, Clover began to sense that something was wrong. "Mr. Pierce?" she said warily.

"Go get some sleep, darling," he said to her.

The Spaniard opened the door for the two siblings. Pierce stepped aside for them to leave. Archie's expression showed that he wanted to protest, say something in his defense, but Pierce raised his hand to stop him. "Just go."

Without argument, the siblings left the wagon.

Once they'd gone, the Spaniard followed them out, closing the door behind him and leaving Pierce alone with Robin.

"I need to ask you a favor," Pierce said the moment the door closed behind him.

Robin folded his arms and arched an eyebrow. "A favor?"

"Aye."

Robin raised his chin a tad and said, "What sort of favor?"

"Time. I'm asking for a little more time."

"Time for what?"

"To find my friend, Indigo Peachtree. Make sure he's safe."

Robin considered.

"Please," Pierce pleaded. "I can't bloody well go anywhere tonight. I'm stuck on this bleedin' rock."

Robin rubbed one of the scars on his face. After a moment, he stepped forward.

Pierce's heart lurched. He backed away, bumping his head on the iron rod where clothes were hanging.

"Take this," the vampire said, reaching over Pierce's shoulder and removing a few clothes from behind Pierce. "The girl's clothes are little more than rags."

The outfit was a shirt, a vest with black buttons, and a tattered looking skirt made from strips of white, pink, red, and black fabric. It also came with tights.

"It looks ridiculous," Pierce remarked.

Robin snorted. "Aye. It belonged to a dwarf who performed with us many years ago. Take them."

Pierce reached for the hanger, trying to steady his shaking hand. "Cheers."

Before he took the colorful clothes, Robin seized him by the forearm and held him tight.

"It doesn't matter where you go, I will find you. Remember that."

Pierce nodded. He bloody well knew.

When he was finally allowed to leave, he mounted his horse. Ramirez watched him from the roof while playing his guitar and singing a Spanish song in that soft tone of his.

"Dead?" Norwich said to the guards, standing in Landcross' room.

"Aye, my lord," the guard that Norwich had sent to the castle to fetch decent clothing for him, explained. "All murdered save for this lot, the captain of the guard, and the house staff." He cleared his throat, his complexion pale and sickly. "Butchered I would say, sir."

"And the prisoners?"

The prison guard, who'd been locked in the cell when he'd been found, spoke up. "Gone, milord."

"Gone? What exactly happened?"

"It was a vampire, milord," a guard with cuts on his face explained. "He pushed us through windows, he did. Killed everyone else."

Vampire? Norwich thought. "Those blasted demons!" He turned to his son, who sat on a chair near a small table with the empty satchel on it. "I'm going to the castle. You stay here and deal with Landcross when he returns."

"All right, Father."

"You three," he pointed to the guards who'd come from the castle, "stay here with him."

The look of sheer relief on the men's faces could not

be mistaken.

"The rest of you," Norwich said to his soldiers, "come with me."

He was the first to leave the room, followed by his tired and worn soldiers.

Despite having the book and masks, things seemed to be unraveling right in front of him, and if he didn't work fast, he'd lose everything.

Had Landcross actually make a deal with Robin of Locksley to save Clover at his own expense? Archie did not want to believe it. He wanted to keep Pierce Landcross at a distance, to see him as nothing more than a worthless thief. But he couldn't deny it. The man had offered his life for the life of another, which proved that there was more to him then Archie had initially thought. His brother, Joaquin, had been right about him.

"What's going to happen to Mr. Pierce?" Clover asked before falling into a coughing fit.

How could he answer her? He didn't want to tell her that Landcross had given himself to a vampire in order to rescue her. She'd be haunted with guilt for the rest of her days.

"He . . . he . . ." Archie began when a familiar voice spoke from behind him.

"Oi, Arch, hold up."

He looked back just as Landcross rode up alongside him. He couldn't repress his smile even if he wanted to.

"Mr. Pierce!" Clover shouted happily.

"One and the same, darling," Landcross said, halting his horse next to them.

Archie shook off his grin. "What happened? I thought you belonged to Robin now."

"I belong to no one, mate. I made a switch, is all. Stay still."

Landcross reached into Archie's coat pocket. Before he could protest, Landcross pulled his hand out, extracting the real stater coin from where he'd hidden it. He quickly tied the rope that he'd replaced the chain with around his neck, then held the coin tightly in his hand, blowing out a breath of relief.

"You had that hidden on me the entire time?" Archie demanded.

"Aye. Ol' Rob would've sensed it on me if I'd kept it. I needed it close by, though, so he'd know that it was around. So I slipped it into your pocket on our way back to his wagon."

"You were still unprotected, though," he pointed out. "Even in that brief moment."

"Aye, what's your point?" Landcross demanded.

Unwilling to explain it, Archie merely shook his head. "Nothing. What now?"

"I'm going back to the hotel for my satchel, and then I'm off to find Indigo. I can't wait 'til morning to look for him with your bloody father on the island."

"What's that?" Clover asked, pointing to the clothes draped over Landcross' saddle.

"A gift," Landcross said, handing the clothes over.

She took them, studying the garments. "They're a little . . . odd."

"Aye, but I'm sure you'll look smashing."

Clover smiled effusively at him.

"Do you know where to look for Peachtree?" Archie asked.

"I have an idea," was all Landcross said before he moved on.

When they returned to the hotel, they used the back way to avoid any unpleasantness with the desk clerk. Archie still had the room key, and he saw that the door was already unlocked, but he assumed Landcross had forgotten to lock it when they'd left. The lamps remained aglow, showing the room as they'd left it, neat and empty.

Clover was the second to enter the room and went directly to the Water Closet, carrying her new clothes with her.

"You two can have this room," Landcross said, walking toward the bed.

"I should say so," Archie said, folding his arms, "seeing that I paid for it."

Landcross grabbed a money purse from the nightstand's drawer and approached him. "Here," he said, handing the purse to him.

"Um, thanks," Archie said, surprised.

As he put the money in his coat pocket, Landcross snatched up the satchel and gave a slight salute. "Cheerio, chum." He started for the open door when he abruptly stopped.

"What?" Archie asked.

Landcross shook the bag. "It feels light." He unfastened the leather flap and looked inside. "Where *is* everything?"

Archie slowly slipped his hand out from his coat pocket. The contents in his stomach turned to sickening poison when he remembered. "Joaquin," he said dryly.

Landcross snapped his head up. "Come again?"

"Your brother was here, in the room with me when I arrived."

Landcross' face flushed red. "You brought him

here?"

"He was helping me look for you," he said, feeling ill. His foolishness to save his sister had utterly blinded him from seeing other possible reasons why Joaquin Landcross would want to help him find his estranged brother.

Landcross dropped the satchel and stomped towards him. Before Archie knew it, the man grabbed him and slammed him up against the wall. "You brought that bastard here and the thought of him taking the book never crossed your mind? How did he even know about the bloody thing?"

"I told him because *you'd* already given me the book, remember?"

"That was a forged copy, chum. I copied the whole thing."

"Why would you do that?"

Dismissing the question, Landcross said, "Now he has the real fuckin' book *and* the masks. Did you make a deal with him?"

"No," he said quickly. "It wasn't anything like that."

"Bollocks!" Landcross shouted, pushing him back and shoving his finger in Archie's face. "You've had it in for me since you and your apes trapped me in Le Havre, haven't you?" He released Archie and went to the door.

"That's neither here nor there," Archie said, stepping toward him. "I—"

"Don't," Landcross snapped, twisting around with a threatening look. "Don't you bloody well follow me. We're done here."

With that, he left. Archie didn't move.

The door to the washroom opened and Clover came out wearing her new outfit. "It fits!" she announced, skipping into the room, the colorful skirt flowing softly with her movements. She stopped and her dark eyes darted about. "Where is Mr. Pierce?"

"He, uh, went to look for the Toymaker. Come on, let's get you your medicine, and then it's off to bed with you."

Pierce's fists clenched in anger. The gall of that little piss-ant! He hated himself for thinking that he was anything more than a disposable tool to be used at Archie's convenience until he was no longer needed.

As Pierce crossed the lobby, there was a scream so ear-piercingly loud that it cut into his brain. The clerk behind the front desk pointed at him as she bit down on her fist. "It's the *madman!*" she shouted.

Confusion rolled around in his head before it finally landed on a memory; Archie and his brother had convinced the hotel staff that he was a maniac.

Instead of trying to explain himself to the hysteretic clerk that he was anything but, he started for the door again.

"Pierce Landcross," someone called from off to his side.

A man dressed like a sailor stumbled out of the hotel's tavern. He held a Colt revolver much like the Oak Leaf model Pierce carried. His staggering gait worried him. That gun could go off accidentally. Pierce recognized the belligerent buffoon as one of Tarquin Norwich's men.

"Think you got me mixed up with someone else, mate," Pierce said, slowly reaching for his own weapon. But his hand stopped the minute three soldiers stepped out of the tavern.

"I don't think so," the drunk said as the men surrounded him. Each one reeked of alcohol. "Take his gun."

"I think this bloke was at the castle," one of the soldiers said.

After Pierce's gun was pulled from its holster, the drunk said, "Let's take him to the stable."

Pierce's heart thumped against his sternum. He didn't imagine he'd live much longer.

"Take him out of here," the clerk shrieked from behind the counter.

"No worries, my lady," the drunk said. "You will never see the likes of him again."

Two of the soldiers grabbed Pierce by the arms and dragged him out the front door and led him around back.

"What's this?" a stable-hand, cleaning out a stall said when they came inside.

"Leave," the drunk ordered, waving his pistol at the boy.

The stable-hand dropped his shovel and headed for the door with his hands slightly raised. The drunk turned to the only soldier not holding Pierce. "Go tie us a noose."

"Aye, my lord."

Pierce didn't like the sound of that. "Listen, lads, there's no need for murder here. We—"

The drunk sank a hard fist into his stomach, sending him to his knees, gasping.

"The legendary Pierce Landcross," the drunk said, shifting the gun around in his hand until he held it by the muzzle. "I can't say that I'm impressed."

The next hard hit was across Pierce's head, making the world spin. He struck the hay-covered floor hard. He thought he was about to pass out and wished he would when heavy boots started kicking him.

He was sure that Norwich wanted him alive to get

him the journal, and even Indigo, since Joaquin had failed in doing so. But Norwich wasn't around, just a band of bloodthirsty drunken sods out for vengeance. Every hit was a mallet tenderizing his internal organs. A sharp blow to his kidneys caused him to moan. When someone got him in the side, he lost his breath a moment. Nearly every kick felt like it was enough to kill him.

"Enough," the leader ordered. "We don't want him to black out on us, now, do we?" He knelt beside Pierce. "I want him fully awake when we hang him."

Pierce shifted his eyes up to the drunk while clutching his wounded ribs. Breathing had become difficult. The kick to his side hadn't been *that* hard. It was as if he'd been severely injured there before. He just couldn't recall when his ribs had ever been hurt so badly.

Pierce closed his eyes. When he opened them again, he was no longer lying on the floor of the stable. He was shocked to discover that he was standing at a bar, looking at a man dressed in a black and red pinstripe suit. The place was full of chatter and stale tobacco smoke. Overhead was a skylight where a cigar shaped flying airship drifted across the evening sky. On the bar was a curious hat. Rabbit skin and feathers.

The man in the suit was a handsome gent with a smooth, almost feminine face.

"How are your injuries?" the man asked him.

Pierce shook his head and blinked rapidly. The man was still there. He rubbed his side. "A bit sore. Hurts to laugh."

"Hey!" the drunk soldier said, snapping his fingers in Pierce's face, drawing him back to the present. "Are you awake in there, Landcross?"

Pierce blinked away the rest of the strange moment,

bringing himself fully around.

Behind the drunk, a soldier threw a rope over a rafter and began tying a noose. The drunk grabbed Pierce and hoisted him to his feet. Pain found every inch of him and wracked his body inside and out. Strong hands clasped his arms, keeping him on his feet.

"I think that once we squeeze the last breath out of you, I'll cut off your head and give it to my father," the drunk man said. "That'll put a smile on my face at least."

Ah, so the drunk was none other than Tarquin's son, Ivor. Another bloody Norwich family member Pierce wished he'd never met.

"Bring him here," Ivor ordered the soldiers.

They pushed Pierce toward the noose. He'd seen men hanged before, the first when he'd been a child traveling through the Netherlands with his clan. A man hanged from a tree beside the road, not burned or disfigured like the corpses the British Guardians would leave, but the message had been delivered all the same. Somewhere down the road, the bloke had made the wrong choice or had merely been in the wrong place. Pierce remembered the horrid ex-pression on the dead man's fat, bloated face. It had been a face of pain; great pain that had portrayed the last moments of his life. His eyes had bulged, with a bloody tongue hanging from his mouth where he nearly bit it off. His face was discolored in shades of purple and yellow. Out of the handful of hangings that Pierce had witnessed throughout the years, that man struck him as the most terrifying.

He struggled against the soldiers, which did little. When they reached the noose, the men turned him completely around, facing him toward the door. There might have been someone who could help just outside those barn doors—if only he had the strength to call out. But he didn't. His wounds held back his voice.

The drunk stood before him with a deranged look on his face. "Do you want to know why I'm doing this, instead of handing you over to my father?"

"'Cause you're pissed off your arse?" Pierce rasped out in a strained whisper.

Something on Pierce's chest caught the drunk's eye. He briefly wondered if it was his necklace, something shiny to divert the bastard's alcohol-sloshed brain.

"Hurt yourself?" Ivor asked, pressing his knuckle against Pierce's healing brand.

He cried out. If the soldiers hadn't been holding him up, the pain would have floored him. It only eased slightly when Ivor removed his hand. Pierce gritted his teeth and sucked in air as tears pooled in his eyes.

"Because the man ruined me," Ivor went on. "He made me put a dagger in my own uncle's chest when I was twelve. I did it right in front of my mother."

The soldiers looked at each other in perplexity.

Ivor grabbed Pierce by the back of the head and pulled him forward, until their heads were next to each other. In a tone drenched in sorrow, he whispered, "Never have I defied the man . . . until tonight. Perhaps when you're dead and his foolish plan dies with you, he'll release me."

He drew away from Pierce and looked him dead in the eye. "I can't wait to hear you choke."

The noose went over Pierce's head. The scratchy rope tightened, and seconds after the soldiers let him go, they hoisted him off the ground.

Norwich and his men finally reached the castle. The moment they rode into the inner courtyard, he dismounted and met the captain of the guard, Gerdi Citroen.

"My lord," she said as he hurried inside the bastion, "I'm sorry, but the prisoners have escaped. There was a vampire and it—"

"I know damn well about the vampire. I want these bodies cleared out and buried somewhere."

"Yes, my lord. Right away."

She stayed in place as he marched on, ignoring the exsanguinated bodies strewn about and the maids crying on the stairs as he raced up them.

Taking a lantern with him, he journeyed up the highest tower to the top of the spiral stairs, where a thick wooden door stood. He quickly unlocked it with a key he wore around his neck, and after taking out his pistol, he entered the room.

The darkness in the curved room was too thick for just one lantern. He went to the center of the room where a spinning wheel sat next to a table, which held a measuring stick and a pair of sharp scissors. He set the book and the masks down on the table with a deep sigh.

Everything was as it should be. Although losing the prisoners was a sizable setback, they weren't part of the main agenda. The real problem was that they could expose what he was doing. He needed to act fast before the authorities came to ask questions.

"Hello, Tarquin Norwich," came a voice from the darkness.

He whipped around and saw a man crouched on the windowsill. How had he gotten up there? Had he been at the window the entire time?

"Who are you?" Norwich demanded, aiming his gun at the intruder. "How did you get in?"

"I came to visit earlier," he said with relish.

"You're the vampire who killed my guards?"

"Not all of them. Just the wicked of heart."

"I see," Norwich said. "Well, as you can see, there's nothing left for you to destroy and no more prisoners for you to free, so be off with you."

"What a lovely collection of death masks you have," the creature said.

"Care to have yours added?" Norwich asked boldly.

"Aye, but I'm not a god, am I? Having a mask of me wouldn't do your plan any good."

"What do you know of it, demon?"

"I know you will fail, like the others who have attempted the same thing before you."

"Away with you, demon," he ordered. "You cannot harm me or even enter this room."

The creature let out a crestfallen sigh. The light was dim, but the vampire's blue eyes could clearly be seen.

"You may have a powerful spell protecting you, but I predict that you will falter and your *witch* will not save you."

With that, the creature was gone, blowing out the lantern with his exit.

When Norwich returned downstairs, he ordered a maid with a swollen nose to follow him into the kitchen. The woman sniffed as she complied. Once they entered the pantry, he went to a storage shelf and brought down a box from the top. He carried the box to the woman and opened it to show her a pink vial.

"Stop your sniffling, woman and listen," he snarled.

The maid sucked in a breath. "Yes, milord."

"What is your name?"

"Pop . . . Poppy, sir."

"Poppy, when you receive my order that it's time to brew tea, I want you to prepare tea and pour this into it."

The maid peered at the vial inside the box queerly.

"Don't ask," he stated, sensing she was going to inquire. "Just do as I say, understand?"

She instantly tightened her lips and nodded. "Yes, milord. It shall be done."

He handed her the box. "Good," was all he said before he left the room. He needed a change of clothes, and then he would return to town to find Landcross and the Toymaker before everything collapsed.

Chapter Twenty-Two
Death Wish

Archie decided to use Landcross' room to his advantage and take a hot bath himself. It would be the perfect conclusion to his rough day.

After Clover drifted off to sleep, he went to the front desk to ask for dry towels.

"Oh," the clerk said, "you were here earlier."

Before he could explain, she said, "So, they finally took him away then."

Her statement made him knit his eyebrows together. "Sorry? Who took who away?"

"Norwich's men," she clarified. "A band of them were in the tavern when that man you were searching for came strolling through. They took him."

"Oh my God," he said, his heartbeat quickening. "Where did they go?"

She shrugged. "To the stable to fetch their horses, I imagine."

He dashed down the corridor, heading for the back exit. Outside, he darted toward the stable doors when the sound of laughter stopped him short. He pulled his gun and pushed one of the doors open. What he saw next made him ice over with horror.

Pierce Landcross was being lifted off the ground by a rope around his neck. He tried desperately to wedge his fingers under the rope to create some slack.

At the center of the murder in progress was Ivor. He was laughing at Landcross, mocking his distress like a spiteful child.

Archie's adrenaline ran high and his blood flowed

thick. He walked in, aimed his pistol at the ceiling, and fired.

The blast startled the three men holding the rope and they let go. Landcross collapsed in a heap, coughing and sucking in air when the restriction around his throat lifted.

"Archie?" Ivor said, squinting his black glassy eyes at him.

"Cut him loose," he demanded, aiming the gun at the men with his brother.

Archie moved in closer, already sensing the conflict that he and his drunken brother were about to have. This was the first time he would go head-to-head with him. Strangely, he almost craved it.

Regardless, his main objective was getting Landcross away from them. Pierce had risked his life to save his sister. Although he'd never told Clover this, she was the one who'd given him a purpose after their mother had died. And despite the cruelness she'd suffered living under her father's rule, none of it had influenced her. She deserved to find happiness. Out of the three Norwich children, she took after their mother the most, which made her loss less painful.

Landcross hadn't just saved Clover; he'd saved the legacy of a good woman.

"I mean it, Ivor," Archie seethed. "Let him go."

"You'd kill me for him, eh?" Ivor challenged.

Archie's finger itched to pull the trigger and end Ivor's cruelty. The urge only grew when Ivor knelt beside Landcross. He snatched him up by his dapper coat collar to help Landcross into a sitting position. He threw his arm around the man, placing his other hand on Landcross' chest. "He isn't going anywhere, little brother. His head belongs to me."

Archie kept his aim on Ivor, but the others were

reaching for their guns. He quickly ordered them to stop. A cold trickle of sweat ran down the nape of his neck. Never had he held a room of armed men at gunpoint before.

"Drop your guns," Landcross ordered in a harsh, raspy voice.

Everyone turned their sights on him and Ivor. Landcross had managed to slip Ivor's own gun out of its holster and jab it under his captor's chin.

"Do it, lads, or I'll open his skull with a bullet, I will."

"Don't do it," Ivor commanded as Landcross stood, lifting him up as well. "Shoot us both down."

The drunken soldiers seemed confused about what to do. They glanced at each other as if to ask what their next move should be.

"Stand down," Archie said, keeping his aim on the soldiers. "If Ivor dies, who here will explain to my father how you were responsible for the death of his beloved son?"

That won them over. The soldiers quickly took out their guns and laid them on the ground.

"Shoot," Ivor ordered. "Damn it, shoot!"

Archie had never seen his brother so careless with his own life before. When his men surrendered their weapons, Ivor began to sweat, tears collecting in his eyes. He struggled to get away from Landcross.

"Stop that," Landcross said, whacking him across the back of the head.

Ivor fell to his knees and stayed that way until Landcross hit him again, sending him to the floor unconscious.

"Landcross!" Archie snapped.

"What?" he said, pulling the noose over his head. "He bloody well hit me with a gun."

With his brother out of commission, Archie turned his full attention to the others. "You two," he ordered the closest soldiers, "saddle a pair of horses. Now!"

The men leapt into action. Landcross walked over to the guns on the floor and picked up a revolver with an oak leaf carved into the grip.

"Are you all right?" Archie asked him.

"I've had better nights," he replied, rubbing the redness around his throat. He sounded like he had sand in his gullet.

Archie studied him. Landcross held his side, his complexion was pale and he wheezed when he breathed. Archie feared that he may have a broken rib. Ivor and his thugs hadn't just put a rope around his neck; they had beaten him as well.

The soldiers returned with the horses. Archie stayed in place, keeping his gun on them. "Mount up, Landcross."

He wanted to make sure that Landcross could get himself on a horse before he mounted his own. Landcross let out a disheartening groan but managed to get on the saddle.

"Go," Archie said.

Landcross said nothing. Archie didn't think he had the strength to speak. He trotted his horse past him and out through the open door.

A moan escaped Ivor.

Archie didn't particularly care for another altercation with him, so he snatched his horse's reins from the soldier who'd brought the animal out, and mounted.

No one tried anything as he turned his horse around and rode swiftly out of the stable.

It took him only a little time to catch up to Landcross, who was riding his horse slowly down the street, hunched over in the saddle.

"Jesus, Landcross," he said, catching up to him, "are you alive?"

Landcross struggled to lift himself up. His words scrapped up past his throat when he said, "I think I'm dying."

"Let's get you to another hotel," he said.

"No, your father may send men to search for us. The beach will be safer."

The trip to the shore took less than a handful of minutes, yet Archie feared he'd lose Landcross in that time. When they reached a good spot on the beach, he helped Landcross dismount and set him down on the soft cool sand. In the distance, a fire burned under a pier.

"I'll gather some wood," Archie said.

"Grand," Landcross wheezed, lying down slowly.

Archie found a pair of homeless men under the pier, drinking by their fire. They told him that the old pier had collapsed sometime back and that the broken pieces of wood were scattered all across the area. Archie paid them for a piece of wood to use as a torch and then searched under the pier for more.

"Yes, I'm still alive," Landcross said when he returned.

Through the light of the torch, Archie saw him lying on his back with an arm draped over his face. At his feet was a hole carved out into the sand.

"Put the wood in the fire pit, lad," Landcross rasped.

"You did this?" Archie asked, placing the bundle of wood down inside the hole. "I thought you were dying."

"Figure of speech. I merely meant that I *felt* like I was dying."

Archie was greatly relieved to hear that. "What

about your side?"

"It hurts like hell. Those bastards put a beatin' on me, they did."

"I mean is anything broken? Any organ damage?"

"Nope."

"Bastard. You had me worried."

Landcross lifted his arm away from his face and looked at him. "Worried, eh?"

Archie arranged the firewood inside the pit and set the torch within the pile. "Maybe."

He rose and went to his horse.

"Where are you going?" Landcross asked quickly.

"I'm going to fetch Clover. She'll be in danger at the hotel."

"Bring some food back, eh?" Landcross said, resting his head back down. "I'm famished."

"Right," he said, mounting the horse. "Keep the fire going, all right?"

With that, he rode away from the beach and back into town. When he reached the hotel, he hurried back to Room 119 and went inside.

The room was pitch-black, which startled him. Then someone struck him on the head from behind. The blow dropped him to his knees. The door closed and hands grabbed his arms. A spark from a match burned to life nearby and moved to a lantern, where the glow grew brighter. Ivor sat on the chair next to the small table, his head bleeding.

"Little brother," Ivor said, "you have a lot of explaining to do when Father arrives."

Chapter Twenty-Three
Keeping the Promise

The wait for Tarquin Norwich's return put fear into Archie as he sat with his brother at the table. Clover remained asleep, unaware of the danger. The medicine had granted her that pleasure.

"I looked into Indigo's book," Ivor said. "The Toymaker certainly is more of a mechanical genius then I thought. What was that strange writing?"

"Don't you know?"

"All I know is that Father is planning to build weapons."

Archie was a little surprised by that. He'd thought their father shared everything with Ivor. "I have no idea what that writing is," Archie replied. "Ask Father."

"Fine."

"Why are you doing this?"

"Doing what?" Ivor asked softly.

"Helping Father?"

"Oh, I'm sorry," Ivor said, turning his head to him. "I didn't see you arguing with him when he sent you off to find that fucking thief."

"That was before I knew what he had planned. You've known this entire time and went along with it anyway."

"Maybe I want what he wants." Ivor brought out his flask and tipped it to his mouth. He threw it down in disgust when he discovered it was empty.

"Or maybe you're just as afraid of him," Archie said.

Ivor's glassy eyes flickered with a mix of anger, sadness, and as Archie suspected, fear. He'd sensed for a long time that Ivor held resentment toward the man who loved him a hundred times over his other children. Archie glanced at the cameo on the flask on the floor. It was an image of their mother, sculpted when she'd been sixteen.

"Mother never wanted this for you," Archie added poignantly.

"Don't talk to me about Mother."

Archie looked back to the bed where Clover was shifting under the sheets. He turned back to his brother. He needed to get him out of the room before Ivor woke her up.

"Let's go to the tavern," he suggested.

There was no argument from Ivor. "All right," he said, standing.

Ivor ordered one of the soldiers to stay at the door and for the rest to come along in case Archie tried anything. The tavern was closing for the night, but Ivor demanded a bottle of gin and two glasses. Considering who he was, the staff had little choice but to comply.

"I don't want anything," Archie said as Ivor poured him a shot. He had long hated alcohol after seeing what it did to his brother. He was certain that if Ivor hadn't chosen to drown his pain, he might have had a chance to become his own man instead of an inebriated mutt languishing at their father's side.

"Drink," Ivor ordered, pouring his own glass of gin.

He decided not to argue and took the shot glass, tossing the drink back quickly. It sent hot coals down his throat, causing him to cough as the temperature rose in his face. Why anyone deliberately drank this stuff was beyond him.

"Another," Ivor said, pouring more. He lifted his glass. "To . . . to whatever."

"To family," Archie said, raising his own glass.

They clinked glasses and drank. Archie threw the liquor straight back, yet his tongue couldn't escape its horrid taste. He began to feel lightheaded.

"She loved us, you know?" he said. "Mother, I mean."

"I don't care," Ivor grumbled.

"It wasn't your fault. It was Father's."

"Shut it."

This was the closest Archie had ever come to talking about that night with his brother. Many times before, he'd wanted to sit down and talk to him about that gruesome night. He remembered the traumatized look on Ivor's face when their father put the dagger in his hand. Uncle Brice was held down on his knees by Tarquin's soldiers. He didn't look afraid. If he hadn't been scared, he should have been. The stabbing was quick, but it took their uncle many long minutes to finally die, all of which they had to watch. It surprised Archie how easily the blade sank into his uncle's chest. Mother begged for mercy and cried the entire time until it was over. Archie had been holding Clover, who screamed so loud it hurt his ear. Ivor had stood in his place, holding the blood-soaked knife. What happened that night changed them all.

"I wanted to do it," Ivor said halfheartedly. "I always loved Father more than Mother anyway. Love him more than any of you."

"Is that what you tell yourself when you're not drunk enough to blot it out?"

"Keep it up, Arch," Ivor growled, "and I'll take a dagger to our dear little sister while you watch."

Archie shot to his feet. Ivor looked up at him from his seat at the table, but he didn't have time to put up any defense before Archie tackled him.

Archie's strength came from rage. He tapped into

something he hadn't known he possessed and over-powered his brother. "Don't ever think of touching Clover, you bastard!" Archie shouted as he punched Ivor's face.

The soldiers acted quickly and yanked him up. Even they had a difficult time trying to control him.

Ivor lay on the floor, bleeding and laughing like the drunken madman he was. "Archie, you nearly killed me," he said, slowly lifting himself to his feet. When he was standing, he looked at Archie, who was being held by the soldiers. His expression turned somber. "I don't think you'd ever fight like that if it was my life in danger, would you?"

If the soldiers weren't holding him, he'd go at Ivor again and finally end his miserable life. But his anger subsided and his stomach wrenched when he heard his father's voice coming from the doorway.

"What's going on here?" Tarquin Norwich demanded.

The room began spinning and Archie retched all over the floor, getting some of the vomit on the soldiers' boots. They let him go and backed away, disgusted. Ivor pointed and laughed loudly at them with blood dripping from his nose.

"Enough!" Norwich bellowed. "I asked what's going on? Archie, why are you here and not heading back to Southampton?"

Archie spit off to the side. "I followed Joaquin Landcross here, sir."

"You did what? Why?"

"I . . . I . . ." he started, struggling for words. He didn't know how to answer his father without endangering his sister. He was sure that his father would harm her if he learned that she was in the hotel.

"I found him in Pierce Landcross' room with

Clover," Ivor said.

Archie shot his brother a deadly look and Ivor grinned with a shrug.

"Clover?" Father said. "She's here?"

"Sleeping away," Ivor said spitefully.

"Where's Pierce Landcross?" Father demanded.

"Gone," Ivor said, finally wiping the blood off his face with a napkin from another table. "I had him, but Archie helped him escape."

"You did what?" Father shouted so loud that it surprised Archie that his eardrums weren't damaged.

"I had to," Archie explained. "Ivor was killing him."

The man's fiery eyes shifted to Ivor. "Is this true?"

Ivor just gave a crooked, half-conscious grin, as if he was testing his father, or prodding him to act out in violence against him.

His father didn't even raise his voice to Ivor. Instead, he returned his attention to Archie, whose stomach twisted again. "Do you know where he is now? Answer truthfully."

Archie knew that tone. If he dared to lie to his father, and if his father sniffed it out, the consequences would be deadly. "I do, sir."

"Sit," his father ordered. "We have some things to discuss."

Archie took in a long breath and approached the chair.

"Ivor, go get yourself and the men rooms," Father commanded. "And clean yourself up."

Ivor flicked his wrist and stumbled out of the room with the soldiers following him. When they were gone, Tarquin took a seat where Ivor had been sitting and poured himself a glass of gin. Archie felt himself turning green.

"You were never one to drink, were you?" his father asked, lifting the glass to his lips.

"No, sir," he answered weakly. His mouth was dry and filmed with a nasty taste.

His father snorted. "That's just about your only good quality."

The compliment had little effect even if it was one of the most favorable things his father had ever said to him.

His father drank his gin and set the glass down. "I'm going to ask you a series of questions and your answers will determine your sister's fate, under-stand?"

When Ivor had threatened Clover, it had sparked Archie into a rage beyond measure. This time, terror filled him when the same threat came from his father. The man was dangerously brutal, a psychopath. Tarquin Norwich didn't believe in the mercy of a quick death, but rather enjoyed savoring the moment of stripping the soul from someone. And Archie was damn sure that his father wouldn't make any distinction between an adult and a child, nor his own offspring or a random youngster. Clover would receive no mercy from him, regardless of her age or blood ties to him.

"Is Landcross waiting for you to return?" his father asked.

"Yes," he croaked.

"Has he come to the island to find Peachtree?"

"He has."

"Does he know where he is?"

"I believe so, but he hasn't told me anything."

"You saved him from Ivor, yes? Saved his life?"

"I did."

"Then he must trust you now."

Archie saw where these questions were leading. "You want me to go back and have him lead you to Peachtree?"

His father hiked up his greying eyebrows as he poured another drink. "Impressive. Perhaps you possess some brain function after all. Yes, go back and stay until morning. When you both leave, we won't be far behind. Make sure I have both Peachtree and Landcross by tomorrow, and I may forgive Clover for her betrayal."

Archie wanted to say something in her defense, but he didn't know how without making things worse. This was the best deal he could get from his father and he couldn't afford to mess it up. "Yes, sir."

His father nodded and took a drink. "Very good. Now, where is he?"

The hardest question yet. When Archie answered, he thought he was going to be sick again. "He's camped on the beach, near the pier."

"Good," his father said, standing up. "Go there. We'll meet up on the morrow."

His father pulled out his revolver and handed it to him. Archie took it and was tempted to fire it in his father's face. Instead, he watched his father as he left the tavern.

Archie returned to the beach where Landcross sat poking at the fire with a stick. He sighed with relief at the sight of him. If Landcross hadn't been here, Clover would suffer for it.

"Took you long enough," Landcross griped as Archie approached the fire. "Where's Clover?"

"She still has a fever so I took her to another hotel. She'll be safe there." He handed a sack of food and a bottle of Scottish whisky to the man. "Here."

"Bloody hell," Landcross said excitably, looking through the sack. "Cheers!"

Landcross brought out bread, cheese, and slices of meat. He quickly made himself a sandwich and began devouring it.

"There's more in there," Landcross said, handing the bag back. "Eat up, lad."

Archie took the bag and made his own sandwich. "I also bought eggs and a pan for the morning."

Landcross nodded as he took another big bite of his sandwich. "Brilliant," he said, his mouth full of food. "Didn't run into any trouble going back, I take it?"

Archie shook his head. "No. Ivor has no idea that you were even staying at the hotel. He was there simply because he needed a bath."

Landcross snorted. "Piss poor luck on my end, eh? That brother of yours is some piece of work."

"He's not my brother," he said bitterly. "Not anymore."

Landcross took the whisky bottle and pulled the cork out with his teeth. He spit it into the fire and said, "Aye. I can say the same thing 'bout my own bastard brother."

"But you risked your life to save him."

Landcross took a drink. "Joaquin wasn't always the backstabbing arsehole that he is now. He watched over me for years when we were youngsters living on our own."

"Really? That was a very drastic act he took against you. Slitting your throat, I mean. And he did so just to keep you from going back?"

Landcross whipped his head around to face him. "How do you know about that?"

"He told me," he said with a shrug. "When I tracked

him down, he told me what he did to you."

"Oh," Landcross said mournfully, "I see. It was the first time he ever attacked me. When he put that dagger to my throat, he suddenly became someone else. It was like something was controlling him."

"Alcohol controls my brother," Archie put in. "After what happened between us; what father made him do."

"Oh, aye, he told me about that nasty business with your uncle just before he threw a noose over my head. Wanker."

"My mother sent letters to my Uncle, asking for help to get us away from our father. Uncle Brice tried leading us to Germany where it would be easier to conceal us and begin a new life. We were halfway to Ringwood when Father and his soldiers caught up with us. To this day, I have no idea how they found us. No one but Mother and Uncle Brice knew where we were going."

Archie stared at his uneaten sandwich. "Ever since Father made Ivor stab our uncle to death, he hasn't been right in the head. Sometimes, I wish he would just talk to me about it."

"He's lost, mate," Landcross said, taking another bite of his sandwich. "Where Ivor is, there's no escape except for death. Freedom's a state of mind, chum. Lose your mind and you lose everything."

Archie bowed his head somberly. "Like Mother," he whispered.

"Sorry, what was that?"

"My mother. She . . . poisoned herself shortly after that. I suppose she saw no other way out, either."

Thinking back on his mother's death, his appetite left him and his stomach filled with grief. Was death the only escape from his father?

Landcross offered no words of comfort; he only

handed the bottle of whisky over to him with a sympathetic smirk. Archie looked at it for a moment.

"The hell with it," he said, taking the bottle.

"To shitbird brothers," Landcross said.

Archie raised the bottle. "To shitbird brothers." He placed the bottle to his lips then added, "And fathers."

He took a drink and handed it back to Landcross. Strangely, drinking with the thief didn't affect him as it had when he'd been drinking with Ivor.

"So, you're married, eh?" Landcross bluntly put in.

Archie gulped at that. "How on earth did you find that out by the way?"

"I read Clover's journal. She's quite the writer, you know."

Archie grunted and snatched the bottle back. "I should've guessed as much." He took a drink. "We thought to leave for America. I wanted to take Eilidh and Clover. Start anew."

"I can relate," Landcross said, taking the bottle for himself.

"Where would you go?"

Landcross shoved the last piece of sandwich into his mouth and said with one chubby cheek, "Any-where."

Archie snorted. "You wouldn't have to run like this if you hadn't tried stealing from the Queen."

Landcross gave him a sidelong glance. "Shut it."

Archie chuckled, clearly feeling the alcohol now. "What? It's funny."

"It's not."

"It is," he argued, taking a bite of his sandwich.

Landcross washed down the last of his food with whisky while Archie laughed. He covered his mouth with his hand, which kept the food from spilling out.

Landcross shook his head. "Pathetic. I think you've

had enough, lad."

Archie lowered his hand to see Landcross swallowing the last few gulps. "Hey!"

He never thought he'd be upset about losing a drink, nor did he ever think that it would be an outlaw who'd have to cut him off. But the bottle ran dry and Landcross tossed it away. He burped. "That'll get me right to sleep."

Landcross lay back with a groan and settled himself into the sand. "You should get yourself some sleep, lad."

Feeling his head swimming blissfully, Archie turned to gaze out at the black ocean, listening to the waves and enjoying the cool sea breeze brush over him.

At that moment, he never felt so free in his entire life. It amazed him how little it took to feel like this. Just a little food on the beach, a fire, real conversation, and some Scottish whisky. Simple things that exposed him to a world he'd never experienced before. He looked over at Landcross, already snoring away. The scoundrel—a thief and outcast—had given him this tranquil moment.

Swallowing the last of his food, he suddenly felt tired. He also settled into the sand and soon fell fast asleep.

Chapter Twenty-Four
'Ello Indigo

Light filtered through Pierce's eyelids, drawing him from the comfort of his dreams back to the cold reality of the beach. He opened his eyes, immediately squinting at the foggy grey morning, then turned to where Archie slept, with hands tucked under his head like a child.

Pierce rose while yawning deeply. When he tried to stretch his arms up, he gasped at the sharp pain in his side.

"Ah, shite!" he groaned, falling sideways onto the sand.

Gathering his strength, he prepared himself for the pain as he gradually got to his feet and headed for the ocean. At the water's edge, he stopped and unfastened his breeches, leaning his head back with a moan as he relieved himself.

The peaceful moment ended when Archie appeared beside him.

"Fuckin' hell," Pierce exclaimed. "Don't do that!"

"It's just me," the lad said, unfastening his own trousers. As he took a piss, he said, "I'll cook up the eggs."

"After you wash your hands first," Pierce said with levity.

Archie gave him a sidelong glance. He didn't seem to be in the mood to joke, no doubt feeling the effects of the whisky.

"No longer feeling the giggles, eh?"

"No," the lad said. "I am not."

Pierce snorted and fastened his trousers. He went back to their little camp. "I'll get the eggs started."

Pierce cautiously lowered himself to his knees and placed more wood into the fire pit. It wouldn't take long to get the fire started up again and the eggs cooked, which sat well with him. He wanted to find Indigo as quickly as possible and get the hell off the island. He didn't give a toss about the book or the reason why Joaquin had stolen it; his main objective was the safety of his friend. That and getting to Le Havre by the end of the day before the Sea Warriors set sail.

By the time Archie returned to camp, the fire was roaring.

"You ought to retrieve your sister," Pierce said to the lad, stoking the flame with a piece of wood. "Go get your bride and start your new life together."

The expression on Archie's face was grave.

"Don't you bloody well retch near the fire, mate! Some of us want to eat without the smell of sick nearby."

"I'm not going to do that," Archie said defensively.

"Bloody better not," he grumbled. He brought out the pan from the sack and held it by the handle over his knee. "Listen," he said, cracking an egg on the edge of the pan, "I'm more then grateful for what you did for me last night, saving my life and all. It's a debt I can never repay."

"I don't want anything from you. I—"

"I ain't finished," he said, tossing away the broken egg shell. "As I said, it's a debt I cannot repay, but I can give you my blessing to leave."

Archie's eyes shifted around for a moment before he said, "Yeah, well, thanks for your blessing and all; but for starters, Clover and I will not be getting a ferry out until this fog clears."

Pierce briefly studied the steely smoky mist that covered the ocean. He was thankful that it obscured the brilliance of the rising sun.

"And I *want* to help," Archie went on. "After everything I put you through and what you did to save Clover, I owe you. Understand? Let me make sure that you find Peachtree. I'll even give you money for the both of you to get off the island."

"You don't say?"

"Yes."

"Well, then let's eat up and be on our way."

Once they finished eating their breakfast, they mounted up and headed down the coast.

"Where are we going?" Archie asked.

"Several miles away to a cave. We'll keep to the shore until we're clear of the town."

When Cowes lay far behind them, they returned to the road and followed it along the coastline for the next couple of hours. Archie said nothing throughout the journey, as if he was deep in thought. It was all well and good for Pierce. His ribs, still sore from the attack, throbbed with every step his horse took. He was sure that none of them were broken, but they might have been cracked. It continued to confuse him how he'd been injured there. It honestly felt like an old injury that had been aggravated.

They reached the end of the road when it veered away from a nearby cliff and headed inland. Pierce rode forward and stopped by the edge. Below them was a wide beach stretching between the cliffs and the ever moving sea. Seagulls soared as if gravity didn't exist for them. A flock also stood about on the beach, squawking over a herd of sea lions.

"Is the cave down there?" Archie asked when he

came up beside him.

"Aye, c'mon."

Archie followed him to a narrow path leading down the side of the cliff. There, Pierce dismounted. "We walk from here, mate."

They slowly descended the rocky, not-so-worn trail. Sometimes the path vanished, forcing them to press their backs up against the rock wall and sidestep over a sliver of land. Weeds sprouting between the cracks in the sandstone provided handholds during those narrow pockets.

Pierce remembered traveling the path in his youth. The cliff had seemed more like a mountain back then. As a wild child, he'd thought the climb was thrilling. A new adventure, as it were. How young and naïve he'd been. At the time, he'd enjoyed his life, living off the land, reveling in every moment of each day, coasting through his existence like a leaf in the wind.

Now he was tired. The failed heist at Buckingham Palace had boosted him to the position of top fugitive in Great Britain, and it was too much, drawing out the last breath of excitement in him for being an outlaw. He was twenty-seven and the years had finally worn him out. If he could make it out of this and get himself onboard the *Ekta,* he would find his own little spot in the world to call his own.

The cool wind wet his eyes, the sun showing through the fog with an unforgiving glow. He reached for another handhold, slowly lowering himself.

"Are you sure he's here?" Archie asked, gripping tightly to the weeds.

"No," Pierce answered truthfully. "But there's nowhere else I can think of."

When he was a few feet above the sand, Pierce leapt off the rocky path despite the sharp pain in his ribs when he landed. He grit his teeth and walked on with Archie following.

"That was a heart-stopping climb," Archie remarked, looking up at how far they'd descended.

"Aye," Pierce agreed. "C'mon, this way."

They traveled over the beach until they came to the mouth of a tall cave. From what he remembered, the cave went back at least a hundred feet or so, but it could possibly go back farther.

He led the way into the cave, watching his footing over the piles of small rocks strewn all over the place. The rocks continued inside, but after a little ways in, they'd been pushed aside, making a clear path into the darkness. He and Joaquin had done it when Indigo had brought them to the cave years ago.

Quietly, he and Archie followed the stone-lined path, allowing the darkness to envelop them completely. The dark didn't last long. After a few minutes of walking blindly, light appeared to brighten their way the farther they went. At the end of the passageway was a round chamber with many ancient cave paintings of animals and people drawn over the walls and ceiling. Indigo had told him that they'd been painted by primitive people who'd lived thousands of years ago, and who'd probably lived there in the cave. The chamber was evidently being lived in again. There was a bookshelf sagging with books, a luggage trunk next to a makeshift bed, and a small table.

Sitting on an old leather chair, with a book in his hand and a pipe in his mouth was a man that Pierce hoped was Indigo Peachtree.

He put his hand on Archie's chest and whispered for him to stay put before stepping in closer. His footsteps were light, for the old man never removed his eyes from the page he was reading.

"Indigo?" he said softly.

The man didn't move an inch, only his eyes as he read each sentence.

"Indigo," Pierce said louder. "Damn it, man, are you dead?"

The old man snapped his head up and a hidden pistol appeared. "No, but you will be if you take one more step, young man."

Pierce stopped and raised his hands. "Whoa, easy mate."

"State your business," the old man said, jabbing the air with his old flintlock.

Old man? Although Indigo hadn't exactly been in his prime when he'd taken in a pair of lost and half-starved boys, he had clearly aged considerably. Back when he and his brother had been in Indigo's care, the grey in the Toymaker's hair had only just settled in at his temples. Now, it dominated his whole head, his hair wild and disheveled, as if he'd just woken. The spectacles he always wore seemed to have grown in size and thickness. His pale skin had lost more pigment and the wrinkles on his face had deepened like cracks in the parched earth. Even his tweed jacket and breeches appeared just as old as the man, as if he'd worn them his entire life.

"My business is to save your old wrinkled arse," Pierce replied.

"Eh?" Indigo said.

"Don't you recognize me?"

The question only deepened Indigo's confusion. "Should I, young man?"

Pierce felt a little pinch in his heart.

"For crying out loud," Archie said from the opening of the cavern, "he hasn't seen you since you were a child."

"Who's that?" Indigo demanded, aiming the gun at the darkness behind Pierce.

"Ignore him," Pierce said, waving off the disembodied voice. "He's a simpleton."

"Hey!"

"Who are you?" Indigo asked again.

"It's me, Pierce Landcross."

The old man's eyes flicked up to the ceiling, as if he were searching for a memory. He picked up a newspaper, studied it, and looked back at Pierce. Indigo smiled broadly, his face lighting up brighter then the whale oil lantern beside him.

"Pierce," Indigo said, lowering his gun. "Pierce, my boy! It is you."

He placed the gun and pipe next to the lantern, dropped the newspaper, and slowly lifted his old bones out of the creaky leather chair. When he was finally on his feet, he stretched out his arms. "Come here and embrace me, lad."

Pierce wrapped his arms around the Toymaker, refraining from squeezing too tight for fear of hurting him, or himself. But it felt good to be in the presence of his old friend again.

Indigo pried himself away and said, "My, you have grown." He leaned in, raising his heavy glasses up from his eyes. "How on earth did you get that nasty scar?"

Pierce quickly covered the scar with his hand. He missed his scarf. Instead of answering Indigo, he said, "Archie, show yourself, eh?"

Archie appeared in the light with a grin. "Hello, Mr. Peachtree."

Indigo set his glasses back over his beady eyes, enlarging them to owl size. Those large dark, wood-stained eyes of his fixed directly on Archie's face. "You look familiar, young man. Have we met before?"

If Indigo recognized Archie as being the son of the man who'd driven him out of his safe haven and now hunted him, it might stop his old ticker right then and there.

Before his memory could place Archie's face, Pierce said, "How the bloody hell did you get all this stuff down that path along the cliff?"

"This?" Indigo said, looking around at the furniture. "I didn't bring everything down at once. It took the course of a few years. I wanted the cave to be my secret place while I excavated the area. And I didn't use the path; I went down the sand dunes."

"What sand dunes?"

"The ones over yonder, about a half mile down the coast. I found them some time after you boys left. Much easier, I say."

Pierce grimaced. "Lovely."

"What do you excavate for?" Archie asked.

The question got the old toymaker excited.

"Ah! Let me show you! You won't believe your eyes."

Indigo seemed to lose years as he sprinted over to the other side of the cave's chamber. He reached behind the headboard of the bed, which was nothing more than a large slab of wood, possibly a broken piece of a boat. What he brought out was a giant skull from some kind of a monster. At first glance, it appeared to be rock mixed with bone. A large eye socket and part of a forehead penetrated the limestone. Indigo set it down on the table.

"Blimey," Pierce gasped, approaching the table with Archie at his side. "What is it?"

Indigo smiled and shrugged. "I haven't the faintest

idea," he admitted, breathing heavily. He seemed a tad winded from lifting the heavy thing.

"This island is littered with bones, large bones from ancient creatures. I've found so many. But this is the first skull I've discovered. It'll take me months to chisel the rock away."

The large skull almost made Pierce forget the reason why they'd come. "We need to get you out of here. You're not safe."

"Are you talking about that horrible man, Tarquin Norwich?" Indigo said, pushing his thick spectacles up his long nose. "Has he dragged you in to hunt for me?"

"He tried," Pierce said with a smirk. "Mostly he wanted me to find your journal."

Indigo's magnified eyes grew even larger and his jaw went slack. "The journal you took from me?"

"I didn't take it," Pierce said quickly. "Not on purpose, anyhow. Yes, that one. How did he find out about the bloody thing in the first place, eh?"

The Toymaker gave him a sheepish look. "I told him," he confessed.

"Pardon?" Pierce said. "You did what?"

"Aye, twenty years ago. It was around Christmas and I was promoting one of my newest automated toys in London. I had the journal with me, and one evening, I was in a tavern when Norwich came in with his oldest son. He asked me for the latest toy for his boy and noticed the journal's contents. I'm sorry to say that I had enough pints in me to open up and tell him everything. *Everything*! At the time, he merely expressed mild interest in the book."

"Well, he's bloody well more than mildly interested now," Pierce declared.

"It doesn't matter. You stole it."

"I didn't steal it," he grumbled.

"He thought my weapon sketches were worthless, and the story behind the masks was an old foolish tale. Then out of the blue, Norwich summoned me to his home under false pretenses; and on the first night that I was there, he began inquiring about the writing."

Finally, Pierce thought. *I'm going to find out about the spell.*

"He wanted to know where the masks were; and that's when I realized that he'd come to believe in the legend."

"The legend?" Pierce wondered. "What legend?"

"Whatever you did with the masks," Indigo said, ignoring his question, "you mustn't tell anyone, understand?"

"Ah," Pierce said, looking back at Archie, who shrugged.

The Toymaker clasped Pierce by the arms and asked in earnest, "Where is the book now?"

Pierce opened his mouth to tell him that Joaquin had it when a voice in the dark said, "It's with me."

He immediately pulled his pistol and aimed it at the void. Archie, who stood just behind him, did the same. A ghost-like figure appeared and soon became a solid form when it came into the light.

"Norwich," Indigo growled.

Never had Pierce heard the Toymaker speak with such venom before. Pierce moved his free arm back, keeping Indigo behind him. To make matters worse, Norwich wasn't alone. Behind him, more ghostly faces appeared. A few he recognized as the drunken soldiers whose idea of a good time was stringing him up. Of course, Ivor was there as well, standing by his dear ole dad and looking all out of sorts.

"I have the book, the masks, and now you, Peachtree," Norwich stated.

A swell of panic formed in Pierce's gut. He'd thought Joaquin had the masks. Had Norwich found Joaquin? Christ, did the bastard have Indigo's *real* journal?

"And you think I'm going to let you take him quietly, eh?" Pierce said with forced bravado. The fact that they were outnumbered and cornered in a cave wasn't lost on him. Even so, he wasn't going to just stand by and let them take Indigo. If he was going to die, he'd die defending his friend.

Norwich didn't seem threatened by him in the least. He looked over his shoulder as a soldier from the back approached with someone small. Pierce saw the gaudy performance dress before he heard her voice.

"Ouch!" Clover cried when Norwich snatched her arm and yanked her in front of him. "Father!"

"Quiet," Norwich commanded. To Archie, he said, "Well?"

An object that Pierce could only assume was a gun, pressed against his head. The click as it was cocked only confirmed it.

"Lower your weapon, Landcross," Archie ordered.

Pierce's eyes went to Clover, who was held in her father's tight grasp. If he tried anything rash, triggering a gunfight, chances were that a bullet would find her. Indigo as well. Once he lowered his gun, they'd surely shoot him dead anyway, now that they had everything they wanted. Perhaps it'd be quick.

He lowered his gun and tossed it to the ground.

A few soldiers approached and went behind Pierce and Indigo with their guns raised, picking up his discarded weapon along the way

"Let's go," Norwich ordered, turning to leave.

Pierce glanced over at Archie, who was kind enough to remove the gun from his head. The lad's sullen expression spoke of his own dire predicament. It became clear that Tarquin Norwich had used his own daughter to control Archie like a marionette. Archie would undoubtedly do whatever was needed to protect his sister's life, and his father was playing into that.

Archie said nothing. Instead, the lad left down the tunnel with Pierce following him, and Indigo and the soldiers trailing behind them.

Ivor was waiting at the mouth of the cave. As soon as Pierce walked by him, the maniac kicked him in the back of the knee, forcing him to drop to a kneeling position upon the stony ground. Ivor pulled his pistol and aimed it at his head.

Could be worse, Pierce thought.

"No!" Indigo shouted, stepping between the gun and Pierce.

Pierce gritted his teeth. If Ivor wanted his father to kill him, shooting Indigo would most certainly prompt that.

"Don't shoot!" Clover screamed, breaking free from her father as if the threat gave her renewed strength. "Don't shoot him, Ivor!"

The girl rushed over and threw herself over Pierce, her tight embrace cutting the air off through his already bruised throat.

Ivor took a step back, his gaze wandering between them. His expression carried both jealously and pain, as if he knew that no one would ever do such a thing for him.

Archie started to approach. "Clover, no! Get away!"

Norwich snatched Archie by the arm and pulled him back. "Ivor, stop this. Put that gun away."

Ivor's eyes were glossy with tears. He slowly turned to his father, whose own expression exposed curiosity.

"What is it, son?" Norwich asked.

Ivor lowered his gun, which would relieve Pierce if Ivor wasn't completely unstable. To prove that, Ivor mumbled something incoherent.

"Come again?" his father said. "Speak up."

"I never . . ." Ivor babbled. "I never wanted to . . ."

Archie approached his brother, understanding what Ivor was trying to say.

"Ivor," Archie said soothingly, reaching out to him with an unsteady hand.

Pierce climbed painfully to his feet. He took Indigo by the shoulder and pulled him back to give the brothers space, recognizing how delicate the situation was, even if no one else did.

Ivor looked over to his younger brother.

"It's all right," Archie said, holding his hand out to him as if he wanted Ivor to take it.

Ivor shook his head. "No, it's not, Arch. I never wanted to kill Uncle Brice. His face haunts my dreams. I can't close my eyes without seeing him. Without hearing his screams."

A sickening feeling settled inside Pierce's gut. He held Clover against his side, wanting to shield her from what might happen, but she wouldn't let him. Instead, she clutched tightly to his dapper coat but she kept watching.

"Brice?" Norwich inquired, "why are you bringing him up now?"

"You should have done this yourself, Father," Ivor said. "After all, *you* did this to me."

"No!" Archie cried when Ivor put the gun in his mouth.

Pierce wrapped himself around Clover just before the blast. A moment passed before he lifted his head to see everyone standing like statues, looking down at

Ivor's body. Archie still had his arm extended, now shaking.

"Take the girl," Pierce whispered to Indigo. He had no idea who Norwich would blame for this, but if Norwich wanted to take his anger out on him or Archie, Clover shouldn't be around to be a part of it.

The Toymaker peeled his owl-sized eyes away from the bloody mess on the floor and lowered them to the weeping child. "Come here, lass."

Clover didn't resist. She let Pierce go and walked over to the soldiers with Indigo. Norwich's face was fixed like an immutable mask on Ivor's body. He looked neither shocked nor angry as he walked up to his dead son, never averting his eyes from him.

"The alcohol drove you to this," Norwich said, as if Ivor didn't have a hole in his head.

"The alcohol?" Archie exclaimed. "Didn't you hear what he said?"

Norwich regarded him as if he was an annoying fly. "Speak another word," he growled softly, where only Archie and Pierce could hear him, "and I will kill your sister right now."

Archie's anger radiated off him to the point where Pierce could feel it. In the lad's state, he might not be thinking clearly enough to take heed.

Pierce came up next to him and placed a hand on his shoulder. "Relax, lad. Don't risk Clover's life over this."

Archie turned. Blood had splattered his face, revealing just how close he'd been when Ivor had pulled the trigger.

Norwich spoke. "Besides, Ivor will not be dead for long."

Both Pierce and Archie gaped at each other, then turned to Norwich, who smirked at their confusion.

"Isn't that correct, Peachtree?" Norwich said.

Pierce's confusion only deepened. Indigo stood in place, his expression as blank as a board. He clearly understood exactly what Norwich meant.

"Pick up my son," Norwich ordered a pair of soldiers. "Carry him back to his horse." To Indigo, he said, "Peachtree, I believe you mentioned another route?"

The Toymaker nodded.

"Then lead the way," Norwich commanded.

Indigo walked ahead of everyone with Clover by his side, while Norwich turned to Pierce. "Go on, Landcross. I have something special in mind for you."

A thousand horrifying thoughts flashed through Pierce's mind in a single instant. He dared not ask what Norwich meant as he left to follow Indigo.

Once they reached the top of the cliff where the horses were waiting, Pierce's hands were bound behind him with rope. Archie needed to assist him onto his horse. Indigo was allowed to ride without bonds. Pierce reckoned that the Toymaker was viewed as less of an escape risk. The soldiers, carrying Ivor's body draped him over the saddle of his own horse. Pierce winced at the sight of the man's brain. When everyone was mounted, Norwich gave the order to move out.

Indigo rode his horse next to Pierce as they headed back to the castle.

"Something you want to tell me?" Pierce asked.

The Toymaker set his eyes on him and smiled fondly. "It is so good to see you, Pierce. How is your brother?"

"Doing better than me at present," he grunted. "Now, would you kindly explain what the fuck is going on?"

"I don't care for your harsh language," Indigo

scolded.

After everything Pierce had gone through, and everything he'd done to save the Toymaker, only to wind up captured and heading to an unknown fate, he was in no mood for a lecture regarding profanity. He screwed up his face in response.

Indigo's hardened expression softened and his shoulders slumped as he gave a deep sigh. "I'm a curious man. In my life, I've always studied a wide variety of things, even dead languages."

"Dead languages?"

"The writing in my journal, it's a spell."

"Aye, that much I know already."

"I discovered that the spell is actually instructions to do something that no one on this earth, or any realm, should ever attempt."

"What does Norwich need you for?" He thought for a moment on his own question. "To translate the writing?"

Indigo nodded. "The spell is written in the ancient language of gods long dead."

That threw Pierce back. "Come again? Ancient dead gods?"

"Yes. The original transcript was in the Royal Library of Alexandria, where most of the world's knowledge was kept at the time. The spell was copied onto a scroll that is said to have been stolen from a book written by a god."

Stealing from gods? What ballsy thief did that? Pierce wondered.

"Somehow, the scroll survived after the library was burned."

"What else was in the book that these gods wrote in?"

"It contained their secrets."

"Secrets? Like a diary for deities?"

"Yes. I suppose. The book burned in the fire but as I said, the scroll survived."

"All right," Pierce said, confused. "Why did you write it down in your journal?"

"I bought the scroll many years back in an Egyptian marketplace. The seller—a strange young man— convinced me to take it and the masks. The spell was written on very old parchment. When I returned home, I jotted it down to translate it more clearly."

"What does the spell do?" Pierce asked anxiously.

Indigo leaned over closer and opened his mouth to speak when Norwich cut him off. "Hold your tongue, Peachtree. We don't want to spoil the surprise." He steered his mount around and rode toward them. "Go on with you," he ordered the Toymaker. "Go."

Indigo narrowed his eyes at Norwich and trotted his horse over to Archie and Clover.

"I don't bloody well like surprises," Pierce said.

"I know that you won't like this one," Norwich replied quickly.

Pierce huffed. "If that be the case, then I can't wait."

Norwich smirked at him. He seemed in high spirits despite having lost his favorite son.

"When I organized the British Guardians, a particular individual volunteered; a German albino with a deformed arm. One Volker Jäger."

Jäger. That name took Pierce back ten years to Germany, where he'd met the beautiful actress, Frederica Katz.

Christ, Volker's alive?

"Ah, you *do* know Jäger?" Norwich said noting his expression. "He knows you, as well. He asked me if I had ever heard of you. At the time, I had not; but that didn't stop him from being my most efficient, and I daresay, most brutal member of the Guardians."

"No doubt, he was responsible for all those hangings and scorched bodies, eh?"

Norwich didn't try to deny the gruesome acts that his Guardians were noted for. Pierce didn't think he would.

"I believe you were his motivation for joining," Norwich said. "Be thankful that *I* caught you instead of him."

Norwich rode back up to the front of the group.

"Fortunate, indeed," Pierce grumbled.

Throughout the rest of the trip back to the castle, he and Indigo weren't allowed to speak to each other, which prevented Pierce from gaining any more insight into what was going on. Still, he wondered why he was still alive.

Spring rain began falling when they arrived at the castle. The sight of the building in daylight made him cringe. Robin of Locksley's victims had been removed from the premises. To shallow graves in a field, Pierce reckoned.

When the gates closed behind them, sealing everyone inside the inner courtyard, it killed any last hope of escape. Perhaps if he was still alive by dusk, Robin would return, find a way to kill Norwich, and get him the hell out. Even though Robin wanted him dead, at least he still had the coin.

The horses came to a halt and Norwich turned to a soldier. "Find a maid by the name of Poppy and tell her that it's time to brew the tea."

"Yes, milord," the soldier said, bowing his head.

Norwich nodded to another soldier, who dismounted, marched over to Pierce and grabbed his arm, yanking him off the saddle and letting him fall to the ground. Pierce's bones shook inside his skin when he landed on the cobblestones.

"Get up," the soldier ordered, giving him a swift kick in the side.

"Stop it!" Clover cried.

Indigo dismounted, rushed over, and shoved the soldier away. "Keep your bloody hands off him," the old man bellowed with fists clenched. To Norwich, who was still on his mount, he said, "If you want me to cooperate, you'd best tell your men to leave him be. Otherwise, you can shoot us both dead right here."

"Uh, wait a tick," Pierce said as he sat up. "I'm not sure I agree with that."

Norwich considered the Toymaker for a moment. He grumbled and dismounted. To Archie, he said, "Take your sister up to her room and then meet me in the north tower." He then addressed everyone else. "Take the prisoners and my son's body inside."

Indigo tried helping Pierce to his feet when the soldier grabbed Pierce by the arm again and hoisted him up. Pierce hissed when a sharp ache exploded like a bomb in his side, spiking pain everywhere else.

As he was led away, Norwich said, "Time to meet your fate, Landcross."

Chapter Twenty-Five
The Moirai

Joaquin rode with eyes half open. The night before had drained him of energy. After stealing the book from his brother, he'd ridden to East Cowes to throw off anyone who might be searching for him. He'd managed to get another hotel room, a low-rent close to the marina.

He'd stayed up thinking about the Dutch woman. It was one of the curses of being a wanted man, never being able to settle down. When it was just him and Pierce, stealing to survive, it had become a familiar way of living. Neither of them had intentionally worked to become fugitives; it had simply turned out that way. And Pierce always thought it was a game.

Now, on the road, he kept himself from falling asleep in the saddle by thinking about the Dutch woman again. He imagined getting praise from the Queen in bringing such critical evidence of what Tarquin Norwich was up to, earning himself money, lands, and perhaps a knighthood. With such newfound status, he'd pardon the Dutch woman if she would agree to tell him her name. She would be so taken by him that she'd allow him to court her, and soon afterwards, they'd be wedded.

The old ruined church was a welcomed sight until he noticed horses near the front entrance. His first instinct was to investigate. Leaving his own horse out of sight, he crept toward the building through the tall grass. He reached the open space where the window once was, peered through it, and grinned.

"Gentlemen," he announced.

They were in the process of building a fire and they

whipped around to face him. Luca Smith opened fire.

Joaquin ducked. "Bloody idiots! It's me, Joaquin!"

He strained to hold back his beast when the sickness pinched his gut.

Now you want to do this?

"Joaquin?" Giles Summerfield exclaimed. "Fuckin' hell, mate, is it really you?"

The sickness subsided and he took a breath and rose back up. "Indeed."

"It is," Luca yelled, smoke from his gun drifting around him. "Thought you'd be on your way to the gallows by now."

"Nope. Nothing that common, I'm afraid. And if you ever take a shot at me again, I'll return in kind, understand?"

The man gulped.

"Go hunt us up some dinner, eh?" Joaquin commanded with a nod to Luca. "Put that gun of yours to good use."

"Aye," he said, grabbing his powder horn.

"What are you doing here?" he asked Giles.

"Coming after you," Giles replied with a smirk.

Joaquin chuckled. "Bloody liar."

"Me and Luca decided the mainland was a bit hot. So we're off to seek our fortunes in pastures new."

"I see," Joaquin said, leaning on the windowsill. "Before you do, let's spend one last night together."

"You don't want to come with us?"

"Not this time. After I get some rest, I'll tell you both everything."

Archie hurried Clover to her old chambers. Once they

entered, he said, "Listen to me. Do you remember where the hidden passageway is up here?" She nodded and he reached into his pocket. "I need you to leave here and head back to Cowes. Wait for me at the port. If I'm not there within the hour"—He placed ten gold sovereigns in her hand—"go on ahead without me. Take a carriage to London and seek an audience with Queen Victoria. Tell her everything."

Clover's chest heaved rapidly. "Why wouldn't you be at the port? Are you saying you might be dead? You can't die, Archie. I won't allow it."

"Shush now. You have to be brave. Like Mother was."

Her breathing slowed, even though the gloss in her dark eyes thickened.

If his father hadn't demanded his presence, he'd make sure she got out of the castle before returning for Landcross. Whatever his father had planned for him, he was certain that Landcross wasn't meant to survive it.

Nothing but guilt and anguish had plagued him since the minute he'd put his gun to Landcross' head back in the cave. He tried telling himself that he'd done what he had to in order to save Clover. Yet thinking on it, he realized that there should have been an alternate option. He should've come up with something other than delivering Landcross and Peachtree over to his insane father. Now he owed it to Landcross to at least go back and try to free him, and send him on his way to Captain Sea Wind's ship.

"Promise me that you'll get to the Queen, Clover Norwich," he insisted. "Promise me."

She stifled her tears and pulled together the bravest face she could. "I promise," she whispered.

"Good," he said with earnest. "Get to the tunnel and

make your way out."

He left the room and hurried to the north tower. On his way, he checked how many rounds were left in his gun.

Pierce felt like a broken automaton, ready to shatter at any moment as he climbed the spiral stairs. If that bloody cocker hadn't yanked him off the horse and kicked him in his wounded side, the climb wouldn't be so difficult. He had to stop a couple of times when the pain marched down his leg, attacking every nerve like bee stings. The first time, the soldier pushed him so hard he nearly fell. It didn't help that his hands were tied behind his back. The second time he stopped, Indigo intervened and helped him on before the soldier had a chance to react.

The locked door at the top was a blessing. It gave him time to catch his breath while Norwich stopped and unlocked it. When the door squeaked open, a cold breeze blew. He shuddered, unable to shake his uneasiness.

They entered a dark room lit only by the grey light coming from a single window. Norwich reached into his pocket, brought out a box of matches, and struck one. He went around the circular room, lighting lamps on the wall. Nothing occupied the room other than a spinning wheel and a table. The table held a pair of shears and a measuring stick, the masks and the journal.

He was relieved to see it was not the original Joaquin had taken, but his copy.

When the lamps brightened the room, Norwich picked up a mask and admired it.

"How in the world did that man get those?" Indigo asked Pierce.

"I got them from where they were hidden so I could bring them to you," he tried explaining. "I thought Norwich might find them."

"Landcross," Norwich cut in, holding up the mask, "do you have any idea what this is?"

Pierce stole a glance at Indigo, who shifted his magnified eyes over to him. The concern on the old Toymaker's face sent a shudder straight up his spine.

"It's a death mask," Norwich said.

"I gathered," Pierce said shortly. "Of an ancient god, no doubt."

Norwich's eyebrows hiked up with surprise. "Very good, Landcross. Do you know *which* god this one is?"

Pierce wasn't amused. His annoyance must have shown because Norwich snorted and said, "This is Dionysus."

He put the mask down and carefully picked up another. "This is the goddess Artemis, goddess of the hunt." He set that one down and lifted the last one. "And this is none other than Zeus, king of all gods."

He carried the masks over to the wall where he hung them on iron spikes.

"How do gods die?" Pierce asked. "Aren't they s'posed to be immortal?"

"Gods can die the same as you and I, Landcross," Norwich explained, hanging another mask. "Would you care to explain the rest, Peachtree?"

Pierce turned to the Toymaker as the soldiers brought in Ivor's body. They carried it between him and Indigo, yet Pierce didn't avert his eyes from the old man.

"Place him there," Norwich ordered, pointing to a spot on the floor in front of the window.

As the soldiers obeyed, a maid entered, carrying a

tray set with a teapot and cups. She breathed heavily as she said, "Here is your tea, milord."

"Good. Set it on the table and leave, Poppy."

"Very good, milord," she said, walking over to the table.

When she spied the bloody corpse, she screamed.

"Set the tea down and leave!" Norwich bellowed.

The dishes rattled as she lowered them to the table. She soon scurried out of the room with her hands clutched to her chest.

Norwich poured tea into one of the cups and walked over to Indigo. "As you were saying," he said, handing the cup to the Toymaker.

Indigo accepted the tea and said, "When Zeus, Artemis, and Dionysus died, other gods created these death masks and used them as a binding tool." He took a drink. "They spent centuries working on the spell to capture the demigods and control how they conduct their affairs by using the masks to bind the gods in one spot outside of their own realm."

"Wait. Control the demigods?" Pierce said, shaking his head as he tried to grasp what Indigo was saying. "What demigods?"

"The Fates," Norwich chimed in as he placed the final mask on the wall. "If the gods were able to capture the Fates and bind them, they could control how long someone lived by prolonging their fate string—or how short their life was by subtracting from it. Zeus and his kin were the first to attempt capturing the Fates. All just to threaten us mortals with sudden death if we choose to follow the new religion that was beginning to take hold at the time."

"Oh, I see," Pierce said. "You're telling me that they were trying to keep their followers from abandoning them, eh?"

"A deity is nothing without its followers," Norwich pointed out. "Without worshipers, they are like any other supernatural being. Like elves, enchanters, or I daresay, vampires."

Another cold shudder danced up Pierce's back. "But they were gods," he said. "Couldn't they just take a life if they wanted to?"

"*Not* these gods," Norwich replied cryptically. "They can kill crops and deliver illnesses, but only the Fates control a person's time of death. When Zeus failed, the Fates crafted special threads just for them to serve as punishment."

"They didn't already have threads? Or was that because they were immortal?" Pierce asked.

"No supernatural being has a thread," Indigo explained. "The Fates only make them for mortals in order to shorten our lives. You see, before they came along, mortals lived for hundreds of years, producing many children that consumed too much of the earth's resources. The Fates put order into mankind's mortality by appointing themselves as judges of life and death."

Mortals? Not *these* gods? What the bloody hell does that mean?

"However, nothing is truly immortal," Indigo went on. "Eventually, power fades. When it burns out, it's done and the energy moves on to another house. Having people worshiping the gods and goddesses, contributing so much of their own vigor to build temples, offering sacrifices, even simply acknowledging them, strengthened the gods' power, keeping them strong."

"And the masks can do that?" Pierce asked. "Hold the Fates?"

"Indeed," Norwich said, shooing the soldiers away

from his son's body, who then relocated themselves near the prisoners. "The attempt to capture the Fates sparked interest in the other gods; and when these three died, they designed the masks to suck out the last of the dead gods' energies, holding their power within their own death masks. Once the spell is recited, it will draw the Fates out of their realm and into this very tower, which will become their prison."

"It seems like a lot of work for the gods to go through just to stay alive," Pierce noted.

Norwich shook his head and said, "Not just alive, Landcross, but to keep existing as a *worshiped* being. And no one wants to give up being a god. As Christianity grew stronger, it took the pagan gods' divinity away as more and more of their followers denounced them. The deities who couldn't adjust died off quicker than those who'd adapted to the changing world. Capturing the Fates was their last attempt to keep their stranglehold on mankind."

Sees Beyond had said something about the spell, thought Pierce. They were deities only because people had crowned them as such. It might have been possible that these supernatural beings had existed as something else before.

"Gods and goddesses have been knocked off their pedestals by new beliefs for centuries," Norwich went on. "They've died, have become other gods, or have adapted into other beings ever since humans began giving so much of themselves."

"How many tried to capture the Fates?"

"No one knows," Indigo spoke up. "It's only apparent that they all failed. Then the masks were said to have been stolen along with the book that the scroll had been from."

"Until some gent at an Egyptian marketplace

convinced *you* to buy the masks, eh?" Pierce surmised.

"I seems that way," Indigo said dolefully.

"Interesting," he mused, although he wasn't buying into any of this nonsense. "Is that the reason why you told me to send the masks away? Were you tempted to use them to capture the Fates?"

"No," Indigo replied, glaring over at Norwich. "Unlike some, I have no desire to live forever."

Pierce looked to Norwich as well, who crouched next to his dead son and placed his hands over Ivor's chest.

"When I have control of the Fates," Norwich said, "I'll have the power to decide who lives and dies. I, of course, will live forever, and my son will return from the dead."

"Right," Pierce said, still very much unconvinced. "If you're going to live forever, then why do you need to build weapons?"

Norwich stood, looking over his shoulder. "Once I have the Fates under my thumb, I'll pick off monarchs from all over the world, as well as those who are next in line to the throne. There will be much chaos. By that time, I will have already eliminated those standing in line to rule England, until the crown is passed onto me. Once I have rule over the British army, we shall use these weapons to march though the pandemonium and take one nation at a time."

Pierce looked at Indigo, who had become very quiet. "And you're s'posed to read off a spell, eh? You're not really gonna do it, are you?"

The Toymaker said nothing.

"Oi! Indigo? Are you there, mate?"

Indigo slowly turned toward him. His eyes weren't his anymore. They were red, with black jagged veins leading to pinprick pupils.

Something was terribly wrong. Pierce had seen eyes like those before.

Indigo appeared hollowed-out, as though his body was awake but his soul slept. Pierce took more notice of the teacup he held and realized that Norwich hadn't touched his own.

"No, he's not there. Not anymore," Norwich said. "And to answer your question, he most likely wouldn't translate the spell willingly, so I added a drug to his tea." To Indigo, he said, "Peachtree, come here."

The Toymaker began moving toward Norwich. The way he walked, it appeared as though he was moving through sludge.

"Indigo," Pierce shouted. "Oi! Stop. Don't listen to 'im!"

Indigo halted and turned back.

"Keep him quiet," Norwich demanded.

Pierce cried out when harsh hands took hold of him, pushing him to his knees.

"Shut your mouth," a soldier ordered, jabbing a gun against his head. Norwich stepped closer, towering over Pierce.

"You don't even know if it'll work," Pierce hissed, consumed by the pain in his side.

Norwich snorted and said, "Then I will end you myself, Landcross. And trust me; it will be a slow and painful death." He shifted his eyes to something behind Pierce and the soldier holding him. "Archie, it's about time you arrived."

Pierce twisted his neck as far back as it could go. From the corner of his eye, he spied Archie in the doorway, aiming a gun at his father.

"Let them go," the lad ordered.

The soldier yanked Pierce up and moved him

around to face Archie.

Although Pierce appreciated the lad's effort, the attempt was piss poor at best. Archie should just shoot his bugger of a father, but the lad most likely had never killed anyone in his life and therefore wouldn't pull the trigger so easily.

Regardless, Archie held his ground, even though the other soldiers were aiming their guns at him.

"Let them go," Archie demanded again. "I *will* shoot you."

"Then you'll lose the chance to be reunited with your mother," Norwich threw back at him.

Without lowering his weapon or even blinking, the lad said, "Don't play me for a fool. Let Landcross and Peachtree go."

"I called you here to witness the resurrection of your mother. You kill me and you will never see her again. Clover will never know her. Do you want to take that away from her?"

"What are you talking about?"

"Simply lower your gun," Norwich said, walking over to Indigo, who stood by the table. "I'll show you." He opened the book.

"Shoot 'im, Arch," Pierce said. "He's fuckin' lost the plot. Do it."

The soldier's gun jabbed under his chin. "Shut it, you."

"Give me a few minutes, son, and I'll bring our family back," Norwich said. "Make us whole again."

Archie blinked. Pierce couldn't decide whether it was in reaction to his father's offer or to the fact that Norwich had actually addressed him as son.

"I don't follow," Archie said. "Bring back the dead?"

"Yes. I have a way." To the soldiers, he said, "Leave

us. All of you."

The young men stood about, glancing at one another in confusion.

"Now!" Norwich shouted.

The gun jolted under Pierce's chin when the soldier holding him got started. Terror shuddered through his body, sweat breaking out on his face. He sucked in a breath as he waited for the gun to go off.

To his relief, the pressure of the pistol lifted, as well as the grasp on his arm. Every soldier filed out, stepping around Archie as he kept the gun pointed at his father. Archie kept a sharp eye on each man as they left. When the last one stepped over the threshold, he kicked the door shut.

Although his posture remained vigilant, his eyes wavered with uncertainty and bewilderment. Archie shifted his dark eyes to Pierce, as if asking him what he should do. Pierce craned his neck over to Peachtree, then to the journal filled with his own forgeries.

"Lower the gun, lad," Pierce said.

Archie shook his head. "I have to get you out of here." To his father, he said, "I'll stay, but let Landcross go."

"No," Norwich said angrily. Apparently, his patience had run out. "Landcross stays right where he is, and so will you. Now lower your gun."

"Lower it, Arch," Pierce pitched in. "He ain't going to cut me loose; and if you shoot 'im, his guards will kill you. Where will Clover be then, eh?"

Archie stared at him, confused.

Pierce winked. "It'll be all right."

What he'd told Archie wasn't a plea for surrender, but common sense. Shooting Norwich would only result in them all dying, including Indigo. Their best solution was to allow this bizarre ceremony to play out.

Archie had clearly begun to lose the courage he had when he'd come into the room. Pierce almost felt sorry for him. With the promise of having his mother returned to him and the very person he'd come to save telling him to lower his gun, Archie caved. He dropped his arm.

"Good," Norwich said, "let us begin."

Norwich clasped his hand onto Indigo's shoulder, causing the Toymaker to jump. His teacup fell to the floor and smashed to bits. "Read," he whispered into Indigo's ear.

Indigo placed a single finger on the page at the beginning of the first sentence. He began to read the words.

The secret door in the kitchen was still open from the previous night when Clover had escaped the castle. She peeked out of the door and scouted the room. No one seemed to be around so she crawled out of the passageway and scurried over to the counter where the knives sat. She snatched one and dashed back into the tunnel.

She rushed through the narrow breezy passageways, heading for the north tower. She'd already lost her mother and her brother; she'd be damned if she lost Archie, too.

The air in the room began to thicken. Pierce wondered if anyone else noticed. His hair began to rise, as if from static. Little snaps of electricity popped against his skin.

"Bloody hell," he complained.

"It has begun," Norwich said.

Pierce had no idea what the spell was going to do, but it most certainly had an effect. As the Toymaker read on, the room took on a yellow hue. It seemed as if Archie saw it as well. He'd been studying his hand before he started looking around everywhere else.

It wasn't that things had simply turned golden, but rather as if some unknown light had doused everything in the room. Electric sparks arced more clearly, crackling here and there in short spurts of bright green and blue.

Then another light appeared overhead. There was no sound to it, just a white glow that started as a speck, spreading out in thin jagged lines, as if someone had rolled up all the lightning in the world into a little ball.

Indigo kept reading from the journal.

The fingers of bright light raced outwards, arcing, snapping, quickening until they formed a perfect circle. Pierce backed up against the wall, away from the aperture forming over his head. The light shone as bright as the sun and everyone shied their eyes from it, except Indigo, who kept reading. The light was so bright that even with Pierce's eyes closed tight, it burned through his eyelids. The sparks became more frequent, popping against him every second. The room seemed to spin.

He almost collapsed when the light was suddenly extinguished. He opened his eyes and turned his head away from the wall. That was when he saw three robed figures crouched on the floor with their arms over their heads.

Chapter Twenty-Six
Just Let Go

Clover quietly slid the stone aside just enough to peek her head out of the tunnel. When she did, she found soldiers chatting amongst themselves down the corridor. To her right were the stairs leading up to the tower.

The tower used to be her and her bothers' secret place, where they had once played silly games, such as princess and knights, fighting off dragons.

If she kept quiet, she could probably make it to the stairs without being noticed.

She slipped out of the tunnel and ran to the stairs. Her footsteps made no sound as she clambered up the steps, the knife clutched in her hand.

The farther she climbed, the stranger the air felt. When she came to a door, she hoped that it wasn't locked, because there were no passageways leading into the tower.

To her relief, the door opened when she pushed on the latch. As the door moved, an unbelievably bright white light lanced through the crack. Its intense glow caused tears to form in her eyes. Ignoring it, she slipped through the doorway and entered the room.

It wasn't long before the light gave out. Starbursts exploded in her eyes like fireworks. When the colors faded and her sight returned, she spotted Archie standing in front of her. He had a gun, which gave her a little more courage. Mr. Pierce was standing by the wall with eyes shut. Her father stood next to Mr. Peachtree behind a table, with his back turned to her.

Mr. Peachtree looked strange. His eyes were a mix

of cherry and burgundy red, and he looked thin, as if he hadn't eaten in weeks.

While her father's back was turned, she dashed over to Mr. Pierce just as he was turning away from the wall, stepping around three women hunched over on the floor.

Pierce became so engrossed in the sudden appearance of the three figures that he now could see were women, that he nearly missed someone sawing through the ropes binding his hands. He glanced over his shoulder and spotted Clover with a knife. He had no idea where she had come from but he was thrilled to see her there. She hacked through his thick bonds, until they started to give.

As the tightness on his wrists loosened, the women rose. Each had olive skin and was dressed in a black tunic. They were tall, slender and young, although they had an appearance of great age. They each shared the same face, yet they had different hair and eye color. The one with red hair had golden eyes, while the blonde's were black. The dark-haired woman had eyes of red.

But as different as they were, their expressions were identical, and they were angry.

The black-haired, red-eyed woman stared directly at Pierce, her teeth clenched and a deep crease between her black brows, which pressed together in anger. If Clover wasn't behind him, Pierce would have backpedaled up to the wall. He shook his head, hoping to let the woman know that he had nothing to do with her and her sisters having been snatched out of their realm. The redheaded one stared at Archie, who only gawked back at her. The third woman with glowing golden locks was looking at Indigo and Norwich.

"Ladies," Norwich said, drawing their attention.

When the black-haired woman snapped her eyes away, Pierce let out a long breath. The rope around his wrists separated. While Norwich was distracted by the otherworldly women, he sidestepped over to Archie, who was still dumbfounded.

"*Psst!*" Pierce hissed to the lad.

Archie unlocked his gaze from the trio and turned to him.

"Look," Pierce whispered.

When Archie saw Clover hiding behind him, his face became firm. "I told you to get out," he said sternly.

Before she could respond, Norwich said, "Ah, the Fates. Clotho, Lachesis, and Atropos, welcome. I am Tarquin Norwich, your new master."

"Things are about to get very nasty, mate," Pierce whispered to Archie. "Best give me the gun, eh? I'll put an end to this."

"No. Just keep Clover safe."

The lad moved away from them and went over to one of the death masks.

Pierce huffed. The idiot wanted to see if Norwich could, in fact, bring his mother back to life. His blasted short-sightedness was putting them all in danger. Pierce looked at the door and wondered if he could get Clover out without being noticed.

"Master?" the raven-haired woman said. "We have no master. We never have and never will."

"Until today, Atropos," Norwich said. "Recognize these?"

He gestured to the masks hanging on the wall. Each was glowing yellow, as if the light had been sucked into them. "These are the gods whose threads you cut. They will forever bind you to this room, and the only power you will ever have is the power I allow you to possess."

"You know not what you do, mortal," the golden-haired woman seethed. "You cannot control us."

"I think I can, Clotho. On my command, you will spin your thread of life whenever I wish. A great general, a worthy servant, even a new bride, you will make it so. Lachesis, you will measure the threads as you have always done, but I will tell you how long they live."

He picked up the shears from the table, snipped the air, and said to the raven-haired woman. "And you, Atropos, will sever those threads. But you will never sever mine."

Pierce looked over his shoulder at Clover and said softly, "Let's get you out, eh?"

She shook her head, her face scrunching up. "I'm not leaving without Archie."

He rolled his eyes and then his head. "Unbelievable," he grumbled.

He couldn't very well argue without Norwich taking notice. Even though Archie had a gun, Norwich probably had one too. The best thing he could do was to keep Clover hidden behind him.

"And you will also repair certain threads that you have severed," Norwich went on. "Bring back the dead, starting with my son."

The women looked at each other and said something in their own language. They didn't sound amused.

Lachesis, the redhead, snorted. "You're not the first fool to attempt our capture, Tarquin Norwich. Everyone who has tried has failed horribly."

"Yes, but they did not have what I have." Norwich again clasped Indigo on the shoulder. "Finish the spell, Peachtree."

Indigo began reading once more. As he did, Pierce held his breath.

The ancient words rumbled off the Toymaker's tongue. Initially he'd read as smoothly as a rose petal. Now he struggled, trembling to finish the incantation.

The masks glowed brighter and began pulsating. Each woman looked at them and became transfixed. Nothing moved, not even the air, which became cold and electric. Pierce's teeth hurt. Archie also watched, smacking his lips at the strange taste in the air. Clover buried her head against Pierce's back, while he stayed focused on the puppet that was his friend, fearing that Norwich would succeed after all.

When Indigo read the last word, he collapsed near Ivor's body.

"Indigo!" Pierce cried, running across the room. He knelt down beside him and lifted his head. Indigo's thick glasses had fallen off and his eyes were closed.

"You all right, ol' boy?" Pierce asked, cradling the Toymaker's head.

"What is he doing free?" Norwich demanded.

Pierce raised his chin to see that he had a gun aimed at his face. As many times as he'd been in this situation before, it never got any less frightening. But the fear of having his head blown off dissipated when Norwich steered his eyes over to his daughter, who still had the knife in her hand.

"Clover," Norwich said, "what are you doing in here?"

Archie quickly moved toward her.

"Indigo," Pierce whispered, patting the Toymaker on the cheek. "C'mon, man, wake up."

"What about Mother?" Archie demanded, standing in front of his sister. "You said you could bring her back."

Indigo gave a slight moan as he opened his bright sea-colored eyes. Apparently, whatever had been slipped into his tea was wearing off.

"Pierce?" Indigo said, blinking a few times.

"Aye, can you stand?"

Indigo nodded and Pierce helped him to his feet. When they were both upright, the Toymaker saw the Fates and gasped in horror. He broke away from Pierce and walked unsteadily to the book on the table.

"No, what have I done?" he said, looking down at the book. After a few minutes of examining the spell, he turned to Pierce with confusion on his face.

The only response Pierce could give with a gun pointed at him was a slow shake of his head to keep Indigo from saying anything.

"You're right," Norwich said to Archie. "Ladies."

The women tore their heads away from the masks and stared directly at him.

"Go to your places," Norwich ordered. "Now."

They only stared back at him. Then they moved. Clotho took her place at the spinning wheel, Lachesis picked up the ruler, and Atropos took the shears in her hand.

"Shite," Pierce muttered.

"Your first task as my slaves is to spin a new thread for Pierce Landcross." He rolled his head over to Pierce with an evil smirk. "And cut it so he'll die right here and now."

Pierce swallowed thickly. "Oh, bugger."

He glanced over at Ivor's body, not knowing whether to be honored or mortified that Norwich wanted him dead before bringing his son back to life.

Clotho started the wheel, spinning the thread on the spindle out onto the table. Lachesis stretched out the thread and measured it with the ruler.

"Father, no," Archie shouted. "Don't do this."

"Shut your mouth, boy." Norwich seethed. "If you ever want to see your mother again, you'd best hold your tongue."

The Fates worked quickly, and before Pierce knew it, Atropos had the thread between her shear's blades.

"Sever it!" Norwich ordered impatiently.

With a snip, she cut the thread in two.

Pierce clutched his pounding chest and fell against the wall. If his life was supposed to flash before his eyes, it didn't happen.

A moment ticked by and his heart kept beating.

"It didn't work?" Norwich said, completely gobsmacked. He swiveled his head back to the Fates. "It *didn't* work!"

"Of course it did not work, you stupid mortal," Atropos fumed.

Norwich looked at Indigo. "You read it wrong, you old fool!"

"No, he didn't," Pierce chimed in. "That ain't his journal. I copied it and altered the words. In fact, I altered the entire book. The whole thing is bloody useless, chum."

Norwich's eye twitched as they shifted to the book.

Pierce returned his attention to the Fates. Atropos was smiling widely at him. They'd known the entire time that the spell hadn't worked and were simply playing along. Sly old birds.

"Looks like it isn't my day to go after all, mate," Pierce said, giving a cocky grin.

He instantly regretted his words when Norwich's twitchy eyes came back to him. "You think so, do you?" Norwich pulled the trigger multiple times.

Two bullets ripped into Pierce's chest and one into his stomach. He looked down at the blood pouring from his wounds before his legs gave out and he slid down the wall to sit on the ground, leaving bloody trails on the stone.

"Pierce!" Indigo shouted, rushing over to him. The Toymaker knelt down beside him and placed a hand over one of his wounds, while holding him against the wall.

Pierce clutched his stomach, blood soaking his hand and oozing from between his fingers. He saw Clover running out from behind Archie.

"No!" she cried, rushing forward when another blast stopped her.

Blood spewed out of her tacky outfit. The ribbons of her skirt fluttered as she fell backwards. The only thing he could be thankful for was that it was a lethal shot. She died before she even hit the ground.

"Clover!" Archie shouted, then raised his gun to point at his father.

Norwich dove for cover as the lad fired repeatedly at him. At the same time, Indigo shielded Pierce with his body.

Norwich shot back once and missed, then tried to shoot again, but his gun clicked on an empty chamber. Archie came out from around the table, pulling the trigger several times, but he was firing nothing. When he finally realized that his gun was empty, he stood there with a blank face drenched in tears and spittle. His father remained on the floor, looking up at him. He seemed to have aged a decade as Archie towered over him like a savage killer looking for his next victim. The Fates simply observed.

"You deserve to lose everything," Archie hissed. "You will never achieve an ounce of what you desire. Ever!"

The lad turned to Pierce and his expression turned

somber. Pierce released a painful breath. Blood from his lungs had reached his mouth and bubbled out on his lips.

Archie dropped the gun and raced to Clover. He lifted her limp body into his arms and held her against his chest. He moaned in anguish. "I'm so sorry," he sobbed. "I'm sorry I got you killed. I only wanted our mother back. Forgive my selfishness. Forgive me!"

Norwich grunted and rose to his feet, just as the soldiers barged into the room with guns drawn. They stopped short at the doorway, gawking at the sight before them.

"This isn't over," Norwich said to the Fates.

"I know it," Atropos said, raising the shears with a sneer. "Useless mortal tools."

The shears, the table, the measuring stick, and the spinning wheel, even the book and tea tray, ignited in blue, green and yellow flames, consuming the items and brightening the room in its glow. As they burned away, the fire contorted, taking the shape of the things it was destroying. The shears and measuring stick remained suspended in midair until Atropos and Lachesis retrieved them. Clotho sat at the spinning wheel, which was constantly moving with the flickering of flames, and spun out a black thread from the bobbin. The thread floated through the air to the next sister, who aligned it with her measuring stick. She nodded to Atropos, who stepped over to it while looking directly at Norwich, her fiery shears raised for him to see.

"A new thread," she said, separating the shear's blades and placing them over the thread. "For you, Tarquin Norwich."

"Wait!" he cried, reaching out to her.

She snipped the thread and it drifted down to the floor.

Norwich grabbed his chest and began to shake. Agony twisted his face. Pierce hoped he'd live long enough to see the bastard die.

Norwich retreated, tripping over his dead son, falling backwards. His back hit the wall and he slid down to the floor, legs over Ivor's body.

There Tarquin Norwich, madman, unworthy husband and father, breathed out his last breath.

After that, Pierce heard nothing more than his own heartbeat slowing. The searing pain had cooled to a numbness that spread throughout his entire body. His spirit was slipping away.

"It's all right, Pierce," Indigo said. "Just let go."

A bright light surrounded the Fates. The masks shook and then shattered. Clotho was holding two pieces of thread, tying them together. Atropos and Lachesis held two other pieces.

As the light became everything, the Fates said, "Not their time."

Chapter Twenty-Seven
Running Out Of Time

When Clover opened her eyes, Archie was the first person she saw. She remembered her father pointing a gun at her just before the blast. There'd been a sharp pain in her chest, then nothing.

"Archie," she said.

He raised his head quickly, his bloodshot eyes searching her entire body.

"Clover?" he said in disbelief. "No. You . . . you were shot. You were bleeding. I saw him shoot you."

"I saw him shoot me, too," she said, lifting herself out of his arms.

When she sat up, the soldiers at the doorway stepped back in astonished confusion. A couple of them made the sign of the cross over their chests.

"I spoke with Mother, Archie."

"What? You spoke to Mother? You actually saw her?"

"She was so beautiful. She told me she's happy where she is. That she's at peace in a place called the In-Between. Mother said she's going to take care of Ivor. She'll help him find a new life whenever he wants to return to this world. She also told me that she approves of Eilidh and wants you both to start having children right away."

Despite crying, Archie cracked a laugh. His smile filled Clover with warmth.

"She did?" he said softly.

"Yes, and Mother wants us to know that she can never return to us because it was her time to die when she did. We need to go on with our lives and not dwell on a past we cannot change."

Archie's face flushed.

"Mother loves you, Archie, and she's proud of you for the years you've spent looking out for me."

Tears rolled down his cheeks. He sniffed and touched her face tenderly. "You really are alive, aren't you?"

The Fates had tied her life's thread together, which had been cut prematurely. They had made it appear as if nothing had happened. Even the blood on her dress had vanished.

She suddenly remembered her friend. "Mr. Pierce?" she said, stepping over to where Indigo held him in his arms.

The Toymaker was watching her in stunned disbelief.

"Is Mr. Pierce alive?" she asked, unable to see him over Mr. Peachtree.

The Toymaker snapped out of his trance and turned his attention to Mr. Pierce. She saw there was no blood on him either, but he remained motionless, eyes half open and mouth slack. As she got closer, she feared the worst.

"Mr. Pierce?" she said softly.

"*Rawr!*" he shrieked, throwing out his hands as if they were claws.

She jumped back with a scream. Mr. Peachtree was so startled that he fell backwards. Mr. Pierce started laughing.

The moment she recovered, she slapped him across the face. "That *wasn't* funny!"

He rubbed his cheek and grinned. "Guess it wasn't our time after all, eh, lass?"

She huffed and smiled back. "I suppose not."

"What are we to do now?" one of the soldiers asked.

"Get the bodies out of here," Archie said assertively. "Bury my father in the family crypt. Today. No wake and no service. My brother as well. Clear out any evidence that people were being held against their will in the castle in case someone talks. Who was in charge when my father wasn't here?"

"That would be the Captain of the Guard, Gerdi Citroen, sir," a soldier replied.

"Find her. If she's sleeping, wake her and inform her of everything. We'll go back to Southampton. I need to telegraph the Queen of my father's death. I'm sure Her Majesty will send for me once she learns the news."

"What about you, Mr. Pierce?" Clover asked.

He got up and placed his hands behind the small of his back and cracked it. "I have a ship to catch, love."

"Pierce, where is the book? The *real* book?" Mr. Peachtree asked as the soldiers collected the bodies.

One of the soldiers had Mr. Pierce's pistol tucked under his belt. When he bent over to grab her father by the legs, Mr. Pierce slipped the gun out of the belt without the soldier even noticing.

"Joaquin has it," Mr. Pierce answered. "Stole it, I should say."

"That book is too dangerous to leave in existence," the Toymaker stated. "It needs to be destroyed."

As Ivor was being lifted up from the ground, his flask tumbled out of his pocket. Clover picked it up and saw the cameo of her mother. She slid her hand lovingly over it.

Mr. Pierce pointed to one of the shattered death masks on the floor. "The masks are broken. No one can try to capture the Fates anymore."

"The book still contains instructions on how to build dangerous weapons," Mr. Peachtree argued.

"I don't have time to chase after that nitwit," Mr. Pierce argued. "My ship leaves today. I have to get back to France."

"I'll go after him," Archie volunteered. "I know where he's going."

"Where?" Mr. Peachtree asked anxiously.

"To London. He wants to use the book as a means to bargain for a pardon."

Mr. Pierce snorted. "Idiot. He'll just be handing himself over to the gallows."

"All the more reason why you should go after him," Mr. Peachtree pressed. "He's your brother and he's heading to his death."

"He ain't no brother of mine," Mr. Pierce said. "You see this?" He slid his hand over the scar on his neck. "Joaquin did this to me. Tried to slit my throat, he did."

Mr. Peachtree stared at him in shock. "*He* gave you that scar? I don't believe it. Your brother would have died for you."

"Brotherly love goes flying out the bleedin' window when you disagree with him, apparently."

"Regardless, we must get the book back. You stole it from me, so you'll help me retrieve it."

"I did *not* steal it. I *accidentally* took it. I can't say that about most things I've taken, but that book I can claim bloody innocence of."

"Pierce," the Toymaker chided, folding his arms.

Mr. Pierce huffed and stomped his foot like a pouting child. "I have to catch a ship."

"Must you travel on that particular ship?" Mr. Peachtree challenged.

"Well, no, but—"

"I'll give you the money for a ticket to anywhere you wish," the Toymaker stated.

Mr. Pierce thought on that. "First class?"

Mr. Peachtree snorted at that, but said anyway, "Aye, first class."

Mr. Pierce chewed his lower lip, obviously weighing his options. "Fine. I want to get something to eat on the way, though."

Pierce didn't care for so much company, yet here he was, sailing back to England with Archie, Clover, and Indigo in tow. Granted, they were heading in the same direction, but they didn't need to join him. He felt that he could take care of Joaquin on his own.

He stood at the railing watching the grey sea, thinking.

Christ, Joaquin, what happened to us?

They had always looked after each other. When they were kids, after their arrest in Abney Park, Pierce and Joaquin were hauled off to the orphanage.

The orphans woke before dawn and were herded by the staff into the cafeteria for horrible watered down porridge. Any child who didn't stay in a straight line formation, even if he stumbled by accident, would get a whack by a switch. When mealtime was over, the children were loaded into carts and taken to various parts of London and set to work.

Pierce and Joaquin were taken to a cotton mill. Pierce worked as a little piecer and Joaquin was put to work repairing broken machine parts. The building was hot and stuffy, and the cotton dust in the air hurt Pierce's lungs and made his eyes itch.

He worked at a very large and loud contraption called a spinning mule. It stretched clear across the room, spinning cotton threads. It had many moving parts, spinning belts, and iron hooks that sorted out countless long lines of cotton threads, stretching from the spindles on a heavy carriage, to a yarn package winding on the other side.

His job as a little piecer required him to repair any broken fibers. He was terrified to stick his hands into the machine. His back hurt from having to hunch over all the time and his ears rang from all the noise. He and another lad, called a side piecer, helped roll the machine back and forth over the dirty hardwood floor on its iron wheels.

He worked for nineteen hours that day. The following day was the same, leaving his lungs full of cotton dust.

At the end of the third day, Pierce and other children went behind the mule to crawl under the machine to wipe it down. The man in charge of holding the break, which kept the carriage in place, accidentally let it loose. Pierce and a few other boys managed to escape as the heavy iron carriage rattled loudly toward them. The rest did not.

The unfortunate children's screams didn't last long, but they were loud enough to be heard throughout the entire factory. It was the first time Pierce had seen anyone die.

It took workers time to get the bodies out and to clean the machine for the spinning mule to resume operation the following day.

After the deaths, Pierce told his brother that he believed he'd be the next to be crushed.

A harsh rainfall poured over the city that night, overflowing canals and rivers. Despite the flooding in the streets, the carts carrying the children made their way to the brick factories, mills, and mines the next day. As they approached the bridge that arched over the river where the cotton mill sat by, Pierce noticed how the water nearly reached the keystone. He didn't think much of it until Joaquin whispered, "We need to jump off the bridge. It's our only chance."

Pierce thought he was mad. But with the water at its current level, the drop wasn't that risky, and the speedy current would carry them away. The only problem was drowning, which considering what could happen to them in the mill, didn't seem so terrible.

He turned to his brother and nodded.

"Right," Joaquin said. "On my say."

The cart made its way slowly over the old stone bridge, and when it reached the height of its arch, Joaquin grabbed him by the arm. "Ready? Set. Go!"

Both of them shot to their feet and leapt over the side of the cart.

"Oi!" one of the staff, sitting next to the cart driver shouted. "Stop, you!"

The man jumped off the seat and chased after them as they clambered onto the ledge of the bridge. Pierce looked down at the rapids below. Even with the waters so high, the fall still appeared to be miles below. He might not have even jumped if Joaquin didn't pull him down with him when he leapt off the bridge.

They spent mere seconds in the air before the water engulfed them. By the time Pierce resurfaced, the current had already carried them away from the bridge. All the other children were standing up in the cart, watching.

Pierce did his best to keep his head up, spitting out water as it rushed into his mouth.

"I got you!" Joaquin said, grabbing him as the water took them toward the River Thames.

The current eventually calmed as it met with the larger river, giving the boys a chance to swim to the riverbank. Mud capped their clothes as they crawled away from the water's edge. They were so exhausted they couldn't even stand.

"See?" Joaquin said, working to catch his breath. "That wasn't too bad."

Pierce collapsed, rolling onto his back, gasping. He felt like he had a chest full of water and muck. "What now?"

Joaquin took in a few deep breaths before he said, "We go look for Mum and Dad." He clasped Pierce by the shoulder. "And whatever happens, just know that I'll always be there to watch out for you."

Pierce frowned and spat into the sea. "Always watch out for me, eh?" Pierce muttered angrily. "You lying cocker."

His nerves were wracked with worry. Other then reeling from the fact that he had come back from the dead, he worried about the encounter he was about to have with his brother as well as the threat of running into any royal guards. Indigo and the Norwich siblings joined him at the railing, tossing pieces of the death masks overboard. Piece by piece, the masks sank into the cold depths.

When they reached the port, they collected their horses and disembarked, then mounted up and headed north.

Pierce believed that Joaquin would go to the ruins of a medieval church on the outskirts of Crawley, which had once been one of their hideouts. If he was heading for London, chances were that his brother would stop there to rest. He only hoped that Joaquin would still be there when they arrived.

It took an hour to reach the old parish. Before approaching the building, everyone dismounted at the forest's edge. The church appeared no different from the last time Pierce had seen it.

The broken building sat in an overgrown field. Butterflies and bees flew busily. Tombstones from the old graveyard, filled with the forgotten dead, peeked over the lengthy grass. Smoke from a fire inside the church wafted out from a large hole in the roof. The key thing that Pierce noticed was the quantity of horses near the front entrance.

"Do you think he's in there?" Archie asked.

"I can't bloody well see through walls," Pierce said icily. "There could be anyone in there."

"Go see then."

"Why me? Why not you?"

"Because, Archie may have to inherit Father's responsibilities," Clover cut in. "Mr. Peachtree is too old and I've already been dead once today."

"I died too, little missy," Pierce returned. "Remember? I was shot three times."

"We'll *both* go," Archie said. "Come on."

Archie took off into the tall grass. With a huff, Pierce followed. They kept low. When they crossed through the graveyard, Pierce's foot caught on a broken tombstone that pitched him forward.

"What are you doing?" Archie whispered. "Get up."

"Oh, I do apologize," he said sarcastically, getting to his feet. "I didn't mean to hold you up."

Archie shook his head and turned to go on when he also tripped over a broken gravestone hidden in the grass. He didn't fall, but Pierce chuckled.

"Shut it," Archie growled.

They reached the wall and both stood on either side of a gaping window. Pierce took a breath and looked in.

A fire burned in the same place where he and Joaquin had always had one: on the short stage in front of the pews. The smell of rotten wood permeated the air inside the building. He spotted three men sitting by the fire, surrounding a small cauldron that hung over the flames.

"Do you see him?" Archie whispered.

Thankfully, he did. He was whittling away on a long stick with a knife. Pierce also recognized the company his brother kept, and they were a pair of faces that he'd hoped to never see again.

"Aye, he's in there all right. He ain't alone, either."

"Do you know them?"

"Giles Summerfield and Luca Smith. A pair of savages, they are. How many rounds do you have?"

Archie pulled his revolver. "I reloaded at the castle. I also brought six additional rounds."

Pierce slipped his Oak Leaf revolver from his holster. "Well then, let's get to it, eh?"

They went around to the front of the building where Clover and Indigo were searching the saddle bags on the horses.

"What are you doing?" Archie demanded Clover.

"Looking for the book," she returned hotly. "If it's out here, then you don't need to go in."

"Is it?" Pierce asked hopefully.

She looked in the bag and shook her head. Indigo did the same.

"Wonderful," Pierce grumbled.

"Stay out of sight," Archie said to both his sister and Indigo.

"C'mon, young lady," Indigo said, stepping away from the animals. "Let the boys play."

"Right," Pierce said. "Ready, Arch?"

"Ready."

Pierce's heart thumped hard. A gap stood between

the old wooden double doors, where one of the hinges was rusted in place. He looked inside to see everyone still by the fire. Luca was melting something inside a ladle. Spoons and some toys lay in a pile beside him. Lead, for sure. They were making shot. Giles held a mold. He opened it and a freshly minted lead ball dropped out.

Joaquin, no longer whittled or held the knife, although the blade was the least of Pierce's worries, especially if his brother carried a revolver. It would seem, however, that the gang only had flintlocks.

Pierce predicted that the door would creak if he pushed it in; and even if it didn't, he'd be spotted when he went inside anyway. He decided to approach the situation at the simplest angle and just go on in.

"'Ello, gents," he said, coming down the aisle with his gun outstretched. "Been a long time, eh?"

"What the bloody hell?" Luca said, dropping the ladle and shooting to his feet as he reached for his own gun.

"Ah, ah," Pierce said, directing his gun on him. "We got you outnumbered in bullets, mate."

"We?" Joaquin said, standing up with the stick.

Pierce scowled, then glanced behind him to find no one there. Archie had backed out on him.

"Fuckin' hell."

"Doesn't matter what sort of gun you're carrying, little brother, it only takes one shot," Joaquin said indignantly.

Through the glow of the firelight, and by the stick he held like a magic staff he seem like an evil wizard. Pierce noted that he also had a bag over his shoulder.

"Pierce Landcross," Giles said, also getting to his feet. "Is it really you, you little bugger? Last time we saw you, you were gagging on the ground with your throat open."

"Aye," Luca said. "I'd be the luckiest man in the world to see that again, eh, Joaquin?"

Pierce was in no mood to go down memory lane with the likes of this lot. "I came for the book, Joaquin."

His brother sighed deeply and rolled his eyes. "I figured as much."

"Hand it over and I'll be on my way."

"And leave us so soon?" Joaquin said sardonically. "We're having such a tender family moment here."

"I mean it, Joaquin. Don't mistake my saving your arse as weakness. I owe you a bullet for what you did, so don't fuckin' test me."

"Hand it over," came a voice from a window frame.

Archie stood outside, aiming his gun at the three.

"Brilliant move," Pierce said petulantly. "Wish you had told me that you were going to do that before I busted in here all on my own."

"I wish you would've told me that *you* were going to bust in," Archie threw back at him.

"You're not getting the book," Joaquin cleaved in. "It's my only way to gain a pardon from the Queen."

Pierce tilted his head. "How'd you figure?"

"By turning in Tarquin Norwich and exposing his plan to build weapons to overthrow the throne."

"Norwich is dead," Pierce stated. "He died of heart failure this morning."

Joaquin almost looked surprised, but more so, he appeared angry. Pierce knew that things were about to get dangerous.

"Fine," Joaquin said, taking hold of the bag's strap, "then I'll sell the fucking thing!"

He threw the stick at Archie, forcing the lad to duck. Giles pulled his pistol—a flintlock as Pierce suspected—

and fired at Archie. The lad again dodged, yet it gave Joaquin time to get his gun out, while Luca aimed his weapon at Pierce.

Before Luca could fire, Pierce dove behind a pew. He knew that the trigger-happy fool would waste his only shot, so he fired off a potshot into the ceiling. Sure enough, wood chips flew from a bullet striking the pew.

He sat up and took aim. Luca was reaching behind him, possibly for another pistol, yet he never got the chance before Pierce pulled the trigger, firing a shot into the man's leg. If it wasn't so damn dark, he would have got him in the head or heart.

Luca fell back, howling. Giles had taken cover as Archie fired on him. Joaquin shot once at Archie, then raced toward the window on the other side and climbed through. Pierce got to his feet and dashed out from behind the rotten pews.

He clambered through the nearest window and dropped down. The moment he landed, Joaquin jumped from the grass with the bag in both hands and swung it at him. The impact to his face sent Pierce falling against the wall. He shook it off and raised his pistol. Joaquin swung the bag deflecting the gun upward.

Another blast sounded. Joaquin kicked Pierce in the stomach. He doubled over and lost his grip on the revolver. Abandoning the weapon, he slammed himself against Joaquin, pushing him away. His brother lost his footing and fell backwards, taking Pierce down with him. Pierce pinned him down and punched him in the face before wrapping his hands around his neck. Heat rose to the surface, igniting his pent-up rage. His grip tightened.

"How could you do that to me?" he shouted as Joaquin's face turned red. "I was your brother!"

A stone struck him in the head, pitching him sideways. Joaquin rolled over to his feet. He tossed a piece of tombstone away, snatched Pierce by the lapel, and hoisted him to his feet.

Joaquin shoved him back and Pierce's heel struck the same tombstone he'd tripped over earlier. Again, it stole his balance and no amount of pin-wheeling his arms could reclaim it. His back struck another tombstone, rattling his brain inside his skull. When his vision cleared, he saw Joaquin slip his knife out of its sheath at his belt.

Joaquin placed it against Pierce's neck. The thin blade was sharper then the last knife that had kissed his throat.

"Why did you have to come after me?" Joaquin demanded through clenched teeth. "I can't control it sometimes."

Pierce shifted his eyes away from his own hands, which were clutching Joaquin's wrist. His brother should have green eyes, but right now, they were red— the same as Indigo's after he'd drunk the tea.

"Joaquin," Indigo called from nearby, "let your brother go."

The knife quivered against his throat. Joaquin kept his burning eyes on Pierce until the red gave way to their natural color. His brother blinked several times before he could see again.

"Pierce," Joaquin whispered. "You . . . you *are* my brother."

He got up, clutching his stomach with a painful gasp, and ran toward the forest.

Pierce staggered to his feet, rubbing the spot on his neck where the knife had rested. "Joaquin, wait!"

He started to go after him when Indigo said, "Don't. Let him go."

Pierce turned to the Toymaker. "What the hell was that? What's wrong with him?"

Indigo shrugged. "I'm not sure, but whatever it is, it's dangerous."

They walked over to where Joaquin had dropped the bag. Pierce crouched down to look inside. To his relief, the book was there. He slipped it out and handed it over to Indigo.

"Here."

Indigo took it. He stared at it in silence a moment before saying, "Let's destroy it together."

When Pierce and Indigo rounded the corner of the church, they found Archie holding both Luca and Giles at gunpoint. Clover said, "Look, Archie, he's all right."

"Pierce," Giles said, standing with his arms upraised, "don't let 'im turn us in to the law, mate. We'll be hanged."

As Pierce approached with Indigo, Luca glared at him angrily from the ground. He sat with his wounded leg outstretched before him, gripping it just above the bullet wound.

"We ought to hang you both and save the lad the trouble of hauling your arses away," Pierce said, placing his hands on his hips. "What do you want to do with 'em, Arch?"

Archie let out an exasperated sigh and lowered the gun. "Get out of here."

Giles didn't have to be told twice. He helped his cousin to his feet and led him to a horse. The wounded man grunted as he mounted. From there, Luca looked directly at Pierce with a fierce expression. "If we ever cross paths again, Landcross, I'll finish the job where your brother left off."

Pierce pulled his gun and shot at the hoofs of Luca's horse. The mount reared up and took off through the field with Luca screaming.

Giles held up his hand. "I need no such sendoff."

He kicked his horse and the animal sped swiftly after the other.

Chapter Twenty-Eight
To The Ship! And to Freedom!

"Where's Joaquin?" Archie asked.

"Dunno," Landcross said with a casual shrug. "Just let 'im be, eh?"

Landcross' soft tone confused Archie. He thought for sure that the man would want revenge. Perhaps he'd killed Joaquin and just didn't wish to admit it?

Then he spotted the book in Peachtree's hand. "What are you going to do with it?"

The corner's of the Toymaker's lips rose. "Let's go to the church."

Inside, where the fire still burned, Archie, Clover, Landcross, and Peachtree surrounded it. Peachtree held the book up. His sad expression told of the labor that had gone into documenting his inventions.

"C'mon, throw the bloody thing in already," Landcross said impatiently.

Peachtree dropped the book into the fire, under the small cauldron. It sat there for a few seconds, the fire curling around it, until finally they latched onto the black leather cover and began eating it away.

"Anyone want to say a few words?" Landcross inquired with levity. He searched the faces around him for a smile. There were none. He cleared his throat, and with a clap of his hands, he said, "Right, I guess this is it, eh? Arch."

"Goodbye, Landcross," Archie said, shaking his hand. He looked down at his feet, unable or unwilling to meet Landcross's gaze.

Now that his father was dead, Archie and his sister

could pursue a new life. He owed everything to Landcross, for if it hadn't been for him, he might not have gained so much.

"Take care of that new bride of yours, eh?" Landcross added.

"I will."

Archie's mood lifted. Eilidh was waiting for him and the thought raised a smile on his face.

Landcross turned to Clover. "Goodbye, lass."

"I don't want you to leave," she said, throwing her arms around his waist and hugging him tight.

Landcross pried her away to look her in the eye. "Hey, it'll be all right, love."

"You can come with us," she said with a sniff. "We'll speak to the Queen on your behalf."

He snorted at that. "Even if there was the slightest chance that she wouldn't put my neck in a noose, the fact is, I have too many enemies in England. My only option is to leave, understand?"

Clover considered that for a moment before she solemnly nodded. Landcross drew her close in a tight embrace. "Take care, darling. Keep up with your writing."

"I will, Mr. Pierce."

"Here," Indigo said, taking a coin purse from his tweed jacket pocket. "Take this for your journey."

Landcross looked at the purse before he embraced the old man. "Farewell, my friend."

Indigo seemed to be caught off-guard. Then he wrapped his arms around Landcross as well. "Farewell, my boy. May you always learn and thrive."

Landcross let Indigo place the purse in his hand.

"Just in case you miss your ship," he said.

Landcross patted Indigo on the arm and walked

toward the double doors. He never looked back. When he was gone from sight, Archie continued to watch the fire steadily consume the book. He too had a whole new life waiting for him beyond the church doors.

It was late afternoon when Pierce reached Shoreham Harbor. After buying a ticket for France, he waited another hour before the ship returned from its last voyage. As he waited, he bought a new hat from a nearby shop, one that would help conceal his face.

When the steamboat arrived, he kept to himself with a new book he'd purchased and tried not to think of the possibility of missing out on traveling with the Sea Warriors. He eased his troubled mind by remembering that even if he did miss the ship, he'd simply get a ticket for another vessel thanks to the money Indigo had given him. Perhaps he'd travel to America and see what New York had to offer.

Given the reputation he'd acquired in Europe, he wondered why he hadn't sailed west years ago. Actually, he did know; he wanted to find his family. He hadn't seen his parents since he was eight years old. For years, he'd scoured nearly the entire continent for them, stealing to feed and clothe himself and getting into loads of trouble along the way. Traveling, however, was in his blood, as it had been in his parents' and grandparents'.

The hope of ever finding them dwindled as time passed. Thinking on it, even if he was reunited with them, his reputation would only put his family in danger. The time had come to cut his losses and move on to new ground.

Today he would bid Europe goodbye forever.

Chief Sea Wind kept watch over the pier from the helm of the *Ekta*. He feared that Landcross was either dead or captured. Both were possibilities. There'd been British soldiers in the area asking about Landcross. But while his instincts told him to wait a little longer, common sense told him otherwise.

A warm breeze swept over him and he knew that time had run out.

His wife suddenly appeared beside him. Waves of Strength also gazed out over the hundreds of people on the pier, but he doubted she was looking for Landcross.

"We must go, husband," she said. "The winds are changing."

"Perhaps we should stay for one more night," he said softly.

"We've been docked long enough. The summer storms will soon be upon the Atlantic. If we are to return home safely, we must weigh anchor now. Even Sees Beyond said as much."

"One more night will not matter. Evening is nearly upon us, anyway."

"You are too fond of that boy. We told him when we were leaving. If he hasn't arrived by now, chances are, he won't. The time has come to set sail."

She was right, of course. They needed to head out before the great winds came and brought the hurricanes over from the west coast of Africa. If they waited too long, it could jeopardize the entire crew.

Pierce watched anxiously as Le Havre came into view. Many ships and boats were docked at the large pier. His eyes darted from one vessel to the next, from steam stacks to masts, searching for the *Ekta*. He began to believe that he'd missed it. Then his eyes alighted on the Apache flag peering just over the other tall masts.

He'd made it! He would be on his way to the islands that the chief had spoken of and . . .

Wait, were they lowering the sails? Bugger, the ship was leaving!

The ferry wasn't even fully docked before he leapt over the railing to the boardwalk below. The fall wasn't far, yet the landing triggered pain in his injured side. Agony radiated out from his side and traveled in lightning strikes down his leg. He ignored it and ran down the boardwalk.

People packed the pier, slowing him. He wove between passengers, sailors, cargo, and livestock to get to the pier where the *Ekta* had been docked. Whenever he broke through to a pocket of open space, he was filled with hope that he'd make it to the ship before it set sail. He ran on, pushing and screaming for people to move aside. Finally, he passed the last ship obstructing his view of the *Ekta*. It had already weighed anchor and was pulling away from the dock.

"Wait!" he called, picking up speed.

The ship's stacks billowed with steam and the fans roared, carrying the vessel far and fast out into the Channel. Pierce dashed down the dock, snatching off his hat and waving it in the air as he ran.

"Don't go!" he screamed as he ran to the pier's end. His lungs burned and his side throbbed. "Chief!" he shouted, waving his arms about. "Come back!"

The ship kept going, slowly becoming smaller as she headed toward the open ocean. Pierce stood there trying to catch his breath. He wheezed and held his side as he hunched over with his other hand on his knee. No one onboard the *Ekta* had seen or heard him. No one had even noticed his presence.

"Pierce Landcross," a strong voice announced from behind him.

His breathing ceased and every joint locked up. He knew that voice.

The sound of guns clicking prompted him to raise his hands and turn around. A pack of royal guards stared at him with an older dark-skinned man standing in front.

"Pierce Landcross," the dark-skinned man repeated. "I am Lieutenant Darius Javan, and I hereby place you under arrest by order of Her Majesty."

A few moments in time, he thought grimly. A few moments had made all the difference between freedom and a trip back to London in shackles.

Bugger.

Epilogue

In her garden, Mother of Craft snipped more chamomile. She sniffed the air, as if it could tell her something. It did and she gasped loudly.

Her daughter, Vela, was cutting roses nearby and heard her. "Mother, what happened?"

Mother of Craft placed a hand over her chest and released her otherworldly breath. "It's done," she said, the corners of her mouth lifting. "Tarquin Norwich is dead."

"Oh," Vela said nonchalantly. "Just like you said he would be." She snipped another rose into the basket. "And that man, Pierce?"

"He is returning to England."

"He's still alive?" Vela asked.

"Yes, unfortunately," she grunted.

"Does he have to die?"

"He does. He is one of the Four, like me, as well as his brother and Frederica Katz. Only one of us can live." She paused in thought. "I may have to be there to oversee his death." She looked at her daughter, who appeared worried. "Vela, what is it?"

"That means you won't be with me," she said pitifully.

Mother of Craft nodded. "Perhaps not, but you will not be alone, child."

Vela swallowed thickly. "Will it hurt?" she asked with a hint of concern in her voice.

"I would be lying if I said no. In truth, I have no idea. This hasn't been done before."

"I'll still be myself, though, won't I? I won't be, you know, *him*?"

"Do you remember the tale, *The Story of the Priest*? As long as the Priest's rules are followed, you shall have dominion over the boy."

Vela thought on that. "The rules are strange."

"They were meant to be."

Vela was a mirror image of her mother, from bright red hair to her unique violet eyes.

"Believe me when I say that once it's over, you will become the strongest being in the world. It's the legacy I leave you. It is a legacy that Pierce Landcross has been granted by the power of his own bloodline. The only difference is that he has no earthly idea of it, which gives us the advantage."

"I just wish that you could be there."

"You will have Mr. Wakefield with you. He is a true enchanter and understands everything that's at stake. Everything will be all right. You must trust me."

"I do," Vela said. "Of course I trust you."

Mother of Craft's heart swelled with affection. "Thank you."

Although many trials still remained ahead, she had confidence that things would happen as they should.

"Will it be easier now to kill Pierce?" Vela asked.

"Easier? Perhaps. The protective spell over him remains strong, which is why I have engineered a long line of misfortunes for him when the time comes. However, his fate thread has been successfully damaged, just as I planned. He is now vulnerable to death." Freya Bates headed for the house. "Come, Vela. Let's go inside. It's time for tea."

Michelle E. Lowe

ABOUT THE AUTHOR

Michelle Lowe is the author of *The Warning*, *Atlantic Pyramid, Cherished Thief,* children's books, *Poe's Haunted House Tour,* and the three part adventure children's series, *The Hex Hunt*. She is also a mother, wife, and painter. Her work in progress is an adventure/fantasy series set in the world of steampunk, titled *Legacy*. Currently, she lives in southern California.

Website: www.michellelowe.net

Facebook.com/michelleloweauthor

Twitter: @MichelleLowe_7

Michelle E. Lowe

NORDLAND PUBLISHING
Follow the North Road.

nordlandpublishing.com
facebook.com/nordlandpublishing
nordlandpublishing.tumblr.com

NORDLAND

www.nordlandpublishing.com

Michelle E. Lowe

Made in the USA
Columbia, SC
21 August 2017